The world loves Jillian Hunter!

"Hunter is a master of her craft."
—Katherine Sutcliffe, bestselling author of *Miracle*

"Jillian Hunter, as always, delivers a great read."
—Jill Marie Landis, bestselling author of *After All*

"She deftly paints riveting stories of passion and adventure. This is an author not to be missed!"
—*Romantic Times* on Jillian Hunter's work

* * *

Praise for Jillian's bestselling **A Deeper Magic**

"Enchanting and suspenseful, *A Deeper Magic* conjures the stirring conflict between the ancient power of tradition and the seductive lure of science. Jillian Hunter has woven a spell whose threads are mystery, deep emotion, and the relationship between the very vivid, very human, very amusing and touching characters of Margaret Rose and Ian MacNeill."
—Kathryn Lynn Davis, bestselling author of *Too Deep For Tears*

"In this highly original, powerful love story . . . Jillian Hunter has written her *tour de force. A Deeper Magic* is compelling, captivating, and enthralling . . . Four and 1/2 stars."
—*Romantic Times* on *A Deeper Magic*

Turn the page and see what everyone's talking about . . .

HE WAS MORE TROUBLE THAN
A WOMAN SHOULD EVER HAVE TO HANDLE . . .

She was standing in a sleeveless chemise and stockings, her petticoats hitched up to her shoulders like a coat of armor. She stared in utter disbelief at Niall for several seconds, then opened her mouth to emit what he suspected would be one earsplitting scream.

"Don't." He moved swiftly behind her, bringing his hand up to her face. "You scream, *chérie,* and I guarantee that your long-suffering husband, who is searching for you even as we stand here, is going to take one look at you half-naked in my arms and assume the worst. Do you understand?"

She jerked her head into a nod, her eyes wide with indignant anger as he lowered his hand and stepped forward to face her again.

In her entire twenty not-uneventful years, Elspeth Kildrummond had never found herself in quite such an embarrassing situation. Caught returning from one of her forbidden escapades by a guest at her own engagement party. In her underwear, to heap shame upon scandal.

Well, she could only blame her own impulsive nature. It wouldn't be the first time she'd brought disaster upon herself.

"Do you mind going outside while I finish dressing?" she snapped when it became clear he had no intention of doing such a socially correct thing on his own.

Niall lifted his broad shoulders in an apologetic shrug that belied the dark mockery in his eyes. "I can't," he said in a stage whisper. "I'm hiding from someone—just like you. And actually, I have to admit I'm very curious to see how we'll get ourselves out of this situation."

JILLIAN HUNTER

GLENLYON'S BRIDE

PINNACLE BOOKS
KENSINGTON PUBLISHING CORP.

PINNACLE BOOKS are published by

Kensington Publishing Corp.
850 Third Avenue
New York, NY 10022

Pinnacle and the P logo Reg. U.S. Pat. & TM Off.

First Printing: October, 1995

Printed in the United States of America

For my sister, Michele Bloomquist,
with all the love in the world

As always my love and thanks to
my husband Jim, my godfather Gordon Thomson,
and my dear friend Kathryn Lynn Davis . . .

GLOSSARY OF FOREIGN TERMS

Scottish/Gaelic

clairschach	ancient wire-strung Irish/Celtic harp
claymore	a large Highland sword
corrie	a hollow circle in a hillside
dollyshop (British slang)	pawnshop
ghillie	attendant
kelpie	a water spirit
laird	a landed proprietor
mail-dubh	blackmail
skene dhu	a dagger worn in the stocking
sporran	purse
strath	valley
targe	light shield
tocher	dowry

French

au diable	the devil (exclamatory)
au revoir	good-bye
bon Dieu	good God
bonté divine	good gracious
chère; chérie	dear; darling
crime passionel	crime of passion
Dieu	God
doucette	sweetheart

grand-mère	grandmother
grand-père	grandfather
je m'en fiche	I don't care
je ne sais	I don't know
je vous prie	I beg you
le bon temps	the good times (days)
ma belle	my beauty
ma chère	my dear
ma foi	my word
maman	mother
ma petite	my little one
mon coeur	my heart
mon Dieu	my God
monsieur	sir; mister
n'employez pas	don't use
n'est-ce pas?	isn't it so?
nom de Dieu	in the name of God; by God
non	no
oui	yes
quelle horreur	what horror
sacrebleu	damn it
sacré nom d'un chien	damn it all
tonnerre de nom	good heavens

Gypsy/Romany

catch-gadjes	police
didakeis	half-breed gypsy
dukker	to tell fortunes
dukkerin	fortunetelling
fambles	hands
gorgio	non-gypsy
hobbiken	trick; spell
O'Del	God

patteran	a secret trail left by gypsies for other gypsies to follow
posh-rat	big (important) man
shannas	trouble

Malay/Hindu

chawat	belt
hantu	haunted
jadoo	Far Eastern magic
kris	wavy sword
leyak	evil fairy; witch
panang	witch doctor
parang	knife; like a machete
shikar	hunt
shikari	hunter

One

Captain Niall Glenlyon had been sitting alone in his host's darkened library for only three minutes or so when the door to the terrace began to rattle. Fortunately, he'd bolted that door to protect his privacy as soon as he had entered the room. For good measure he'd also drawn the drapes to block out the annoying glare of the bright fairy lanterns strung outside. He really hated parties.

The sash windows shook next, glass reverberating against wood.

He scowled and slowly sat forward, tossing his fresh cigar into the unlit fireplace. He'd spent most of his life in Burma and Indonesia, growing up in a jungle mission, then serving in the Queen's Native Infantry before ending up as a soldier of fortune in a privately supported army. He wondered for a moment if this could be an earthquake. It seemed improbable on a brisk October evening in Scotland.

The door vibrated again as if a demon were demanding entry. *Dieu,* was he witnessing an attempted burglary? Or had that obnoxious British journalist finally figured out where he was hiding?

The damned radical press had been on his tail for over a fortnight, hoping to sniff out a juicy scandal about the first of the infamous Glenlyon pride to return to civilization. Unfortunately, Niall's reputation, however undeserved or exaggerated, had preceded him.

Even now he cringed at the stories they'd written about him. Seducer of trembling virgins he'd never met. Harem bodyguard. Far Eastern jungle hero and dabbler in dark magic. Louisiana lumberer and priest gone bad. There was just enough truth in the assortment of fairy tales to get him into trouble. In fact, the last Niall had read, in the ludicrous fictionalized version of his life penned by the reporter who persisted in following him, he was purportedly sharing a cave in Bali with a holy man, a deposed Siamese princess, and a dragon lizard.

Well, hell. It sounded better than the social torture he was trying to escape—some pointless engagement party for an aspiring English politician and his fiancée, a young woman who was apparently too spoiled and ill-mannered to have so far bothered making an appearance in her own drawing room. Niall had a private terror of crowds and enclosed places anyway. He'd only been able to tolerate fifteen minutes of pretending he was a polite person before that reporter had arrived at the party.

An intriguing silhouette behind the drapes outside caught his attention. Rising from his comfortable armchair, he walked soundlessly to the window.

"Blast and hell!" a voice whispered on the terrace. "Some nodcock's bolted the door, and the windows are warped tight! Now what am I going to do?"

Being the nodcock in question, Niall stood back between the drapes and looked outside. The irate female had dropped to her knees to struggle with the window. Yes, she was definitely female. Grinning, he stared down at the well-rounded derrière that wriggled directly in his line of vision. The bold creature had evidently hoped to disguise her sex in a pair of baggy tartan trousers, an oversized vest, and a battered velvet bonnet.

Not a burglar. Not a press reporter. Probably just a

maidservant sneaking home from a rendezvous with a neighboring footman. His heavy black eyebrows arched in anticipation, Niall unbolted the door for her and casually returned to his chair.

Far be it from him to thwart the course of true love, or lust for that matter. This impromptu performance would add a little spice to what promised to be an interminable evening.

The window groaned open. The little adventuress with the shapely behind poked her head through the dark brocade curtains. Apparently she was assisted by some unseen companion lurking out in the garden.

"Hurry up, Elspeth," an anxious male voice whispered. "I left the cart out in de street—"

She—Elspeth—worked half her body into the room only to freeze in apparent horror as a small collie came tearing across the terrace to bark at her rump.

Unnoticed, Niall scooted his chair back against the drapes and sat quietly to analyze this interesting turn of events.

"You idiot, Clootie!" Balancing at an awkward angle on her hipbone, Elspeth swatted her hand at the dog's ears. It's only *me*—get your miserable hide back into the kitchen before Cook hears you and I catch merry hell!"

The kitchen. A scullery maid, Niall thought as the collie reluctantly turned and trotted back to the wrought-iron railing, stopping once to look at Niall watching through the drapes.

"What happened, Elspeth?" that nervous male voice demanded from the darker reaches of the garden.

"Just a stupid old dog." The daring Elspeth had dropped into the room with a muffled *ooof,* and Niall could only hear but not see her as she fought with the drapes to squeeze herself out from behind a small piece of furniture.

"Ouch, dammit! I just broke my big toe on that ridiculous rosewood whatnot."

"Rub some spit and crushed comfrey leaves on it." Her companion sounded more afraid than amorous. "I really got to go before de catch-gadjes come. You get me hanged for dis, girl."

"I didn't ask you to see me home in the first place, Samson," she said testily. She straightened and limped past Niall, muttering over her shoulder. "It's not as if I don't know the way, and George is going to kill me if anyone saw us together. Now hurry back to camp before Delilah turns up at the front door demanding to know where you are. And don't forget to give Ali Baba that bran mash."

Samson? *And* Delilah? Niall grinned into the darkness at the odd characters in this young woman's world. George, he guessed, would be her cuckolded husband—the butler or possibly another footman. The poor unsuspecting sod whose young wife sneaked around in trousers having secret trysts with a nervous young man named Samson.

Dejectedly, the woman yanked off her old bonnet and squatted to massage her toe, heedless of the heavy blond braid that fell down her back. She sighed. The sound hinted to Niall of a despair that no amount of illicit adventure could lighten. Raising her head, she sniffed the air in disdain.

"Stupid men and their vile cigars. Why anyone would smoke something that smelled like powdered pig manure is beyond me."

Niall swallowed a laugh. Then just as he thought he'd finally get his first good look at the face of this lower-class Venus, she sprang to her feet with such a horrified shriek that he half rose in reaction himself.

She whirled toward the terrace door. "Oh, my God," she whispered. "My bag—Samson, you dim-witted dumpling, you forgot to give me my bag!"

She'd just wrenched the door open when Niall heard footsteps behind him in the interior hall, and a key turning in the lock of the library door. Then a man's voice asked in a frantic undertone, "Elspeth, are you in there?"

Panicking at the sound of that voice, she fled out onto the terrace, down the steps, and into the garden. Niall stood up. Staring after her, he debated how he would explain *his* presence to an angry husband and how it could be used against him, being caught in the middle of a domestic embarrassment.

He didn't exactly have a saint's reputation. Who in his right mind would believe his innocence?

Impulsively he hurried out onto the terrace. Turning down the path the errant Elspeth had chosen, he took refuge on a bench hidden behind a trellis at the end of the rose garden where he'd last seen her. The evening breeze felt refreshing, rustling the fallen leaves at his feet, and he allowed himself to relax.

A few moments later he spotted her again. Crouched behind a moonlit statue, she was tugging off her oversized trousers with one hand, rummaging through an old duffel bag on the ground with the other.

So that explained the bag's importance. It contained her clothing. Realizing she was about to change back into her normal household attire, Niall watched in unabashed fascination. He was only a man, after all, no matter what had been written about him.

Besides, he was curious to know exactly what this Elspeth and Samson had been up to.

Apparently so was her husband. Niall frowned as he noticed a well-dressed man emerge onto the terrace. His voice was low and he seemed understandably upset.

"Elspeth Victoria, this is absolutely the last straw, do you hear me?"

At that moment Clootie, the old collie, chose to return. Racing across the garden, he skidded to a stop and began circling the rosebushes whose straggly branches sheltered Elspeth. The man on the terrace strode to the stairs, his head cocked suspiciously at the dog's behavior. The young woman herself muttered several unrepeatable words and tried to shoo the dog away with her bonnet. It was quite a dilemma.

"Show yourself this instant, Elspeth," the pompous man on the terrace ordered, but to no avail. He only succeeded in temporarily distracting the dog.

He sounded, Niall decided, too damned imperious for a footman—definitely a butler. Elspeth could be the pastry cook, perhaps some temperamental Parisian-trained upstart from the slums whose culinary talents would play a crucial part in tonight's supper party. The passionate creature must have really thrown the household into an uproar.

"I can't believe you're doing this to me, Elspeth." The man on the terrace was pacing now, and Niall began to think he looked disturbingly familiar. "Everyone is waiting for you to perform."

To perform? A performing pastry cook? Niall frowned, perplexed that he'd failed to solve this preposterous mystery. And even though as a rule he disapproved of infidelity, he felt an inexplicable empathy for this misguided young woman and her predicament.

He'd been forced to hide a few times himself in his life. Not in a town garden with a toothless house dog at his heels, it was true. But he *had* run for cover in sweating rain forests with poisonous thorns ripping the rags from his back, and native man-traps making every step a life-or-death calculation. He'd never forgotten the black terror of those days. The remembered fear of being caught and tortured rippled in his blood even now. But he wasn't sure why this ridiculous woman should remind him of his earlier trials.

Aware he would probably regret it later, he cupped his fingers around his mouth and emitted the deep mewling growl of a jungle panther. The old dog pricked its ears in alarm and warily backed away from the bushes. The man on the terrace threw up his hands in disgust and spun around, muttering to the slender man who'd come to stand in the library doorway behind him.

"It was only a bloody dog and cat in the bushes. I don't know where the hell she's got to."

She had, Niall noted, taken advantage of the diversion to scuttle like a crab up the low semicircular steps of the dilapidated summerhouse behind her. Then she had vanished inside.

He chuckled, silently applauding her audacity. But his amusement soon degenerated into irritation at the appearance at the far end of the garden of the very man he'd been trying himself to escape all evening.

Archie Harper, the persistent pot-bellied press reporter for *Le Bon Temps* magazine. The abrasive pest had been waiting on the docks of Southampton six weeks ago when Niall and his valet had arrived by steamer from Singapore via Marseilles. Undaunted by Niall's refusal to grant him an interview, Harper had followed Niall here after he'd received word his uncle in the Highlands was gravely ill and wished to see him.

Niall had cut short his London stay and traveled north, pausing only the past two days in Falhaven to finalize business arrangements for his fledgling coffee plantation with the mercantile firm of Kildrummond and Westcott— the hosts of this evening's entertainment. Tomorrow he'd be on the road to the Highlands proper. Within two months he hoped to God to be on his way back to his unknown little island in the Malay Archipelago.

"Captain Glenlyon?" Harper's irritating nasal whine, with a touch of Cockney origins, set Niall's teeth on edge. "I know you're out there 'aving a smoke. Just want a few minutes of your time to set the record straight about poor Rachel."

Rachel. Poor Rachel. God, not again.

Niall's reaction was instinctive. In one fluid move, he dove behind the screen of fading autumn roses and swung in a semicrouch into the summerhouse. Reminded of Rachel, his ever-present anxiety over her, he'd failed to take into consideration the other young woman whose furtive antics had so entertained him until he straightened. Turning slowly, he found himself face to face with the misadventurous Elspeth herself.

She'd taken her braid loose, and her hair was the wildest, most sensual mane he'd ever seen on a woman—a waist-length tangle of dark blond pre-Raphaelite curls that made her look like a naughty wood nymph. Her face was sweet. Finely drawn, it had a patrician nose, and a ripe, soft, red mouth as tempting as a strawberry. Her eyes, however—the luminous golden-green of an enraged tigress—held his imagination at bay before it could get the better of him. Or the worse. His reaction to her was intensely visceral.

Her physical appearance was far from perfect. Those dark scowling eyebrows and cleft chin were too strongly defined for the rest of her face, but Glenlyon doubted that any normal man would be able to resist looking at her.

She was standing in a sleeveless chemise and stockings, her petticoats hitched up to her shoulders like a coat of armor. She stared in utter disbelief at Niall for several seconds, then opened her mouth to emit what he suspected would be one earsplitting scream.

"Don't." He moved swiftly behind her, bringing his hand up to her face. "You scream, *chérie,* and I guarantee that your long-suffering husband, who is searching for you even as we stand here, is going to take one look at you half-naked in my arms and assume the worst. Do you understand?"

She jerked her head into a nod, her eyes wide with indignant anger as he lowered his hand and stepped forward to face her again.

In her entire twenty not-uneventful years, Elspeth Kildrummond had never found herself in quite such an embarrassing situation. Caught returning from one of her forbidden escapades by a guest at her own engagement party. In her underwear, to heap shame upon scandal.

Well, she could only blame her own impulsive nature. It wouldn't be the first time she'd brought disaster upon herself.

"Do you mind going outside while I finish dressing?" she snapped when it became clear he had no intention of doing such a socially correct thing on his own.

Niall lifted his broad shoulders in an apologetic shrug that belied the dark mockery in his eyes. "I can't," he said in a stage whisper. "I'm hiding from someone—just like you. And actually, I have to admit I'm very curious to see how we'll get ourselves out of this situation."

Elspeth clutched her petticoats a little tighter, narrowing her eyes to examine him more carefully.

She'd never met a man who exuded such a potent combination of humor, self-confidence, and unabashed sensuality. His gaze drifted over her in a look that categorized all of her physical assets and deficits—and left her uncertain whether she should laugh at his presumption or belt him across the chops.

He was tall, with longish blue-black hair, and a muscular frame that shouldn't have looked as elegant in evening clothes as it did. His sun-burnished face reminded Elspeth of one she'd seen stamped on a foreign coin in her father's desk, a face that hinted of exotic lands and dangerous ports-of-call.

Giving him her coldest glare, which unfortunately seemed to have no effect on his composure, she crept sideways to duck behind the fan-backed wicker chair which held her evening gown.

"You don't have to watch me, do you?"

He grinned, his even white teeth an attractive contrast

to his dark complexion. "But I've been watching you ever since you broke into the library window. A charming scene."

She scowled. "There's an expression for men like you— men who like to watch people doing private things. My sister read it in a magazine—something that started with a naked woman on a horse."

"I believe you're thinking of a Peeping Tom."

"That's it," she said quickly. "That's what you are."

"I certainly am not," he retorted, looking annoyed for the first time, which gave Elspeth a small measure of satisfaction. "Your sister should find a more productive pastime than reading such rubbish."

Elspeth privately agreed, but she wasn't about to tell him that. "Are you going to leave so I can make myself decent?"

"Not yet. But just to prove I'm no Peeping Tom, I promise I won't look."

He smiled and turned to stare outside while she struggled into her dress. His face—in all its sardonic amusement—was burning in her mind. His features were cleanly sculpted, a strong browline and hawkish nose, the firm mouth of a sensualist above a square-hewn chin. But it was his eyes, those sad, soulful gray eyes, that saved him from being relegated to the realm of practiced rogues and crass businessmen who paraded in and out of her father's house.

She hadn't met him before, even though Duncan Kildrummond was an established shipbuilder and importer of foreign goods who entertained a remarkable mixture of exotic visitors. No, she'd have remembered such an impertinent man, she was sure.

She bit the inside of her cheek, peering out from the curtain of hair that fell across her face. She was well enough versed in etiquette to realize he might be a foreign dignitary—she tried to place his country of origin by his burnished skin and compelling physiognomy, but her boarding-school geography failed.

He'd spoken both in English and French. An ambassador from Morocco, perhaps? Some sultan's arrogant bastard son? Or a mere sea captain from Quebec who sold lumber? Whoever he was, he offended every decent feeling and made her aware of some indecent ones as well.

She finished fastening the hooks at her back, thinking distractedly that if she continued to eat and drink as she had earlier in the evening, she'd never fit into her wedding gown. "I don't know where you come from, *monsieur,* but in this country, it's exceedingly rude for a man to impose his presence on a woman in the middle of her toilette."

"In my country it's considered so rude for a woman to cuckold her husband that he's justified in throwing her into a live volcano."

Elspeth's mouth dropped open.

Niall pivoted slowly, his eyes widening at the transformation her change of clothing had made. "You're not the pastry cook, are you?"

"The what?" She frowned and stepped out from behind the chair, hastily twisting her dark-gold braid into a knot at her nape.

He studied her in curious silence. Oh, that poor husband of hers. No wonder he couldn't control her behavior. She needed a much firmer hand—Niall had enough experience with wild creatures himself to see that.

She kicked her discarded outfit under the wicker chair and swept barefooted past him with her bag. Her chin was held so high in the air, Niall privately feared she'd step off the uppermost step of the summerhouse and hurt herself.

Instead, he turned deliberately so that she walked right into him. "Wait *chérie,*" he said softly. "There's someone coming."

Elspeth looked up slowly, suppressing a shiver of apprehension. Face to face, he was even more intimidating than when he'd remained at a safe distance in the shadows. Handsome seemed too tame a word to describe the masculine energy he exuded. Once before in her life Elspeth had fallen for another man who looked like a dark angel and who extracted a devil's toll from her soul and reputation.

"You're beginning to seriously overstep the boundaries of the invitation extended you this evening, Mr.—" She stepped back in sudden alarm, her voice rising. "Wait a minute. Three houses have been burglarized in this square during the past week. Just what were you doing in the library with the lights out anyway? Who are you?"

"Niall Glenlyon," he said quietly, unoffended that she thought him a thief. "And you?"

"Elspeth!"

From outside the summerhouse came the sound of footsteps, a man calling furiously, "Fergus said he saw you out here, Elspeth. If you make a fool of me tonight . . ."

His voice faded into a whisper of wind, the dry leaves of ivy that embraced the summerhouse shivering lightly.

Niall stared down into the worried face of the young woman he'd detained. "Ah, not a servant at all—you're one of Duncan's daughters, and that's George the fiancé you've got on a goose chase." His gray eyes amused, he plucked a piece of straw from her hair. "Dear, dear. A roll in the hay cart with Samson right before our own engagement party? It doesn't exactly portend well for a lifetime of wedded bliss now, does it, Miss Kildrummond?"

Two

With a playful gesture, Niall flicked away the straw from the bridge of Elspeth's nose. Appalled at his impertinence, while at the same time reluctantly impressed by the invaluable ruby ring on his right hand, she drew a breath and swatted his fingers away. "If it's any of your business, Mr. Glenlyon, which I assure you it's not, I was helping to walk a colicky colt with friends."

"Really?" He widened his eyes. "Then why all the bother with the secret disguise and athletic climb through the library window?"

Elspeth took another breath to counteract the sense of intimacy mounting between them, dimly aware of George calling her again from the other side of the summerhouse. For all his lighthearted banter, this was apparently a man who enjoyed flirting with danger. George not only had a black temper, he was also an excellent marksman, a skill perfected during the frequent hunting parties he hosted on his forested Devon estate. Personally, Elspeth detested the sport, as she did George's obsession with guns. But everyone else seemed to think her fiancé was a master of the most masculine pastime.

Masculine.

The man standing in front of her gave worlds of dimension to the word.

She pursed her lips. "Neither my fiancé nor my father

approves of my current choice of friends, and I'm quite sure they wouldn't approve of our conversation either."

Niall blinked. "Well, I wasn't the one running around in a provocative state of undress—accusing innocent strangers of perverted acts." He dropped his voice to a conspiratorial whisper. "These friends of yours are criminals, perhaps? Swindlers and prostitutes?"

In his irreverent mockery, he'd come closer to the truth than Elspeth could believe. "They're gypsies if you must know," she confessed, not knowing why she felt obliged to answer him at all. "Horse dealers who are camped on the outskirts of town, and we're trying to raise a racehorse for the Duke of—"

She stopped herself before she could reveal her most personal dreams, scowling at the delighted smile that brightened his swarthy face and deepened the grooves on either side of his mouth. He was the most dangerous sort of man, the type who seduced young women in his sleep with his false sincerity which no doubt hid the ruthless motives of a wolf. He was gorgeous, a dark well-muscled god whose smile alone might have melted Elspeth's heart if it had not been so tightly guarded.

Fortunately, she was immune to such devilish charm. She'd be married in two short months, a fact which to her fiancé's constant irritation she too frequently forgot, and she intended to leave all her adolescent mistakes and romantic hopes behind her. Respectably wed, she could concentrate on scraping up the money to restore the deteriorating Highland home that was her *tocher,* or dowry, to Sir George Westcott. George had been recently knighted for his success in foreign business affairs, in tea and teakwood, and he hoped to win a seat in the House of Commons next year, with an eye on a cabinet position. And he'd promised her that if he won, they would stay at Liath House whenever he wasn't in Westminster.

But George knew nothing of her secret scheme with

the gypsy couple Samson and Delilah Petulengro and the eccentric Duke of Kengownie who bred horses on his sprawling Tayside estate, where he lived with his mistress, a widowed countess from Avignon. George had no idea Elspeth had struck up these strange friendships through a bookmaker at a horserace two years ago outside London. To this day, he believed that Elspeth had been taking badly needed deportment lessons from the impoverished French countess, whom he'd employed to give his betrothed that "Continental flair."

Gypsies, prostitutes, gin and gambling parties. The countess had given Elspeth quite an education, all right.

No. George knew nothing of the colt named Ali Baba which the five unlikely partners intended to enter in the Derby and the St. Leger next year. He would die a thousand deaths if he did.

"Gypsies?" the man with the Scottish name and mysterious origins exclaimed, his mischievous eyes intent on her face. "Children of the night—fortunetellers and pickpockets. Your betrothed must have a heart of stone to deny you such innocent company."

She narrowed her eyes. "Are you making fun of me, Mr. Glenlyon?"

"*Ma chère,* how could you think such a thing?"

He managed to look genuinely insulted, but the wicked sparkle in his heavy-lidded eyes confirmed her suspicions. Unfortunately there were times when Elspeth herself wondered if George had much heart at all, not to mention one made of stone. His saving quality was that he seemed to love her, and Elspeth had come to believe that loving her required the forbearance of a saint. Of course, if George had known about her horrible fall from grace three years ago, he wouldn't have wanted her as his parlormaid, not to mention as his wife.

They had practically grown up together in the sleepy crofting village of Glen Fyne that lay sheltered in a foothill valley of the inhospitable Cairngorm Mountains. For several happy years they'd spent every summer together, she and her younger sister Catherine, the adored granddaughters of the laird, Ronald Kildrummond; George the only son of an English financier who packed him away each year to stay with his dour Scottish relatives. George's uncle had managed the small moorland estate that bordered the sheltered Kildrummond lands which for centuries had supported a poor farming community.

Every magical summer, until she turned seventeen, Elspeth and George had hunted, fished, swum and savored life's sweetness together. Then George's father had pulled a few strings and secured a position for his son in the Royal Navy as a midshipman. Several weeks after George went away, Elspeth's mother, Helen, caught a cold which developed into pneumonia. She died at sunrise one bright July morning before the old doctor could even be roused from his own bed to attend her. Devastated by the cruel swiftness of Helen's death, Ronald Kildrummond and his son Duncan could barely struggle through the following weeks of anger and raw sorrow, let alone spare comfort on Helen's two young grieving daughters.

To cope with her own pain, Elspeth had thrown herself into the running of the estate. This proved a formidable task since oat crops had failed two years in a row, and starvation threatened the tenant farmers. In other outlying areas, hunger riots had erupted, but Elspeth remained confident that the poor families who regarded her as one of their very own would not turn against the Kildrummonds. Besides, her grandfather was slowly impoverishing himself to feed them.

"Your thoughts are a hundred miles away, Miss Kildrummond," Niall observed quietly, his voice too compelling to ignore. "And very disturbing thoughts they are, if I'm to judge by the look on your face."

Elspeth glanced up into his dark gray eyes and felt a

moment of irrational panic, as if somehow his perceptive gaze did indeed have the power to probe her most private secrets. Shaking off the disturbing sensation, she edged around him to the steps. She supposed it was part of his charm, to pretend sympathy when in all likelihood, he had only one thing on his mind.

Seduction.

His deep voice mocked her attempt to escape him. "Everyone is entitled to have a few secrets, I always say. And I'm in no position to judge you, *ma belle.*"

Elspeth paused, her breath trapped in her throat. He meant it as a joke, but if only he knew. She had her secrets, all right. Secrets that might shock even this man with all his worldly experience.

In the August of her seventeenth summer, a young sheriff's substitute named Robert Campbell had been sent by his superiors to Glen Fyne to find out whether the Kildrummonds needed any officers to prevent rioting among their tenants. Elspeth was outraged at the handsome officer's suggestion of disloyalty, exhausted from the physical work of weeding and clearing stones from the unproductive soil.

Everyone called her an angel for her selfless devotion to the glen. But the truth was, she had needed an outlet for her sorrow. She'd also needed a shoulder to cry on, and Robert Campbell contrived to offer her his massive shoulders at every opportunity.

Vulnerable and inexperienced, she'd succumbed at first to his subtle expressions of compassion, then to his rugged charm. A month later, when he returned to his headquarters in Inverness, she had learned that she was pregnant after their first and only night spent together.

One night of impetuous pleasure, and she would pay for the rest of her life. And she was too humiliated, too afraid to ask for help. Her grandfather and father would disown her and murder Robert. Catherine was too young to understand. And George, well, George was playing sailor at sea.

Anyway, a woman didn't exactly ask the man who loved her to overlook this sort of mistake.

No one had known her awful secret except her grandfather's trusted old gamekeeper and a few of the tenant families who cared about her. In fact, they'd cared about Elspeth so much, they had sent a band of indignant young farmers after Robert to bring him back to marry her at musket-point.

Elspeth smiled ruefully at the memory. She hadn't loved Robert, not really. And as it turned out, her dear friends had been forced to return to Glen Fyne without Robert anyway, after discovering he was already married with five small children to support. Later, she'd learned that they had held a lottery to see who among the unmarried farmers would ask for her hand. But it had never come to that. She had lost the child.

She exhaled slowly. Her shoulders tensed as the past slipped away and the present, with all its problems and temptations, intruded. Glenlyon had walked up behind her; his cool breath brushed her cheek as he broke the silence. The pleasant sparks of sensation that rose to the surface of her skin reminded her she couldn't afford a moment of inattention in his presence. Even his formal black evening attire couldn't hide the primal energy of the man.

"You couldn't possibly have any truly dark secrets, Miss Kildrummond. Not with the sheltered life you've led. Now me, on the other hand"—he lifted his shoulders in an elegant Gallic shrug—"well, my past is as murky as mud."

"You'll forgive me if I don't find that hard to believe."

He laughed, too delighted by her cranky outlook on life, too attracted to her, to take offense. "On the contrary. You're wise to be wary of my shadowed past."

She sighed. She didn't care to imagine the encyclopedia of sins he'd committed, but she did wish she could put her own humiliating memories behind her. Still, perhaps it was better to remember. As long as she did, she wasn't liable to fall under the spell of a man like Niall Glenlyon.

"You're a funny little thing, did you know that?" he asked unexpectedly.

"A funny little thing?" she repeated, turning stiffly to stare at him. "Is that supposed to be a compliment in your country, Mr. Glenlyon?"

"I'm not sure whether it's a compliment or not," he said, completely honest now. "It's certainly not an asset in European society." He lowered his voice. "I do know I've never met anyone quite like you before."

Elspeth sighed again. "Well, you're not exactly seeing my best side. I'm a bit at odds tonight, what with the colt and the party and the—the weather."

She frowned, rubbing her forearms as if she'd just realized how cool the breeze had become. It *was* odd that she hadn't noticed before, but then this Glenlyon character had gotten her so agitated it was no small wonder she hadn't felt the autumn bite in the air.

"The weather," Niall repeated slowly, glancing out into the garden, but not with any real interest. *"Oui,* there's something brewing off the sea, I'd have to agree."

"My grandfather would say the fairies are whipping up another spell of wickedness to unleash on this evil world," Elspeth murmured.

Niall took advantage of their momentary truce to study the exposed line of her throat, the tantalizing hollow where her pulse beat beneath her finely grained skin. "Well," he said, forcing himself back to the subject, "the world is generally an evil place, and no doubt your *grand-mère* was a wise woman to warn you of it. My valet is a great believer in the spirits himself."

"Is he?" Elspeth asked to be polite, but she was suddenly more intrigued by the way his eyes could darken from the impenetrable gray of Highland mist to pewter.

"Oh, indeed," Niall answered. "He's probably burning a few offerings even as we speak."

"Dear me."

"He worries over me like a mother hen," he confided.

"I can well imagine."

"He has it in his head that our journey to Scotland is some sort of mystical quest."

Elspeth compressed her lips into a disapproving line. This was a preposterous conversation to carry on with a stranger, and she knew better than to encourage it.

"I'm going inside now, Mr. Glenlyon."

Niall was suddenly reluctant to let her go. Their charming interlude had been like a breath of fresh air to chase away his despondent mood, and he wasn't ready to return either of them to the perils of reality quite so soon.

But, no. He was getting carried away, searching for excuses to avoid that boring party. And she *was* right. Some indefinable energy hummed in the air.

She took a step down, feeling his gaze follow her nervous retreat. "As unspeakably thrilling as it's been to meet you, Mr. Glenlyon, I'm afraid I have to run inside to finish dressing now."

"Of course." His deep voice was politeness itself, and he was irritated that for a whimsical interval, he'd managed to disregard the fact that she had a fiancé, and that they were both playing truant from a party to celebrate her engagement.

"Don't forget to brush the rest of the straw from your hair," he couldn't resist calling after her.

She touched the twisted knot at her nape in annoyance. Her shoulders stiffened.

"And put some proper shoes on those restless feet, Miss Kildrummond."

She glanced back at him, too indignant to think of a reply.

He grinned shamelessly. "Well, I'd hate for you to stub

your big toe again on that ridiculous rosewood whatnot," he explained in a solicitous tone.

"You're too very kind—"

He raised his hand abruptly to silence her, his grin fading. Elspeth looked around in confusion, feeling the nerves in her spine tingle at the warning on his face. Then without explanation or apology, he caught her elbow and dragged her back up toward him, staring over her head to some unidentified threat outside. She swallowed a cry as he forced her flush to his chest. Her breasts pressed against his black evening jacket and the wall of iron muscle and sinew that lay beneath it.

"Do you bloody well mind?" she demanded.

"Be quiet!" he whispered calmly. "And don't pull on my jacket again—I've only got it on loan. The damn thing goes back to the pawnbroker in the morning."

A pawnbroker. Dear lord, he was a pauper, and proud of it. She leaned back and renewed her efforts to break his hold.

He shook his head in warning and gripped her even harder until she gasped, pinned against him as helplessly as a captive butterfly.

"Behave yourself, Miss Kildrummond," he murmured with an amused smile.

Seconds later she heard what Glenlyon's sharper senses had already detected—the tread of footsteps on the secluded path to the summerhouse. It was too late. George had found her, barefooted and standing in the arms of a strange man. Mortified as she imagined the scene that would surely ensue, she looked up and glared at the square line of Glenlyon's closely shaven chin.

"I know you're in there, Elspeth," George said, huffing like a bull. "This little prank has gone too far."

Niall glanced down at her, frowning at the colorful emotions that crossed her face: alarm, resentment, embarrassment. *Bon Dieu,* why should he bother to save her from making a spectacle of himself? She struck him as haughty and defiant and more than a little deserving of some old-fashioned discipline if she didn't want to find herself in really serious trouble one day. Look at his own damn foolish behavior tonight, and he'd only just met her. Her unstudied sensuality brought out all his reckless impulses.

And Niall minded his own affairs. No jealous fiancés, no outraged husbands, thank you very much. But as he stared down into her sweetly anxious face, something of her inner turmoil communicated to that place in his heart where he had suffered his own share of torment. To his astonishment he felt such an unexpected infusion of tenderness and unbridled desire for her that he would have cheerfully murdered her fiancé on the spot.

How many times had he been forced to trust a stranger's compassion? How many times, in how many improbable places, had he hidden from enemies with his very life at stake?

It couldn't hurt to help her once.

He dipped his head toward hers, pressing his mouth to her ear. Her skin smelled delectable, of rose water and woodsmoke and woman, and his body tightened in response. At any other time he might have been tempted to take her into his arms and investigate just what lay beneath her shield of touch-me-not tartness. Instead, he whispered, "Hide behind the chair again. I'll take care of the nuisance for you."

She bit her lip, backing away from him. The sexual hunger in his eyes had not escaped her notice. But neither had his sympathy or wicked humor, such a devastating combination. She was going to pay for accepting the charming devil's help. She just knew it. But the alternative, one of George's frightful lectures . . .

"Elspeth!" George's voice had dropped to its most thunderously low-timbered pitch, the same tone he practiced in front of her for his anticipated oratory arguments in Parliament.

She crouched behind the chair, her heart in her throat as he climbed into the summerhouse and stared blankly into the shadows. He'd burst a major blood vessel if he discovered her hiding from him like this.

"Captain Glenlyon," she heard him say in surprise, obviously not expecting to find the other man alone in the summerhouse. "We haven't formally met, but I'm Duncan's partner from Devon."

"Sir George Westcott. Yes, I believe we passed each other in the hall earlier."

Elspeth watched them shake hands.

"I was looking for my fiancée Elspeth," George explained in an exasperated voice. "I've run out of excuses to explain her absence."

She saw Niall pull a cigar from the pocket of his black satin vest and light it. His voice was admirably casual as he suggested, "Perhaps you should check her bedroom. You know how young women like to preen. The poor *petite* is probably so excited, she can't decide which color dress to wear."

Elspeth rolled her eyes at Glenlyon's preposterous evaluation of her character. *Captain* Glenlyon—probably a pirate, as well as a pauper, she thought with a disdainful sniff. That would explain his predatory air, and what was his association with her father?

"I did check her room earlier," George admitted, venting a frustrated sigh. "Her maid told me she was resting for her violin recital and didn't want to be disturbed."

"Your missing fiancée is a musician?" Niall asked in obvious disbelief.

George hesitated. "Actually, musician is a term that doesn't begin to describe what Elspeth does with a violin."

"How intriguing," Glenlyon said politely. "But as talented as I'm sure this young lady is, I'd really prefer to discuss the profitable East European market Duncan mentioned today."

Their conversation turned to business. Elspeth heard the word "coffee" repeated and something about an island plantation, although she wouldn't have been surprised to learn that the mysterious captain made his living luring little Scottish children into some faraway slave trade. She suspected that George had dealt in the past with other such disreputable characters in foreign ports, as much as he denied it.

The thought reawakened the anxiety that had been building inside her as her wedding day approached. Bridal nerves, her older thrice-married cousin Susan reassured her. But Elspeth had secret doubts. George had changed so much since moving to his posh West End townhouse in London two years ago, and his obsession began with the House of Commons. He was stuffier and more concerned about money and how society viewed him than she could believe.

But he loved her. At least he loved her. And no one under seventy with a full set of teeth had yet to ask for her hand, a problem she'd never really tried to remedy because it had been understood since childhood that she and George would end up together.

Her legs had gone numb from the prolonged crouch. Wiggling her toes, she worked up the courage to peer around the chair again. George was drifting back toward the steps; his face was blocked from her view by Niall Glenlyon's wide shoulders.

She was taken aback at the comparison between the two of them. A well-built man in his late twenties, George looked rather nondescript, even a little plump, standing beside the disgustingly gorgeous man who towered over him like a mountain. The moonlight emphasized the dark contours of Glenlyon's face, his broad shoulders and elegant stance.

As she watched, he flicked his cigar into the garden and put his hand on George's shoulder in a gesture which might be interpreted as an overture of male understanding, but which in reality actually succeeded in forcing George down the summerhouse steps.

"Women," Glenlyon said in a low voice laced with an undercurrent of irony Elspeth suspected was meant for her to hear. "Who, Sir George, can explain their whims and multi-faceted moods?"

George grunted. "If only it were that simple. A woman's moods can be dealt with, Captain. Outright defiance is another matter."

"I'll send the misbehaved Miss Kildrummond on her merry way should I run into her," Niall promised as George blew out another sigh and began to trudge back toward the house. "And if I were you, Sir George," he added loudly, "I'd keep a tighter rein on her in the future, maybe even take her over my knee—"

He slapped his hand down on his thigh for emphasis, grinning over his shoulder at Elspeth as if to reassure himself she could hear him. Fuming in helpless silence, she listened to George give an answering snort of agreement.

"All clear, *chérie.*" As George strode away, reinforced by the troublemaker's advice, Glenlyon pivoted, whistling as if he didn't have a care in the world with his big hands buried in his pockets. "Come out, come out, wherever you are. I took care of—"

She shot up like a cat attacking a canary, blood rushing into her cramped limbs. "I heard exactly what you did." She strode forward, jabbing her forefinger at the ruffles on his white lawn shirt. "Don't expect any thanks from me. And stop trying to impress me with those embarrassing French endearments."

"Ma foi, we are touchy, aren't we? I was only trying to help."

"Well, George doesn't need any encouragement or helpful hints on how to manage my behavior. You'll just make everything worse."

Niall frowned, noticing the taut lines of tension that appeared around her mouth whenever she mentioned her fiancé. "Then why marry him?" he asked simply. He put his right hand to his cheek in feigned horror. The ruby he wore winked in the moonlight. "Or do you have to?"

She gave him a look to wither a fig tree and swept around the chair. Her anger unexpectedly subsided as she reached one of the marble pillars that supported the summerhouse. The breeze had grown stronger. She could barely hear faint strains of conversation drifting from the drawing room of the classical pink granite mansion that dominated the square. She should be there now, at George's side, smiling and acting as if she was enjoying herself, nodding like a simpleton when someone whispered what a lucky girl she was to have snared such a fine man.

"You couldn't possibly understand," she muttered. "George and I have known each other forever."

"Forever seems a bit of an exaggeration, doesn't it?"

Elspeth shrugged her shoulders. "When we were younger, I was George's only champion," she said in a reflective voice. "I used my influence as the laird's granddaughter to defend him from his uncle's demeaning verbal abuse. I used my fists to protect him from the unkind taunts of the tough-bred tenant children who mocked him for his Sassenach softness."

Niall studied her, regretting that he had never known the fierce loyalty of such a friend—or—lover in his life.

"As a child George was afraid of so many things," she went on quietly, "of wild animals and of being alone in the dark."

"And as an adult?" he prompted, not giving a damn

about George but too fascinated by this facet of her character to care.

She shook her head. "I've said too much."

The unpalatable truth was that as an adult George's fears had not disappeared but had taken sometimes disturbing outlets. The bullied boy had become a bully himself, and those creatures he had feared had become the victims of his "masculinity."

Niall came up behind her, his voice softer now. "He's a little chubby around the middle. Are you really in love with him?"

She tensed, wondering why she was wasting her breath trying to explain her muddled life to this impertinent person. "I'm not sure I believe in love, Mr. Glenlyon. Or that it's necessary to ensure a good marriage."

Actually Niall didn't think so either, but it bothered him to hear his own cynical views coming from a woman who surely hadn't shared his miserable experiences. "That doesn't sound very romantic."

"Well, we can't all be Romeo and Juliet now, can we?" she snapped.

Niall was silent, and Elspeth instantly regretted her outburst, which revealed more of her misgivings than she cared to acknowledge even to herself. There probably wasn't anything wrong with George. The fault lay with her own unconventional nature and the impossible dreams and desires that possessed her. She'd been unsettled since her father had uprooted her and Catherine almost two years ago from their beloved Highland home. And then when her grandfather had died unexpectedly last November, the warmth had faded from her world.

"This is more serious than I realized, Miss Kildrummond," Niall murmured into her hair. "Perhaps it still isn't too late to change your mind about this marriage."

She started, Glenlyon's low teasing voice bringing her back to the moment. Turning slowly, she was alarmed at how close together they were standing, at how difficult it had suddenly become for her to breathe. If the breeze outside were brewing a storm, it was warm and cracking with dangerous sparks inside the summerhouse. What a beautiful man he was, she thought irrelevantly, all chiseled elegance and virile power. She resented him for making her so aware of the fact.

"This—this is an entirely inappropriate conversation to be having with a stranger in a summerhouse."

"Nonsense. A stranger is like a priest, and confession is good for the soul."

Elspeth eyed him warily. "I'm not a Catholic."

"And I'm certainly not a priest," he said with a self-deprecating laugh, "no matter what the press may write."

She caught her breath. "I *have* to go."

"Don't marry him," he warned her. "Wait."

She folded her arms across her chest. "For what?"

"Another man might sweep you off your feet," he continued quietly, and he had no idea what he was saying, but he felt an inexplicable urgency to warn her just the same.

"Another man," she repeated, her voice dubious, and even though she suspected this was all part of his routine seduction, she couldn't bring herself to end it quite yet. The heat radiating from his body had a soporific effect on her ability to reason, rather like lying on a warm sandy beach on a summer day. His skin smelled of Castile soap and smoke, of the starch used on his lawn shirt.

"Is George going to tolerate your little adventures after you and he are married, *chère?*" he asked shrewdly.

She smiled coldly. "Would you?"

He gave a silky laugh of surprise. "Hell, no, but then I'd make certain you had enough adventure at home that you wouldn't need to seek it outside."

"Are you proposing I marry you, Mr. Glenlyon?"

He looked so aghast at the suggestion that she had to

laugh, and then he was staring at her mouth, her arms fell to her sides, and the amusement she had felt turned into a sweet panic that immobilized her mind.

"You're making a mistake," he said in an undertone.

She moistened her lips. A subtle languor had invaded her senses—or rather her common sense, dulling the mental reflexes which should have put her on guard against this man. Yet, unfairly, her physical awareness of him had intensified to a horrifying degree. She could feel little sparks of excitement erupting through her body like a fireworks display as she faced him. The flurry of sensations alarmed her, leaving in their wake a trail of shivering heat, but she told herself it was only her temper igniting.

She was strong.

She was going to take one step around him, then another and another until she reached the brightly lit house behind them that glowed like a beacon of sanity. Her home, her house, but she hated it.

"Wait," he repeated softly, edging just a little closer.

"Wait . . . for what?" she asked quietly.

"Wait for something better, *chérie.*"

"Is that your personal philosophy, Mr. Glenlyon, to avoid commitment in general, or just sage advice for me based on the great depth of our relationship?"

Glenlyon didn't answer, didn't touch her. He didn't need to. He was seducing her with his somnolent gray eyes. His gaze was claiming possession as if he were a predator watching his unwary victim in the forest. Her skin burned from the subtle change his face underwent, the teasing humor darkening to an elemental hard-edged hunger she couldn't possibly misinterpret.

He smiled with satisfaction. "If you didn't have your own doubts, you wouldn't be standing so close to me that I could kiss the sadness from your mouth."

"Mind your own damn business!"

"You'd like me to kiss you, wouldn't you?"

"I'm going inside now," she said firmly, realizing how foolish it sounded when he'd made no real attempt to stop her. "Can I trust you to keep what happened tonight a secret?"

She was so adorable, so touchingly solemn that Niall felt ashamed for letting the game go this far. He hadn't enjoyed himself so much in ages. "Do I look like the type to kiss and tell?"

She bristled. "Do I look like the type who would know— or care?"

He braced his arm against the pillar, leaning closer to her but still careful not to take that irretrievable step over the physical boundaries of socially acceptable behavior. It was the intangible ones, however, that had Elspeth worried.

"Kiss me once and find out, Miss Kildrummond," he teased softly. "Kiss me and see if I carry tales out of school."

Three

She shifted her weight, shrinking back from him only to find herself resting against the perilous support of his forearm. At the accidental contact, she straightened her spine and schooled her expression into cool disdain to hide the forbidden excitement that tingled along her nerve endings.

"You need a lesson in manners, Mr.—*Captain* Glenlyon."

"Niall," he said in an amused voice, bending his sun-burnished face toward hers, "and you need taming, *ma chère,* with a firm but gentle hand."

Slowly, as if in anticipation of tasting some precious nectar, he slid his free hand up her shoulder and caught her chin, drawing her face to his. She was staring up at him with the same mesmerized fear that a doe's eyes reflected before a hunter moved in for the kill. Guilt knifed through him, a confusing counterpoint to sexual impulse, and he attempted to suppress it, more intent on seducing her mouth with a slow teasing kiss that would teach her not to flirt with dark, dangerous men . . . least of all not with someone like him.

But as his lips hovered a mere breath from hers, as he lowered his arm to pull her toward him, he was unprepared for his own reaction, not just the powerful urges of his body, but of the unexpected tenderness that tightened his heart. "How sweet you are," he murmured, frowning

intently as if he didn't want to believe it. And it was true.
He *didn't* like the sudden turn his feelings had taken. He
never liked it when anything threatened his sense of self-
control.

"Oh," Elspeth whispered as he kissed her. The earth
was opening up beneath her feet, the stars in the mid-
night-blue October sky dipping and dancing across her vision. He brushed his lower lip back and forth across her
mouth until her breathing quickened, until tendrils of longing unfurled deep in the pit of her belly and ensnared her
senses. She closed her eyes. She curled her bare toes into
the floor to keep from straining into him.

He dragged her harder against him, and the bolt of excitement that shot through her resisting body broke the
spell. She forced her eyes open, trying to focus on his
face. "You big . . . you French—you presumptuous foreign *bastard!*"

Niall pressed his forehead to hers and laughed helplessly at the look of fury on her face, while his own heart
beat hard with an unnerving combination of desire and
bittersweet emotion.

"Stop looking at me with those huge wounded eyes,
mon coeur," he said huskily. "Run back to your papa and
Georgie-Porgie before I change my mind and devour you
morsel by delicious morsel."

Elspeth swallowed over the aching knot in her throat.
What was wrong with her? She didn't need another heartache in her life, didn't need to flirt with fire when she
had George. Safe, predictable George, who might never
inspire any burning passion in her heart, but he wouldn't
break it either.

"Capt'n Glenlyon!" a triumphant male voice shouted
into the heavy silence that had fallen. "I've finally found
you. I shoulda known a man of your experience would
'ave 'unted down a pretty female before the evening was
over. Who's your quarry then—the saucy little laundress?"

Niall jerked his arm away from Elspeth and looked up, his eyes blazing with resentment. *"Dieu,* that disgusting man again." He raked his fingers through his long black hair, unable to believe he'd been so engrossed in this woman that all his normally alert senses had gone to sleep.

"That's Archie Harper," Elspeth whispered, staring around Niall in sudden panic. "He's a vile press reporter for the most lurid magazine, and he's made a fortune writing about the private lives of scoundrels and harlots. George must have invited him here to cover our engagement party."

She paused to give Niall an accusing frown. "Not that he'll want to marry me if Harper writes about how he caught me alone with you."

Niall's mouth curved into a sardonic smile. It didn't seem a good time to tell her that *he* was one of the miscreants that Harper had made money on with his libelous articles about Niall's allegedly intriguing life.

"Scoundrels and harlots," he murmured. "Oh, hell . . ." Out of habit he started to draw another cigar from his vest pocket, then stopped, surprised to discover his hand was unsteady from his foolish dalliance with Elspeth Kildrummond. And he thought he was teaching *her* a lesson. "I knew there was a reason why I hated parties."

Elspeth pushed away from the pillar, hardly trusting herself to look at his darkly handsome face. "I can't imagine you're invited to many," she said under her breath, "not if your usual behavior includes seducing the host's daughter."

"If I *had* seduced you, you'd be leaving here in a far better mood—or maybe you wouldn't want to leave me at all." He grinned, his blood stirring at the thought. "Maybe you'd be begging me to get rid of Harper so we could finish what we'd started."

Before Elspeth could respond to that outrageous remark,

Archie Harper appeared, wheezing slightly as he mounted the steps. He was extremely stout, on the short side, and had thinning black hair and protruding hazel eyes. On first sight he reminded Elspeth of a little storybook frog in his long-tailed green velvet frock coat, black breeches, and outdated buckled shoes. When he saw her, he popped a licorice pastille into his mouth and gave her a lascivious grin.

She couldn't believe her sister Catherine's claim that Harper had a brilliant mind and that he truly cared about the masses, that he was dedicated to exposing political corruption and social injustice. The only article of his Elspeth had ever read had been entitled *"The Heartache of a Soho Harlot."* Lies and libel, he'd once written in an editorial, were perfectly acceptable literary devices if they helped to get a beneficial message across to humanity.

Her face wary, Elspeth watched him hike up his baggy woolen trousers to approach her. Aware by his sly grin that he would assume the worst of her encounter with Glenlyon, she started to pull even farther away from the pillar.

"Don't you dare move an inch," Niall told her quietly. "Don't give him the impression this was anything more than a chance meeting."

"It *was* a chance meeting," she whispered back indignantly.

"Was it? My valet wouldn't think so. And Harper here would leap at the opportunity to describe our misbehavior in his magazine."

"Your misbehavior, you mean."

"I was merely an innocent bystander, *ma chère,* but if you keep whispering in my ear that way, the man is really going to assume there's something between us."

And so Elspeth stayed, her face strained, her senses still in chaos, while Glenlyon lounged back against the pillar, appearing only mildly irritated at the intrusion. A chance meeting, indeed.

"Well, well," Archie murmured. "What 'ave we here? The world-famous jungle 'unter and the lively Miss Kildrummond." He planted himself between her and Niall. His buggy eyes shone with glee as he glanced from one to the other. "Do I smell a scandal brewing, Captain?"

Niall smiled darkly. "Anything you smell is probably wafting from your own foul imagination, little man." He pretended to sniff the air. "Or is that your cologne?"

Archie chuckled appreciatively. "Captain Glenlyon *and* Elspeth Kildrummond. Dear me, what a pairing. But I sense I've interrupted a tender moment. Does Sir George suspect, or was this unusual romance unplanned?"

Elspeth sucked in her breath, twisting her hands in her skirts so she wouldn't be tempted to shove him back down the steps. The tension between her and Glenlyon couldn't be so obvious that a clod like Archie Harper could sense it. And yet she knew it was. She knew instinctively that the combination of two such strong-willed characters as her and Niall had created a dangerous alchemy to be avoided at all costs.

"Sir George and your father are beside themselves with worry over your absence, Miss Kildrummond." Archie flashed her a gummy smile. "I guess it took the infamous shikari himself to find you."

"Infamous shi—" Elspeth looked exasperated. "I haven't the faintest idea what you're talking about."

"Don't you read the papers?"

"Not the rubbish you write."

"Your charming sister does."

"My charming sister doesn't have the brains God gave a goose when it comes to literary taste," Elspeth retorted.

Archie pursed his mouth, not the least bit perturbed. "If you'd had an interest in international news, my dear, you'd know that Captain Glenlyon is a jungle tracker—"

"And if you'd had an interest in the truth," Niall interrupted, "you'd know I've been retired for years. I'm a boring planter now, and there's a Dutchman on Java who's a better tracker than I ever was."

Archie shook his balding head and began jangling a handful of loose change in his trousers pocket. "I can't imagine Sir George will be pleased to 'ear I caught his fiancée 'iding in the summerhouse with a bloke who once worked in a brothel. Can't imagine it at—"

"Worked in a—a *what?*" Elspeth's shocked gaze flew to Glenlyon's face, but he refused to look at her. His expression was unreadable. Well, that was the end of her now. She was finished. A pauper, a pirate, *a brothel.* It was too bad. It was unbelievable. It could only have happened to her!

Glenlyon drew himself up to his full height, his face tight with warning. Elspeth's reaction to his past history had not escaped his notice; it shouldn't even have fazed him. She wasn't the first young woman to find him attractive only to run hiding behind her papa's back when she discovered the ugly truth about Niall's life. And he told himself he didn't care. He wanted nothing to do with her anyway.

Still, he couldn't deny the plunge his spirits had taken at the revulsion in her eyes. The sense of sweet conspiracy between them had suddenly become tainted. And it hurt. Damn her for making him so aware of his unworthiness. Damn her for making him hope, even for an instant, that her penchant for peculiar companions would include someone as tarnished as him.

"It might be beneficial to your continued good health if you didn't tell Sir George anything about tonight, Harper," he said in a dangerously soft voice.

"I—I'll make a deal with you, Captain Glenlyon." Archie's voice cracked with the nervous strain of withstanding Niall's basilisk stare. "Your life story to leave this young lady's name outta the magazine. I mean, it's not as if she can weather another slur on her social standing."

Elspeth stared at him in shock. Harper had an uncanny ability to unearth scandal, but he couldn't possibly have learned about her ill-fated love affair that tumultuous summer in the Highlands. What he probably had heard was the gossip that she'd been spotted attending a horse race last spring with several women of disreputable character, the gypsy fortuneteller Delilah and a few local prostitutes who'd wanted to invest their earnings in her racehorse scheme.

It wasn't that Elspeth sought such colorful characters out on purpose. She'd just never had much luck mingling with the other women of her own class. Their hypocrisy infuriated her. Their preoccupation with such soul-stirring pursuits as playing charades and reciting love sonnets to their lap-dogs made her want to scream aloud in annoyance.

"I think you're proposing blackmail, Mr. Harper," Glenlyon said slowly, straightening his broad shoulders in his borrowed coat. "What makes you think I give a damn about what you write at all?"

"Well, now, Capt'n, there's Miss Kildrummond to worry about—"

"I suggest you start worrying about your shortened life expectancy," Niall broke in grimly.

Elspeth put her hand to her throat and ventured closer to the steps. If Glenlyon was going to murder Archie or destroy what was left of her name, she couldn't stop him. Anyway, she'd begun to feel sick from the dandelion wine she'd drunk with Delilah, and more than a little anxious over her prolonged absence from the house. It was fashionable to be a trifle late, but you didn't arrive two hours into your own engagement party.

"Your fate is in his hands, Miss Kildrummond," Archie said with a dramatic sigh.

She glanced up again at Glenlyon. He was scowling at her as if it were all her fault his overamorous inclinations had gotten them into this mess. Her own earlier escape to the Romany encampment had been carefully planned for a week, a business venture as she saw it. Even George wouldn't be able to object to her subterfuge once he realized she was secretly plotting to make them rich.

But this scapegrace Captain Glenlyon could ruin it all, and she might have taken the opportunity to put him in his place if he hadn't looked quite so forbidding. His harsh moonlit face gave no hint to what he was about to do. A brothel. Good God. A man like that was capable of anything.

He chuckled unexpectedly, dispelling the dark images running rampant in Elspeth's mind. "My goodness, what a pair of stormy petrels you are. If we were in the jungle, Harper, I'd feed you to the crocodiles. And you, Miss Kildrummond"—he shook his head—"out of sympathy for your future husband, I suppose I'll have to answer this man's silly questions."

Archie chortled, then pulled a pencil and diary journal from his coat pocket.

"Go!" Glenlyon widened his eyes at Elspeth. "Don't you have the sense to know when to escape?"

She did, backing down the stairs only to catch her breath in surprise as the breeze sent a pile of fallen leaves dancing around her feet. She could hear the press reporter firing personal questions at Glenlyon, questions that would make a decent person blush. And even though she had no interest in the sordid details of the captain's life, she slowed as she reached the pathway to the house, listening intently despite herself.

"Is it true that you studied for the priesthood in Louisiana, Captain, that your experiences in a Mandalay brothel and as a jungle soldier so sickened your soul that you turned to religion as an antidote?"

She heard Niall's low cynical laughter. "Do I look like a particularly spiritual man, Mr. Harper?"

No, Elspeth answered silently, you do *not*.

"But the American papers reported that you'd entered the seminary somewhere in Louisiana."

"That sounds like something my headstrong older brother would do," Niall replied, sounding bored. "For a laugh."

Archie seemed confused. "And he's the priest?"

"The last time I saw Alex was about two years ago—when I served as his second in an illegal duel over some New Orleans debutante. You may think I'm an endless source of scandal, Harper, but my brothers have outdone me." Elspeth imagined him taking a long draw on his smelly cigar. "My uncle was a missionary-priest in Siam, and yes, I spent a few months in the seminary. I suppose that's where that particular rumor got started."

"There was another brother then," Archie mumbled, clearly disappointed.

"My younger brother Dallas. He's either struck it rich in the Far Eastern lumber trade by now, or he's dead."

"And Rachel Glenlyon?"

Elspeth frowned and pivoted involuntarily at the note of interest in Archie's voice. Even across the distance she could feel the sudden intense silence before Niall growled out a surprising reply.

"Ask me about being a voodoo lumberer and helping slaves escape through the swamp. Ask me about the army and getting malaria, or about leading idiot Europeans on suicidal treks into the jungle. But leave that part of my personal history the hell alone, Harper. Do you understand?"

Four

Rachel—could that be the name of the infuriating man's wife, his mother or even his sister? Elspeth's frown deepened. Whoever this mystery woman was, she certainly evoked a strong emotional response from Niall Glenlyon. And in what capacity could he have worked in a brothel?

Pondering the few intriguing tidbits of information she'd overheard about his life, she turned back toward the house. And looked up with a start into her fiancé's unsmiling face.

By most standards George was an attractive man, with clean masculine features, expressive brown eyes, and a full-lipped mouth that could look sulky when it wasn't trained into a smile. A few years ago, before business and then politics had taken over his life, before he'd been knighted for his commercial trading ventures in the Orient, he'd been an avid horseman who had shared her passion for racing. Now he only rode during one of the famous hunts he held on his well-stocked estate, and his athletic frame had begun to soften as a result of his sedentary life. Still, he was considered quite a catch, and Elspeth was well aware that half of Falhaven wondered how she'd managed to land a titled bachelor with a future in Parliament.

Looking at him now, she found it hard to believe that they'd ever stayed up all night together chasing hedgehogs in the glen, or in the village kirkyard on All Hallows Eve to prove to George that the ghosts wouldn't rise from their graves. This was the same dear boy who'd kissed her when she had the mumps and spoon-fed her barley water, who'd fainted at her feet when she had showed him the adder she had found, the same boy who had cried for her in his coach when he went away to sea.

But that George had left Glen Fyne and never returned, and she missed her old companion, hoping against hope that he would reappear when his obsession with politics ended. Otherwise, she wondered how they could possibly be happy when he thrived on his boring social life in London, and she adored riding free in the hills with her unlikely collection of forbidden friends.

She forced a bright smile. "George! I thought you were locked in a furious card game with that old lecher Martin MacDuff."

"So you remember who I am," he said in a clipped tone. "I suppose it's too much to hope you also remember we have an engagement party planned for the evening? Supper has been delayed so long that your father was reduced to serving light refreshments. The guests are at the hors d'oeuvres like a pack of wolves."

She leaned down to pluck a piece of gravel out from between her toes, praying he wouldn't question the guilt that was surely written all over her face. His reference to wolves reminded her too well of her embarrassing encounter with Niall Glenlyon. But when she straightened, sneaking a glance toward the summerhouse, both Niall and Archie had disappeared, presumably to finish their fascinating conversation in private.

George narrowed his eyes, noticing where her attention had wandered. "Where have you been all evening anyway?"

She waited until he looked away to brush another piece of straw from her hair. "Practicing my violin." She held up her bulging duffel bag for inspection.

"Outside?"

"Well, yes." And it wasn't exactly a lie. Old Milo had let her play his fiddle for a few moments around the gypsy campfire before the complaints about her performance from the other Rom had grown too vocal to ignore.

George compressed his lips, examining her too-bright face, her lopsided chignon, then finally—the damning evidence—her filthy bare feet. "My coachman thought he saw you riding down the street in a gypsy wagon."

"I told you the old coot was getting senile—"

She broke off with a squeal of alarm as he gripped her arm to drag her against him, glancing back toward the house to see if anyone was watching. "You absolutely reek of smoke and horse sweat—you were with those damned cairds again on the Hill. For God's sake, Elspeth!"

"Really, George, reek is rather an exaggeration."

"What if you fell off one of those untrained horses and broke your neck? What if those gypsies drugged you and sold you into white slavery?"

He was so serious that Elspeth started to giggle; he'd gotten too worked up to even notice.

"What if somebody important saw you with those wretched beggars?"

"They're not beggars," she said defensively. "They're honest gypsies, horse-traders and fortunetellers."

He snorted in disgust. "Honest gypsy is a contradiction in terms. I can't believe how naive you can be." Shaking his head in affectionate exasperation, he caught her chin in his hand. "Give me a little kiss before we go inside, and I'll try to forgive you."

Elspeth frowned as she stared up at his face, surprised when that other man's image sprung into her mind. Dark, mocking, temptation personified. Disturbed by the too-fresh memory, she shook herself free. "I have to go inside to make myself presentable before the party."

George sighed. "I can't argue with that. You realize you

won't be able to behave like this in London. *Lady* Elspeth. Good Lord."

"You promised me we'd spend all our free months in Glen Fyne."

He nodded slowly. "When the old house is made habitable and the grounds are stocked with game so my friends can come shooting."

"The house is fine the way it is," she said with stubborn loyalty. "Anyway, I can't say I'm looking forward to entertaining a lot of fat-bummed Englishmen who think it's jolly good sport to blow off all the poor deer's heads."

George rocked back on his heels, looking as if he might faint. "They're my friends, Elspeth, and your language is appalling. Furthermore, Francis assured me the house isn't fit to live in."

Elspeth felt her temper begin to rise as it inevitably did when George launched into a defense of his peculiar Scottish cousin. "I don't give a tuppenny damn what Coffin Face says."

"I forbid you to call him that."

"He makes my flesh creep, George," she said, crossing her arms.

"He's a good man, a pious man, and you ought to be grateful he agreed to take care of that godforsaken estate."

"A pious man?" Elspeth gave a derisive hoot of laughter. "Catherine and Aunt Flora said they saw him sneaking around the waterfront bawdy house just the day before yesterday."

George sniffed. "Your sister reads entirely too many of those lurid romance novels and magazines."

At any other time Elspeth would have been forced to agree. But George's remark brought up an intriguing point: her sister did cram her head with worthless social trivia, some of which might include whatever had been written about Niall Glenlyon.

A deep lyrical voice spoke behind her.

"I apologize for interrupting such an intimate conversation, but unfortunately you're standing in the middle of the path, and I really don't know of any other way to return to the party."

Elspeth almost jumped out of her skin at the sound of that low-toned voice, a voice that might have been conjured out of her private thoughts. Glancing past George, she saw Captain Glenlyon standing a few feet behind them in his black evening attire. An ironic smile crossed his face as he met her gaze. He had, she thought in reluctant admiration, not only the manners, but also the tread of some wild animal, to sneak up behind them unnoticed as he had.

"What do you want?" she said rudely.

"The poor man is clearly trying to move around us, Elspeth," George said in embarrassment. "I can only hope he didn't overhear you. I daresay he was probably shocked insensible by your bad language."

"Bad language?" Niall stared at Elspeth in exaggerated chagrin. "Surely not from this charming young woman?"

George frowned as if sensing that something was a little off about the situation. "I'm forgetting my manners," he said slowly. "Elspeth, this is Captain Niall Glenlyon of—well, I'm not exactly sure where he's from, but he's recently purchased a coffee plantation on a British Protectorate island in the Malay Archipelago. He's just signed a contract with our company."

"A coffee planter?" Elspeth uncrossed her arms, a little disappointed that her villainous assessment of Glenlyon's character had been so far off the mark. "And here I was thinking he looked for all the world like a French privateer or a procurer of young women for a sultan's harem."

George glanced uncertainly at the other man. "Elspeth is Duncan's daughter and my fiancée, Captain. I'm afraid you'll have to forgive her that rustic sense of humor. She was raised in the Highlands, you see."

"By that he means I'm a savage," Elspeth explained. "I've left my claymore in my room, but I'll probably have cause to use it before I run up and down the dinner table slaying guests."

Niall hid a grin as he took her hand. He would, he decided impulsively, forgive her almost anything for another chance to taste that sweet mouth of hers or even for a few more minutes of flirtatious banter. The thought stirred him more than he liked to admit. This one was trouble. She was the cat who wouldn't be tamed, the tigress who would lead the hunter on a *shikar*, a hunt, of the most hell-raising heights. Fortunately for everyone involved, Niall had retired from the chase and no longer accepted dangerous challenges.

Still, the temptation hung in the air like the smoke of some exotic incense.

"The pleasure is mine, Miss Kildrummond." He grazed her knuckles with his lips, his voice impersonal. "It isn't possible that we've met before, is it?" he questioned softly.

Elspeth gave him a stern look. "No, it isn't."

"You've never been to Singapore?" he persisted. "Perhaps as a guest at the Raffles Hotel?"

"Never."

Niall narrowed his eyes. "Bombay. That's it. You were a guest at the consul-general's lawn party last summer, weren't you—the girl with the pet elephant?"

"I've never been out of Britain in my life," she said crisply, all the while aware, far too aware, of the flames dancing in the depths of his eyes, seductive, dangerous, drawing her into his game.

He sighed deeply. "I could have sworn . . . there's something so familiar about your face. Ah, well, I must be mistaken."

Elspeth could have kicked him. "You must."

Oblivious to the undercurrent of conflict between her

and Glenlyon, George glanced pointedly at his pocket watch. "I suggest you follow us back inside, Captain."

"Yes. Of course." As Glenlyon released Elspeth's hand, his mouth lifted into a sheepish smile. "Imagine my having to ask for help finding the way through a city garden."

"Just imagine," Elspeth said dryly.

"You'd never believe the amount of money I was paid to lead people in and out of jungle swamps."

George started to walk toward the house, slowing when he realized that Niall and Elspeth were not following. "You'll excuse us, Captain. Elspeth is giving a musicale in less than twenty minutes and needs a moment to prepare."

"More like a year of moments," she said under her breath as she wheeled to hurry after him. Then, without knowing why, she glanced back over her shoulder at Glenlyon.

It was a mistake.

The old Biblical warning about looking back at sin flashed across her mind. Not that God did anything so dramatic as turn her into a pillar of salt like Lot's wife, but the expression on Niall's face, the emotion unveiled in his eyes because she'd caught him in an unguarded moment, touched a sympathetic chord inside her.

Just for an instant he looked so alone and out of his element, like a wolf who'd wandered out of the woods and was afraid of human contact while craving companionship with his own kind. Lost, she thought. The man who made his living finding others looks utterly lost, and she could almost feel sorry for him except that she knew how dangerous he might prove.

"Elspeth?" George called impatiently.

The illusion of emotional vulnerability in Niall's eyes— she told herself she'd imagined it—vanished at the sound of George's voice. She backed up another step, aware of a strange ache in her breast when she tried to break Glen-lyon's gaze.

And then he winked at her. The audacious character actually dared to give her a seductive wink that sent tingling warmth all the way down to her naked toes, that sent every ounce of sympathy she'd felt for him straight out of her gullible heart.

She whirled in embarrassment, expecting to find George witnessing the ridiculous interchange. But George didn't look at her or Niall at all. He was wholly engrossed in watching a stooped old man with matted white hair limp painfully across the garden toward them.

A stranger, the old man had either sneaked in through the servant's yard as Elspeth had earlier, or he'd been lying in wait for them to pass. Something about the dignified grace of his painful gait stirred Elspeth's memory, but she couldn't say she recognized him.

"Stay here," George said quietly. "I'll take care of this."

Elspeth frowned, conscious that Glenlyon had moved to hover directly behind her so that if she turned even slightly, she wouldn't be able to escape him. Protector or predator, she couldn't tell which. But the heat and latent power of his body, the sheer energy of his presence, made her almost forget the intruder who'd paused to rest his leg at the fountain.

"Looks like a spot of trouble for dear George." Niall shifted casually to stand in front of her. "Perhaps it's an unhappy constituent-to-be, or is that poor fellow another of your social diversions, *chère?*"

Elspeth refused to dignify the comment with an answer and concentrated instead on trying to hear what George and the old man were saying. It appeared they were arguing—the intruder kept shaking his head and trying to push around George. The only side of his face visible to Elspeth had been badly disfigured by what must have been a horrible accident. The black eye patch and tattered plaid and trews he wore made her ache with guilt for the good health and creature comforts she took for granted.

Niall glanced back at her and grinned. "Maybe he's trying to wangle an invitation to your supper party. You do have interesting friends on the other side of the gate. Samson, Delilah . . ."

Elspeth flushed but forced herself to stare straight ahead. "It's more likely he's a vagrant, or a crippled sailor looking for employment. George was in the Navy once himself."

"Hmmm. They do appear to know each other."

"Perhaps he's a displaced crofter who's drifted down from the Highlands to find work," Elspeth murmured. "So many families have been evicted from their homes by greedy landowners."

"The old fellow looks upset, doesn't he?"

"Wouldn't you be upset if your home had been torn down and your family broken apart?"

"Yes, *chérie,*" Niall said solemnly. "I'd be upset enough to commit murder if my loved ones were threatened." He hesitated, his gaze distant. "In fact, I have."

His stark declaration gave Elspeth pause and she looked away, shivering as a gust of wind raced through the garden. She could easily believe he harbored the potential for such violence . . . and passion. The forbidden thought slipped into her mind, and she shivered again, wondering where on earth it had come from.

Niall noticed how she hugged herself against a reaction that might have been caused by cold or apprehension, and he resisted the urge to take her into his arms. Once again, to his annoyance, she'd managed to touch him on a more emotional level than he usually allowed, and she hadn't even tried, he was sure. But the surprising concern in her voice over the old vagrant's welfare had made him deeply ashamed of his own attempt to find humor in another person's misfortune.

He knew better. No stranger to poverty himself, he'd been frequently reduced to begging for food and shelter in his younger years after his Scottish soldier father had been ambushed and assassinated by Burmese royalists, and the Glenlyon family had fled into the jungle. Yes, Niall *had* killed, starting with the two enemy soldiers who were chasing his mother and sister into a swamp.

But how deep did this pampered woman's apparent sweetness run?

For his money, Niall would bet Elspeth Kildrummond was the shallow sort who claimed a social conscience, who cried into her scented hanky at the sight of starving children in the street. Yet he doubted she'd do anything more to help them than toss a few pennies their way.

He knew her type well. He avoided young women like her whenever he could. Stubborn, sheltered, spoiled, with a fairy-tale view of the world from what they'd read in some silly book. They were the inexperienced young things whose name was legion and who still believed in heroes and happiness.

In Niall's opinion, neither existed.

"My grandparents were evicted from their croft holdings in Ross-Shire and forced to emigrate to America," he said reflectively, shifting his train of thought back to a safer topic. "Some of my unknown cousins are scattered throughout the Highlands."

Elspeth smiled sweetly. "Why then, Captain, perhaps that old man is one of your relatives. You aren't missing a father by any chance?"

He threw back his head and laughed. She had fire in her soul—he gave her that. "Do you see a resemblance between us?"

She couldn't resist sneaking another look up at his face, curious enough about his background to temporarily forget the scene at the fountain. "How does a man from the jungle happen to speak French and claim a Scottish heritage anyway?"

He hesitated, as if he were uncomfortable discussing his personal history. "Maman, who is from a French Jesuit family in New Orleans, and her surgeon father, had come to Edinburgh to recruit young doctors for the hospital that Grand-père hoped to build in Rangoon. My father, Lamont Glenlyon, was in town at the time, an arrogant army recruit looking for a last fling before being sent as a guard to the British Consul-General in Bangkok." He smiled into her eyes. "He and Maman fell in love on the long steamship voyage over."

Elspeth tried to ignore the suddenly erratic rhythm of her heartbeat, the effect of his unexpectedly self-conscious smile. "Then you weren't born in Scotland?"

"No. I was born in a crocodile-infested black mangrove swamp outside Rangoon while my father led a regiment in the Burma Wars."

"Let me guess the rest," she said wryly. "Your parents abandoned you at the tender age of seven, and you were raised until adolescence by a family of man-eating tigers. That would explain your predatory nature."

He grinned in delight. "Go on. I can hardly wait to hear how you imagine I spent my puberty."

"The possibilities boggle the mind. I suspect your brothel must have played quite a substantial part in your education."

Niall inclined his head. His wolfish smile was only serving to verify the voluptuous images of his misspent youth that Elspeth couldn't prevent from stealing into her thoughts. Which, she realized with grudging amusement, was probably the very effect the shameless man hoped to create. But he was just the kind who by a look alone made a woman aware of her own secret longings, who by a look alone suggested he could satisfy them.

Raising her chin, she refocused her attention on George

in time to see him give the white-haired vagrant a vicious shove toward the garden gate where a footman had just appeared. Elspeth cringed inwardly at the cruel act, which from her vantage point had seemed unprovoked. Straightening his neckcloth, George made a covert motion for the footman's help while the elderly man struggled to rise from his knees.

Niall scowled and started forward, torn between staying at Elspeth's side and rushing over to help the fallen man. He remembered very well what it was like to be kicked like a dog because you were dirty and different and didn't belong. Imagining the old man's humiliation, he clenched his fists and envisioned cracking George's perfectly squared jaw in two like the joints of a puppet. The sudden urge for violence surprised him, but not any less than what—who—had provoked it.

He glanced down in renewed appraisal at Elspeth as the rising breeze sent the sweetness of roses from her skin toward him. Damn if the little rebel didn't look ready to wallop George a good one herself. What a character she was. What a package of unawakened sensuality and spice.

Take care, chère. *The world is just waiting to destroy noble idealists like you. I know. I fought it until it damn near broke me.*

But he didn't fight it anymore. *Non.* He avoided people and their endless problems like the plague, and if he wasn't happy, he could at least pretend to enjoy a lonely peace.

"It appears our future duly-elected isn't in a charitable mood tonight," he remarked dryly, deliberately redirecting his attention across the garden and away from Elspeth Kildrummond's unpredictable future and the protective instincts she stirred in him.

And Elspeth couldn't bring herself to defend George's behavior, not even to this stranger, thinking that "duly-elected" would be a matter of contention. Catherine had heard rumors that George intended to sway his voters with free beer and transportation to the polls next year. Of course George denied it.

Suddenly the footman grabbed the old man by the arm, jerking him to his feet. Elspeth took an involuntary step forward only to freeze in indignation as Niall caught her hand.

"Just who the devil do you think you are?" she demanded.

"Stay where you are."

"You——"

"Stay," he said, his voice rough with genuine concern.

He yanked her back against him when she resisted, and she whipped around in reaction, raising her free hand in a fist to his chest. The dangerous gleam in his eyes stopped her cold; it dared her to lose control and pay the consequences. Taking a breath, she lowered her hand and stood in apparent submission at his side while inwardly she struggled to subdue her temper.

"That's so much better, Miss Kildrummond," he murmured with an infuriating smile. "I'm gratified to see you do respond to the proper handling."

"I'll gratify you, you—crocodile-swamp blackguard."

Niall lifted his eyebrow at the double entendre, and she twisted around, wanting to bite off her tongue for giving him exactly the opening he needed.

"Please release my hand," she said coolly. "I'm going to pretend you don't exist."

He didn't and she couldn't, intensely conscious of the dangerous friction between them. Her pulse kept jumping at the continued pressure of his warm brown fingers on her forearm. He felt so solid, damn him, so strong and threatening at the same time. And true to his word, he refused to let her go until he could release her back to George, who was too shaken to notice the peculiar fact that Niall had taken it upon himself to physically restrain his fiancée.

"Get back in the house." George's mouth was white around the corners. "That man is a lunatic—too dangerous to be left wandering around."

Elspeth glanced past him, puzzled by his reaction. The old man was leaning against the fountain basin, muttering to himself and wiping his single eye on his tattered plaid. The footman had made several attempts to remove him from the grounds, but the vagrant was holding him off with a surprising display of strength, splashing water and sporadically swinging his deformed fists in the air like a man fighting the entire world and all its invisible demons.

The footman finally retreated a few steps. At the reprieve, the old man instantly swung around and managed to hobble to where Elspeth stood. She held her breath, more in pity than in fear.

"Miss Elspeth," he said in a labored voice. "Help me, lass. I'm nae well."

She took a tentative step toward him, throwing off George's hand as he reached out to stop her.

"He's mad," he warned in an undertone. "He doesn't know what he's saying. Stay away from him, do you hear me?"

Niall shifted his weight forward. His own relaxed stance gave no indication that every muscle in his body was tensed and prepared to spring into action if necessary. "Good heavens, Miss Kildrummond," he said softly, "the poor old man does know your name."

"Every bloody beggar in town knows of Elspeth and her sister's foolish generosity by now," George said, pulling a handkerchief from his vest pocket to wipe his upper lip. "For God's sake, both of you, get inside the house before the other guests come out to see the engaged couple arguing over a drunken tramp."

"How do you know me?" Elspeth called over to the

vagrant, trying to move around George to examine the man's face. "What can I do to help you?"

The man didn't answer, glancing around him in apprehension as two other footmen, who'd been checking the lanterns on the terrace, came running to help oust him from the premises. Elspeth resisted the urge to intervene while they dragged him away.

She looked up accusingly at George; she was certain he was keeping something from her. "He went to a lot of trouble to see me for a drunken tramp. He didn't wander over our garden wall by accident."

George pushed a lock of his hair back from his face. "If you don't want vagrants invading the privacy of your home, then you shouldn't commune with them in the street, or in that wretched soup kitchen, which only attracts a horde of shiftless ne'er-do-wells anyway."

"You're deliberately misunderstanding me, George. How do I know whether I want him in my home or not when you're preventing me from talking to him?"

George flushed. "I was protecting you, for pity's sake. You're not only tainting my name with your silly charities but endangering your own welfare. I'm sure Captain Glenlyon would agree."

Niall looked displeased at having the matter laid at his feet. Etiquette demanded some sort of response. "Actually, I think, um, I suppose it's wise for well-bred young women to avoid strange men whenever possible. However," he added diplomatically, "the world needs all the charity it is offered."

Elspeth shot him an annoyed look. If he hadn't restrained her a little while ago, she might have gotten to the heart of the matter herself. If she hadn't let herself be drawn under his dangerous spell, if she hadn't let him intimidate her, she would have confronted the old fellow alone.

She glanced thoughtfully at the garden gate, then spun

around on the path and started to run toward the house as if it were a haven instead of the lonely shell that she tried to escape every chance. She ran as if she could not only leave behind George and her commitment to him, but also the dark yearning in Niall Glenlyon's eyes and the temptation he had reintroduced into her life.

Niall and George stood together in a silence made all the more awkward by their unexpected abandonment. In fact, neither of them spoke or moved until Elspeth slowed farther up the path to curse as her duffel bag slipped from beneath her skirts and hit the ground with a resounding plunk.

"Dear God," George said, and shuddered. "She's carrying her violin in that bag, despite the fact she has a perfectly good case for it. The wretched instrument is worth more than my carriage alone."

Was worth, Niall thought, suppressing a chuckle out of sympathy for the man as he watched George stride away.

His hands in his pockets, Niall turned slowly onto the path to saunter after George. But a few moments later, some inner prompting forced him to stop and take stock of his surroundings.

A man accustomed to obeying his instincts, he pivoted and searched the shadows for a clue to what had unnerved him. Nothing unusual lurked in the orderly lay-out of privet, trees, and parterres. No more vagrants, gypsies, or beautiful young tigresses. There were no cannibals, hill bandits or soldiers either, the fearful enemies of his own tumultuous past.

Only the strong upsurge of a breeze from the North Sea stirred the falling autumn foliage.

The spirits trying to warns you, Tuan—he could imagine his Malay valet and mentor's voice whispering the words. And Niall hadn't survived his entire life in a hostile environment under a witch doctor's tutelage without developing a keen scent for impending danger.

The deceptively ordinary garden setting trembled with dark overtones . . . desire, greed, and even death. He could feel the air around him pulsing in protest, and from a long-abandoned habit, inculcated in him during his early years in a French Jesuit mission school, he lifted his hand to his chest to cross himself as protection against what he did not know. Elspeth's grandmother might have been right, the fairies were plotting wickedness tonight.

The spirits always warn you before they strike, Tuan Captain. The wise man know to listen to their subtle voices.

He lifted his face to the evening sky, telling himself he didn't care what happened to such a disordered family as the Kildrummonds. What had come over him tonight, to flirt so outrageously with that little troublemaker? *Dieu,* after watching Sir George deal with that deranged old vagrant, he felt tempted to find another mercantile firm to deal with. But that meant breaking a contract, staying in the Lowlands until he found another company to oblige him, and Niall couldn't spare the time.

"What is it now, Captain Glenlyon?" George called curtly from the terrace.

Niall shook off the unwelcome mood and strode toward the stairs. "It's going to rain tonight."

George turned away, his voice impatient. "It's always raining in this accursed country. I'm surprised no one warned you what to expect."

Five

Niall stifled a yawn in his palm and glanced at the clock in the corner of the crowded drawing room. Only a few more hours of inane conversation and confinement, of nibbling on pâté and toast points that were too insubstantial to nourish a sparrow, save a full-grown man. By dawn he'd be on the road to the Grampian Highlands to visit the uncle he'd never met, but who had written to summon him on a mysterious matter of "grave" importance. By the urgent tone of the letter, from a man well into his seventies, Niall had concluded this would be a deathbed meeting.

Not a pleasant prospect. But only afterward would he feel free to forever turn his back on this bewildering world of boring conversation and inexcusable rudeness. If he didn't die of hunger first himself.

He felt trapped. A few guests, who evidently not only read but believed Archie Harper's scuttlebutt, circled Niall as if he were a curiosity on exhibit in a museum. They disturbed him less than those who actually dared talk to him. Honestly, he'd rather be standing in a lagoon full of fertile leopard frogs during a wet monsoon than amidst these stuffy, pretentious people who never said what they meant and yet still managed to say too much.

"Good Lord, Alfred, did you hear the way he snarled at me when I asked him if he employed slaves on his plantation? How was I to know his politics? The man is positively barbaric."

"Well, his coloring *is* unusually dark, his manners appalling. Perhaps he's part aborigine himself."

"His clothes are five years out of fashion. Why, I haven't seen a coat like that since *Waterloo!*"

Niall grinned at his reflection in the candlelit window. Five years out of fashion, eh? Hell, that little rat at the pawnbroker's shop had assured him it was only three. Besides, Niall didn't think he looked that conspicuous. All right, he needed to have his hair trimmed. True, Hasim had forgotten to polish his boots again. And he was the tallest person in the room. But it wasn't as if he had a scimitar stuck between his teeth.

No, he was convinced he owned some invisible quality that imbued him with this dark distinction, the tarnished essence of all his past sins that followed him like a shadow.

"Did you see how many toast points he just took?"

"I don't know where he's putting it all."

"In his pockets, probably."

Niall stared with fierce longing at the door, planning an escape. He'd knock over that braying woman in blue silk if he made a dash for it; she might engage him in aimless chitchat if he tried more politely to pass her. He wasn't sure which was worse.

The damned "musicale" had been delayed, and so had supper. Starvation did not improve Niall's temper. The next time someone asked him if he wore a tiger-skin loincloth in the jungle, as some cartoonist had depicted him, he was going to walk right out of this hot, overfurnished house, business be damned.

He knew this feeling too well, being the outsider, the foreign devil. He couldn't recall a time or a place where he'd ever felt he belonged. But after almost thirty years of living estranged to the majority of the human race, he'd begun to take his stray-cat status for granted.

No, he didn't belong in Scotland. He'd never belonged

anywhere, except now perhaps on his distant island and for one brief summer long ago, at the House of Many Joys in Mandalay, where he'd been taken after collapsing from hunger and heat exhaustion in a filthy market street with pariah dogs sniffing at his face.

Carry him to the ricksha, girls. Lady Su Ying will know what to do with him. Perhaps he's one of the hill bandits' captives who was being held for ransom.

Perhaps he's a prince, or a palace slave.

He had tried to roll back into the gutter, away from the sharp prodding fingernails and curious painted faces of the Burmese Courtesans. He'd been ready to die, broken in body and spirit.

Look at his eyes! He's one of the Invulnerables, girls, a white devil! Don't touch him or his spirit will contaminate you.

He's a dead boy unless Lady Su Ying decides to help him. That's for certain.

Niall claimed a glass of champagne from the marble sideboard behind him, smiling at the bittersweet memories of his sixteenth summer. In Mandalay he had lost what remained of his youthful innocence and belief in his own invulnerability. He had never planned to stay longer than a few weeks in the House of Many Joys, just long enough to regain his strength, but then one of the girls convinced him that she remembered seeing Rachel in the vicinity a month earlier. The household of a tribal warrior had accompanied a young white girl in a palanquin carried by fierce-looking slaves.

Rachel—adopted into the family of a pagan warlord? Inconceivable. He knew it couldn't possibly be true.

But he had stayed anyway. And he had served as a bodyguard to the sad young courtesans who'd befriended him, all the time waiting for the glorious day when his little sister would magically appear on the dusty road that wound into the mountains beneath his window, and they could both run down to the river to wash away the years of pain and degradation.

But Rachel had never appeared.

As he took a sip of champagne, he glanced inadvertently at the windows overlooking the garden. No doubt Elspeth Kildrummond thought herself very daring with her gypsies and horse-racing schemes. But a young woman of her hoity-toity sensibilities had never dreamed of the things *he'd* seen and done. *Dieu,* the horror in her eyes when Harper had mentioned the word "brothel."

Until that cursed moment Niall was convinced she'd shared the sweet attraction for him as he did for her, the start of sexual chemistry that hinted at something even more powerful under the surface. But now he'd never find out.

He didn't know why he kept thinking about her. Perhaps her innocence and sense of fun had appealed to the remnants of his own soul which had not perished yet from self-isolation and years of emotional neglect. Intellectually, he was offended by her frivolous manner. He'd been so stupid, so uncharacteristically careless, to toy with her. The sooner he left Falhaven, the better.

He looked away from the window as an attractive ginger-haired woman drifted from her husband's side to "accidentally" drop her fan at Niall's feet. Now, *this* woman, with her seductive walk and experienced eyes, was more his sexual equal. She appeared to be about thirty-five, full-figured, with a sweet face that showed a hint of a double chin to come. She'd been eyeing him on and off all evening, like a sweetmeat she wished to nibble.

Swinging down gracefully to retrieve the fan, she managed to give him a provocative glimpse of her fair neck and shoulders, freckles poorly concealed beneath a coating of rice powder. She reminded Niall of a milkmaid turned social matron, and he admired her directness, if nothing else.

He put down his glass and bent, hiding a smile, to save her the effort of picking up the fan. He wasn't as impartial to a pretty woman's charms as he'd like; the interlude with the spirited Miss Kildrummond in the summerhouse had reminded him of that, but he had no time for love play tonight even if he were inclined. Which strangely in the case of this flame-haired woman he was not.

"Madame," he said solemnly as they straightened, assessing each other over the top of the fan before etiquette required they must move apart. "Don't trouble yourself."

She gave him a naughty smile. Her teeth were sharp-pointed, like a vixen's, and slightly crooked. "It was clumsy of me to drop it."

Niall grinned slowly. "I thought so."

She narrowed her eyes and took the fan, pretending not to realize she'd been insulted. "I'm Susan Dweeney—Duncan Kildrummond's niece. My husband is an accountant for the firm."

Bon Dieu, he thought. Elspeth's cousin.

"Niall Glenlyon, Mrs. Dweeney," he said politely, leaning back against the sideboard.

"Yes, I know who you are, Captain Glenlyon. We all do, actually. You must find our little soirée boring after your exciting life."

"It doesn't compare to sitting around a cook pot with a bunch of cannibals, madame, I'd have to agree."

She laughed, ignoring the plaintive look her husband sent her, although it made Niall feel uncomfortable. "Rumor has it that the famous hunter is in Scotland for romantic reasons, Captain. The papers report you're looking for a bride to carry back to your jungle hideaway."

Niall's grin became strained. He knew where that particular rumor had started, and he intended to squelch it once and for all tonight, just as soon as he got the big-mouthed miscreant alone. "You can't believe everything you read, Mrs. Dweeney."

"But it was your own valet the newspaper quoted, Captain. Don't tell me not even one woman in Scotland has tickled your fancy?"

Niall was saved the embarrassment of a reply by the appearance in the doorway of his host, Duncan Kildrummond. A trim, vital man of medium height in his fifties, Duncan had an amiable face, flushed at the moment, framed in grayish-brown hair and bushy sideburns. He took one look at Niall and Susan, then frowned, cutting a swath through his chattering guests to interrupt them.

As he reached them, Duncan nodded to Niall and gave Susan a dismissive pat on the arm. "Don't let those newspaper accounts of Captain Glenlyon's exploits frighten you, my dear. He was a priest trying to convert the heathens before they converted him."

Niall didn't bother to correct him. Hell, they could think he was a whirling dervish for all he cared. He blanked out their conversation, but just as he'd managed to filch another handful of toast points from a passing footman, he found himself eavesdropping against his will.

"Where the deuce has your cousin been all evening, Susan? She'll be late to her own funeral, to say nothing of an engagement party that's costing me an arm and a leg."

Susan scrutinized Niall over the ribs of her fan. "Fergus said he thought he saw her sneaking back into the house earlier. And the gypsies are passing through town again. I know because my maid is going to the fair to have her fortune read in the morning."

Duncan's face darkened. "Elspeth has been expressly forbidden anywhere near those vagabonds." He turned without warning to Niall. "You were outside earlier yourself, Glenlyon. You didn't see my wayward daughter dallying about by any chance?"

Niall swallowed the toast whole, unprepared for the direct question. "As a matter of fact, I, uh, did run into her and Sir George in the garden. There was a bit of trouble with an intruder, some old vagrant, who'd wandered onto the grounds. But gypsies—I don't think so— No, quite impossible."

"An intruder?" Duncan frowned, glancing toward the window.

Susan shuddered delicately. "There was another house broken into on the square just last week. And a woman like myself whose husband is always away on business is so very vulnerable, don't you agree, Captain Glenlyon?"

"I suppose that depends on the woman, Mrs. Dweeney."

There was a brief lull in the conversation, with Duncan looking preoccupied and Susan absentmindedly scratching a mole on her cheek with the fan. Niall glanced up. His eyes narrowed in unconscious dislike at the sight of Sir George working his way toward them. *He* certainly didn't want to be implicated in Elspeth's earlier disappearance.

George gave the group a tight smile, sharing a quick look with Susan that Niall shouldn't have caught, but did. He suppressed a sigh. He knew a sexual message when he saw it, and that furtive exchange definitely had a palpable basis in shared bedroom experience. Lord, what a family. He didn't blame Elspeth for trying to escape.

"I need to see you a moment alone, Duncan," George said quietly. "We've run into an unexpected problem with the Highland account."

"The— Oh, God." Duncan scowled, already turning toward the end of the room. "What sort of problem?" he demanded as the two men moved away, heads bent together in private conversation.

Niall was mildly curious to hear George's answer, but Susan started to talk almost at the same moment; it crossed his mind that the distraction was deliberate, family secrets an outsider wasn't supposed to overhear. As if he cared.

"Another boring business detail," Susan murmured with

a sigh of annoyance. "That leaves you and me to entertain each other, Captain."

He reclaimed his glass from the sideboard. "I was under the impression that the evening's entertainment had already been planned."

"You mean Elspeth and her sister's recital. Well, I can't guarantee how entertaining their music will be, but as for Elspeth, she is quite a diversion unto herself. Isn't she?"

"I wouldn't know," Niall replied guardedly.

"Of course you would." Susan pried the glass from his hand and drank from it before he could object. "Fergus also saw you and Elspeth ducking into the summerhouse only moments apart," she said slyly. "I simply neglected to mention that to Duncan."

"Observant man this Fergus."

She smiled, sipping the champagne.

"It was an accidental encounter, Mrs. Dweeney," he added, frowning at her.

"Ooh, but isn't that the most exciting kind?" Susan's eyes sparkled. "It's a good thing Elspeth is leaving town tomorrow with George and her aunt. She's a headstrong woman, and I consider it my duty to watch over her until she's married."

Niall glanced across the room at George's departing figure. "Headstrong is rather an understatement. And isn't your association with her fiancé taking the concept of chaperone a little far?"

She lifted her chin, not bothering to deny the charge. "I'd think a man of your liberal background would understand."

Actually he didn't. Heaven knew he was the last person to cast stones, but there had been something so profoundly innocent about Elspeth Kildrummond that no matter how much of a problem she was to her family, she deserved better than to marry a man of George Westcott's cruel sophistication. Anyway, in Niall's view, love, commitment,

and fidelity were hopelessly intertwined. Which was probably why he'd avoided all three so far.

"What does the 'Highland account' mean?" he asked
without thinking.

Susan glanced away to wave at a group of women who
were gaping at Glenlyon. " 'Highland account'? It could
mean biscuits or bacon. I wouldn't know. I haven't a clue
what Duncan and George deal in these days. As long as
they turn a profit, I don't think I care."

There was a sudden hush over the room. Niall noticed
heads turning away from them. As he glanced around himself to see what had caused the fuss, he couldn't hold back
a smile. A small appealing figure had just been spotted
trying to sneak in through the side door—Elspeth Kildrummond in a demure rose velvet dress with a white-lace collar,
her wild angel's hair dutifully tamed into a figure eight at
her nape. Not beautiful, no. But she had something, an inner
spark, a wellspring of exuberance, that would attract men
all her life. He felt himself pulled toward her like an iron
bar to a magnet.

His smile faded as she finally noticed him, and before
he could stop himself, he took a step toward her, completely forgetting the other woman at his side. The flirtatious attraction between him and Elspeth earlier was
nothing compared to the deep stab of desire that pierced
his composure now. He felt like pushing everyone else out
of his path just to stare at her.

He forced another smile to hide his own disconcert-
ment. Elspeth's eyes widened in apprehension as if she
were terrified he'd announce to everyone what had happened in the garden. It irritated him that she would doubt
his word, but, of course, he couldn't blame her. He didn't
trust himself half the time.

All at once the other guests converged on her to block
Niall's view. Her fiancé and father were in the fore. The
last image in Niall's mind before he glanced away was

that of George hovering over Elspeth like a hawk claiming a woodland creature. He wished suddenly for another drink. He needed something to numb the onslaught of emotions he had no desire to experience.

Besides, he really hated parties.

"Their marriage will be a mistake," Susan said softly, her gaze riveted to George and Elspeth.

Niall's mouth thinned. "If he continues to carry on with you, madame, I suppose it will."

"He won't. George and I are finished." She tossed her head, looking up at Niall with a brittle smile. "I've no idea why I've confided so much in you, Captain. Perhaps because you were once a priest. But I'm certain you're not at all trustworthy."

"You should always obey your instincts, ma'am."

The other guests had begun to seat themselves at the far end of the room in the rows of light cane-backed chairs curved in a semicircle around a carpeted dais. Susan's gray-haired husband, twenty years her senior, stood awkward and alone several feet away from her and Niall, dressed to the teeth in his grandfather's Highland soldier regalia. A smile pasted on his bearded face, he waited with touching patience to escort his faithless wife to her chair.

Niall tried his best to merge into the crowd assembling for the musical recital, tact not usually his strong point. "I think we should find our seats, Mrs. Dweeney."

She turned and touched his arm, her blue eyes dark with childlike appeal. "I live only minutes from here on Rose Street near the bleachfields. My husband is leaving early in the morning on a trip North—"

"So am I," Niall interrupted her in a low dismissive tone. Discreetly, he shrugged off her hand and claimed an aisle seat in the last row where he could slip away if necessary, forcing her to continue without him. A footman handed him a printed programme and he stared down with a grin at the names imprinted on the front. Elspeth Victoria and Catherine Margaret Kildrummond. Several guests had paused at one of the windows to comment on the rising wind.

"It's going to rain before midnight."

"—before supper at the rate this affair is dragging along."

The temperature in the room had dropped several degrees, prompting more than one woman to send for her shawl. The lanterns strung on the terrace rocked and threw quavering shadows of gold at the window. Around Niall, servants hurried about lowering lights and drawing drapes to block out the disturbing scratching of a hornbeam tree against the eaves. And the feeling of menace he had sensed earlier wrapped itself more tightly around the house as the first notes of the recital began.

Six

The musicale was sheer torture, the caterwauling of a dozen tomcats on a hot summer night. Elspeth performed as rigidly as a prisoner facing a firing squad. In Niall's opinion, however, it was her audience who suffered the most. Fretful squeaks, passionately misplayed chords and embarrassing silences while she put down her bow to scratch her nose, squint at the music sheet, or scold her sister, who attempted to accompany her on an ill-tuned piano. Catherine Kildrummond was a younger version of Elspeth with even fairer coloring and that same dauntless air of innocence.

The program featured a medley of Bach's sonatas—complex rhythms interspersed with dense passages and jarring climaxes that resounded out of the blue just when the listeners dared to relax a moment.

Niall touched his left ear and wondered if it were possible to go deaf during a violin recital. How did the others stand it? He leaned forward, chuckling softly as he noticed the thick wads of lamb's wool that Susan, Duncan, and George had stuffed into their ears.

The recital, mercifully, did come to an end. The audience clapped and clapped as if it had not just been subjected to head-ringing insult, or perhaps because the torture had finally stopped. Niall jumped to his feet and applauded too—it took nerve to play that badly in public.

Elspeth looked up at him, frowning suspiciously as she forced her violin back into its wooden case.

"Wonderful, Miss Kildrummond!" He remained standing while the crowd of hungry guests gathered around Duncan and George at the blazing fireplace. "Encore!"

"You fool," she said softly, ducking her head to hide a smile.

That smile disappeared as her father quieted the room and motioned her to George's side to announce their engagement. Niall found another glass of champagne and wandered over to the window. He was still standing alone even after several congratulatory toasts had been made and the other guests began drifting in pairs toward the dining room. A servant extinguished the lamps and left. Niall sighed, enveloped in darkness and disturbing memories.

Marriage and champagne toasts. Formality and infidelity. The mere thought of such entanglements depressed him, and he supposed he should be grateful that the only woman he'd ever planned to marry had changed her mind four years ago in a small chapel in Marseilles.

Yvonne Lenclos, the daughter of an affluent silk merchant with connections in the Far East, had wanted desperately to marry Niall when she mistakenly believed she was pregnant with his child. But she hadn't been, admitting as much in a frightened whisper as they stood together to repeat their wedding vows at the altar. And if the shock of her confession weren't quite enough for Niall to absorb, she had then thrown her bridal bouquet at his feet and run from the church, leaving her embarrassed family to explain that poor Yvonne had confided only the night before that perhaps she was too delicate to withstand life on the savage island. Perhaps if Niall offered to stay and work as one of Papa's clerks, she would reconsider marrying him.

Yvonne still wrote to him from time to time. He always tossed her letters into the sea without opening them. And it wasn't because she'd broken his heart. It was because he'd come within minutes of making a mistake that would have ruined both their lives. Boredom, lust, loneliness. He didn't know what had drawn him and Yvonne together. Obviously they hadn't loved each other enough to compromise. Still, sometimes he wished they'd tried. He would like his own family to fill his empty plantation house. As Hasim had told him a hundred times, a witch doctor did not substitute for a wife. But who in God's name would take Niall as a husband after the life he had led?

He turned slowly, aware of another presence in the darkened room.

Elspeth Kildrummond stood in the shadows of the doorway. His mood lifted instantly. A smile of ironic anticipation broke across his brooding face.

Staring at him solemnly with her luminous eyes, she darted back to the dais to pick up her violin case. She reminded him of a cat: independent, lithe, distrustful. And like every feline worth her salt, she was too attracted to danger for her own good. Why else had she returned to this room?

"Papa's afraid someone might sit on it," she explained hastily, backing away from him with her precious instrument of torture clutched to her chest. "It's very expensive. One of a kind."

"Yes." He cleared his throat. "Well, you play so—so—"

"—so horribly," she laughed, her golden-green eyes crinkling at the corners. "Signor Francelli swears there's no word in either the English or Italian languages to describe my playing. Whenever I pick up the violin, he just puts his head in his hands and weeps."

She bumped back up against the door. "Oh, by the way, thank you for keeping quiet about what happened." She frowned, her eyes widening at the intense look on his face as he started to move toward her. "Captain Glenlyon, is something wrong? You look a little peculiar. I—I noticed you were putting away that pâté like a condemned man at his last meal."

"Dieu," he murmured softly, and even to Elspeth's ears, the word sounded more like a prayer than profanity.

She dropped her violin case and groped behind her for the doorknob. She must be losing her mind, returning to this room when she suspected—no, she *hoped*—she'd find him still alone. Danger signals had rung through her brain the instant she had seen him again. She'd ignored them. Even stronger, more alarming, impulses had raced through her body. She had denied them. There was no reasonable answer for why she'd felt compelled to see him again at all.

He was everything a woman of decent upbringing should despise. But against all logic, against all weight of her past experience with Robert Campbell, she'd been drawn back to this dark room, to this even darker man. She had been haunted by the image of him standing alone at the window while everyone congratulated her on the coup of landing George.

She had told herself she'd returned only for the reassurance that Glenlyon wouldn't reveal to anyone where she'd spent the earlier part of the evening. She told herself that she really cared about rescuing her rotten old violin.

But the lies mocked her uncharacteristic attempt at self-deception. And now she regretted obeying whatever inner prompting had lured her back here. No one had ever looked at her with such raw need before. No one had ever made her so aware of how little she knew her own emotions.

"Little fool," he said quietly, "why did you come back here anyway?"

Her voice sounded abnormally loud in the room. "I came to get my violin."

"I don't think so. I think you came back because you liked kissing me."

"I detested it."

"Did you?" He was staring at her mouth, fascinated by

the pouting fullness of her lower lip. "But you *did* come back," he said softly. "You came back to see me."

She couldn't seem to draw a breath. "All right. I admit I was curious about you. You looked sad standing there all alone at the window while everyone else was laughing and joking."

A cynical smile played across his sun-burnished features. "So I'm a curiosity, am I? An oddity, an object of passing amusement like an animal in a zoo to be added to your bizarre collection of friends?"

She exhaled in a rush. "I don't intend to 'add' you to anything in my life, Glenlyon. I feel a little sorry for you, that's all and—"

"Oh, for God's sake. Save your pity for the soup kitchen."

"You're rather rude, aren't you?"

"Shall I swing from the chandeliers while peeling a banana between my toes?" He began to advance on her, anger and amusement warring for domination on his face. "Shall I shoot a poisoned blow dart into someone's bum during dinner?"

She didn't blink. She didn't flinch. In fact, she gave no sign that her heart had lodged in her throat, preventing the cry for help she would probably be wise to attempt before he came another inch closer.

"Do as you like, Captain," she said with a self-composure she certainly didn't feel. "It might enliven a tedious evening, but please don't use my bum as your target. I hope to go riding early tomorrow morning."

He stared at her, a little surprised. Then he started to laugh, and the movement brought his large body against hers for a moment. The inadvertent contact paralyzed him, tempted him to force her back against the door and meld their bodies together, to prolong the irresistible friction that he felt every time he looked at her.

It had affected her, too. He saw the dark panic in her

eyes, the awareness, the need. The tension between them alarmed her, as well it should. And he couldn't stay angry at her even though the thought of anyone pitying him made him wild. But he shouldn't blame her. She was too brave, too honest, standing up to someone like him when anyone could see she was shivering in her slippers.

She jerked away. Her heart began pounding in a painful clash of anxiety and sinful anticipation. "Do you mind telling me what's so damned amusing?" she asked crossly.

"You are."

"Why?"

"Why? You wish to know why? *Ma chère,* even an un-educated soldier of fortune like me knows that a young woman isn't supposed to ask *why.*"

"Captain Glenlyon, I'm not even supposed to be talking to you."

"More is your shame then, mademoiselle."

He sobered, shaking his head, almost wishing he'd met her another time, under different circumstances. Before the corrosion had reached the core of his soul. For now, he could only warn her away, offer her his lukewarm con-gratulations on her impending marriage.

"You're putting temptation in my mind again," he said quietly, the amusement wiped from his face. "I think you should rejoin your family."

"Yes. Yes. Of course. You're right. Everyone is no doubt wondering what's become of me—"

Her nervous chatter faded away just before he reached her, and the truth was, he hadn't heard a word she'd said. His mind was floating in a weird haze, disembodied from the physical urges he was trying to subdue. Yet as clearly as if looking at a portrait, he looked down into her en-chanting face and saw with unbelievable clarity the prom-ise of a thousand silly-intimate moments just like this. He pictured them together, entangled in sex-scented sheets, walking in leafy lanes, with children running up behind them. Lovers and friends. Joy and tribulation.

The vision pierced his heart. The glimpse into the gentle pleasures that a man like him would never know made him grieve, made him achingly aware of simple human needs, to bond, to share, that he had convinced himself he had conquered.

He drew in his breath, aware he was frightening her, but he was frightened too. Then just as mysteriously as it had struck him, the spell of premonition passed. In the Far East they called it kismet. But Niall knew it for the deceptive stirring of physical desire that it surely was. It had to be—he'd never experienced such a powerful stirring of emotion before.

Elspeth reached down clumsily for her violin case. "Well, thank you again. I—"

She broke off, startled, as a surge of wind blew the French doors behind them open and a shadowed figure moved against the yellow brocade curtains. Cold air rushed into every corner of the room. The violin case remained on the floor.

Niall spun around. The same old man they'd seen earlier in the garden stood behind them, but since then he had obviously been beaten severely about the face by the footmen. An egg-shaped knot protruded through the filthy hair on his forehead, and blood had caked in the deep wrinkles around his mouth. He made an inarticulate sound of distress in his throat, blinking to see into the room.

"What do you want, old fellow?" Niall asked gently.

The man ignored Niall, limping forward several steps. "Do you nae remember me, Miss Elspeth? I didna want to scare ye wi' my face."

"You don't scare me," she said slowly. "In fact, I ask your forgiveness if you've suffered on my account. Let me see your head."

Entranced, Niall witnessed her unthinking transformation from a flighty young miss who flirted with strangers into a compassionate woman who could humble herself for a vagabond. His heart ached with jealous longing to experience her tenderness firsthand.

Still, he felt more than a little alarmed for her safety when she moved past him to study the intruder, asking in concern, "Do I know you from town? Let me fetch my father and have him help you. He'll be furious when he sees what the footmen did."

"No! No, ye musna tell him ye've—"

Sudden panic filling his eyes, the old vagrant bolted back into the garden at the same instant the drawing room door opened behind Elspeth, and George strode inside, glancing from her to Niall with his eyebrows raised.

"Well," George said, swallowing hard. "Well. What have we here?"

Niall stood unmoving, deliberately not looking at the curtains, which still stirred in the wind. The pathetic old man had nerve, and although he was obviously disturbed, he hadn't struck Niall as the dangerous character George claimed him to be outside. If anything, the intruder had addressed Elspeth with a deep affection that did suggest a prior acquaintance. Unless of course, he was mad and, in that case, a genuine danger.

George looked around the room. "If I didn't know better, Captain, I'd suspect you were trying to detain Elspeth on purpose. This is the second time tonight I've found you two in the same vicinity under questionable circumstances."

Niall shrugged in irritation. "Your fiancée returned for her violin, Sir George. And, ill-bred foreigner that I am, I hadn't made my way to the dining room yet."

"Her violin." George frowned down at the case lying on the floor; this lapse in Elspeth's behavior apparently made enough sense to pacify his suspicions. Shaking his head like an indulgent parent, he held open the door to usher her into the hall. "Hurry up then. Come along. We at least want to arrive before the consommé is served." He smiled over his shoulder at Niall with the easy charm he could exude when everything went his way. "She'll settle down in London when she has a household of her own to manage. It's all the excitement over our engagement. She'll settle down soon enough."

Niall just smiled back while his gaze trailed the tawny young tigress who marched before him with her violin case banging against the wall. I wouldn't count on it, George, old man, he thought. I wouldn't count on a docile wife at all.

Seven

Elspeth's upcoming wedding in November dominated the talk of the supper table. The matrons present offered advice on the hiring of domestics—beware those cheeky Irish grooms, the Welsh girls work well in the kitchen. The younger women discussed fashionable bridal attire while the men argued business and politics. Elspeth strived to sound interested, but the truth was, the wedding plans bored her to death.

She was more concerned with how she could sneak out in the morning to meet the duke at the gypsy encampment before she, George, and Aunt Flora, acting as chaperone, boarded the stage to Devon. George was hosting a fox cub hunt at his modest country home there to encourage the political support of his wealthier neighbors.

Elspeth dreaded the event, fully intending to devote her energy to helping the unfortunate little foxes escape the hounds. Anyway, tomorrow was the day Samson turned over the training of Ali Baba to his young gypsy cousin, Gethel Petulengro. The boy was a little too rash and concerned with impressing young girls for Elspeth's liking, and she wanted to reassure herself Samson's faith in him was well deserved.

"Will you be here for the ceremony, Captain Glenlyon?" she heard her younger sister Catherine asking the dark-haired foreigner who had remained silent throughout the meal.

"Of course he won't," Elspeth said, embarrassed by the question. But Cat had just turned sixteen with no suitor in sight. She was a hopelessly romantic bookworm with bold green eyes and a sweet heart-shaped face framed in fluffy blond hair. She probably thought Glenlyon cut a dashing figure compared to the other men present. Which, Elspeth admitted grudgingly, he did.

He smiled at the younger girl. "I'm returning home at the end of the month."

"I understand that you're looking for a bride yourself," Catherine blurted out without warning.

Niall took a quick sip of wine to choke down a laugh while several disapproving *tsks* sounded from the older women at the table. Yet for all their shocked murmurings, these matrons were interested enough to interrupt their own conversations to await his answer. Even the footmen standing against the wall stopped their sly whispering to listen.

Those brazen Kildrummond girls, Elspeth could imagine them gossiping later. So unrefined, so spontaneous. No mother to temper the uncouth ways of their father, who thought that money, music lessons, and elaborate supper parties could buy prestige.

Niall still hadn't answered, aware that everyone hoped he'd say something to shock them, aware that the details of his personal life, from his sexual habits to his failed military career, were public knowledge.

As the popular rumor went, he had risen from his position as brothel master to army captain only to be dishonorably discharged from the military for inventive sexual indiscretion with a general's daughter.

The far less titillating truth was that he'd earned his superior officer's disfavor by criticizing the British army's treatment of its native captives. For several months Niall had even been expected to face a court-martial. But in the end, out of respect for his late father's rank, Niall's superiors had granted him an honorable discharge and a token pension.

But the taint of disgrace still clung to him. Admittedly, he hadn't helped matters by taking a mercenary position afterward in the East India Company because he was bored and broke. Nobody cared for a solider of fortune.

He stared across the table, his dark face inscrutable.

Catherine put down her fork, too excited to take note of his forbidding expression. "I read that the captain's bride should be strong enough to bear him at least five sons and intelligent enough to teach them herself because the jungle would be their only school."

"My, my, isn't it a shame that Queen Hippolyta of the Amazons isn't alive for his inspection?" Elspeth asked archly.

Niall raised his napkin to his mouth to cover a smile. "The truth is that there aren't many European women who'd choose to live on a lonely pagan island, and I don't blame them. It seems I'm destined to remain a bachelor."

Curiosity overcame Elspeth's determination to pretend he didn't exist. "Why don't you marry a native woman?"

"Elspeth, really." George interrupted the intricate carving of his lamp chop. "How rude."

Glenlyon merely shrugged, swirling his wine glass between his long tapered fingers. These people deserved to be shocked, scrutinizing his every move during this endless meal as if they expected him to disgrace himself by eating his mashed potatoes with his soup spoon, or God forbid, with his hands.

"According to the culture," he said to his enraptured audience, "a man on my island can't take a native wife unless he's collected a few heads to prove his manhood."

Silence crept across the table like a shadow. Elspeth looked into his eyes, feeling an unwilling smile form on her lips, a spark of surprising camaraderie in her heart. Oh, he was very bold, very bad.

Apparently the speechless guests thought so too.

Then Duncan snorted in amusement and reached for another buttered bun, diffusing the sense of scandalized delight that held his guests spellbound. Archie Harper began scribbling on the notebook poised on his thigh. Marjorie MacDuff, matron of matrons, leaned back in her chair with her eyelids twitching; the subject of headhunting was so barbaric at a civilized supper table, it could only have come up at the Kildrummonds' house.

Only Catherine dared to break the silence, staring at Niall in blazing admiration. "I simply stopped breathing when I read how you singlehandedly saved that colonel's daughter from the rhinoceros stampede."

Niall looked up in alarm. "I did *what?*"

"Now Captain Glenlyon can't be expected to remember all 'is exploits, can 'e?" Archie Harper asked smoothly, having written that particular account which relied more on imagination than factual information.

A footman whisked away Elspeth's plate and set a platter of imported fruit before her. As she reached for a small blood orange, Niall caught her eye and gave her a warm intimate smile.

A quiver shot up her spine, part sensual response and something even more treacherous that felt like empathy. *Rescue me from these people,* the rogue's sad gray eyes seemed to plead. Or perhaps she was merely projecting her own social insecurities onto him because she sensed his unease, and understood it.

She studied Niall's face from beneath the tangled fringe of her lowered gold-tipped lashes. Who were his distant ancestors on the Scottish side of his family? Warriors and tribal chieftains? Had they clashed with hers on some ancient heath? Did the animosity he stirred in her go back through the mists of time? But what if it wasn't animosity she felt for him at all? she wondered uneasily. What if the little flashes of emotion she fought to ignore had another meaning altogether?

"We have fresh fruit on our island all year long," Niall said unexpectedly, watching her fingers close around the orange. "Do your tastes run to the exotic, Miss Kildrummond?"

Doing her best to pretend she hadn't heard him, Elspeth reached for her knife, but hit the table with her elbow instead. The orange bounced off the plate and into her lap before rolling to the floor. Sighing in exasperation, she ducked under the lace tablecloth. Catherine leaned down a few seconds later to see what had happened.

"Susan said you were alone with *him* in the summerhouse," Catherine whispered, her eyes shining like green marbles.

Elspeth frowned. The orange had rolled too far across the floor for her to reach it without creating a fuss. In fact, it sat trapped right between Niall Glenlyon's wellworn black boots while he pushed it back and forth with the ball of his right foot, as if daring her to retrieve it. She'd be damned if she was going to crawl between the insolent man's legs for a piece of bruised fruit.

"Captain Glenlyon is the most fascinating person," Catherine continued quietly. "I read his life story in a serial novel last year."

"Catherine, you feather brain, everyone knows that a novel is a work of fiction. Captain Glenlyon is no more a hero than—than George."

Catherine considered this. "Well, he's certainly more intriguing. I hope that doesn't offend you."

Elspeth slid down onto the floor; now she'd dropped her napkin. "Why the dickens should it offend—" She lowered her voice an octave. "I don't suppose you remember reading anything about someone named Rachel Glenlyon, do you?"

"Why, of course, I do. That poor, poor girl. She was

the captain's missing sister. You see, their father was killed in a native skirmish outside the military compound in Burma. Mrs. Glenlyon and her children fled for their lives into the jungle, but somehow the young daughter disappeared. Captain Glenlyon and his two brothers spent years trying to find her."

Susan, pretending to rearrange her skirts, leaned down to poke her head under the table, hissing, "For heaven's sake, the pair of you! Can you not sit through a supper like a pair of normal people for just once?"

Chastened, Elspeth and Catherine straightened in their chairs just in time to overhear the conversation in progress between Glenlyon and George. So Rachel was his sister. How sad, Elspeth thought with another tug of reluctant empathy. She had lost people she'd loved, too.

"Wouldn't your brother's lumber production increase if he made better use of the native slaves?" George was asking, money always foremost on his mind.

"Dallas doesn't use slaves," Glenlyon answered succinctly. "Anyway, what he really needs are more elephants and skilled mahouts to guide them through the jungle. A teak log can weigh up to four tons."

One of the men at the table, a retired banker, looked down his nose at Niall. "I imagine you'll be returning to your island with countless ideas for social improvement from what you've seen here at home."

Niall hesitated, running his index finger along the edge of his knife before he replied. "Which social improvements do you suggest I carry back to the pagan people of Kali Simpang? Should I tell them to take their children from the rice fields and put them into sweatshops? Or should we tear down our waterfalls to make way for distilleries and factories that would defile our blue tropical skies?"

"I believe you're actually a social reformer at heart, Captain," Catherine said shyly.

George leaned forward on his forearms, his mouth pursed in disapproval. "Are you suggesting we return to the Dark Ages then, Captain Glenlyon?"

"Not at all," Niall replied. "I'm suggesting that in many aspects, we have never left them."

Archie Harper gave Niall a mock salute with his wine-glass. "Reformed sinners make the best moral crusaders, eh, Capt'n?"

"George is quite an expert on sin himself," Elspeth murmured. "In fact, he's written a proposal to Parliament to have a law enacted against women undressing with their blinds left open."

Once again there was silence, followed by a low buzz of cautious approval. Niall looked directly at Elspeth.

"How is it to be enforced?" he asked, quirking his brow. "I mean, who would volunteer for such a distasteful task as checking the bedroom windows of naked women?"

Elspeth hazarded a glance at her fiancé, pretending not to notice the icy warning in his eyes. "Oh, dear. You haven't thought that far ahead, have you, George? Captain Glenlyon does have a point."

George gave her a tight smile. "Captain Glenlyon obviously has little experience with life in a civilized culture."

"Oh, but they couldn't possibly have that sort of problem on the captain's island," Catherine said innocently. "The women there hardly wear any clothing to begin with—isn't that right, Captain?"

A violent blast of wind banged against the windows and overturned a potted plant outside, serving to divert attention from Catherine's unsuitable observation. The garden lights flared from behind the curtains, then went out one by one. Mrs. MacDuff put her hand to her breast and gave an appropriate shriek of feminine alarm.

Niall frowned and reached up to loosen his cravat. His gaze unwillingly returned to Elspeth's face as conversation turned to the prospect of an early winter. Bored, he indulged in a dangerous little flight of fantasy. He imagined freeing that wild dark-blond hair and spreading it over her white shoulders and breasts. He imagined tasting that sweet impertinent mouth again, savoring the cries of pleasure it would yield when he laid her beneath him.

He frowned and leaned back in his chair, amused that while he was letting his imagination drive him mad, the object of his fantasy was more interested in polishing off a handful of nuts than in flirting with him across the table.

No, she wasn't aware of him at all, but Niall suddenly decided that he would have to change that. Just in the name of good fun, of course.

Elspeth stared at the window and nibbled on a sugared almond, thinking of that one-eyed man outside in the storm, that wretched husk of a human being who, unless he was truly mad, appeared to know her.

Where had she seen him before? Not at the soup kitchen. Not at the old Soldiers' Hospital where she and Catherine staged musical recitals, which the poor old souls pretended to love. There had been something so poignantly familiar about his disfigured face.

No. She knew him, *she knew*—

She popped another almond into her mouth; her concentration began dissolving as she noticed Glenlyon studying her from under his brows. The look in his eyes alone was enough to warn her what he was thinking. In fact, it was probably all he ever thought about. Her face warm, she swallowed the almond whole only to find it refused to go down, choking her so she couldn't draw another breath.

George stared at her in horror, no doubt thinking of the social embarrassment. Catherine passed her a glass of water. Most of it went sloshing over Elspeth's gown before she could drink it. Duncan calmly leaned over the table to give her a hearty thwack between her shoulder blades. But Elspeth still couldn't breathe. She rose from her seat with her hand pressed to her throat, her eyes dark with apology and panic.

Then somehow, she hadn't even noticed him move around the table, Glenlyon was behind her, occupying her chair and pulling her over his lap. In helpless humiliation, she felt herself thrown over his massive thighs with his knee pressed into her diaphragm. She might have been a pagan princess taken captive by a barbaric chieftain. She had never suffered such indignity.

"Do not panic, Miss Kildrummond." The thread of irony in his voice made her fully aware of how much the rogue was enjoying this. "My valet has a pet monkey who is forever choking on brass buttons."

Elspeth twisted her head around and glowered up at him for all she was worth. His gray eyes glittering, Glenlyon matter-of-factly pushed her head back down and braced the heel of his hand between her shoulder blades, thumping several times while lifting his knee against her. The almond dislodged itself and went down.

"Better now, *chérie?*" he asked quietly, leaning back to allow her to make a dignified escape from his lap.

She jumped up. All around the table the guests gaped at her in varying degrees of consternation. Archie was furiously recording the mishap, possibly hoping for a more dramatic outcome; Elspeth wouldn't have been the first person to choke to death at a supper party, a fish bone being the usual cause of demise.

As usual, she'd made a spectacle of herself. While another woman might have choked and elicited sympathy for the harrowing experience, Elspeth had committed the social crime of having a pariah come to her rescue. And that pariah was sitting back in his chair as imperturbably as Satan himself, when it was his fault she'd swallowed the almond whole in the first place.

George had risen slowly, having taken the time to dab a spot of chestnut trifle from his mouth with a napkin.

He walked around the table at Elspeth's chair, leaning over her with a look of concern. "You need to take a few moments to compose yourself, my dear, while the gentlemen retire to smoke."

"It was only an almond, George. I am composed."

He lowered his voice. "Well, your hair isn't, and there's water all down the front of your gown. Everyone is staring at you."

Elspeth glanced across the table, feeling Glenlyon's amused gaze on her face. "The next time I'm choking to death," she said in a louder voice than she intended, "I'll strive to do so in a ladylike manner."

Someone at the table tittered at that; it sounded like Susan's husband, and George smiled uncertainly, as if taking credit for a good joke, while Elspeth excused herself and rose from her chair.

At the door she heard the wind chasing through the garden, followed by a faraway echo of thunder. Against her will she glanced back into the room—and looked at Niall Glenlyon. He wasn't looking at her, though. His dark head was turned toward the window, and Elspeth wondered if he was thinking of the vagrant and his strange mutterings. He had treated the old man with a gentleness which had surprised her.

The doorknob twisted under her fingers. Startled, she swung around and stared at the tall, gaunt figure in brown fustian who stood in the doorway before her. It was the last person in the world she hoped to meet.

"Old Coffin Face," she said before she could stop herself, and a chill shot through her as it always did when she looked into his oddly slanted amber eyes. "Why aren't you on your way back to Glen Fyne before the weather worsens?"

He studied her for several moments, his mouth stretched into a humorless smile at her customary bluntness. His proper name was Francis Barron, and he was George's

Scottish cousin on his mother's side, a man in his late twenties, although Elspeth held to the belief that Francis had been born a hundred years old.

Uneducated but shrewd, he worked for the Kildrummond family as a factor at Liath House. Periodically he came down to Falhaven to order supplies and meet with Duncan. He was strangely devoted to George, and his father had gone as mad as a March hare, living like a hermit in some Highland cave and claiming to be the reincarnation of a druid. Francis thought that his father was possessed by demons. Elspeth suspected that madness ran in the family.

His childhood sweetheart had mysteriously disappeared one stormy night in Glen Fyne, and the crofters still whispered that he'd pushed her off a bridge because she was planning to leave him for another man. Francis only referred to her as "The Misguided Child" and her body was never found. Rumor also had it that he infrequently visited the lowest brothels, and that even the most desperate of prostitutes refused to be alone with him, citing unspeakable abuse.

Despite his religious zeal and pretensions to piety, Elspeth thought Francis's spiritual facade concealed a cruel, perverse nature. Even years ago at Liath House, whenever a horse or a trapped animal needed to be put out of its misery, it was Francis who volunteered for the job. Elspeth had given him his nickname because of his oblong-shaped face, perpetually grave expression, and bone-white complexion.

"Good evening, Elspeth Kildrummond," he said sourly. "I hear ye've been embarrassing my cousin again."

"I choked on a bloody nut."

"I believe it more likely ye were choking on yer own foul language. Besides, I was referring to yer unfortunate association wi' that Philistine Delilah Petulengro. Ye were seen sitting barelegged on her wagon this very afternoon."

She took his bony wrist and propelled him back into the hall, closing the door behind them. "Coffin Face, I know you and I don't often see eye to eye, but you wouldn't want to ruin my engagement party by repeating that to anyone, would you?"

Francis shook his head. "Wretched woman, ye'll be the downfall of my cousin, I'm certain. Change yer sinful ways before it's too late. The day of your damnation is verra near."

"I can always count on you for the uplifting word."

"I speak the truth."

"I'll bear that in mind."

"Ye ought to spend yer idle time praying on yer knees instead of running about like a hoyden."

"But I do pray, Francis."

"I cringe to imagine what ye petition the Almighty for, Elspeth Kildrummond. Horse races, most likely."

"How did you know?"

She dropped his wrist and backed away from him until she reached the bottom of the staircase. Then with an impudent grin, she whirled around and ran up to her room, shivering as he followed her with his gaze from the darkness of the hall. She was going to oust Francis on his ear the very minute she officially became lady of Liath House.

Inside her room, she had to pick a path through the mountains of sporting magazines, shoes, and petticoats on the floor to reach her dressing table. Things had gotten pretty bad since the maids refused to tidy the place after finding a family of wee mice in the cupboard. In fact, even by Elspeth's own relaxed standards, the room was a disgrace.

As her eyes became accustomed to the darkness, she knocked over a bottle of rose water and pack of playing cards before finding her brush. A box of powder went next. Sneezing, she vowed to clean the puddled mess in the morning. She couldn't be bothered with a candle or lamp, and there seemed little point in worrying over her appearance anyway.

Cosmetics, coiffures, clothing. Nothing helped much. She still had those black scowling eyebrows and a Norseman's chin, thanks to some long ago mismating of a Celtic ancestress with a marauding Viking.

She lifted the brush to her hair only to freeze as in the mirror she noticed a shape shifting behind her on the bed. Dear God, she thought in horror. Could those wee mice have possibly grown into rats?

She pivoted, her heart hammering in her ears. Then the shape wagged its tail and jumped to the floor. It was only the old dog, that silly Clootie who'd curled up on her pillow and left muddy paw prints all over the blue satin comforter.

"Get back into the kitchen, you mongrel! What is the matter with you tonight?" She shook her head, closing her eyes a second to relax. What was the matter with *her?*

The collie skulked to the door, then trotted back to her side. Elspeth sighed and quickly changed from her water-spotted dress. The dog persisted in clinging to the skirts of the drab green silk she'd pulled haphazardly from her wardrobe. The dress was quite wrinkled, and there was a pearl button missing from the sculpted bodice, but she didn't suppose anyone would be rude enough to remark on it.

Except Niall Glenlyon. The memory of his mocking face brought gooseflesh to her skin. The unwelcome thought popped into her mind that they made a fine pair of misfits, she in her outdated dress and he in his dolly-shop coat. But she didn't intend to give him the chance to notice the comparison. In fact, the farther she stayed away from him, the better.

She could hear the guests milling below in the hall, and she hurried down to join them, with an old collie and the scent of roses in her wake. Tonight was supposed to be a celebration, the start of her new life. Why then did she feel this tightness in her chest, the nebulous fear that something awful was about to happen? Why was she suddenly so tempted to curl up with Clootie on the landing and hide there for the rest of the night?

Eight

The women guests drifted in a chattering group down the candlelit corridor toward the small drawing room to take tea and gossip. Lagging several feet behind, the men argued hunting and horsebreeding. Their destination was the oak-paneled smoking room where mellow Glenlivet whisky and walnuts would be served by an ample-bosomed Irish parlormaid in a frilly white cap.

Elspeth managed to merge without notice into the noisy stream of guests, glancing around her as she did. She half expected that the old vagrant would pop up again before the evening ended. And seconds later, when she heard several explosive curses from the men gathered in front of her, underscored by a collective gasp of astonishment from the ladies, she was afraid that the poor man had given her father justifiable cause to have him arrested on charges of housebreaking.

She stood on her tiptoes to see above the crowd.

"Dear God." The diminutive Mrs. MacDuff was fanning the fake pearls on her shrunken chest like a pigeon about to take flight. "There's a *heathen* in the hallway."

"It's a bloody Indian." George was so taken aback he didn't bother to apologize for using bad language in mixed company, or even to chastise Elspeth when she gave him an unladylike poke in the ribs to get a closer look at who was causing so much consternation.

To her relief, it wasn't the earlier intruder at all. It was a rather peculiar if pleasant-looking brown-skinned man of indeterminate age, his head wrapped in a white cotton turban with a large ruby in its center. His face held an unusual appeal—flat nose, broad cheekbones, and eyes as liquid and dark as brewed tea. He appeared unaffected by all the attention, perhaps even a little proud of it, as if it weren't at all odd to find a native wearing a short black jacket and a batik sarong in a Scottish hallway.

"Isn't he cold?" someone whispered.

"It looks as if he's wearing some sort of Indian kilt."

"Perhaps he's from the Hindu Highlands."

"You oughtn't to antagonize him. One never knows what these foreigners will do."

"Poor bugger is turning blue."

"I freezings," the man affirmed with a boyish grin. "Tomorrow I wear socks under sarong like Scottish butler. And waistcoat over my *kris.*"

Still grinning, he flipped open his jacket to reveal an ominous-looking wavy sword strapped to his waist. The sight elicited several shocked oaths from the men and forced the ladies to scurry back like frightened field mice.

His friendly grin faded, however, the moment his gaze encountered Elspeth. Moving apart from the crowd with the authority of a prince, he fixed her with a long silent stare that seemed to view all her secret hopes and yearnings, to penetrate the obscure shadows of her past and future.

"Yes," he said quietly and smiled into her eyes. "You are the one."

"Am I?" she asked, unable to look away.

"Yes."

Elspeth didn't know quite what to make of that. Puzzled, she merely smiled and stepped back into the crowd, a little shock of pleased annoyance going through her to find Niall Glenlyon at her side. His hand brushed hers, and she was certain it wasn't an accident.

She pulled away. He edged closer.

The native sketched her a courtly bow.

Niall chuckled. "You should feel honored, Miss Kildrummond. That's the same bow he practiced endlessly on our sea voyage over in the hope he would run into the queen."

As the native straightened, the winsome grin returned to his wrinkled face, and he lifted his gaze to Glenlyon.

"Who?" he asked imperiously.

"Miss Elspeth Kildrummond," Niall answered in an undertone, and Elspeth was surprised at the respect in his voice as he addressed his servant. "She's our host's eldest daughter."

"Ah. This one very, very goods, Tuan. Heart of tigress."

Elspeth glanced up at Niall. "Goods for what—or shouldn't I ask?"

Niall scratched his eyebrow, hesitating for so long that Elspeth decided he was more nonplussed by the native's cryptic remark than his cynical nature would allow him to show. "You definitely shouldn't ask."

Her father pressed forward to stand next to her and Niall. "I take it this is your man, Captain Glenlyon?"

"Hasim is my—" Niall foundered for the correct English word to describe the Malay shaman who was far more mentor and friend than valet.

The Malay servant looked pointedly at Elspeth again. "I am Hasim," he explained. "Cook, valet, witch doctor. Sometimes butler." His eyes crinkled in amusement. "Headhunter before I met Tuan Captain, but now I civilized. Only take heads during war."

And leaving his stunned audience to absorb that revelation, he began to remove Niall's black evening coat and replace it with the charcoal-gray silk smoking jacket slung over his arm.

"You also supposed to wears this, Tuan," he said with great self-importance, producing a tiny blue-velvet smoking cap with gold tassels.

Niall frowned. "No, I don't think so, Hasim."

"Yes, Tuan. It very propers. Ladies like."

Niall glanced in embarrassment at Elspeth, his frown deepening at the smile she made no effort to conceal. "That will be all, Hasim."

"Not all, Tuan. Man in pawnbroker's shop said you have to wear pretty hat if you smokes with gentlemans."

"You're excused now, Hasim."

"But pretty hat—"

"—makes me feel like that damned monkey of yours."

"Headhunter . . . *witch* doctor?" Mrs. MacDuff had shrugged off her husband's hand to approach her host. "I find this in remarkably poor taste, Duncan."

Duncan looked at Niall. "Perhaps he's having us on."

"No, I'm not." Glenlyon smiled, his wide shoulders straining against his shirt as he thrust his arms into the jacket. "Hasim is a *panang*—yes, a witch doctor, and he raised me and my brothers for six years after we washed ashore on his island."

"Then he's your factotum, Captain Glenlyon," Catherine Kildrummond said brightly. "Just like Robinson Crusoe's man Friday in the book."

"Well, not exactly."

"His soul has been saved?" Mrs. MacDuff asked in a high-pitched voice that quavered between hope and horror.

Niall shrugged, apparently unconcerned by the question of his valet's immortal soul. "I'm not really sure. The subject has never come up in our conversations. But he has been received by a duchess in Aberdeen. In fact, he gave her a mummified frog to cure her sore throat, and she gave him in return— What was her gift again, Hasim?"

"*Chawat,* Tuan. Very elegants." Hasim raised his jacket again to show off the white cashmere necktie he wore knotted around his slender waist to drape like a tail.

Elspeth started to laugh, but the sound died into an

uneasy silence as George brushed past her toward the door of the male sanctuary.

"I hardly think Her Grace intended her gift to be worn in such a vulgar manner," he said with a contemptuous sniff.

"Don't be so stuffy, George," Elspeth said. "You're just jealous because you don't have the flair or figure to wear a necktie around your waist."

He turned slowly to study her. "You are a damnable brat, Elspeth," he said with a reluctant smile. "It's a wonder I'm so in love with you."

"Are you?" she asked in a low strained voice, certain that Glenlyon, with his hunter's instincts, could hear them.

George's reply puzzled her. "Never doubt it, darling." His smile disappeared. "No matter what I may have——"

He wasn't allowed to finish. The men began propelling him into the smoking room, the women moving past the doorway in pairs. Niall stepped around Elspeth with a faint smile on his face.

"That was very touching, Miss Kildrummond," he murmured, pretending to wipe a tear from his eye with his knuckle.

She gave him an icy smile. "How very crass of you to eavesdrop on a private conversation."

"Crass or not, I don't think I liked the sound of that little *tête-à-tête* between you and George at all."

"Really?" she asked dryly.

He lowered his head to hers. "You didn't tell him about 'us,' did you?"

She glanced around them in alarm. "There are people listening, you—you troublemaker. And there is no 'us.' "

"There isn't? But this is too cruel, too sudden . . . no 'us'? Not even after I saved your life at supper?"

Color flooded her face. "Don't remind me of that horrible incident. I've never been so humiliated in my life. Well, almost never."

"It's my coat, isn't it?"

She stared at him. Something that felt horribly like laughter came welling up inside her. "I think you're quite mad, Glenlyon."

"You're missing a button, by the way," he said under his breath.

"Trust you to notice."

"Ma chère, I've noticed nothing but you all night."

She started past him. He sidestepped her, studying her angry face with wicked enjoyment.

"The men are going to wonder what's become of you, Captain. I'm sure they're all just dying to hear about your exploits."

"Je m'en fiche," he said quietly. "I don't care. I'd much rather hoist you over my shoulders for a romp in the summerhouse than sit in that room with those stuffy old relics."

Elspeth closed her eyes. A romp in the summerhouse. He was too much.

"Well, what do you think?" he whispered, smiling innocently as Duncan glanced out at them from the doorway. "We can sneak away together to your gypsy encampment and dance barefoot around the campfire. I'll even clamp a rose in my teeth for effect, shall I?"

Her eyes flew open, shooting sparks. "I think you're insufferable."

He smiled archly. "But you're tempted all the same, aren't you?"

"What I'm tempted to do, Captain," she said in a scathing whisper, "is to murder you on the spot."

A servant bustled past them pushing a tea-trolley. George shouted to Niall from the depths of the smoking room.

"Are you going to join the men or have tea with the ladies, Glenlyon?"

Niall straightened reluctantly. "I meant it when I

warned you about George, Miss Kildrummond. The little baronet didn't get that manure on his boots from walking through a field of wildflowers. I'd be suspicious if I were you."

"Well, you aren't, Captain Glenlyon, and I suggest you not strain your imagination by putting yourself in my place. In fact, once again, I suggest you mind your own damn business."

He grinned like a satyr, backing into the doorway. That's splendid advice, *darling.* I think I'll take it."

Elspeth remained rooted to the spot, shaking inwardly as he turned away. It would have been far easier to shrug off his warning if it hadn't echoed her own deepest feelings about George.

"Unprincipled rogue," she muttered.

"Who, George?" Catherine said behind her.

"No. Oh, never mind."

The corridor was empty now, but the two sisters lingered there on purpose as had become their habit, fascinated by the salty male conversation which drifted from the smoking room and which Society deemed too disturbing for their delicate ears.

"Look at that stag's head above the fire, Captain Glenlyon. I'll bet my uncle's balls ye've never shot anything like that, have ye?"

"Hmmm. No, sir. You're right. I haven't."

"Sir George shot that himself on his estate as a present for his future father-in-law. Few men can outshoot him, ye ken. Pretty impressive beast, wouldn't ye say, Captain?"

"Well, the antlers are blunted. I'd say it was an old animal and couldn't have withstood much of a chase."

"You'll be heading north just in time for a wee bit of

deer shooting yourself, Captain. I'd like to see how those big-game skills of yours fare in our tamer Highland hills."

One of the men started to close the door. Elspeth and Catherine were leaning so far forward to listen, they almost toppled into the room. Elspeth stuck out the toe of her shoe as a wedge just in time.

From inside the room Niall raised his brows at the two pretty faces he'd glimpsed peering at him through the crack in the door. What a handful. "I'm not on a shooting expedition, gentlemen," he said casually. "I have personal business in the Highlands to attend to."

"A woman? Aye, well, it is still rutting season," Martin MacDuff commented, giving the passing parlormaid a pat on the rump. "Come on, Moira, lass, a wee drop more. That's right, hen. Lean a little lower so I can see those big white breasts of yours. Why, I do swear they've grown since last month. You've been eating your oats, lassie."

Catherine burst into helpless giggles, then gasped as Elspeth gave her a sharp pinch on the arm to quiet her.

George had moved to the fire, one leg planted on a footstool as if he were posing for a portrait. "Well, Captain, give us an answer. Is Martin right or not?"

Niall stared down into his whisky glass. "Since I haven't met Moira before tonight," he answered slowly, "I'm not exactly qualified to judge whether she's grown or not."

Several men guffawed. George nodded in reluctant amusement. "I was referring to Martin's earlier question. Do you have a romantic interest in Scotland?"

"Elspeth? Catherine?" a woman's voice trilled from down the hall, the gossip group apparently just realizing it had lost its most constant source of scandal, those ill-bred Kildrummond daughters.

Elspeth glanced around in annoyance, whispering, "Just a moment! I've dropped my earring," before she turned back to the door to learn whether Glenlyon did indeed have a mystery woman hidden in the Highlands.

"I'm traveling alone," she heard him answer, "except for Hasim, and he's nobody's idea of a paramour."

Suddenly Catherine sneezed, not once, but three times in rapid succession; she couldn't help it. The smell of rice powder and rose water on Elspeth's hair was overpowering. There was an interval of disbelieving silence in the room. Then George left the fire and wrenched open the door with such a look of outrage, you'd have thought they had been caught spying on a secret government cabinet. Elspeth fell forward onto her hands and knees between Glenlyon's long outstretched legs.

Duncan, recognizing his daughter, covered his eyes in embarrassment.

"Elspeth." George looked mortified. "I should have known."

She didn't even try to defend herself, staring past him into the room. In fact, she really didn't hear him or her cousin Susan calling again from down the hall. Their voices receded like the echoes of a dream.

She heard only the low deep laughter of the man whose dark elegance dominated the room, the man who obviously found everything about her so very amusing. She tried to look away, but she couldn't. And the strange thing was that neither did Niall, his laughter suddenly subsiding into the uneasy hush around them.

Try as he might, Niall couldn't bring himself to stop staring at the woman practically sprawled out at his feet like a pagan offering he was too tempted to accept. The mere sight of her sent his mind spiraling in dangerous circles. His own languid posture belied the tension that immobilized him. He was aware of everyone staring at him, expecting a reaction, and he didn't care.

Look at that sweet, scowling face. Just look at her. Why, give her a spear and shield, and she could be mistaken for a Valkyrie on a Viking battlefield. The submissive femininity of her pose stirred his blood. The fire in her eyes fascinated him.

In fact, it fascinated Niall so much he hoped Kildrummond had possessed the foresight to place Niall's bedchamber on the opposite end of the house from his she-devil of a daughter. Niall needed to sleep tonight, not lie awake craving a woman who belonged to someone else.

He put his fingers to his cravat. *Sacrebleu* but this room was hot. Didn't the domestics believe in ever opening the windows? Was everyone too afraid of gypsies and vagrants breaking in, or of the incorrigible Elspeth escaping? He was going to suffocate, stew in his own juices.

"Captain Glenlyon," one of the men said in amused concern, "is something the matter?"

And Niall couldn't even answer. Raising his glass, he downed the whisky in one burning swallow. Was something wrong? No, not yet. Not ever if he got the hell away from the house in time.

Elspeth Kildrummond, your mouth is sweeter than sin. Keep far, far away from me if you know what's good for you.

It was her sister who finally saved Elspeth from a complete scandal, helping her to her feet and out into the hall. The door closed resoundingly in their faces. The snorts of muffled male laughter fell like an insult in the silence. Strange that she didn't hear *his* voice again. But the deep unforgettable resonance of it still rang through her mind.

"Why on earth were you two staring at each other like that?" Catherine whispered in fascination.

"I wasn't staring at him." Elspeth jabbed a pin back into her hair with a trembling hand. "He was staring at me."

"But you were. Oh, you were. It was so dramatic. I should have loved to sketch it. You looked exactly like Proserina carted off to Hades and sprawled at Pluto's feet."

"Pluto's feet. Hades. Dear God. Is there a full moon tonight?"

"I wouldn't know, Elspeth. I've been inside all evening practicing at the piano while you were running about having your adventures without me."

"He's leaving tomorrow," Elspeth mumbled, leaning back against the door. "Thank God. This is horrible. What was he thinking, to stare at me like that in front of everyone?"

"Yes. It's not as if he could have been blinded by your beauty."

"Thank you, Catherine."

"Come on, Elspeth!" Susan called from the drawing-room door. "We're dying to hear about the trousseau Duncan's ordered for you from Edinburgh."

Edinburgh. A trousseau. Elspeth felt a mild panic, unable to picture her upcoming marriage in her mind. She could only picture that devil's face in all its mesmerizing darkness. Yes, thank God he was going away. The man had a way of dominating her thoughts.

As she hurried down the hall after Catherine, an unconscious frown creased her forehead. She didn't know what was wrong with her. She felt as restless as a raven before a rainstorm.

She wanted to blame Niall Glenlyon for her edginess, for aggravating her usual good nature in the garden with his untoward behavior, his outrageous charm.

She wanted to blame George for her peculiar mood, George who grew a bit more pompous every time he returned from London, who became more and more a stranger, who criticized and struggled to change the unconventional aspects of her character that he had once admired.

She wanted to blame her father, for forcing her and Catherine to take music lessons when everyone knew they were tone deaf and hopelessly untalented, for thinking he could buy and bluff his way into the rigid strictures of Society.

But more than anything she just wanted to run outside, to ride back to the gypsy encampment to escape the unsettled feeling that kept growing stronger.

Something horrible is going to happen. Something I can't control.

She shook off the ominous thought and took a deep breath outside the drawing room before she opened the door to greet the small group of women assembled in front of a fire screen which depicted *The Rape of the Lock.* They stared back at her with a censure that felt like a slap across the face. And yet despite their blatant disapproval, a strange rush of fondness for them swept through Elspeth; they were comforting in their familiarity for all their flaws, forever trying to refine her when she could have told them it was a hopeless cause.

Then right on the tail of that wave of inexplicable affection for the old battle-axes came a sudden fear that she would never see them again after tonight. Not miserable Mrs. MacDuff or even her own silly harlot of a cousin, Susan. Deep in her marrow she sensed that her life was about to be irrevocably altered, and she would be torn from the common world she knew. The impulse to run away seized her again, but to where, from what?

The clock on the mantelpiece chimed nine times as if to emphasize the passage of time. A shiver of fear shot through her.

Somebody make it stop, a frantic little voice screamed inside her head, but nobody else heard it. No one else shared her irrational terror.

"What is wrong with you tonight, Elspeth?" Susan asked in an undertone.

"Nothing." She frowned, rubbing her forearms. "I'm fine."

"Perhaps the poor thing is overwrought with all the excitement," someone murmured.

"Perhaps it's the weather. These late autumn storms are so unsettling."

"Do you have a fever, dear?"

"Why, it's no surprise she's taken ill with the company she keeps. There's cholera raging again in the slums."

"For heaven's sake, I'm fine!"

Stunning them into silence with her outburst, she plunked down on the window seat and threw back the lace undercurtains to stare outside. All their fussing about fevers reminded her of a resolution she'd made to herself earlier in the evening. George would throttle her, but she was going to sell the Navy medals he'd given her from his treasured collection to buy medicine for the Romany children who couldn't afford a doctor's care. With winter on its way, and the gypsies camping on the unsheltered Scottish moors—

"Elspeth, wake up!" Susan said sharply. "Marjorie has asked you the same question three times in a row now."

Elspeth sighed, letting the curtains fall back against the window. "The trousseau. Yes, well, the gown is ivory satin with—"

"Not the trousseau," Marjorie interrupted her slyly. "We want you to tell us everything you know about Captain Glenlyon."

"Me?" she said in astonishment. "How the hel— how the hellebore would I know anything about him? I never read the papers."

"Come now, Elspeth. Don't be coy. Susan told us about the interlude in the summerhouse. Surely you learned something about the fascinating man?"

Elspeth hesitated, tempted to shock them into oblivion with a detailed account of what had really happened between her and Glenlyon. But then the clock on the mantel chimed the hour again. Heads turned. Conversation stopped. Elspeth could not breathe for the anxiety crushing her chest.

"One of the housemaids must have dropped it when she was dusting," Susan said, turning back to Elspeth with a shrug of annoyance at the interruption. "Go on, Elspeth."

The clock wasn't broken. Elspeth knew that, but none of them would understand. It was only trying to warn her how little time she had left, and there was nothing she could do but wait—for what she did not know. Something dark and faceless watching through the windows. Something that carried the scent of death on the wind.

Nine

Catherine spread the popular periodical open on her sister's bedchamber carpet, making as much noise as possible as she flipped through the pages. When Elspeth didn't react, pretending to be sound asleep in her bed, Catherine rose to her knees and shook her by the shoulders.

"Listen to this, Elspeth!" she whispered urgently.

Elspeth rolled to the other side of the bed, cocooning herself in the coverlet that Clootie had decorated with muddy dog prints.

"It's a matter of life or death," Catherine added as a last resort.

Elspeth slowly unraveled herself from the bedclothes and reluctantly opened her eyes to stare up at her sister's animated face. "If it's another sordid confession of a country girl lured into a life of prostitution by her uncle, it'll be a matter of death, all right. Yours."

"Let me read it to you."

"It better not be another story about a young orphaned chimney sweep dying in the gutter with the clatter of coach wheels drowning out his heart-rending groans."

"Just listen."

Catherine stretched upward to place the candlestick on the nightstand between them before she started to read. Elspeth sighed in resignation and flung her hand over her eyes. Dear God, it must be past midnight. She had to sneak out before dawn to meet Samson and be back at breakfast to catch the coach.

Catherine began, her voice quavering with excitement, " 'If Niall Glenlyon's name has become familiar in the male military and mercantile clubs of the European community in the Far East, it is positively legend in the female social circles whose members take delight in discussing his exploits, most of which Captain Glenlyon claims are patently untrue.' "

"Fascinating." Elspeth swallowed, suddenly wide awake despite herself. "Are you finished?"

"No." Catherine returned to the article, ignoring Elspeth's loud succession of sighs. " 'They say he communes with the spirits of the animals in whose savage world he lives: the tiger, the leopard, the white-tailed eagle. Yet according to the Rajah of his island, Glenlyon has deliberately hunted to kill only one animal—a man-eating tigress that had stalked the jungle village for almost a year.' "

Elspeth stared up at the shadows the candle flame threw against the wall. "I don't suppose it mentions anything about him working in a brothel?" she murmured.

"A brothel?" Catherine's hand flew to her mouth. "Good Lord. I must have missed that week's installment."

Elspeth slid down on the floor, frowning, and started to read the magazine for herself over Catherine's shoulder.

They say that the witch doctor who rescued the three Glenlyon boys on his remote heathen island spirited them away to his jungle hideaway and taught them the secrets of jadoo, *Far Eastern magic; that the unruly trio learned how to seduce women with only a smile, and how to hear the private music of the wind and sea while others hear only the muffled clamor of their own minds.*

They say that Niall Glenlyon ravished the daughter

of an army general on a billiard table in the British
barracks in Rangoon, that his subsequent refusal to
marry her, to explain his misbehavior, cost him an
involuntary retirement from the army, and the threat
of a court-martial.

"A billiard table!" That was the last straw. Elspeth
jumped up in disgust and blew out the candle, then dove
back into bed while Catherine peered like a mole at the
rest of the article. "Honestly, Cat, Papa would die if he
caught you reading such—such prurient material."

"Look who's calling the kettle black. *The Racing Cal-
endar* isn't exactly known as classic literature." Catherine
shook her head in amazement. "The man knows magic,"
she whispered. "Why, he could be casting a spell over
you even as we speak."

"I wish he'd put a spell on you. A spell of silence."

"Ooh, I wonder if he was putting the evil eye on you
in the smoking room. Can you imagine, Elspeth?"

Elspeth snorted into her pillow, infuriated that she'd let
herself be drawn into her sister's fantasy world. "He was
caught with his breeks down on a billiard table, and I daresay his cue stick wasn't pointed at a corner pocket. Imagine
that, Catherine."

The sharp pinging on the balcony woke her less than
an hour later. Assuming that the storm had erupted during
the night, she snuggled down deeper under the covers and
tried without luck to return to her wonderful dream.

Ali Baba had been forging across the finish line. They
were going to be filthy rich!

The *ping-ping-ping* on her small private balcony persisted, as loud as hailstones. Throwing off the comforter,
she eased out of bed. As she opened the balcony door, a
spray of damp wind washed over her, and she averted her

face, swallowing a cry. She lived in constant terror that Samson would show up one night to tell her Ali Baba had taken ill.

And then she realized it probably wasn't the rain that had awakened her at all. It was probably that damned rogue Glenlyon hoping to play Romeo to her in the dark. She grinned reluctantly at his perseverance.

She had completely forgotten her earlier premonition of disaster. She'd even forgotten about the old vagrant until she saw him again. Her grin vanished, a shadow stirring in her memory.

Catching her breath, she stepped closer to the railing. He stood directly below her balcony, rain pelting his long gnarled hair. He was reaching down to collect another handful of gravel from the footpath to throw at her door.

"What do you want?" she called down softly, shivering from cold and apprehension.

"Miss Elspeth, I didna want to frighten ye, but I tried all evening to find ye alone." He lifted his scarred face to the balcony, letting the gravel dribble through the lumpy flesh of his fingers. " 'Tis Tormod, my dear. Tormod Mac-Queen. Do ye nae remember yer granddad's old ghillie?"

"Tormod. Oh, my God. I didn't recognize—" She couldn't finish, shock and sympathy choking off the words. Dead. The dear man was supposed to be dead. What had happened to his face and hands? Was he a ghost? Where had he been the past months she had been quietly mourning him?

He forced a smile. "Aye. I'm changed, ye ken. Gruesome to look at, but at least I'm still alive. Do ye recognize this, my dear?"

He reached under his plaid to show her the jewel-gripped *skene-dhu,* or Highland dirk, that Elspeth had coveted every day of her confused adolescence. It was the companion to the broadsword her great-great-grandfather had carried to Culloden Moor, reputed to have been blessed by a white

witch to give his wife courage in his absence. The knife
was worth a small fortune. Its ebony grip was inlaid with
gold and set with garnets to represent the blood that would
be spilled in battle, pearls for the bones of those who would
sacrifice their lives.

"I recognize it," she said, swallowing hard. The rush of
memories, of questions its appearance raised, were too
painful to assimilate.

"I've kept it fer ye. Kept it safe from thievin' hands
who have no respect fer the old times."

Anger blazed inside her as the gist of what he was
saying penetrated her mind. She raised her hand to wipe
away the raindrops that trickled down her face. They
might have been tears. But she was too shocked, too upset
to cry.

The precious keepsake had been promised to her and
Cat by their grandfather, Ronald Kildrummond, a decade
ago. But after Ronald's death, Elspeth's father had ordered
Francis to sell off whatever valuables he could, purportedly for the upkeep of the impoverished estate.

Her father had told her the dirk had been sold to a
collector of antiques from Inverness.

Her father had also told her that Tormod had burned
to death last August in an accidental fire in his home.
Tormod, her grandfather's gamekeeper and most trusted
friend, the gentle, patient man who'd taught her to ride
and dance her first Highland reel, who'd vowed to stand
by her during the awful days of her illegitimate pregnancy.
The man who stood below her now in the garden, dirty,
disheveled, disfigured. But not dead, and no ghost either,
she thought grimly.

She gazed down, away from Tormod, at her father's private office where so many clandestine late-night meetings
were conducted. Duncan and George's senior partner had
died last winter, accusing both men of embezzlement, but
no one had listened because Arthur MacAllister had been

an unpopular old curmudgeon who'd distrusted his own wife. Now, for the first time, Elspeth wondered about the man's deathbed claims, and about the "fires" at the waterfront warehouse two months ago, the whispers of insurance fraud. The firm had recently lost several important overseas accounts. Yet mysteriously, last summer, right after George had proposed to her, all the company's longstanding bills had been settled. Duncan and George had become visibly more relaxed.

Tormod hobbled closer to the balcony, his gruff voice urgent. "I need to speak wi' ye tonight. There's been so much trouble at home. The others claim ye were part of it, but I couldna believe it. I had to find out fer myself."

Part of what? she wondered in bewilderment. She stared back down into his scarred face and felt that earlier fear clawing back into her awareness. She wanted to call him a liar, to deny the suspicions he'd planted in her mind.

She loved her father, and he loved her. There had to be an explanation. Her life, its most important relationships, could not have been built on lies.

"Wait. Don't say any more, Tormod." She backed away from the railing, shivering. "Meet me in the summerhouse. I'll be down as soon as I fetch my shawl."

Ten

Niall was by nature and necessity a light sleeper, accustomed to the incessant rhythm of tropical rain. He had opened his eyes the instant the first particle of gravel had struck her balcony. It sounded incongruous with the natural cadence of the storm. In the interval that followed, he knew instinctively that Hasim had awakened too, curled up on the carpet with his superstitious disdain for proper beds.

They didn't speak, only listened to the series of sounds that told a story. Elspeth's balcony door creaking open, the gravel assault from below coming to a sudden stop. The faraway murmur of voices in the rain, male and female, low with the familiarity of a long-time association.

He closed his eyes, smiling to himself as he heard her rummage through her armoire, placed up against the other side of the wall that separated their rooms. Then her outer door opened and softly closed; she had to be making one of her many furtive escapes downstairs.

"She's sneaking out again, that misbehaved girl," he said quietly, and to his surprise the thought both annoyed and aroused him, sent a hot pulsing of blood through his deeply relaxed body. "Is she meeting her stuffy fiancé George, do you think, or her gypsies again?"

Hasim lit a cigarette and stared in fascination at the configuration of smoke rings he blew up toward the plaster angels floating across the ceiling. "Why you cares,

Tuan? Said lady too spoiled, play bad music, marry stupid man. Sneak out of house to ride horses with social inferiors. Tuan Captain too pure to defile his character with such very bad womans."

"You know, Hasim, if you fall asleep with that cigarette dangling from your lips, you're liable to burn our host's house down."

"Not such a bad thing to happen, Tuan. Very evil spirits in this house. I leave offerings in every corner to protect us."

"I hope you remembered to leave our clothes out for the morning."

"Tuan, I leaves your clothes out. I waterproofs your boots and wash my feets in vinegar water like it say in *The Domestic Valet's Directory.*" Hasim glanced toward the window, his voice solemn. "She has very strong heart, Tuan."

"She also has a fiancé, Hasim, and I say he's welcome to her."

"She going into very big troubles, Tuan. This the spirits tell me."

"Probably so, Hasim. But there's nothing we can do about it."

Hasim sat up and crossed his legs, staring in silent disapproval across the room until Niall felt compelled to shift onto his side to look at him. "You not going to even try to help her, Tuan? Save her from this very bad things?"

"What 'very bad thing'? She'll stub her little toe sneaking down the stairs? A constable will apprehend her on the corner and drag her home to Papa?" Niall exhaled quietly. "What I'm going to do is take her advice and mind my own business. I strongly urge you to do the same."

* * *

Elspeth hurried through the garden. Rain went splashing down onto the thin paisley shawl she'd thrown on over her white muslin nightrail. As she passed her father's office, George suddenly appeared at the window, staring outside with a worried expression on his face. She drew back against the wall beneath him and slowly edged out of view. Her bare toes sank in the mud. She felt sick with fear that he'd stop her. She was going to marry him, and suddenly she didn't know who he was.

She had no idea what Tormod wanted; she might even have been a little afraid of him, his strange appearance and behavior, if she weren't so furious at George for callously evicting him from the garden earlier. George surely had recognized him—he and Tormod had talked at length, had argued. For years she and George had lived in the man's shadow, those bittersweet bygone times when she'd run around the glen like the pagan she was at heart, and George had wandered the lonely grounds of his uncle's estate like the priggish lordling he'd become. And Tormod had brought them together, an impossible pair.

She started down the path to the summerhouse only to whirl around in alarm as something tugged hard at the muddied hem of her gown.

"Not you again, Clootie!" she whispered in relief, kneeling to scratch his ears and give her racing heart a rest.

Despite the impatience in her voice, she was honestly glad of the old collie's company, more nervous about meeting Tormod than she liked to admit. But the dog refused to be petted, backing away from her and whimpering in distress.

"Don't you dare start barking, Clootie. Och, I'll carry you with me just in case."

Yet when she went to lift him, the dog scooted free, circling her several times and pushing his muzzle against her as she straightened.

"Look, I'm not going to stand here in the freezing drizzle trying to placate you," she said sternly. "Go back inside where you belong!"

The dog made several more attempts to head her back toward the house before he disappeared. Disgusted, Elspeth continued on and ran up the steps of the summerhouse, hesitating before she stepped inside. Apprehension crawled up her spine, but she ignored it, impatient to absolve her father of any wrongdoing.

Tormod had hidden himself behind one of the pillars at the back of the summerhouse. He didn't emerge until she called him twice by name. His hands, the fingers deformed with scar tissue, trembled as she clasped them in her own. She could feel his ribs, the knobs of his shoulders, when she tried to draw him against her to embrace.

He eased away, his head lowered in shame. "Ye'll not want to touch me, my dear. I smell like a pig and havena had a decent wash since I left Glen Fyne." His mouth twisted into a bitter semblance of a smile. "The White Glen, named for the briar roses that once covered it in spring, the snow that falls in winter. Aye, 'tis whiter now than ever. The bastards will nae have to rename it."

A wave of cold fear broke over her. Part of her wanted to run back to the house and pretend she hadn't met him again. He made no sense, and yet there was a chilling logic in his voice that compelled her to stay. "What are you saying?" she whispered hoarsely.

Tormod's single eye glittered with a hatred that was almost unholy. "Ye promised ye'd come home. Yer granddad left the land to ye because you were the one who loved it best. He trusted ye to take care of us. Aye, I trained ye myself to do his job."

She started to shiver as the cold air cut through the insubstantial folds of her nightrail. "I was coming, after the wedding in November."

Tormod limped to the arched entryway, contempt in his

voice. "He waited for ye on his deathbed. He asked where ye were every hour."

She shook her head, tears of helpless remorse in her eyes. She had been in London, at George's insistence, while her grandfather was dying. "I didn't even know he was ill."

"He'd been dying for months."

"No one told me." She hugged herself. Guilt and grief welled up uncontrollably as she closed her eyes against the image of her beloved grandda dying alone, believing she didn't care enough about him to make the journey north.

"He wanted ye there. He needed yer help to try to stop them."

She lowered her arms. "What help? To stop who, Tormod? I don't understand—"

He turned around with the jeweled dirk drawn from its scabbard and catching dark glints of moonlight. "Swear on this." He strode up before her and caught her chin with one hand, the other lifting the knife between them. A spasm of alarm passed through her, but she couldn't move, wondering if he were really mad as George had insisted, wishing now she had heeded his warning.

"Can ye swear to me ye didna know what yer father and Georgie Westcott were aboot?"

She swallowed over the constriction in her throat. Dear God, what *had* they done? Sold her land, her inheritance, her dowry? No, they couldn't have.

She shook her head, frightened and confused, afraid of whatever he wanted to reveal. "I don't know anything," she whispered. "Oh, dammit, Tormod, tell me. Does it have something to do with what happened to your face?"

He nodded slowly, tears filming his eye.

"Tormod," she prompted gently, "please put the dirk down and talk to me."

"Aye," he said, his voice rasping, but before he could

lower the dirk, there were footsteps on the outer steps, a man rushing from the darkness toward them.

"Get away from her, you lunatic!"

Elspeth could only stare. In fact, she almost didn't recognize George at all. His face was distorted by unspeakably dark emotions.

"Get out of the way, Elspeth," he ordered her in a voice that also did not sound like his, but that gripped her with chilling fear.

She couldn't think; sheer instinct compelled her to step around Tormod, to shield him. Through her daze she registered the fact that her father was slowly mounting the stairs into the summerhouse. His startled gaze met hers for only a fraction of a second before he turned to stare at Tormod, disbelief and pity registering on his face.

And standing behind Duncan at the bottom of the stairs was Francis Barron. His amber eyes blazed, blaming Elspeth for this scene. Like a buzzard on a moorland crag, his presence could only portend evil. She began to shake. The inner voice that she had tried to ignore all evening now began shrieking wildly inside her head.

Something horrible is going to happen.

She saw the cold metallic gleam of a pistol in George's hand as he charged toward her. The sight of it appalled her; she couldn't comprehend what he intended to do. George shot poor little animals. Not people. Please God, not people.

She tried again, her movements awkward, to position herself between him and Tormod. The strange light in George's eyes terrified her. But Tormod only forced her back against the rocking chair. His shrunken frame shook with the intensity of his emotions.

"I lost my family in the fire, and my own life means nothing anymore." He held the dirk out to her, fumbling with his other hand to find the sporran he wore under his filthy plaid. "Take it. And the scabbard, 'tis here, kept for ye as promised. Aye, old Tormod kept his promise. Now 'tis up to you to do the same. Use the dirk's courage, remember its history, and go home to help the others."

He thrust the knife toward her, the garnets glistening like blood in the moonlight. Then just as she lifted her hand to grasp the hilt, George forced himself between them, shoving her off to the side so hard that she gasped, slamming back against the chair. Stunned, she heard Tormod swear, saw his fingers curl around the jeweled hilt as he turned on George.

George raised his arm, the pistol level with Tormod's chest. "Come at me, would you, you old bastard."

"No," she cried, her voice hoarse. "God, no, George, you can't—"

She pushed herself away from the chair to stop him, but someone grabbed her from behind. Francis, his scrawny arms like bands of steel.

She kicked back against his knees, and heard him grunt in surprise at her strength. His grip tightened until she couldn't breathe, until she felt like an animal caught in a trap. Even then she banged her head into his chest, so wild to free herself she didn't hear his voice.

"Did I nae warn ye, Elspeth Kildrummond? Pray now if ye've ever prayed before."

But all she could do, shaking her head, was to whisper, "George, don't, don't, don't—" And another voice joined her litany, a man's voice which might have been her father's or Francis's. It could even have been both.

"George, don't . . ."

But he fired the pistol anyway, and its reverberations resounded like a tidal wave through the blood roaring in her head. "Oh, no, George. I don't believe you did this." She had sagged back into Francis's arms, and didn't realize it. She was speaking without any idea whether she made sense at all, shock giving her voice a flat conversational tone. "Papa, did you see what George did? You should have stopped him. I can't believe you didn't stop him."

Tormod took an involuntary step toward her, a look of disbelief and panic on his face before his features crumpled into complete relaxation.

"Remember," he whispered. That was all.

Then he fell across the chair. And Elspeth relinquished her faint hope that he could have survived being shot at such close range. She began to shake, bile rising from the pit of her stomach. The dirk lay at her feet.

"God forgive you, Georgie," Francis whispered, staring down at Tormod's body. As if Elspeth were a serpent, he released her and thrust her away from him.

Blood rushed back into her arms, stinging her veins, but she was too numb to even notice. She made a despairing sound in her throat and knelt. The hem of her nightrail brushed the small puddle of blood on the floor. Knowing it was futile, she felt for a pulse in Tormod's wrist, pressing the heel of her other hand to the wound in his chest.

Murder. Cold-blooded murder. She swallowed a sob and drew him into her lap, cradling him and thinking how insubstantial he felt, the pride and dignity, the very soul gone from his body. He and his ailing wife had promised to adopt and raise her baby if her father had refused to let her keep it, and their kindness, their unconditional love had been her sole comfort before she miscarried the child.

Tormod's only daughter, with two sons of her own to feed, had offered to pass the child off as her own to spare Elspeth the shame. More than once Tormod had carried her and Catherine to the burn in the middle of the night to bring down their fevers when they were bairns. He had been a golden thread in the fabric of Elspeth's often troubled life.

Tormod had taught her to love the land, to trust her

instincts, to overcome the limitations the world would place before her. He had taught her how to open her heart, to embrace life.

"I'm sorry," she crooned, rocking him back and forth like a child, tears slipping down her face. "Oh, my friend. Hie ye awa' to Magh Meala, the Plain of Honey you taught us about as bairns where only the bravest men are allowed."

"Elspeth," George said, but he didn't move. He looked as shocked as anyone by what had happened.

She tossed back her head, her hair falling across her anguished face. "Why? Why did you have to kill him?" Her voice broke, and she glanced past George to her father, standing with his hand shielding his eyes. "He saved your life once, Papa, when you were sick and lost in a snowstorm. You always said he was the brother you never had. *Why did you allow this to happen?*"

Duncan brought his hand away from his face. There were tears in his eyes too, but she didn't care. She was in too much pain to care. "Lower your voice, darling," he said heavily. "The houseguests might hear you and we've trouble enough on our heads as it is."

George knelt down beside her, speaking in soft urgent tones. "He was going to stab you, Elspeth, and look how he turned on me. Don't you understand? He came here tonight to *kill* you."

"Why? Why would he want to kill me, George?"

"God only knows, darling. A deranged mind cannot be understood. I'm just grateful I got here when I did. In another few moments—"

She shook her head, shrinking away from him when he reached for her hand. "Don't touch me. You killed him on purpose—he wasn't going to hurt me at all. Murderer. You murderer." Biting her lip against more tears, she defiantly tore off her Paisley shawl, the fringe hitting George in the face, and gently pressed it against Tormod's chest.

George glanced up at Francis, making a covert gesture with his hand. "Elspeth, listen to reason. The man was mad."

She rose clumsily to her feet, pressing back against the pillar as she had earlier in the evening to escape another man. But Glenlyon's flagrant attempts at seduction, his potent charm, which had seemed so perilous at the time, took on an almost wistful innocence in contrast to what had just happened.

She ground her teeth together to stop their chattering. "He was about to tell me about Glen Fyne. About what you and my father had done."

George's expression did not change, but her father glanced up slowly, his face grim, gray. Francis was hoisting Tormod into his arms with an awkward finality that turned Elspeth's stomach, that forced her to look away. There would be no lykewake to speed her old friend's soul to heaven. The man who had observed tradition all his life deserved so much better than this.

"Tormod was mentally unbalanced," George said quietly. "He'd lost his home and family, including two grandchildren, in a fire last year, and the shock unhinged him. He went wild with grief and refused to leave his home even when the walls were caving in on him. The authorities had to commit him to a lunatic infirmary for his own protection."

"An asylum?" she said, stunned.

"Apparently he escaped."

"You told me he was dead, that he'd died in that fire."

"My dear," Duncan said, his voice deep with sadness, "I didn't want to upset you and Catherine, or spoil the memories you had of the old man. The Tormod we knew did die in that fire."

Elspeth shook her head. "You're lying. He and his family could always have lived in Granddad's lodge. He had no home to lose."

Duncan's brows pulled together in concern. "I had to ask Francis to force him out last February. Tormod had become a rebel, demanding rights I could not meet. He moved into one of the poor crofts, even though his pension could have brought him a decent home in the Lowlands."

"The Lowlands?" she cried in disbelief. "He'd been with our family for fifty years."

"He was a dangerous, unpredictable man," George said tersely, rising from the floor. "He crippled a constable, in a drunken rage. This is a matter of public record, and Francis can verify it."

"I'm afraid it's true, Elspeth," Duncan said solemnly. "I did not want you to know until you were settled down in your new life."

She buried her face in her hands, so confused she didn't know what to believe. What if they were telling her the truth? Why should she not trust her own family over an old friend? Tormod's disfigured face flashed across her mind. *You're needed at home.* Yes, madness had burned in his gaze, but the gentle compassion she remembered had been there too, and all her instincts had urged her to trust him.

She lowered her hands, rushing forward as Francis began carrying Tormod's inert body outside. "Where are you taking him?" she asked in alarm.

Duncan placed his hand on her shoulder. "We'll handle this. You're not to worry."

"But what about his family?"

"They're either gone or dead," Duncan said grimly. "The asylum won't want the expense of burying him. Francis will do the right thing."

George came up behind her, gently pulling her back against him. She went rigid, staring down through fresh tears at the bloodstains on the white muslin skirt of her nightrail.

"Poor darling," he murmured, massaging the stiff muscles of her shoulder. "It was such a traumatic thing for you to witness."

"Don't 'poor darling' me, you vicious little swine."

He drew a breath. "Your father and I will take care of everything, I promise. But we'll have to keep this in the family, Elspeth. I can't afford a scandal, you understand."

"We don't want to upset your sister," Duncan added in an undertone. "She's at an impressionable age, and she always adored the old man."

"Think about our upcoming wedding, darling. Put this behind you."

Elspeth twisted away from them, rage and revulsion at their cold logic deepening her voice. "You *killed* him, George. You can't just pretend it never happened because he was of no consequence to society. Dear God, I believe you're more concerned about your miserable election than over ending that man's life."

George didn't answer, turning abruptly from the sight of her pale stricken face to the figure that had suddenly appeared on the summerhouse steps.

"Susan," he said tightly. "In God's name, why did you not stay in the office?"

"What is it?" she whispered, lifting her hand to the diamonds at her throat. "Shall I call for help?"

"It was the vagrant we evicted earlier from the garden," Duncan explained, not meeting her gaze.

"Oh—the—Oh, I see." Susan glanced at George, her voice low. "My maid will have heard that shot, too, George, and perhaps the others in the east wing."

"It was a clap of thunder," he interrupted her. "Or the stable door banging in the wind."

Strangely, as upset as she was, or perhaps because of it, Elspeth was acutely attuned to the easy intimacy that George and Susan shared. They look at each other like lovers, she thought with an irrational urge to giggle, the realization inconsequential, not even surprising compared to the tumultuous events of the past half hour. Or perhaps she was in such a state of shock that little else could faze her. Her defenses had been annihilated by Tormod's death.

George and Susan. Damn the dirty pair. Of course it was true. There had been little signs all along which she'd been too dense or preoccupied to understand. Susan at the warehouse. George stopping by to see Fergus late in the evening. She should have noticed. Perhaps if she'd cared more, she would have.

She caught a final glimpse of Francis disappearing into the unused carriage house with Tormod slung over his shoulders like a broken doll. The rain was falling harder now, and it seemed to intensify the lingering smell of gunsmoke and blood in the summerhouse.

She put her hand to her mouth, shuddering as her stomach muscles contracted. She needed to get away, find help, be alone. The sense of panic closing in on her had become unbearable. With Tormod's death, she had lost her last living link to innocent memories, and her final hope of a future with George.

"I'm . . . going to be . . . sick."

George turned to clasp her hands, chaffing warmth into her wrists, but she couldn't stand his touch. She swallowed the sourness that burned in her throat. "You'll look at this differently in the morning, Elspeth. Let me take you inside. You've had the fright of your life."

She reared back. "Fetch the authorities, you big-assed bastard, killer. Liar . . . fornicating liar."

"Hush now," Susan said, tears in her eyes as she fussed over Elspeth with her typical maternal concern, patting her arm, stroking her hair. "Goddamnit, George, she's in shock. Goddamn your secrets, your guns. Come into the office with me, Elspeth, and have a wee drop of laudanum to help you forget. Come quietly, sweetheart. I know it was a ghastly experience, but we'll not want that press reporter to catch wind of it."

"Why not?" Elspeth asked, backing away with a half-hysterical laugh. "Maybe he could find out the truth for me. Maybe I should stand under his hotel window and shout for him. What a story this would make."

"Jesus," George breathed, glancing at Duncan in alarm. "I think she means it."

But in the end she did allow Susan to lead her through the garden and into the office, moving like a sleepwalker while the rain washed down on them. Slumped minutes later in the maroon leather chair behind her father's desk, she watched Susan make a mess of his inkblotter as she tried to pour them two glasses of laudanum-laced brandy from Duncan's private cabinet.

Poor Susan. Her hands were shaking so badly she could barely pull the stopper. Elspeth felt like laughing at her just for the release of tension. Instead, she stared down blindly at the dirk balanced across her lap. The memory of that single gunshot reverberated in her mind. Flinching, she pressed her fingers to her temples, but it didn't stop. The horror echoed endlessly.

"Bastards!" she shouted without warning at the window, bending forward to clasp her knees. She had started to suffer terrible cramps, spasms that gripped her belly in a vise and stole her breath.

The dirk clattered to her feet. Susan jumped like a rabbit, bumping back into the desk and sending her overfilled glass flying. Rivulets of drugged brandy rolled across the polished mahogany surface and splashed onto Elspeth's nightrail.

"Sweet heaven, Elspeth! Och, look what you've made me do."

Elspeth sniffed and wiped her nose, staring down at the mess in her lap in sick fascination. She felt horrendous, her hair like a collapsed haystack, blood and brandy staining through her muslin nightrail. She took a deep gulp of the drink Susan handed her, then deliberately let the rest dribble from the glass onto the Oriental carpet. It was her father's favorite, very pricey, he always warned her. Money mattered too much in this house.

Remember, Tormod had said. Oh, God, as if she'd ever forget.

Susan began pacing before the door, her face powder smeared, her hair disarrayed. "Sneak upstairs and change before one of the servants sees you. Dear Lord, what a night. What is it about you that attracts trouble like a magnet, Elspeth? Why couldn't you have stayed in your room and slept like any other respectable woman would have done?"

Elspeth forced a cold smile. "When you use the word 'respectable,' Susan, is that how you'd describe your behavior with George—making the two-humped beastie behind my back?"

Susan stopped in mid-stride, her fist pressed to her mouth. "Oooh, what a vile thing to say—"

"—and do." Her lips compressed in contempt, Elspeth slammed down her glass and came to her feet. "I feel like an utter fool for not seeing it all along. All those accidental meetings between the pair of you at the warehouse. No wonder you're so free with advice on how to sneak upstairs to avoid the servants—you've had plenty of practice. Oh, for pity's sake, Susan. Don't start. You're really going to disturb the household with that bawling."

Expelling a frustrated sigh, she strode across the room and put her arms awkwardly around Susan's shoulders, an act that took considerable self-control because she would have much rather strangled her. Although Susan had less brains than a turnip and the sexual morals of a she-hare, she really deserved to be pitied for having married Fergus Dweeney who was arguably the most boring man in the world. In fact, Elspeth suspected that Susan carried on her outrageous affairs in the hope she would shock Fergus out of his lethal blandness. And Susan had lived a difficult life, abandoned by her drunken parents when she was three and shunted back and forth between abusive foster homes. Perhaps she would hate Susan tomorrow. But for now she almost pitied her.

Susan sniffed loudly. "It didn't mean anything, you ken. We—we were going to stop before the wedding."

"How considerate. I'm touched, Susan. I truly am."

Susan's childlike face crumpled again, and that ridiculous sense of guilty affection crept back into Elspeth's anger. Her eyes dark with worry, she consoled Susan with a few absentminded pats on the back and stared across the room at the window. God, what a night. What a nightmare. She didn't know who to trust, who to believe anymore. Murder and betrayal—her father, George, Susan. The dirty stinking lot. She didn't need them anyway, but Tormod, poor Tormod.

"Y-you're going to stain my gown with the brandy on your nightrail," Susan said with another noisy sniff after several moments had passed. She patted Elspeth on the shoulder and hiccuped, disengaging herself to smooth down her white satin skirts. "You'd better go upstairs to change, dear. Just in case."

Elspeth swallowed the temptation to make another scene. Just in case what? In case a police inspector arrived to arrest them all in the middle of the night? In case George decided to spirit her away to a foreign country and keep her locked away for the rest of her life in a gloomy turret so she couldn't testify against him?

"Do you know why Tormod wanted to see me?" she demanded.

Susan blinked nervously. "I'd heard rumors that he was mad, that's all."

"What about Liath House? Fergus does all the accounts.

Have they sold my home behind my back? Did they tear the old place down?"

Susan hesitated. "From what I understand, the estate is worth more now than it ever was. Your father has always looked after your interests."

"I wonder about that, Susan. After tonight, I wonder about you all."

Her anguish was compounded by the fact that she didn't know who to believe, Tormod—or George and her father. What if, for God only knew the misguided reason, Tormod *had* meant to kill her with her grandfather's dirk?

"Where will Francis take Tormod?" she asked abruptly.

Susan swallowed. "He's supposed to leave for the Highlands in a day or two. Perhaps he'll take him back home to his family burying-place. That would please you, wouldn't it?"

"The only thing that would please me is to have him alive again," she said quietly. She exhaled, suddenly exhausted, overwhelmed, and leaned back against the door. It would be ironic but almost impossible for Francis to cart a corpse back home without attracting notice. Besides, Francis had no compassion in him. If he had, he'd never have shot her favorite horse in the head, then burned the body while she and Catherine were here in Falhaven visiting Auntie Flora. Elspeth hadn't believed his claim five years ago that the stallion had broken its leg falling down the hillside, and she didn't believe it now.

She brushed around Susan to retrieve the dirk from the floor, then returned to the door. A peculiar numbness was creeping from her brain into her body and bringing a detached sense of calm.

"You're not going to tell anyone about George, are you?" Susan whispered anxiously behind her.

"I haven't decided what I'll do, Susan," she said in a distant voice, hesitating at the door.

In fact, she was halfway up the stairs before she thought

to wonder whether Susan meant Elspeth shouldn't tell anyone that George was carrying on an adulterous affair with her fiancée's cousin, or that he had just murdered a man.

Eleven

Elspeth walked down the hall in darkness, waiting for the events of the night to overcome her, but she felt nothing beyond the lingering disbelief and horror of Tormod's death. Her emotions lay dormant beneath a protective veil of numbness which a distant inner voice tried to warn her was a symptom of shock. Her movements were unthinking; some deep-seated instinct propelled her forward.

She wouldn't allow herself to think about George and Susan, conducting their secret liaison under her nose, their betrayal. She would concentrate on uncovering the truth for herself, answering the questions Tormod had planted in her mind.

She had to focus on that. The truth. Her breath caught on an unexpected sob. Was this a nightmare? Had she really been laughing and worrying about disgracing herself during supper only a few hours ago? Dammit, she couldn't afford to cry.

She had to concentrate—

A door swung open in the upper hallway as she mounted the last step of the winding staircase. She froze, still holding her breath and squeezing back against the banister to avoid detection. She couldn't face one of her father's boorish houseguests now. She couldn't face her own sister after what had just happened.

* * *

The pistol shot, muffled by the heavy downpour of rain, had gotten Glenlyon out of bed and half dressed before he even remembered where he was. A musty guest chamber in Scotland. Not home in the airy whitewashed plantation house on the jungle hill he owned.

His reaction was instinctive. He buttoned on his light woolen trousers and hurried out onto the balcony, rain falling against his bare brown chest. Predictably Hasim had preceded him, staring in silence through the blurred shadows of the garden. It was well past midnight.

They glanced only once at each other. Years of shared experiences had forged a strong psychic bond between them. Hasim dragging Niall and his brothers from the shipwreck when the boys had been chased out of Burma, hiding the three of them in the deepest reaches of the rain forest because he believed they had been sent as a sign of favor from the gods to replace the three children he had lost to cholera. Niall rescuing the little witch doctor from the jaws of a crocodile. Nursing each other through recurrent bouts of malarial fever.

"Trouble, Tuan," Hasim murmured.

Niall narrowed his eyes. "It's none of our concern," he said softly. "I have other plans."

"You know better, Tuan. The spirits likes to play sometimes."

"And sometimes, Hasim, you and your spirits are a proper pain in the ass."

With a cursory glance down into the garden, Niall returned to his bed, reminding himself he needed rest for the long journey ahead. The old collie jumped up from the floor and sat on his chest, whimpering in distress. Softhearted Hasim had apparently let the dog in a few minutes earlier. Niall couldn't help noticing the animal's nervous energy, the way the dog's eyes never moved from the door.

"Been out chasing a bad cat in the rain, old fellow?"

he asked quietly as he began stroking the damp fur of the collie's neck.

The dog whined, thrusting its muzzle under Niall's chin. Niall frowned, finding himself suddenly unable to sleep, that pistol shot echoing in his mind.

The spirits likes to play sometimes.

No. Let Hasim be wrong for once.

His face grave, Niall scratched the collie's ears for a good half hour and stared resentfully across the room into the dark. Dammit, he deserved peace. He'd earned his right to solitude, required it as other men did food and sex and air. In his mind he saw himself riding away from this small seaport town, into the hills. Business deal made. No need to return, to dwell on the shot he had heard, the scene in the summerhouse last night.

And then she crept back into his thoughts. Not for long. Perhaps only a few seconds, but the intensity of the intrusion, the impression she had made on him, forced him to grin. Mischievous golden-green eyes, insecure smile, horrid little temper. And that wretched violin music.

He could not remember when a woman had made him feel so many powerful emotions at once. He'd never met one who gave as good as she got, or better. He knew there had never been another woman before who'd actually tempted him to lie about his life to impress her.

The spirits likes to play sometimes.

"Not with me." His gravelly voice defied the silence that seemed to mock him.

Hasim chuckled impishly from his sea of smoke rings. Niall could have wrung his skinny neck, praying that for just once the little shaman had misinterpreted his spirit guides' advice.

He closed his eyes, his breathing deliberately slow and deep, but no sooner had he begun to relax than he heard footsteps on the stairs. A woman's almost inaudible sob, a heart-wrenching sound in the deep silence of the night.

He sat up slowly. From the corner of his eye, he noticed that Hasim had extinguished his cigarette and sat cross-legged in an attitude of expectant listening.

Ignoring every logical argument that presented itself to his mind, Niall pushed the dog from the pillow and left the bed to walk silently across the room. He could no more ignore the distress in her voice than he could force his own heart to stop beating.

Twelve

He spotted her instantly, a slender figure in white pressed up against the banister. She saw him, too, staring up in disbelief at his face before she dared to dart up the remaining stairs and whisk past his door to her own room. Her attempt to pretend he didn't exist would have been amusing—under different circumstances.

Actually, Niall was half inclined to let her pass without acknowledging his presence. As it was, he'd lost enough sleep over her nocturnal adventures to make the prospect of tomorrow's travel extremely unappealing. But he could feel Hasim watching him from behind the door like an anxious grandfather. He remembered her cry of distress.

And all noble intentions aside, he didn't like to think she could ignore him quite that easily.

"I heard a pistol fired about an hour ago," he said quietly, just before she reached her room.

Elspeth turned woodenly toward him, her face so white and washed of its appealing vivacity that Niall felt a cold prickle of concern crawl down his spine.

"It must have been the stable door banging in the wind," she said in a remote voice, evading his sharp gaze. "I'm sorry if it disturbed you. The undergroom was supposed to have nailed it shut before the party."

He looked puzzled. "It was a pistol," he said slowly. "Perhaps I should alert your father—or go outside to investigate myself."

"No. Please," she whispered, alarm flashing in her eyes. "You'll only get the boy in trouble."

"And you? I take it this is another of your unauthorized adventures?"

Niall was only teasing her, trying to bait her into another lively conversation, but to his disappointment she didn't respond, not with her earlier cynical humor or anger or much of any other discernible emotion either. He frowned, scrutinizing her as closely as he could in the dimness. Her hair was loose. Raindrops had soaked into the tangled strands. Her stare kept eluding his, and the bruised look in her eyes reminded him of the lost persons he had found wandering in the jungle. *Bon Dieu,* could she be suffering from shock?

His gaze traveled rapidly from her face down her nightrail, taking in the dirk she held gripped in the muslin folds and stopping at the dark stains on her hemline. Before she could protest, he knelt and rubbed his fingertips across the ruffles. When he rose again, staring down at his hand, his mouth was pinched tight with alarm.

Yes, there was the expected mud from the rain, but the deeper splotches around her knees were definitely bloodstains.

Had she been raped, or injured? Could *she* have killed someone? He imagined her walking in on Sir George and Cousin Susan at an adulterously inopportune moment, a pistol fired during what the French called a *crime passionel.* But where had the peculiar-looking weapon come from? What was its significance?

"What happened?" he demanded, drawing her by the shoulders into the more private doorway of his room. "Are you hurt? Will you let Hasim help you? He's very talented, discreet, and gentle."

His low voice washed over Elspeth like a warm rippling wave, penetrating the coldness that had seeped into her system. It was lulling, his voice. In a detached corner of her mind, she decided the claim of his talent with animals was probably the truth.

"Leave . . . me . . . alone."

He dug his fingers into her shoulders, staring down into her face. She was shaking uncontrollably, and he did not delude himself into thinking his masculine appeal had caused such a powerful reaction. "Your skin is like ice, *ma belle,*" he murmured. "Come inside the room and tell us what happened."

She twisted back against the doorjamb. His kind persistence was nearly breaking her fragile shell of strength. "Nothing happened."

"Do you take me for an utter fool? There's blood all over your gown."

"I-I left the house to help my friends with a foal."

"An incredible birth to judge by your appearance," he said grimly.

She clenched her teeth, tears of fear and frustration gathering in her eyes. "Why can't you mind your own damn business?" she whispered fiercely. "Just pretend you never met me, all right? Go back to your tigers and your magic and your—billiard tables."

She shook away from him, backing into the hall. He watched her helplessly, resisting an overwhelming urge to draw her back into the protection of his arms, to comfort her and learn what had upset her.

"Let me help you," he insisted again. "There's little I haven't heard before."

She stared past him into his room, at Hasim sitting on the floor with the old collie, at the dressing table spread with the amazing amount of food Niall had managed to charm out of the scullery maids.

But he had the unpleasant feeling she didn't really see him, or a single object inside that room. Her gaze had turned inward to some private horror he could only guess at. His sense of frustrated concern mounted. He couldn't reach her.

"Please, *chérie,* let me help you."

She looked up at him once again with those wide frightened eyes before turning and hurrying into her own room and closing the door firmly behind her. Whatever dark secrets she guarded about this night, she had taken them with her.

Niall told himself he ought to feel relieved and let the matter rest, accepting his dismissal with a clear conscience. But he was too full of helpless anger at whoever had hurt her. It enraged him to think of her protecting the man who had mistreated her, assuming that was what had occurred. *Dieu,* he'd like to get his hands on him.

He closed the door, staring fiercely across the room. "Whatever happened, she wants to keep it to herself, Hasim. She said the noise we heard was the stable door in the wind, and that she'd been out helping to deliver a horse." As he spoke, returning to his bed, he tried to convince himself to take her story at face value.

"Wounds not always show, Tuan. Deepest one leaves no blood."

"Well, there was blood, all right," Niall said tightly, easing down onto the bed. "As long as it wasn't hers, I'm not going to worry. I guess we'll have to wait until tomorrow to see whether Sir George's obituary turns up in the morning paper."

"She not kill man, Tuan," Hasim said confidently. "Evil heart not in her horoscope."

"How the hell—"

A storm of muffled sounds from the next room diverted Niall's attention. Frowning up at the ceiling, he listened as Elspeth began rummaging through her belongings.

Drawers were being carefully pulled out. The armoire door was opened one creaky inch at a time.

Several minutes later there were footsteps in the hall, a discreet knock at her door, the murmured pleas of her father to let him in, which were answered with utter silence. Well, things couldn't be too bad, Niall reasoned. Perhaps the little hellfire had been telling the truth, after all, and her papa had heard about her sneaking back into the house. But her face continued to haunt him, and the thought that she was in some kind of trouble weighed heavily on his mind.

Still, he managed to snatch another few hours of sleep. When he opened his eyes again, it was dawn. Rubbing his jaw, he got out of bed and walked without thinking out onto the balcony, stepping over Hasim, who had slept on the floor with a carpet wrapped around his compact body.

The rain had stopped. A fresh wind promised to blow away the lingering vestiges of the previous night, the storm, its secrets. As Niall drew a breath, he caught the scent on the air, the primal smell of fear and desperation, a wounded creature taking flight. You didn't survive in the jungle for as long as he had without learning how to listen to the chorus of mystical messages that lay beneath life's surface.

"She's gone," he said unnecessarily to Hasim, stirring behind him. "Your tigress is gone, Hasim."

Hasim emerged from the carpet like a snail reluctant to leave its shell.

"She'll be over her pique and be back home before tea time," Niall added heartily, taking reassurance from his own prediction as he strode back into the room for his morning shave. "Ring for some hot water—oh, never mind. Just sneak down to the kitchen again and wangle a tasty packed luncheon out of that kindhearted cook. Shall

I leave Miss Kildrummond a box of chocolates, perhaps? She looks the type to enjoy sweets, doesn't she?"

His hands clasped behind his back, his face worried, Hasim followed Niall back inside. "Not my place to say, Tuan."

Niall turned from the shaving stand, his heavy eyebrows arched.

"Personal advice on such things is for wife to give, Tuan. Hasim is cook, valet, witch doctor. Sometimes butler, but never wifes."

"Perish the thought."

Niall glanced back at his reflection in the mirror, bending at the knee to lather his face with soap and cold water, while Hasim began to sharpen the razor against his leather strops. "By the way, Hasim, if it does turn out that Miss Kildrummond killed her fiancé last night, you're not to say a word about me talking to her in the hall, do you understand? She'll be in enough trouble without having associated with the likes of me."

Hasim looked sullen. "She already in big trouble—"

He stopped at the frantic pounding on the door. Niall straightened, rubbing his face off automatically with a towel. "Who is it?" he called, catching a glimpse of Hasim's concerned face in the mirror.

"It's Elspeth's sister, Captain Glenlyon," Catherine Kildrummond said in an urgent whisper from the hallway. "Please, sir, you'll have to come downstairs straight away. Something horrible has happened."

Thirteen

Niall leaned forward in the leather armchair drawn beside Duncan Kildrummond's desk, his gray eyes narrowed in disbelief. Hungry, unshaven, and in a hurry, he was not exactly at his social best. "You want me to *what?*"

Duncan looked up, bleary-eyed, his head cradled in one hand. "Find my daughter before she gets into serious trouble. It's what you do, is it not, find persons gone mission in foreign lands?"

Niall shook his head in confusion. "I *used* to find people—the occasional cartographer or botanist, an intrepid traveler or two. But never spoiled young women who ran away from home because of a family dispute. I assume that's what this is all about—a quarrel with her fiancé?"

Duncan was quiet for a moment, possibly debating how much he should confide in Niall. "Yes," he said quietly, the lie obvious to them both. "She had a misunderstanding with George after the party last night. Perhaps it was all the strain. Elspeth's never been one for social functions."

"I noticed. But I'm hardly in a position to help."

"George has sent his cousin after her. You might remember him from supper." Duncan frowned. "My daughters refer to him by the unappealing nickname of Coffin Face."

Niall held back a smile, fishing a cigar from his vest pocket. "A formidable fellow. Yes, I remember him. He looked capable of bringing your daughter back home. It would seem my services are superfluous."

"I don't want *him* to find her, Captain. I'm not sure I even want George to find her after what went on last night. Anyway, George is hosting a hunt in Devon and cannot beg off at such short notice."

Niall sat in silence, studying his unlit cigar. Duncan and Sir George were business partners, so last night's crisis must have wreaked quite a bit of emotional havoc to destroy not just a personal but a financial venture.

He sat forward suddenly, alarmed by a purely selfish thought. "This isn't going to affect the contract we drew up for my coffee, is it?"

Duncan gave him a mildly disgusted look. "Your interests will be taken care of, Captain Glenlyon. In fact, you could profit from my misfortune. I'm prepared to offer you an additional ten percent of the profits to bring my daughter home discreetly." His breath soughed out on a heavy sigh. "Never mind discretion. I'll settle for having her home."

"I don't think so."

"Fifteen percent then. And I insist you take this cash allowance for your expenses." He pushed a heavy purse across the table. "There'll be another thousand pounds on her return."

Fifteen percent. A fat purse. A thousand pounds. It was more than tempting.

"Look, Captain Glenlyon, you're traveling north to the Grampians yourself, aren't you? It can't be more than a three or four day detour from Glen Fyne. For a man of your talents, finding Elspeth will be no more than a slight inconvenience."

"Glen Fyne?"

"Elspeth is obsessed with the place, has been ever since she was old enough to walk. She'll go there, all right."

"Who owns this glen?"

"My father left it to Elspeth, and I am trustee until she marries, at which point it goes to George. All this, of course, is irrelevant to you, Captain."

The wounded tigress always return to her lair, Tuan. The words were a distant echo of Hasim's voice from a long-ago morning when Niall had set off on what was now a renowned hunt for a mortally wounded tigress. It was a story that Archie Harper had pounced on and peddled all across Europe. Niall thought it strange that it should come to his mind now.

"I want my daughter stopped before she reaches Glen Fyne," Duncan continued quietly, his face shadowed with strain.

"Why?" Niall asked, more and more disliking the air of mystery surrounding Elspeth's disappearance. And he was haunted by the suppressed horror in her eyes, those bloodstains. *Dieu,* he had to stop this. He kept telling himself to believe her story, that she had been birthing a horse, that people did not go around firing pistols in pleasant Scottish gardens.

"Why?" he demanded again.

"Places, people change, Glenlyon. Elspeth will be in for a nasty shock if she arrives expecting to find everything at home as she left it. We've had no time to prepare her."

"What sort of changes are you referring to?"

"Progress," Duncan said, the succinct reply discouraging further discussion on the matter, but not the questions forming in Niall's mind.

"Why don't you go after her yourself?" he asked with a faint shrug.

Duncan paused. "I have concerns here to smooth over. With George away, I can't afford to go traipsing up into the Highlands unless I wish my business to suffer."

Concerns? Niall tossed his cigar down onto the desk, thinking of that pistol shot in the garden which could indeed have led to certain disturbing concerns. "Do you really think a stranger will be able to persuade your wayward daughter to come home?" he asked skeptically.

"This is too private a matter to involve anyone local, Glenlyon. And while it's true that the Scottish Highlands don't pose the same physical dangers as your jungles, there are hazards nonetheless. Winter storms can strike without warning in those secluded foothills, and a young woman alone on the road invites trouble under the best conditions."

"I'm very sorry." Niall rose from his chair, alarmed by the faint softening he could feel in his resistance. "I really don't think I can help you. But if it's any consolation, I understand that runaway wives and daughters in these cases usually scurry back home as soon as their spending money is gone."

"Not Elspeth," Duncan said softly.

Niall began to edge away from the desk. "I haven't even finished shaving—" He broke off as Duncan picked up the purse and tossed it to him. Niall hated the instinct in himself which would not refuse the insulting offer; his fingers were already reaching down to the desk.

"Keep the money, Glenlyon, whatever you decide. You look like you can use it."

"I suggest you hire a retired police detective in a larger city," Niall said slowly. "Really, how far can she travel unnoticed?"

Duncan was silent until Niall reached the door. "When Elspeth was twelve years old, Glenlyon, I came upon her out in the barn sneaking a smoke on my pipe. As usual I had more important matters on my mind than my daughter's misbehavior, so I pretended not to see her, and went back to the house. You could say I've been pretending not to see her ever since." He paused, his voice laden with worry and remorse. "I'm afraid Elspeth and I are both about to pay dearly for my neglect. I'm afraid this time she may well burn down the barn."

Quelle horreur.

Niall had been unable to resist sneaking a peek around Elspeth's room, hoping to appease his conscience by finding a clue to prove his assertion that she had run off on some immature impulse and would soon return.

Indeed, what he saw was the messy domain of a spoiled creature who apparently had nothing more burdensome on her mind than an appointment at the milliner's the next day. Certainly she did not concern herself with domestic harmony. The cluttered opulence had him shaking his head in relieved chagrin.

Of course she had run away, the impetuous female.

There were letters, no doubt years old and unanswered, stuffed into the drawers of her writing desk. A pair of stockings dangled from the pleated sun-blinds. A forlorn hanging fern gasped for water in a tarnished brass pot. Brown fronds curled up at the ends like shriveled little tongues. Tea-stained sheets of music, and sporting magazines with betting tips circled covered the red velvet ottoman. The room reeked of roses and rice powder, a scent Niall found disturbingly alluring by association of their conversation outside the smoking room the night before.

He poked around the armoire for a moment, his brows gathering into a frown. No shredded dresses. No evidence of the temper tantrum he might have expected if she had indeed caught George and Susan in the act. If she'd packed, she hadn't taken much for a strenuous winter journey. A cloak perhaps.

It should reassure him. She hadn't planned an extended trip—unless she'd been too upset to *plan* anything at all. Unless she'd been motivated by sheer emotion, by whatever had caused that traumatized fear in her eyes.

His frown deepened as he backed into the center of the room, unprepared for the feelings of pain and confusion that lingered in the shadows. He told himself again that the whole affair would probably prove no more serious than a three-day sojourn at a female friend's house while her papa fretted and fumed.

Pivoting, he stared down at the porcelain chamber pot on the bed. A twisted gold betrothal ring gleamed in its empty basin. He laughed softly. Well, that was to the point. George couldn't fail to miss such an eloquent message.

"Are you going to find her, Captain Glenlyon?" an anxious female voice whispered at the door.

He glanced around to see Catherine Kildrummond's pale face poking into the room. "Do you know where she is?" he asked.

"Papa thinks she's gone to Glen Fyne. It belongs to her, you see. Grandda left Papa all his money and this house, and I'm to have the townhouse in Aberdeen. But the land went to Elspeth because she loved it so."

"It's a daunting journey for a young woman to make alone."

"Oh, but you don't know my sister." Gazing up at him with worshipful eyes, she slipped into the room. "You will find her, won't you, just as you found that deposed Siamese princess who wanted to make you her consort?"

"No," he said softly, moving around her with an embarrassed smile. "I'm sorry, but I can't find your sister. I have prior obligations."

Her soft anxious voice stopped him again as he reached for the doorknob. "Something very bad happened to her last night."

"What do you mean?" he asked without looking around.

"I-I found her nightrail and burned it in my grate. There

were bloodstains on it, Captain. Bloodstains and b-brandy, and I found it stuffed under her bed early this morning."

Niall turned reluctantly to face her. "I understand she was off with her gypsy friends again during the night."

"No, she wasn't. Samson was prowling around the stables waiting for her at dawn. They had some sort of appointment, and she missed it."

This was *not* what Niall needed to hear to lay his own concerns to rest. "Did you see Sir George this morning?" he asked quietly.

"Yes. He left for Devon two hours ago. She didn't kill him if that's what you're thinking."

"Susan?"

"She was still alive over a gargantuan plate of sausages and eggs at breakfast," Catherine said wryly.

"She told me she'd helped deliver a foal during the night," Niall said, the scene still vivid in his mind. "If she'd wished for my interference, she could have asked for it then."

"Perhaps she was too afraid."

"And what is there in this house to be afraid of, may I ask? Another ghastly musicale? An evening at the opera?"

Catherine's chin trembled. "Mock me if you will, but I know something unspeakable must have happened to Elspeth, and now George has sent that horrid monster of a man after her."

Niall almost smiled. "Perhaps it takes a 'horrid monster of a man' to bring your handful of a sister home."

"Francis Barron is rumored to have drowned his own betrothed in Glen Fyne, but George refuses to hear a single word against him."

"Rumors are best not believed, Miss Kildrummond," Niall retorted, convincing himself that Barron was probably no more a villain than he was himself a hero. "You might have misjudged this man."

"I'm certainly beginning to think I've misjudged *you.*"

"I'm sorry," he said, and meant it. "I can only hope your illusions heal." Then giving her a stiff bow, he turned the doorknob and let himself out into the hall.

Catherine stared after his receding figure, her voice so faint he barely caught her astonishing farewell. "I took you for a man of unusual sensitivity last night at supper, Captain. I defended you to my sister. I should have known better than to ask the decent thing from a man who can't keep his—his cue stick under control."

Fourteen

If Elspeth had not proved so easy to trace, Niall would have left town without giving her another thought. At least, that was what he told himself as he paid off the dour cab driver, giving him instructions to wait at the corner, and followed the man's directions down a cobbled wynd that wended between several large warehouses and ended in a gloomy court.

Following Elspeth was like tracking a falling star, all careening impulse and dangerous sparks. She'd made quite an impression on the locals during her late-night flight, cursing a blue streak at the sausage-roll vendor for running over her bags, accusing the young cabbie, who had reluctantly driven her to this disreputable part of town, of overcharging her.

Everyone remembered Elspeth. Everyone thought it was a shocking shame that another foolish young woman was running away from home to take refuge in a brothel, and what was the world coming to that a well-bred young lassie would resort to this?

For Niall it was the ultimate irony, having sworn he'd never set foot in another whorehouse as long as he lived.

"Are you coming in with me?" he asked Hasim.

"Me, Tuan? No. I stays outside and talks to birds. Not go in bad house."

Niall narrowed his eyes. The three-story granite house of ill repute sat at the end of the court, tucked well away from the bustle of the harbor. Still, it was close enough that you could hear the muted screech of gulls and rumble of dray carts; you could smell the iodine tang of the sea and the oil from the paddle steamers mingled with the fishy scent of hot eel-pies.

Niall judged it to be a second-rate house, as far as brothels went, the sort of place frequented by clerks and medical students, and he smiled wryly at the sign posted above the door: MRS. GRIMBLE'S FINISHING SCHOOL FOR YOUNG LADIES. CLEAN LOGINS. AB-SOLUTELY NO CREDIT ALLOWED.

And Elspeth wondered why her papa questioned her choice of friends, he thought, chuckling softly as he let the brass knocker drop. There was a considerable wait. Then a hump-backed old man in mismatched servant's livery cracked open the door after standing on a foot-ladder to size him up through the fanlight window.

"Aye?" the man said, scratching at the owl-like tuft of hair on his left ear.

Niall peered down the empty hallway where a maidservant listlessly pushed a mop through a puddle of dirty water. "I'm looking for a woman with blond—"

"Eh? What did ye say?"

"Never mind," Niall said politely. "Could I please have a word in private with Mrs. Grimble herself?"

"Five shillings a night, mister."

Niall sighed. "May I come in?"

The footman emerged to circle him on the doorstep as a gnome would a giant, scratching his ear so persistently Niall suspected it must harbor a flea. "Ye're an Australian," he guessed, finally motioning Niall to follow him down the hall. "I can tell by yer clothes, ye see. It's a talent I've acquired over the years."

"Actually," Niall said as he entered the house, "I'm—"

Before Niall could finish, the peculiar footman gave him a friendly shove into a drawing room that was decorated to resemble a Far Eastern bazaar. Pots of peacock feathers occupied the corners. Red silk curtains fell in lush folds to the floor where tasseled cushions were piled invitingly. A gaslight chandelier popped sporadically in the silence. There were several low chenille couches on which a few women sat avidly reading penny periodicals and nibbling at a communal box of sweetmeats. It was obviously a slow morning.

Niall glanced past them to the woman he'd pegged to be the establishment's procuress. Dressed in a canary yellow silk gown, her height boosted by a pair of morocco slippers with brass heels, she had the austere face of a schoolmistress and the beefy forearms of a stevedore. She was applying that strength to massage the neck of a stout man reclining on a chaise lounge—*Bon Dieu,* it was that little frog journalist again, Archie Harper.

"Well, well, well." Archie twisted around, grinning at Niall from ear to ear. "Are you 'ere as a customer, Captain, or are you making a nostalgic visit?"

Niall smiled blandly. "I granted you your interview, Harper."

Archie swung his short legs to the floor, smoothing back his thin disheveled hair before he drew Niall toward the window. "This wouldn't be about the body, would it?" he said in a hushed voice.

Niall started to jerk his arm away, then froze. His dark gaze pinned the other man. "What body?"

For a moment Archie appeared to search his face, possibly gauging whether Niall could be trusted with such a dangerous tidbit of information. Or perhaps he'd been only testing Niall, trying to trick him into revealing evidence he could distort into another lurid story. To his frustration, Niall could not read the little bastard's mind.

He decided to call Harper's bluff, hoping deep in his heart that this "body" had nothing to do with Elspeth's disappearance. "How do you know about the body?" he asked in an undertone.

But Archie was apparently smarter than that, pretending to laugh off the matter and leaving Niall more confused, and concerned, than ever. "Almost 'ad you there, didn't I, Captain? Well, you can't blame a bloke for trying, eh? It's been a thin month for scandal."

"Harper—"

Archie gestured effusively to the prostitutes seated around the room. "Ladies," he announced in a blaring voice, "I'd like you to meet one of your very own—a fellow graduate from a School of Venus. Captain Glenlyon 'ere worked in the 'ouse of Many Joys in Mandalay some years ago."

"Mandalay?" A woman in her thirties, with lacquered blond ringlets and wearing a schoolgirl's pinafore, looked up blearily from her paper. "That's in Wales, isn't it?"

Archie rolled his eyes at Niall and started to move back to his chaise, but Niall deftly sidestepped him, his voice intense. "What body?" he demanded.

"Body? Crikey, did I say body, Captain?"

And suddenly Niall didn't know what to believe. He couldn't decide whether Harper had heard about that pistol shot from a Kildrummond servant and was fishing for clues, or whether the man was all brass and bluster.

"Mandalay, was it?" asked a husky-voiced woman behind him, breaking his train of thought.

He swung around to find the brothel's procuress sizing him up with a cold but experienced eye. "I don't suppose ye're looking for a job?"

"No."

"You're not a she-shirt?"

"No, madame, I'm not."

"What do ye want then?"

He forced a smile. "A woman."

"A woman?" She seemed a little surprised, which in itself surprised Niall, considering the milieu. "Of course."

He sensed the other women in the room begin to study him with half-hearted interest, and all of a sudden his thoughts traveled back through the years to the morning he'd regained consciousness in that flimsy teakwood palace in Mandalay. Semi-delirious, he had jumped up from his palliasse and nearly frightened his female rescuers to death, a half-naked foreign boy brandishing a long knife, all muscle and feverish madness as he tore through the house shoving aside one bamboo curtain after another to save his sister from horrors his naive mind could only dimly imagine.

"What type of woman do ye fancy?" Mrs. Grimble's voice brought him back to the present, and to the inexplicable urgency to find Elspeth and send her home to the safety his beloved sister had been denied.

"She—"

"A man of yer background would probably like a more exotic girl," Mrs. Grimble suggested in a businesslike tone. "How about a nice Chinese?"

Before Niall could refuse, the woman snapped her fingers and a petulant-looking girl with dyed black hair cut à la Oliver Cromwell glanced up from her box of sweetmeats. Her blue eyes had been lined with kohl to give them an Asiatic slant, and Niall decided she was from the Far East all right, the far eastern end of the local harbor.

She picked a piece of walnut from her teeth with her thumbnail. "We go uppee stairs?" she asked unenthusiastically.

He choked back a rude snort of laughter and glanced down at Mrs. Grimble. "You misunderstood me. I'm looking for Elspeth Kildrummond."

He saw a door slam in the woman's eyes. "Kildrummond? Never heard of her. And if ye don't see anything else to yer taste in this room, I'll thank ye to leave my establishment."

Niall stared at her for several seconds, taken aback by the fierce protectiveness in the woman's voice. So, Elspeth Kildrummond inspired that sort of loyalty among her low-class friends. Intriguing.

He reached into his vest pocket. "I suppose I'll have to pay."

"And I suppose I'll have to have ye thrown out into the street," she retorted, crossing her arms over her chest. "Do I make myself clear?"

Niall straightened his shoulders, glancing once at Archie Harper's openly amused face. "Quite, madame. I'll find my own way out."

Elspeth lowered herself onto the musty unmade bed only to shoot back to her feet as a floorboard creaked outside the door. She'd spent half the night trying not to imagine what lurid acts had taken place in this very room. It was her first actual experience inside the brothel. All her previous communication with the girls had either been conducted in stolen moments at the race tracks or in the charity hall.

She'd been halfway out of town only a few hours ago when she'd realized Francis Barron was following her. All she could think of was the young village woman he'd murdered, the dispassion on his face when he had carried Tormod through the garden, the blame in his eyes when he'd looked at her. Realizing how vulnerable she'd be once she reached the lonely country roads, she had decided impulsively to take Mrs. Grimble up on her standing offer to visit the "Finishing School."

Of course, she couldn't hide out here much longer. But the girls had been so warm and protective of her, hunting through their wardrobes to come up with the embarrassing disguise she wore; many of them had entered the life to escape abusive fathers and husbands at home. And they weren't trying to convert her. They simply supported her decision to break off with George after she'd told them about his affair with Susan, the excuse she'd used for leaving home.

But as much as she trusted her friends, she couldn't bring herself to tell them everything. Not that George had killed a man. She couldn't bring herself to implicate her own father in a murder when in her heart she needed desperately to believe in his innocence. She might not condone his business practices, but she still loved him and owed him at least that small loyalty.

And when the door she was staring at slowly opened, she half expected to see her papa standing there, come to take her back home and reassure her that everything would be all right, that by some miracle Tormod wasn't really dead.

The hope perished instantly in her heart as she recognized the dark figure in the doorway, even more forbidding in the gray light of morning than she remembered him from the previous evening.

Glenlyon. She'd almost convinced herself that she had imagined him too, that their dangerous flirtation hadn't been the prelude to a tragedy which might destroy so many lives. But he was real, and she shivered at the raw power of his presence as he swept into the room, his face inscrutable, his shoulders draped in a black woolen greatcoat that had seen better days.

He's wearing his own clothes, she thought irrelevantly. And he looks like—like a thief accustomed to breaking into a woman's bedroom.

And Niall took one look at her, at the hideous red wig perched on her head, at the clinging gray silk dress that reminded him of the curtains his mother had determinedly brought to the jungle from France, and he stopped cold, his emotions in an uproar.

Exasperation, amusement, relief. And yes, even a little admiration for her efforts.

"Take that absurd object off your head," he said quietly, walking straight past the bed to the window because he was afraid he would laugh in her face. "It looks like a dead fox."

She sat in a shocked trance and stared at the door. Her heart had begun to beat so hard that she felt lightheaded. Although he pretended to stare down into the street, she knew perfectly well she wouldn't make it halfway across the room before he intercepted her. The mere thought of all that strength unleashed paralyzed her.

"I told you to take off that godawful disguise, Elspeth," he said impatiently. "It's incredibly atrocious."

"How the blue blazes did you find me, Glenlyon?"

He glanced around, his mouth lifting wryly at one corner. "It was almost as easy as tracking an elephant in the snow."

"I don't think I care for the analogy." She twisted around to face him, her knees drawn to her chest, her heart drumming in her ears. "But then perhaps you weren't looking for me at all. Perhaps you just dropped in for a morning's bawdy entertainment. If so, I suggest you find another room."

"What for? You're as 'entertaining' a woman as I've ever met."

She wrapped her arms around her knees in a self-protective gesture as he sauntered back toward the bed; a menacing amusement lit his eyes. "Take your lustful urges down the hall, Glenlyon."

"Lustful urges?" He gave an insulting snort of laughter. "Obviously you haven't looked in a mirror this morning. You're not exactly an irresistible temptation with pastry crumbs on your chin and that moth-eaten creature perched on your head."

She forced herself not to flinch when he finally reached her. His movements were as graceful as those of the lethal jungle cats he probably kept as pets on his island. And like those beautiful beasts he was unpredictable.

Alarmed by his nearness, aware of the blatant vulnerability of a woman posed on a bed used solely for sexual purposes, she bounced onto her feet and stood to face him.

"Sit down, Elspeth," he said with a frown. "I don't trust you."

Her insides began to tremble. "You don't trust *me.*"

"Sit," he repeated calmly, bracing the heel of his hand against her shoulder to give her the imperceptible push necessary to send her sinking back down into the lumpy mattress.

She hurled what remained of her sausage-roll at his shoulder. Her voice was husky with panic as she announced, "One more step, Glenlyon, just one more step, and I'll scream bloody murder."

"Go ahead." He leaned down, his eyes dancing with dark humor, and plucked off her wig to toss it across the room. "They'll just assume we're having the time of our lives. Now, you and I are going to have a nice little talk, eh, *chérie?*"

Elspeth rubbed her chin against her shoulder, catching her breath as he sat down beside her on the bed. For a moment she was fascinated by the sheer size of him. His big shoulders dominated her view. Her palms grew moist. If she weren't so scared and exhausted, she might have felt more ashamed of what she had been reduced to, wearing a harlot's dress in a bawdy house and sitting on a harlot's bed with the most disreputable person she had ever met. But she was a woman pushed beyond the limits of shame. She was spitting angry.

"Men don't usually go to brothels for pleasant little chats," she pointed out tartly.

"And young women usually don't take shelter in them unless they intend to become permanent residents." He felt a reluctant stab of compassion as he stared down at what he could see of her face through that tangled skein of golden hair. Anger, fear, and the valiant struggle to hold ground against him; the dark violet smudges of fatigue under her eyes, which even now brimmed with the secret horror she refused to divulge and the tears she was too proud to shed. "Never mind what you and your sister have read in your novels. Life in a place like this would kill you, *chére.*"

She affected a sigh of bored sophistication. "While I may not be anywhere as knowledgeable about the subject as you, Captain, I'm not entirely stupid."

He settled into a more comfortable position. His muscular thigh was pinning her skirts to the bed. Schooling his features into a stern expression, he told her, "You're worrying your papa sick."

"He sent you after me?" she said, blinking in disbelief.

"That's right."

"He had no business involving a stranger in a family matter!"

"I thought the same thing myself," Niall admitted uncomfortably.

She swung her gaze down to the floor, but not before Niall had felt the bittersweet impact of the panic and bewilderment in her eyes. Hell, he thought darkly, there had to be more to this than a lover's spat.

"What did Papa tell you had happened?" she asked in an unsteady voice.

"Enough—enough to make me delay my own plans to

chase after you all morning." He hesitated. "Why don't you explain what he didn't tell me?"

She remained silent, her eyes bright with suspicion. No, she wasn't stupid. She wouldn't snap at such obvious bait. She wouldn't trust him with one tiny thread of that secret she guarded so closely. And if he had any sense at all, he'd be thankful he wasn't involved.

He lowered his voice and glanced away. "Why don't you start by telling me what happened to the body?"

Her face went blank, drained of color and expression. For his life Niall couldn't discern whether she was utterly terrified by the question, or whether he was so far off target that she couldn't grasp his meaning.

"Body?" Her voice was a raspy wisp of sound. "Now who's been reading too much fiction, Glenlyon?"

"No one can hide behind a tough facade forever," he said softly. "Sooner or later, even the hardest shell will crack under the strain."

"And then all the king's horses and all the king's men will have to put me together again, won't they?"

He sighed and extracted a thin black cigar and match from his vest pocket. Before Elspeth realized what he intended to do, he'd picked up her left foot to strike a light on his lucifer match against the heel of her side-laced riding boot.

Indignant, she peeled her foot from his hand and scooted all the way back to the headboard, her skirts still imprisoned by his thigh. "I don't remember giving you permission to smoke."

He laughed softly. "You're not going to attract many customers with that attitude, *ma chére.*"

"Glenlyon, I don't give a—"

She didn't finish, distracted by the sight of their reflection in the cloudy oval mirror of the old wardrobe standing beside the door. The tawdry image fascinated her, her disheveled hair, the beautiful man on the bed, blue smoke wreathing them in a cameo of dreamy sensuality.

"Oh, dear Lord," she said under her breath, a bolt of forbidden excitement breaking through her anger. "This is what they mean in those novels when a woman falls into decadence."

Niall snorted derisively. "Well, this is one moral decline I can't take the blame for."

She forced her attention away from the provocative image in the mirror. "Tell my father I'm not coming back."

"You consider this place an improvement over your home?" he asked with a cynical glint in his eye.

She sniffed in disdain. "Your cigar is offending my nose, Glenlyon."

"How much do you plan to charge for your services?"

"Very amusing," she said sourly, "but you needn't lose any sleep on my account. I don't plan to stay here indefinitely."

He flicked his cigar onto the scarred wooden floor and ground it out under his bootheel. "I've heard those words before."

"I don't doubt it."

"I've *said* those words before."

"Tell it to the press reporters, Glenlyon."

He averted his eyes. "I buried girls from the joy house who were younger than you, girls who were strangled by their customers."

"Stop trying to frighten me," she whispered, swallowing over the knot in her throat.

"I pulled brutes wild with lust off their broken little bodies."

"I—" She bit back the automatic sarcasm, more shaken by the concern in the cunning devil's voice than she could bear. It wasn't as if she enjoyed being in this wretched situation. "You seem to be under the illusion that I'm as innocent as the proverbial lamb led astray, Captain. You ought to save your sympathy for someone who needs it."

He blew out a soft frustrated sigh. "So you're not innocent, are you?"

"No. I'm not," she said coldly.

"I see."

"Good. Then go away."

"If you're not innocent, you must be *practiced,*" he said slowly, savoring the word on his tongue. "You must have acquired a certain experience."

She shrugged, uncertain what this conversation was leading to, her face mutinous and uneasy. This was a man who had killed people for a living, she remembered with a jolt of alarm. Who did she think she was to outwit him?

He studied her for several moments in silence until Elspeth began to fidget, pretending to tug a loose thread from her sleeve to deflect the burning intensity of his stare. From beneath her lashes, she stole a startled peep at him as suddenly he got up from the bed and strode to the wardrobe against the wall. His face merciless, he threw open the door and reached inside to rifle through an eye-widening selection of costumes, including several sable boas, lacy corsets, stockings, a shepherdess's smock, a nun's habit.

A skimpy maid's white apron landed in Elspeth's lap. "Take off everything except your stockings and put that on," he ordered her over his shoulder. "Ah, here we are. This goes on under it."

Elspeth stared down in horrified amusement at the abbreviated black lace corset that hit the bed. It didn't look anything like the serviceable whalebone stays she was loath to wear. This *thing* was shamelessly designed to emphasize a woman's bum and thrust her bosom up to her eyebrows. Why, it was more titillating than the bust improver Susan had bought in London last year.

"Men adore black lace, Elspeth," Niall confided in a

low voice. "Oh, and leave your boots on, too. It's a nice erotic contrast."

Elspeth looked up quickly, a blush creeping up her neck to burn the tips of her ears. She knew exactly what he was doing, hoping to shock her into running home. And she was shocked, too, but she'd never let on how much.

"Well?" he said, leaning back against the wardrobe with a puzzled look. "Is something wrong, or are you less experienced than you like to pretend?"

"Not really." Throwing him a sunny smile, she hopped off the bed with the corset clutched in one hand while reaching back to unhook her own gown with the other. Her fingers were shaking; she couldn't believe her own brass or pigheadedness, but the man needed to be shown he could be taught a lesson too, and Elspeth, for better or worse, had never been able to resist a challenge.

"I'm having a wee bit of trouble with the last hook," she murmured, glancing back at him with her eyebrow demurely raised. "Captain, would you mind?"

He reached her side in one determined stride. The look on his face was so ominous, she took a reflexive step toward the door with her back toward him, and wondered with a stab of trepidation if she hadn't gone too far.

He brought his hands down onto her shoulders; she stilled like a deer in terror of its life and closed her eyes to suppress the shivers of dangerous excitement that the feel of his strong fingers set off along her spine.

He stood unmoving for several moments, amazed at her ability to reduce him to pure animal impulse. "I can't deny I deserved this," he mused with a reluctant smile of acknowledgment for her small victory.

Elspeth drew an involuntary breath as his rough woolen coat brushed the exposed skin of her shoulder blades. The sensation was unbearably intimate. She tried to exhale, only to find her throat had closed in an instant of unbearable suspense.

"You did deserve it," she said without daring to turn around.

"But what if I can't help myself?" he asked quietly, his fingers tightening slightly. "What do we do if your little display of nerve backfires, and I simply can't resist you? What if you've driven me to the . . . edge?"

He felt her shoulders stiffen. "What edge?" she demanded in a suspicious voice.

"Why, the edge alluded to in all those novels, *chérie*. Surely a woman of your vast experience has walked more than one man to that dangerous precipice?"

His voice was hoarse, mockingly seductive. The pressure of his fingertips, moving against her tense muscles, unleashed a hypnotic lassitude inside her. Slowly opening her eyes, she glanced up, transfixed again by their reflection in the mirror. Niall's face was drawn into a stark mask of desire; his powerful body, cloaked in black, overshadowed hers, loomed as large and impressive as legend would make him.

And she couldn't believe how she looked herself, half-undressed, her shoulders bare, leaning back against him as if he owned her. They might have been two people she'd never seen before, a man and woman who resembled Elspeth and Niall in every way except that they were playing out their darker sides and sins, their darkest fantasies.

Her scalp tightened with a sensation that might have been anxiety or anticipation. "Please," she whispered, and even her voice was not her own, sultry and belonging to that daring woman in the mirror.

He gripped her shoulders, certain she had no idea of the moral battle raging inside him. He was afraid to set her back on the reckless path she'd taken. But he was more afraid of what could happen if he didn't let her go, if they suddenly gave in to the primal impulses charging the stillness between them like the rumblings of an electrical storm. Entranced, he studied the delicate curve of her neck, the slope of her shoulder where his fingers created stark white imprints against the creamy grain of her skin. She thought she was so strong, so clever, that sheer audacity would carry her through any trial. He'd believed the same thing once of himself.

Every breath he struggled to draw brought the fragrance of her into his blood. Reason could not compete with the hot rush of anticipation through his body.

He wished he could believe the flagrant lie she had told him. He wished she had not been so brazenly naive and that he could court her with compliments, with promises he might or might not ever keep, that he could take her without compunction. A vision of her lying beneath him on that rumpled bed flashed like wildfire through too many sere months of self-denial.

"You should never gamble such high stakes against a more experienced player, Miss Kildrummond," he said, exhaling quietly.

"Get knotted, Glenlyon. You sound like someone's lecherous old uncle."

He blinked. The insult pierced all the patience and mature restraint he had called into play to handle the matter. So much for gentleness and understanding, he thought with grim humor. Before he could stop himself, he had brought his right hand down between her breasts to wrest the corset from her fingers. She bit the back of his wrist and rammed her elbow back into his diaphragm, a blow he dodged by instinct.

The corset dropped to the floor; Elspeth seized advantage of the moment by making a dash for the door. She didn't get far, though. Niall stuck his foot out to trip her, then gently snagged her by the forearm to break her fall. Her legs got entangled in her loosened gown as he caught her.

"Charming," he said wryly, dragging her around in a half-circle to face him. "If your papa could see you now."

"You're despicable—pulling a dirty trick like that to trip me!"

"Do you really want to go running down a brothel hallway with your pretty white breasts exposed?"

"My—" Mortified, she tugged her gown back up over her chemise.

And Niall made no pretense of looking away. No, he was done with cosseting the holy terror. Instead, he studied her with an open enjoyment fully intended to give her serious doubts as to whether she wouldn't be safer in the hall after all.

"Shameless, Miss Kildrummond," he chided softly. "Shameless and rather gauche for a woman of such . . . experience."

She glared at him. He smiled back. His gray eyes reminded her of ice with irises of flame, and that was how she felt as she stood before him, struggling to make herself decent; she felt frozen with a delicious terror and melting with a strange internal heat at the same time.

"Dieu m'aide," he murmured with a frown gathering between his heavy black brows. Expelling a deep breath, he put his hand under her chin to nudge her resentful face up to his. "Suddenly I seem to be losing this game, and I can't say I like it."

"You started it, Glenlyon."

"Yes, I did, didn't I? But it was only to teach you a lesson."

"Was it?"

"You didn't have to play along," he murmured.

"Perhaps I thought you needed to be taught a lesson as well."

He couldn't resist chuckling at that. "Well, Elspeth, who knows? Perhaps an even higher power is making fun of us both. But how far would you have carried this act, *chère?"* He traced the stubborn angle of her jaw with his thumb, his voice lowering to a lazy whisper. "You'd never need a costume like the one on the floor to arouse a man."

She suppressed a violent shiver as he drew his hand away. "I don't intend to 'arouse' anyone, Glenlyon. In a costume or otherwise."

"Would you really have put it on to spite me?" he asked in amusement.

"If I thought it would have gotten rid of you, I would have."

He pursed his lips. "That's a pretty high price to pay to get rid of someone. Either I'm an exceptionally hateful person, which I concede is possible, or you're more desperate than I realized."

Elspeth didn't know how it had happened, but all of a sudden the sexually charged atmosphere between them was intensifying into something even more intimate. She told herself she was overtired; she hadn't slept but an hour and then only in fits. Tormod's death had been dominating her broken dreams.

She told herself she hadn't even had time to marshal her defenses against this strangely attractive man who was trying to dress her in indecent underthings and pry out her family secrets. But he was more than she could fight; she was a heartbeat from breaking down.

She swallowed, closing her eyes, and sagged back against the door in temporary defeat.

Niall's smile vanished. Disquietude replaced the satisfaction he should have felt at the sign of her weakening. "You're exhausted, Elspeth, in body and spirit, and don't give me that Banbury tale about delivering a foal in your nightdress." He frowned, resisting the urge to take her back into his arms. "What really happened to you last night?" he asked slowly.

"Nothing." She summoned the nerve to open her eyes

and look him dead in the face. "George and I had a quarrel, that's all."

"Your fiancé has sent a man called Francis Barron after you." He was watching her so closely he couldn't fail to miss the fear that flickered in her eyes at the mention of Barron's name. "Your father doesn't seem to approve."

"I can take care of Francis," she said stoutly.

"Oh, really? The same way you took care of me? *Nom de Dieu,* sweetheart, what are you running from? I can't help you if you're not honest."

There was a brisk *rat-tat-tat* at the door. Elspeth spun around, raising her arms to her unbuttoned gown as a freckle-faced young sailor poked his head into the room. His gaze traveled from her startled face to the corset on the floor, the selection of enticing costumes piled on the bed.

"Uh, sorry! I seem to have gotten the wrong room." He gazed at Elspeth for a long moment, a hopeful grin breaking out on his homely face. "I'm not in any hurry though. I think I'll sneak back downstairs to have another tot while ye finish up here. I do enjoy a spirited lass."

Niall gave the man a dark smile. "Oh, she's a spirited one, all right."

The door closed, and Elspeth thought she might die of shame, swiftly rebuttoning her gown while Niall walked backward to throw himself down onto the bed, his large shoulders convulsed with mocking laughter that resounded insultingly in the quiet.

"You should . . . you should have seen your . . . face."

"Belt up, Glenlyon," she said, white-lipped with humiliation. "Just bloody belt up."

He rolled back onto his feet, circling her with another infuriating snigger of laughter. "Admit it—you were horrified. And isn't it a damn good thing I was here to make sure nothing happened?"

She stared back at him in silence, but something in her eyes, something vulnerable and wounded, made him suddenly regret teasing her when she was probably at the lowest ebb in her life. And damn it all if he didn't desire her anyway, if he hadn't felt like kicking that idiotic young sailor halfway down the stairs for even daring to hope he could touch her. No, Elspeth didn't need black lace to excite a man. She had only to stand there with her wild mane of hair and her brave heart in her eyes to turn him into the veriest fool.

He gestured to the door. "Get out of here before you find yourself in really serious trouble," he said with a weary sigh. "The world isn't usually kind to women who venture away from home."

"I am going home," she replied in a muffled voice, and it didn't occur to him then that she was referring to anywhere but her father's Falhaven house.

He nodded slowly, disappointed and at the same time relieved their association had come to an end. "Good girl. I'll watch you from the window. There's a cab on the corner waiting for me. Tell the driver I want him to drive you straight home."

The spark of defiance in her eyes should have put him on guard. Naively, he chose to believe she would obey him.

"Here." He tossed her back the ugly red wig as she reached the door with her cloak and traveling bag, even her violin case, clutched under her arm. "You might as well stay in disguise until you're safely home. That pest Harper is hanging about downstairs."

She was quiet, too quiet, he thought uneasily. But perhaps the scene with the sailor had embarrassed her more than he realized. "What are you waiting for now?" he asked as she hesitated at the door.

"Just tell me one thing, Glenlyon," she demanded softly.

"Did my father pay you to help me, or did you do it out of the kindness of your black heart?"

He gazed down at her serious little face. He knew he should probably lie to save her feelings, to appear more the gallant, but in the end it wouldn't matter what she thought of him. In the end it was probably better that she learned to stay inside the comfortable chimera of her pampered life. "He offered to make a slight modification to my advantage in our contract. And, yes, he gave me a little spending cash to bring you home."

She said nothing, she did not blink an eyelash, and Niall flinched inwardly at a surprising sting of regret. The cynicism on her expressive face was so blatant that he almost wished he'd bothered to lie. Once again she had managed to wound him with that look of shattered innocence. Once again she'd reminded him that he was really nothing more than a mercenary soldier, an unsuccessful one at that, a cowardly failure who had broken his last promise to his father and watched his family disintegrate as a result.

"Well, what are you waiting for now?" he said impatiently. "That snot-faced sailor is going to come panting after you in the streets if you don't hurry home to your papa."

She drew back at the raw emotion on his face. "I'd almost forgotten how crude you are."

He forced a laugh and picked up the costume she'd dropped earlier, plucking loose one of the black silk thongs laced across the bodice. "You've no idea, *mon coeur*," he said in a remorseless voice. "Now get out of here before I decide to enlighten you—get out of here, or I swear I won't be responsible for what will happen between us."

He turned toward the bed, his shoulders taut with the tension that had tied his muscles into burning knots. Only when she slammed the door and he heard her footsteps receding down the hall did he uncurl his fists and let the scandalous costume float to the floor.

Fifteen

Well, that was that. Niall watched down from the window with a rueful grin as Elspeth hurriedly emerged from the brothel into the street. She looked so preposterous in her lopsided flame-red wig and revealing whore's dress that he was suddenly afraid the driver would refuse her passage. But after a few moments of understandable indecision, the cabbie apparently elected to take her aboard.

Niall mouthed, *"Au revoir,"* and waved down at her with uneasy satisfaction as the driver neatly circled the court. Elspeth returned the gesture by thumbing her nose up at the window while the cab disappeared from the wynd.

And not a moment too soon. The tail end of the cab was still visible as a horseman clad in brown appeared riding from an opposite alleyway.

Francis Barron. Niall leaned back against the window-frame, frowning in displeasure. Had Barron come here in search of Elspeth, or in her own enchanting turn of words, was he here to spend a "morning's bawdy entertainment" in the brothel?

Niall was so engrossed in following the Scotsman's movements that he didn't bother to turn around when the door behind him opened and a woman quietly entered the room.

"Captain Glenlyon," she said in a wry voice, "why is it I'm no surprised to find ye still skulking about in my house?"

He smiled at her over his shoulder. "You'll have to excuse the state of your room, Mrs. Grimble. I had a spot of trouble, but it's taken care of now."

Raising her plucked half-moon eyebrows at the disordered clothes on the bed, she walked forward to join him at the window. "Dear God," she exclaimed in alarm as she looked down into the street, "it's Coffin Face. Dinna tell me he's coming to my house again. That's the second time this month."

"I take it Francis Barron isn't one of your favorite customers?"

"My girls refuse to be alone in a room wi' him," she said nervously. "They swear he doesna have the desires of a normal man. Some of them even refuse to work afterward and run off without a word."

Niall felt a cold wave of disgust wash over him; she didn't need to go into sordid detail. He had witnessed the results of enough perversion to last a lifetime.

"Elspeth was afraid he'd come after her," the woman said quietly as they stepped back simultaneously from the window.

Niall suppressed a pang of anxiety at the thought. "Yes, but it doesn't matter. I've sent her back home."

Mrs. Grimble's gaze drifted back to evocative disarray of the bed. "Apparently it was quite a farewell. Ye're sure she's safely away?"

"I saw the cab drive her away myself."

The woman picked a sable boa up from the floor before she moved back to the door. "Aye, well. That's the end of it, isn't it?"

"Yes." He didn't like the doubt in her voice at all. "That's the end of it."

"And ye're certain ye don't want a job as bully boy, starting wi' getting rid of Francis Barron for me?"

"Yes, madame. I'm certain." He followed her to the door. "Do you have a back passage I could use? I suspect your friend Mr. Harper is lying in wait downstairs with his venomous pen poised."

And two minutes later Niall found himself standing alone in the back wynd behind the brothel, waiting impatiently for Hasim to reappear. He didn't know why he was suddenly in such a dark temper, unless the sight of a pair of street urchins scrounging for treasures in the gutter reminded him of his past humiliations.

He should be in a cheerful mood. He shouldn't feel like he was standing under a thundercloud. Within the hour he'd be on his uncomplicated way again. Elspeth Kildrummond would be ensconced in her papa's big house, her foolish misadventure forgotten, and Niall could conclude his own affairs, his business contract improved, his conscience appeased because he had saved her—

From what? Ah, that was the question. Had he saved her from the religious wrath of Francis Barron? From a career in harlotry? Or had he saved her only from himself and the painful yearnings she had raked to life inside a heart that had been denied love and laughter for far too long?

"You look very sads, Tuan."

"Yes, well, I am sad, Hasim, but that's what I get for listening to you and playing the good Samaritan, isn't it?" He cast a disgruntled glance around the gloomy tenements that leaned over them like gigantic tombstones. "Come on. Let's get out of here before someone decides to divest us of all our worldly possessions."

Hasim refused to follow. "You not save ladies, Tuan?"

"I sent her home. She's gone."

"But you not save her?"

"Sacré nom d'un chien! What is wrong with everyone? I delayed my own journey to come here, didn't I? I gave her a scathing lecture, frightening the hell out of us both in the process. I embarrassed myself with my behavior. Am I supposed to wrap her in tissue paper and carry her

around in my pocket? I scared the wits out of her. Yes! *I sent her home.*"

Pivoting on his well-worn bootheel, he strode down the street without any idea where he was headed. Hasim fell into a belligerent step behind him, not uttering a word. In fact, the Malay servant's silence only served to amplify the mocking voice in Niall's mind.

But you not save her, Tuan. You scare her. You embarrasses yourself. You send her back to evil house of her father. But you not save her from very bad thing.

Sixteen

"Scottish heiress, my sweet arse." Muttering to himself, the dour-faced driver maneuvered the cab into the stream of traffic heading out of town, coaches and beer carts for the country, broughams on pleasure rides along the picturesque river road.

Only as they approached the quieter outskirts of the small northeastern seaport did the cabbie slow and turn around on his box to look down at his unusual young passenger.

"The foreign gentleman paid me to take ye directly to Windsor Place, miss. I shouldna disobey him."

Elspeth wriggled back up against the seat and drew her first complete breath since spotting Francis riding past the cab. Thank God the nasty creature hadn't recognized her. She made a covert attempt to readjust her lopsided red wig; only gradually did she acknowledge the driver's critical scrutiny.

"Ye're not in trouble wi' the law, are ye, lass?"

Elspeth stared up into his heavily lined face, affecting a confidential tone. "Do you really want to know the truth?"

"Probably not."

"Well, I'll tell you anyway. That foreign gentleman who paid my fare is from a pagan island where men are allowed to keep as many wives as they please."

"Och, dinna take me for an utter idiot!"

"And he wants to spirit me away for a heathen wedding with his headhunter valet as best man, and my father's agreed and—and before Christmas, I'll be languishing away in my husband's private harem, and they'll probably change my name to Fatima and teach me to do lurid dances with silk veils."

A horrible silence followed her outburst. Elspeth stared down in nervous suspense at her hands and waited for him to toss her out on her backside. She was shaking at how easily she had maligned Glenlyon's character, rationalizing that with his reputation he'd never even notice another shovel of mud slung his way.

"Ye're a runaway, aren't ye, lass?" the man said with a compassionate perception that caught her off guard.

She didn't answer. She was suddenly too busy wondering whether Niall Glenlyon had remained in that musty little room, whether he'd summoned one of the girls to finish what he'd started with her. She supposed she should be grateful that he'd forced her to escape when he had. Thanks to him she'd missed an encounter with Coffin Face by mere seconds. And if Francis hadn't come to Mrs. Grimble's looking for her, it was for other more depraved reasons than she cared to contemplate.

But she wasn't grateful for the emotional turmoil Glenlyon had stirred in her troubled-enough heart, for tempting her to trust him with the truth. He'd already proven himself unworthy of her trust by taking her father's side, and he'd accepted money for it. Why had she hoped for even a second that he had come after her of his own inner urging?

Mercenary. Vulgar man.

The memory of her standing half-undressed in his arms smoldered in her blood like the melody of one of the Moorish love songs the gypsies played around the campfire. She could almost feel the pressure of his strong brown arm curved around her bare shoulders, the sensual tingling in her breasts as he had looked at her. Oh, the *way* he had looked at her.

She closed her eyes, appalled at the turn of her thoughts when there were more critical matters at stake. Captain Glenlyon had probably forgotten her by now, romping around in that room with a sea of obliging women in naughty costumes. It was a perversity in her nature that she kept thinking about what might have happened had she stayed with him.

The cabbie's voice forced her back to a more mundane reality. "I canna go any farther, and neither should ye, lass. There's a band of cairds camped over the hill, and no proper young girl wants to associate wi' their sort."

Elspeth refrained from pointing out that he'd just whisked her away from no less decorous a place than a brothel. Peering out the window at the gaily painted wagons gathered about the hillside, she felt an enormous shudder of relief ripple over her. She wasn't too late.

She began to rummage in her bag for the money hidden beneath the food she'd filched from home. "I know there's a shilling in here somewhere. Well, here's a sixpence anyway."

"Och, keep it," the cabbie muttered. "The foreigner overpaid me, to tell the truth, and ye'll need all yer siller if ye're a runaway."

"Thank you," she said, her voice soft with embarrassment.

"Ye'll not do anything stupid not like run off wi' the gypsies, lass? It canna be so bad at home—"

"Please," she broke in, "please don't tell anyone where I am."

He vented a sigh. "I never clapped eyes on ye, lassie."

She tucked the sixpence back into her bulging bag, then gave him a cheeky grin and climbed out of the cab. Halfway to the top of the hill, she spotted her Romany friend Samson and began to wave wildly, but he didn't budge an inch toward her. In fact, a scowl of suspicion was spreading across his face as she hoisted up her drooping skirts to complete the climb.

Samson slowly unfolded his arms, taking an involuntary step back in alarm at the oddly familiar woman who waved and clambered toward him. "Who in the name of *O'Del—*"

Elspeth steeled herself for a grueling interrogation, a very probable rejection, and a sea of complaints. Her defenses were so impaired from her interlude with Glenlyon, it would be an exhausting effort to manage even a muscle-bound moron like Samson. And didn't he have nerve to stare at *her*—he who looked like a street vendor's trained monkey in his little red cap and burgundy velvet jacket, his mustard-yellow silk neckcloth and tartan trousers?

"That isn't you, Elspeth?" he asked in an insultingly hopeful undertone.

"It's me," she said flatly, tramping over a clump of heather to dump her bag, her violin, her cloak, at his feet. "I'm here."

He stared at her in dismay. Defiantly she stared right back, and between the pain of them, she couldn't have decided who was the most conspicuous.

Still, she loved Samson Petulengro with her entire heart. She had never quite figured out why.

He was thirty years old, with curly black hair that grew down the back of his neck and shoulders like squirrel fur. Despite this peculiarity, he was quite attractive in his own way. A proud Roman nose, expressive brown eyes, swarthy skin, a handshake that crushed the feeling out of your finger bones. In fact, Elspeth thought he would be a very impressive personage if he didn't belch so much in public and lack an eye tooth. But any man who had trained three horses that had won all their races had to be forgiven a few minor flaws.

"Yer late, Elspeth," he pointed out. "De duke, he waited for over two hours." He subsided into another wary silence, sliding down a muddy furrow to heft her belongings into his brawny arms and help her up the hill.

"I had a crisis," she mumbled, avoiding his eyes.

"A crisis?"

Circling her slowly, he took in her lopsided wig, her wrinkled revealing dress, the shadows of exhaustion under her eyes. He touched his single gold hoop earring with his free hand, his tone nervous.

"A crisis?" he repeated. "I know I shouldn't ask yer. I know I'm not gonna like de answer, but what kind of *shannas* you get yerself into now, girl?"

Seventeen

The crisp November weather had already begun to deepen into the chilly mists of an early frost by the time Niall reached the ancient market town of Arbeadie. There, fed up with sitting in a crowded public coach all day discussing cow disorders with his bucolic companions, he hired two horses for the remainder of the ride toward the blue haze of the Grampian Mountains in the west.

He didn't allow himself to think of Elspeth Kildrummond much. And when he did, it was usually at night, when his mental armor was removed, sitting alone in a remote village taproom before a pungent peat fire. The flames reminded him of her, dancing lights like an imp in the dark and dispelling the deepening coldness of the Scottish evenings. She would steal into his awareness like woodsmoke and shroud his common sense before he even realized it.

Her vivid face would flash into his mind, and he'd have to smile at the memory of their last meeting. What an enchanting mess she was. He almost wished—no, he didn't. She and her nasty baronet were probably planning their honeymoon at this very moment he sat here tormenting himself with his morose fantasies.

He decided what he should wish was that Elspeth and her fiancé enjoyed a good life together, but he didn't wish that either. He hoped she left the pompous bastard in the lurch. She deserved someone better than Sir George Westcott, and if Niall had met her under different conditions,

if his own soul hadn't been immersed in darkness for
more years than he could count, he might have considered—

He refused to follow the thought to its dangerous conclusion. And so his late-night musings went, until he ended
up laughing aloud at himself, weaving up to his room half-
drunk on raw Highland whisky and unacknowledged
dreams, terrified to admit that the longing Elspeth Kildrummond had awakened in him stemmed from a source that
could never be fulfilled.

And two days later, just as he'd begun to convince himself she was fading into nothing more threatening than an
intriguing memory, Niall received an unexpected shock.
He'd been having the horses reshod for the rest of the
strenuous upland journey when he met Francis Barron outside the village smithy. Hasim had gone for a walk in the
woods to wangle some good weather out of the spirits by
tossing a charm or two into the waters of the local tarn.

The two men stared at each other in surprise and mutual
dislike. Niall was on the verge of simply looking the other
way to avoid a confrontation when an unpleasant suspicion
struck him.

Francis Barron hadn't come all the way to this isolated
Highland hamlet to sample the local ale. And if he were
on his way to Glen Fyne, it did seem an odd coincidence
that they would meet in such an unlikely spot.

"You aren't following me, Barron?" he asked coolly.
"First Mrs. Grimble's house, and now here."

Francis narrowed his eyes and gazed past Niall to the
two horses tethered outside the smithy. The pounding of
an anvil against a forge played a counter harmony to the
music of a blind piper on the hilly common behind them.

"That would depend, Captain Glenlyon," he replied

dourly. "Are ye traveling alone, or do ye have Elspeth hidden away inside that tavern?"

"Hidden away? If—" Niall couldn't finish.

He felt as if one of the anvil blows had caught him on the side of his head. The realization that she had not returned home after all took him off guard and touched off a chain of emotions he couldn't control. He didn't believe it. Yes, he did. It was completely in character for her.

What he couldn't believe was his own reaction, the instinctive fear mingled with anger and a sort of perverse admiration for Elspeth's defiant flight. Damn if the clever little feline hadn't managed to elude the lot of them so far. That is, if she weren't lying in a gorge somewhere with a broken neck. The possibility brought a lump of anxiety to his throat.

"I don't make a practice of spiriting away other men's fiancées," he said tersely.

Francis's mouth pulled into a crooked parody of a smile. "But you're not above seducing them in a brothel bedchamber? Aye, I know ye were the one who helped the little witch escape. The devil takes care of his own."

"If I had any idea what you were talking about," Niall said in a deceptively even voice, "I believe I might have to consider myself insulted. And then I believe I might be forced to demand an apology, for myself and the girl. Isn't it fortunate for us both that I haven't understood a single word you've said?"

Francis swallowed, his Adam's apple working. "I'd expect a man like you to resort to physical force. Vice and violence walk hand in hand. But the Lord is on my side, ye see."

"Do tell."

"I'll find Elspeth Kildrummond," Francis said solemnly, "and I'll do whatever I must to save her and her soul from its race toward hell. This is my cross to bear."

Niall hardened his heart to the fierce protective instincts that clamored inside him at the thought of Francis Barron subduing Elspeth's irrepressible spirit in the name of divine salvation. She had brought this trouble on herself—or had she? She was safe enough with her loved ones. Or was she? The doubts began to pile up like a thunderhead that weighed too heavily on his conscience.

This wouldn't be about the body, would it?

He glanced up distractedly. A band of gypsy children had suddenly appeared in an unsupervised swarm on the winding street that rose into the lane behind them. Clad in colorful tatters of discarded clothing, faded plaids and tartans, they banged the copper pots they carried as they began harassing the shoppers gathered around various merchants' stalls.

Niall watched them in silence for several moments until they splintered into strategic groups to hawk their pots and clothes-pegs, apples, nuts, and eggs.

"Filthy little beggars," Francis said with a frown. "Somebody's hen house and orchard was robbed during the night." And noting the amusement on Niall's face, he added, "But then I suppose ye condone their pagan ways, Captain, having lived wi' the savages all your life."

Niall slowly turned his head. The look of warning in his eyes was so unmistakable that the other man took an involuntary step backward and wondered whether he *had* finally come face to face with the devil himself.

"You might find out just how pagan I am at heart if any harm comes to that girl," Niall said quietly.

"This is a family matter, Captain."

"And you're not family yet," Niall retorted. "Not until Cousin George actually drags Miss Kildrummond to the altar. Now I really have to end this delightful conversation. I have a sudden craving for stolen fruit."

He pushed around the long gaunt man, noting that Francis's mouth trembled with suppressed rage as their shoulders brushed, but he didn't raise a hand in retaliation. And as Niall waved over a pig-tailed gypsy girl, buying her entire basket of hazelnuts to add to his supplies, he felt Francis staring at him with those unholy amber eyes.

Ciel, he only hoped that Elspeth had as much cunning as she did courage. She was going to need it.

"Come have yer fortune told in the dukkerin wagon," one of the gypsy girls coaxed Niall, tugging at his frayed coatsleeve.

"No fortunes for me," he said with a strained smile. "I get more than enough soothsaying from my valet."

"I'll find her before ye do, Captain," Francis promised as Niall began to walk away.

"I don't doubt it," Niall said without breaking his stride. "You see, I have no intention of chasing after her at all."

"Her wickedness must be stopped, Captain," Francis called in a louder voice, oblivious to the mocking faces the gypsy children were pulling behind his back. "Someone has to save her from herself."

A red haze of anger swam before Niall's eyes, but he didn't allow himself to stop or to analyze Barron's threat. He didn't allow himself to acknowledge the deeper emotions building like water behind a floodgate where for years he had felt nothing.

If he did, he might lose control and turn on Francis Barron before anyone could stop him. He quickened his pace, breathing hard. His face became expressionless except for the pain of realization and self-denial in his eyes. His temper had always frightened him. It had frightened his family when he was a child, and later in life the men in his regiment. He needed to get away, be alone before he started to lash out from that place inside him that was as wild and unpredictable as his jungle origins. . . .

Before he started to care.

Her wickedness must be stopped.

The words still echoed like the dark refrain of a Gre-

gorian chant in the back of Niall's head two hours later
as he cantered from the hamlet. Behind him, Hasim struggled to keep up. His heels were banging against his horse's
sides along with the newly bought copper kettle that Niall
had noted but chosen not to comment on. God only knew
when Hasim had made friends with the gypsies.

They slowed their pace on reaching the main road. The
distant flat-topped peaks of the Grampians diverted Niall's
attention, and he thought of the mountains of his jungle
home. Not that he expected to stay on the island as much
as he loved it now. He never stayed anywhere for long.
After a while the restlessness overcame him and he found
an excuse, any excuse to move on, always trying to escape
the emptiness inside him that was like an ever-widening
chasm. But no matter where he went he understood wildness, solitude, the laws and challenges of nature. It was
the workings of the human heart that bewildered him, and
none so much a mystery as his own.

Even now as he stared off toward the mountains, enshrouded in an aura of mist and magic, he sought a desperately needed peace in their wild beauty to calm the
turmoil of his thoughts. His senses avidly drank in the
soothing wash of coolness and muted color, the blues, pur-
ples, and tarnished golds. But his mind would not relax.
Over and over it returned to that rebellious face, those
tempting tigress eyes, pride, fear, and desire in their depths.
Where had the damn girl gone? And why, why? How had
she managed to elude Barron this far? Certainly it would
be too dangerous, too conspicuous, for a young woman to
ride these rough highways alone on horseback, no matter
how experienced a horsewoman she was. Stubbornness or
desperation? Yes, someone desperate enough would find a
way. He knew that from experience.

He pressed on, not slowing again until they reached a
crossroads, and the decision had to be made whether to
take the well-traveled highway into the Grampians, or to

take a detour into the less popular remains of a military road that led to the northeast. It would cost him a day, but the delay might be worth it to avoid meeting anyone. Or to chance finding her.

As he studied the bleak moorland that rose into the gloaming shadows, he drew a cigar from his pocket. If everyone assumed Elspeth was running to her former home in Glen Fyne, then why didn't Barron simply ride ahead to await her arrival? What was the point in trying to intercept her?

He looked up in sudden alarm as Hasim produced one of his unreliable homemade matches from his tiger-skin pouch and stretched precariously across his saddle to light Niall's cigar. The sulphur tip flared like a miniature bonfire between them, eliciting a shriek of excited laughter from Hasim before he flung the flaming match back over his head.

Niall struggled to subdue his nervous mount. "Next time, Hasim, I suggest you buy us some decent matches instead of another kettle."

"Kettle for making coffee," Hasim said, sneaking his own cigarette from his waist pouch. "For making very bad drink that Tuan hopes makes us very rich."

"Well, we won't get rich if I waste my time chasing after that woman," Niall said somberly, his mind refusing to leave that perplexing subject. "Kildrummond said the weather can turn brutal in those heights without warning. I'll bet they intend to get Elspeth back home in time for the wedding. A blizzard would make travel virtually impossible."

"Impossible," Hasim echoed, frowning at the peculiar moorland landscape that seemed to stretch without end. No trees. No brightly colored birds or orchids. Just weird configurations of gray rocks and strange little plants that scratched his private parts when he sat among them to answer nature's call. Evil spirits definitely in this place called a moors.

"Tuan, your grandfathers born in this land and gives you their blood. The spirits here welcomes you. I don't think they likes me very much."

"Give them time, Hasim."

They resumed riding toward a granite ridge whose rocky overhang looked to Niall as if it would provide decent shelter for the night. "Why did you buy that kettle from the gypsies anyway, Hasim?" he asked. "You know I have one in my saddlebags. Don't tell me you felt sorry for the little thieves."

"Me, Tuan? Why not possible. My heart as hards as yours."

It was just past gloaming when they reached the overhang. In a matter of minutes they'd kindled a small fire of heather twigs and furze, and stretched their bedrolls out to absorb the heat. Niall glanced out across the hills to the blurred smudges of gold where the fires of a gypsy encampment burned, luring gullible villagers to fortune-telling wagons. Hasim proceeded to dig through his rosewood medicine chest for an offering to placate the spirits of the cold wind: dried dragonflies and tiger balm, desiccated python and polished volcanic stones, various pots of colored clay and the phials of quinine he and Niall took as a preventative.

"I remember Maman telling us she liked the gypsies," Niall murmured, closing his eyes. "She envied them their freedom, their ease at traveling from village to village. She always said—" He sat up suddenly. A smile of smug realization broke across his face. *"Par Dieu,* Hasim, how could I have been so stupid?"

Hasim gazed at him through a haze of frangipani incense. "I wonder that myself sometimes, Tuan."

Niall laughed and leaped to his feet, jamming the shirt-tails of his blue muslin shirt into his buckskin trousers. It was a costume that in Hasim's opinion was vastly inadequate for the biting Highland night.

"We going homes, Tuan?" he asked hopefully, huddled inside his ankle-length sun-bear cape.

"We're going on a shikar, Hasim. For a young tigress."

Hasim cast a skeptical glance across the barren moor that surrounded them. "Excuse me, Tuan. This is a jokes?"

"No joke, my friend," Niall said cheerfully as he climbed down a natural staircase of rocks to splash freezing water from a burn onto his face. "Call down your jadoo spirits, Hasim. You might have a chance to trade professional secrets with your gypsy friends."

Twenty minutes later Niall stood at the perimeter of the gypsy encampment, chuckling dryly as he focused his field glasses on a gaily painted wagon with a scrolled placard on the panel which read:

—SAMSOM PETULENGRO—
WORSHIPFUL COMPANY OF FARRIERS
HORSE TRAINER
PRIZE FIGHTER
CURER OF WARTS

—DELILAH—
HIS WIFE
FORTUNETELLER EXTRAORDINAIRE
SELLER OF CLOTHES PEGS

Eighteen

"Tonight, Elspeth, I will reveal to you all my deepest, darkest secrets to reading de future."

"Reveal to me how to make this blasted jackdaw stop squawking first."

"Sneak a few drops of whisky into his water, but don't yer dare tell Samson. My husband, he dotes on that damn bird." Tapping her brown bare toes with impatience, Delilah gestured Elspeth closer. "Stop looking outside, and just sit down at de dukkerin table. Hey, did yer know if you have sexual relations with de devil, you'll be able to predict de future—You think this is a laughing matter?" she demanded indignantly at Elspeth's muffled snort of amusement. "You think just any idiot can read de ball?"

"Of course not, Delilah," Elspeth answered somberly. "I've never thought of you as just any idiot. Now tell me about Glen Fyne again."

"You mock my powers?" Delilah asked with a sly grin.

"I'm in absolute awe of your powers, Delilah. I'm in awe of anyone who can sleep in a wagon this size with Samson and three boisterous male children."

"Not to mention an ungrateful runaway with no respect for all de unseen powers of de universe."

Her face resigned, Elspeth adjusted the smoky oil-lamp that hung on the wagon hook. A moment later she had settled down on a heap of old sheepskin rugs and threadbare quilts.

The *vardo,* or wagon, was as crowded as a bazaar, furnished with a small black coal stove, a chest of drawers, and a wall of overfilled cupboards whose contents more often than not tumbled out onto the feather bed when the outer wheels pitched into motion. Every bare space was taken up with willow baskets of clothes pegs, swatches of fragrant herbs, tangles of tarnished jewelry. A table made from a fat peeling oak stump, draped in a red silk shawl, separated her from her dear friend Delilah Petulengro.

On the table sat a crystal ball which Delilah claimed had belonged to a powerful Scottish sorceress who wielded great influence during the days of King Robert the Bruce. This Elspeth doubted since she had seen entire stalls of the same crystals last year at a Cheapside market in London. But never mind. The ball exuded a certain mystical aura if you didn't notice its numerous little chips, and the fact that its artist had thought it amusing to fashion a cigar pouring volumes of smoke from the mouth of one of the pair of winged pewter dragons that embraced its base.

Elspeth sat up with a start of surprise. Without warning Delilah had launched into a weird ritual of undulating her hands above the ball and rolling her eyes back in their sockets until the whites showed. Then suddenly she froze, fingers stiff in the air like a starfish taken out of water. A low moan issued from her throat.

Elspeth slowly lowered the bottle of malt whisky she had pinched from Samson's cupboard for a wee nip to fight the damp moorland cold. "Good Lord, Delilah, that's overdoing things a bit, isn't it?"

"You think it's easy to contact de spirits? You think dey gonna listen if yer just whisper and whine?"

Elspeth passed the bottle across the table. "I doubt any self-respecting spirit would come within a mile of you. Why, you've probably scared them straight back to the otherworld."

Delilah took a deep drink, wiped her hand across her

lips, and leaned forward in an attitude of intense concentration. Elspeth stared at the silver crucifix nestled in the hollow of her friend's throat and listened idly to the prattle of a husband and wife practicing their Punch and Judy show somewhere outside the wagon. She felt the sharpness of cold in the air more keenly tonight, despite the fact that she and Delilah had stuffed moss into the window sill and floor planks.

Delilah snorted in exasperation. "It's still de same, Elspeth. De only thing I can see when I think of that place is a swirling gray mass of something. Like ghosts." She jerked her head up, her eyes dark with drama. "What if all yer people is dead?"

"And you call yourself a mystic. How could an entire village have ceased to exist after centuries?"

"Maybe dey got under a curse."

"Delilah, please."

"Maybe a dreaded disease wiped everyone out and no one survived to tell. Look, I'm better at doing love lives. Don't you want to know about yer romantic destiny?"

Elspeth leaned across the table to scrutinize the crystal. "You ought to polish this thing once in a while. I think those swirling gray masses you keep seeing are fingerprints."

Delilah paused to slide her spectacles back up her slightly hooked nose and peer critically at the crystal. As she leaned forward, her golden hoop earrings glinted against the tumble of black uncombed curls that framed her elfin face. Her father-in-law Abel was the tribe's chieftain, and he treated Delilah like a princess.

"Hey, I think yer right, Elspeth. My children musta sneaked in here today. Ugh. It feels like grouse egg."

Elspeth studied her vivacious friend with a pang of envy. Delilah was only five years her senior, but she had an exciting life with three delightful sons and a loving husband who would disembowel any man who looked at her twice. She and Elspeth had been friends for two years now, since the stormy afternoon when Elspeth had paid for and brought her family's own physician across the moor to make an emergency call on Delilah's mother.

Fortunately, Delilah was a better friend and mother herself than she was a fortuneteller. Imagine Glen Fyne having ceased to exist. It was inconceivable, and Elspeth firmly rejected the thought and the cold feeling of fear that accompanied it.

"I can't believe people actually pay to hear this nonsense," she grumbled, twisting her finger around a lock of her hair, dyed by Delilah to a hideous mud-brown blond with an infusion of walnut leaves. It was part of her "disguise" which included a thick padding of quilt worn at her waist to give her the appearance of a pregnant gypsy wife. Her own skin, never properly protected by a parasol or bonnet while she rode or went boating with Catherine, was not so pale as to attract notice. Anyway, intermarriage among gypsies and other Scots was not uncommon.

"On second thought, Delilah, I don't think I have a talent for this sort of thing. Wouldn't it be easier if I just played my violin at the fairs instead of fortunetelling?"

Delilah blinked, her horror palpable. "Talk about attracting attention. Just pretend to concentrate on de crystal, and remember de young girls like to hear dere's a handsome man in the future. De older women care less what a man looks like, but he oughta be rich. If de woman is very, very old, he just have to be alive."

Elspeth looked appalled. "I can't believe you'd accept money for telling such a pack of lies."

"And who am I to warn some stupid girl with stars in her eyes that de handsome prince she's to marry will be a big oaf or worse in ten years less?"

Delilah tossed back her hair and hunched over the ball again, her concentration broken as her husband gave a loud belch outside the wagon window. "That proves my point.

Forget de crystal, Elspeth. Let me see yer fambles, and for heaven's sake, don't forget to ask for de coin first."

"I'd never have the nerve."

"No telling you get paid if yer don't dukker good then."

Elspeth reluctantly held out her hands for a palmistry lesson.

"Ah, lady." Delilah heaved a sympathetic sigh. "De lines of yer palm tell me yer a woman who has suffered too much in her short life."

"I'm suffering now. Phew, Delilah, your breath is as bad as my old sheepdog Clootie's. You really shouldn't chew so much garlic before you read palms."

The gypsy woman grinned, showing perfect pearls of teeth, and prodded the fleshy pad of Elspeth's thumb with her ragged fingernail. "This is what we professional fortunetellers call de Mount of Venus. When it's as plump as yours, it means—"

"Mount of *Venus?* You made that up."

"I did not." Delilah's pretty face tightened in annoyance. "It's supposed to mean you have a highly sensual nature that can cause you all sorts of problems. In your case, though, it's probably yer big mouth that's going to bring you trouble."

"Problems." Elspeth sighed. "Well, that part is true enough."

"You also got small proportioned palms which tells me yer impulsive to a fault. De middle finger is ruled by Saturn, and I even see a star there, Elspeth—that could mean big danger. Over here, it would mean a shipwreck."

"Over where?"

"Here."

"That isn't a line on my palm, Delilah. It's a horse hair. You need to clean your spectacles along with your silly crystal."

"Strange markings," Delilah said, frowning. "I never seen such lines."

Elspeth swallowed, aware that Delilah no longer seemed to be pretending. "From yer wrist to dere is yer life line just. Now, a small thumb means a weak-willed individual. Dem I don't cheat too much. Dey got enough problems before."

Delilah glanced up, devilish humor lurking in her dark eyes. "Yer want to know why you should beware of men who got big long thumbs?"

"No, not really. But go on. Tell me anyway. Why should I beware of men who have big long thumbs?"

"Because . . ." Delilah leaned back, each successive word escaping her in a little dragon snort of laughter. "Because dey—dey also got big long . . ."

"You said that," Elspeth said primly.

". . . big long male . . . parts."

"How could you possibly know that?" Elspeth whispered.

Delilah grinned sheepishly. "Hey, I got seven brothers. I got eyes."

Elspeth stared at her friend in appalled silence before she dropped straight back against the carpets, clutching her padded midsection in a paroxysm of convulsive laughter. Disturbed by the racket, Samson's pet jackdaw woke up and began hopping around its cage. Only dimly did Elspeth notice her gypsy friend's laughter die away as the wagon steps outside creaked with a considerable weight.

The heavy muslin curtains across the arched doorway parted. Damp night air swirled into the eerie silence that had fallen, a silence throbbing with a sudden perceivable tension.

Delilah's eyes rounded as she stared up at the uninvited guest. *"O'Del,"* she whispered, unconsciously putting her hand to the crucifix at her throat.

Elspeth reluctantly turned her head, her own amusement subsiding. Even before she looked up at the silent man gazing into the poorly lit wagon, she knew who it was by the change in the air, by the constrictive fear in her own body that trapped the breath in her lungs, the unnerving charge of male energy that sent little shivers down her nape to her spine.

Glenlyon. Niall Glenlyon. The impact of his presence immobilized her. It sent panic signals streaking through her brain like lightning bolts that burned away her ability to reason.

She stared at his long booted legs, at the black woolen greatcoat, glistening with mist. She couldn't say it was a complete surprise to see him again. From the moment they'd met, she had known he possessed predator instincts, the devil's own intuition.

Still, it was a greater shock than she expected when she mustered all her courage to look up into his lean sardonic face, and then there was nothing to do but brazen it out, hoping against hope that the man had not come here seeking her at all, but rather, as improbable as it was, to have his fortune told. Hoping that he would accept her for what she pretended to be—a pregnant gypsy collapsed on a pile of carpets with hair like a multicolored ball of yarn stuffed under a scrap of paisley kerchief.

For a heart-stopping instant, she almost allowed herself the dangerous luxury of believing he hadn't recognized her, that his appearance here was coincidence.

His gaze, as cool as mist, skirted over her and settled on Delilah, sitting with her mouth agape like a dead carp and her hand lowering to her breast. When he finally spoke, his deep-timbered voice hit every nerve in Elspeth's body and reawakened all of the delicious antagonism of their last confrontation.

"Delilah Petulengro?" His mouth lifted in the faintest smile. "Fortuneteller Extraordinaire . . . Seller of Clothes Pegs?"

Delilah snapped her mouth shut. "You want a love potion? No, a man looks like you don't need no potions. You want me to read yer palm?"

And the instant she said that, both she and Elspeth glanced down inadvertently at his thumbs; big, powerful, long thumbs, in perfect proportion to the rest of his physical presence which overwhelmed the crowded little wagon.

Niall released a long-suffering sigh. "I've come to take her home."

Delilah, bless her heart, didn't so much as blink. "Who? What, you lost a sweetheart, yer wife or someone?" She waved him away. "Come back in de morning, mister. De crystal is too tired tonight to help yer."

He ducked his head to avoid cracking it on the lintel and stepped into the wagon. His broad frame was shadowing the expression of expectant horror on Elspeth's face as he looked right down into her eyes. "If you want to change out of that ridiculous costume, you have three minutes to do so," he said quietly. "I'll be waiting outside. And if you aren't ready by then I'll haul you out of here however I have to."

Elspeth bolted to her feet. "Why can't you just leave me alone? You've been like a foxtail in my foot ever since the moment I met you!"

Niall's eyes widened as the prominent bulge of her false pregnancy sagged to her knees. Defying him silently to say a word, she hoisted it back into position where it promptly sank to rest at half-mast against her hipbone.

"You've gone from bad to worse, *ma belle,*" he said with a woeful smile. "It seems I'm not a minute too soon."

"I thought I'd seen the last of you, Glenlyon."

"And I thought you'd gone home like the clever little girl you obviously are not."

"It seems to me we've exhausted the subject, Captain. Or could you possibly have forgotten our last meeting?"

A dangerous flame flared in the depths of his eyes. "I'll

never forget that morning if I live to be a hundred," he said in an undertone.

Elspeth closed her own eyes for a moment to compose herself. What audacity he had to follow her, to barge in here in that long black coat and those tight buckskin trousers, the wicked beauty of his features accentuated by several days' growth of beard and a look of mounting impatience that boded ill for her plans.

"You've already wasted more time than I can afford," he told her curtly. "Get dressed. Or undressed . . . whatever it takes to make you presentable for the stagecoach ride back to Falhaven."

Elspeth fought back a sense of desperation as she glanced over her shoulder at Delilah. "Perhaps we should warn Captain Glenlyon that your husband was the heavyweight boxing champion of 1836."

"It was 1835 actually," Delilah murmured, still in awe of the man standing in her doorway.

Niall gave Delilah a disarming smile. "You might prefer to wait outside, Mrs. Petulengro. It appears your pigheaded friend here needs a little private persuasion. And by the way, your husband is a charming man. We had a very enjoyable chat by the campfire."

Elspeth clenched her hands. "Now you know for certain that he's lying, Delilah. Samson would never invite a *gorgio* to sit around the fire with them."

"But he is very dark," Delilah observed, giving Niall a favorable once-over. "Perhaps he's a *didakeis,* Elspeth, a half-breed himself."

"I only wish I could claim to share such distinguished heritage," Niall said politely, "but then again, who knows? My mother *was* from the South of France." He directed another intimate smile at Delilah. "Mrs. Petulengro, a few moments of privacy, if you please."

Delilah nodded, defenseless against his charm, and reluctantly heaved herself to her feet.

"Don't you dare leave me alone with him," Elspeth said in a frantic undertone. "The man is perverse."

Delilah's dark gaze swung back to Niall. "Perverse?" she whispered. "In what way?"

"There's no telling what he might do if we're left alone," Elspeth said in a panic that wasn't wholly contrived.

Delilah, in fact, did wish devoutly to stay, but this man appeared a little too determined to cross. Giving Elspeth an apologetic shrug, she crept around the table toward the doorway. Halfway there, her gaze fell inadvertently on the crystal globe that glowed in the lamplight. No, it couldn't be! Excitement surged through her at the strange spectacle of images that were solidifying within the center of the glass.

It was incredible. The lousy crystal, which Delilah would have been willing to swear on her firstborn's soul could not have manifested the psychic powers of a flea, was literally seething with demonic possession.

The presence of the dark man who blocked her doorway had unleashed a metaphysical maelstrom in the murky glass.

"O'Del," Delilah whispered with her stare transfixed on the miniature crystal-encased representation of the very man and woman who stood before her in her wagon. Crosscurrents of emotion were colliding between them. In truth, Delilah had never experienced a genuine vision in her life. Why, until this moment she'd believed herself incapable of it, a harmless little fraud who fleeced the gullible *gorgios* out of money they usually deserved to lose.

But *this*.

She tugged at Elspeth's elbow, her voice shaking with the terrifying wonder of it. "Do you see de crystal, Elspeth?"

"Yes, I see it," Elspeth snapped, but she didn't—at least not the mystical vision evolving at its core. "And I'm about to hit this man over the head with the blasted thing if he doesn't leave me alone."

Delilah leaned over the crystal, her eyes agog behind her wire-rimmed spectacles. At first the image had been encircled in a ring of fire. But now there was water, so much turbulent water around the dark-haired man and woman, immersing their figures, forcing them to take refuge in each other's arms, and the aura of sexuality that surrounded them warmed her own shivering body, took her breath away. But there was something else hovering in the background, a shadow, a force of darkness that sent a cold shaft of fear through her.

"I'm having a vision," she shouted, clutching her palpitating heart. "It's finally happening to me."

Elspeth yanked off her kerchief and threw it at the table. "Get your husband in here now, Delilah, and make him bring every last one of his throwing knives!"

"Samson and my valet are at the van right now examining that splendid Arabian horse," Niall said calmly. "It seems the poor creature has developed a bad case of shin inflammation, and Hasim is a skilled healer of animals as well as people."

Elspeth looked stricken. It was the worst thing he could have told her. Shin inflammation, he'd said. Arabian, her Arabian . . . lame. Elspeth refused to believe it, preferring to think he was lying just to upset her. "I'm going outside to see the horse for myself," she muttered, starting around him.

"Oh, no, you aren't." And before she could take even a tentative step, he had shifted his position to obstruct her path. "We'll go outside together after you've changed into something more appropriate for the ride home."

"I suppose you'd prefer a sable boa or a French's costume with black lace stockings?" she asked tartly.

"I might." Shaking his head, he raised a hank of her hair to the light. "Perhaps the dead fox wig wasn't such a bad idea, after all. Whatever you've done to your hair has made it one hell of a nasty sight."

"You're not exactly the image of elegance yourself, Glenlyon," she retorted, trying to pull away from him. "Did the pawnbroker find those trousers in his grandfather's attic?"

He chuckled, tugging playfully at the strand of hair he'd wrapped around his forefinger. "Poor Georgie-Porgie might change his mind about the wedding himself if he could see you now."

George. The name flooded Elspeth with a wave of conflicting feelings. Her first instinct was to wish for the comfortable familiarity of their long-standing friendship. But then in a dark rush of memory the details of everything that had happened that night returned, George holding that pistol, murdering a man, George and Susan. She shook her head slowly as if in denial and looked right through Niall. The last moments of Tormod's life played through her mind with agonizing clarity.

Niall frowned at the dark shift in her expression, lowering his hand. "What is it?" he asked in quiet concern.

She refused to meet his gaze. Her voice trembled with something he suspected ran even deeper than anger. "Delilah, if you don't bring your husband in here now, I won't be held accountable for what happens."

Delilah blinked as if snapping out of a trance. The vision in the crystal had vanished. Regretting that she'd miss even one moment of this juicy drama unfolding in her wagon, she straightened and squeezed her voluptuous frame through the tiny space that separated Elspeth and the masterful foreigner. Talk about *shannas!* Later she would tell her husband that the sparks of friction between those two singed the ends of her own hair.

With Delilah gone, Elspeth's battered defenses began to crumble. What if Ali Baba really had been injured? What if this horrible man meant it when he said he'd make her go home? His persistence was beginning to frighten her; he was more than capable of carrying out his threats. Pressing back against the cupboard door, the jackdaw trying to peck at her hair, she buried her face in her hands and tried to think. She didn't have the energy to weep.

"I want you out of my life, Glenlyon," she ground out. "Now. Forever."

"Chasing after you isn't exactly my idea of a pleasure excursion either, *mon coeur*," he said in annoyance. And yet, as he stared down at her downbent head, he found himself more affected by the sight of her distress than he dared show. "You lied to me, and I don't like that. You promised me you'd go home."

"And I was going home," she said fiercely, dropping her hands from her face. "I was going back to the only real home I've ever known, and if we were there now, my friends would punish you for trying to abduct me—they'd string up your miserable carcass by the thumbnails for the ravens and kestrels to feast on."

"Abduct you? *You?* Do you think I'm insane?"

"The possibility has crossed my mind."

His mouth curled in disdain. "I intend to put you on a coach bound for Falhaven the first thing in the morning, even if I have to hand-tie you to my own horse to make sure we catch it in time. I've never met such an incredible pain in the neck in my entire life."

The jackdaw had gotten hold of a lock of her hair and was drawing it into the cage like a worm. Elspeth tried to pretend she didn't notice, but the stinging tugs at her scalp brought tears to her eyes. "What makes you think I won't get off at the first stop?" she demanded between gasps of pain.

He took a menacing step toward her, his eyes like flint. "Because I plan on using some of the money your papa gave me to pay passage for my valet to deposit your troublesome derrière at your doorstep."

"You're not coming with me?"

"Not for a million pounds."

She sniffed, pulling her hair from the bird's black beak. Niall could practically see the cogs of her devious mind working, planning another escape. He thrust his forefinger under her nose.

"Hasim was a headhunter before he started cleaning my boots, and if you think all his savage instincts have been subdued, you're making a serious mistake."

He gave her a long threatening look, then whirled around. His black greatcoat brushed her skirts. Elspeth had just dared to release her pent-up breath when he paused at the doorway.

"On second thought, I won't wait outside for you to dress. I don't trust you not to escape through the window." His eyes glinted with unholy humor in the hazy lamplight. "I will turn around though, *chérie,* before you start accusing me of being a Peeping Tom again."

She stared at the broad slope of his shoulders, at his black-swathed figure filling the doorway. Damn cold-hearted mercenary. He didn't care a whit about what happened to her. He just wanted his coffee contract and his hunting-for-hire money. She meant no more to him than ". . . another poor animal to be tracked," she muttered under her breath, "another empty-headed woman to take to his bed, or billiard table. He probably isn't particular."

He chuckled, raising the curtain at the window to gaze out at the gypsy campfires blazing in the mist. "You do pick your friends," he mused.

"I pick my enemies too."

"I wasn't criticizing your choice of company," he murmured. "As far as I'm concerned, there isn't a discernible difference between a princess and a prostitute."

"You being a character expert on the latter."

He smiled. "I have nothing personal against you, Elspeth."

"I'll bet Henry the Eighth said the same thing to Anne Boleyn."

"Hurry up, child. You'll have the entire ride home to compare me to historical villains."

"Napoleon."

"I believe I'm taller."

"Bluebeard."

"He wasn't real." He glanced back over his shoulder. "I've never been married, either."

"Attila the—"

He spun around, the movement sending the jackdaw into a cawing frenzy. "Do I have to come over there and help you undress again?"

"You might not be laughing at me when Samson shows you what made him a heavyweight champion, Captain."

"But I wasn't laughing at you now," he said quietly. "I never laugh at unhappiness . . . or fear." He hesitated a heartbeat. "You are afraid of something, aren't you, Elspeth?"

He stared at her for several seconds before he returned his brooding gaze to the doorway. Elspeth swallowed over the sudden tightness in her throat. She almost preferred his casual mockery—it gave her an exterior focus for her pain. But his understanding, the glimpses of infrequent compassion in his character, only confused her and made her wonder if she'd misjudged him from the start. Not that she'd be dense enough to let herself be swayed by a few kind words, whether sincere or not. She was clinging to her sense of righteous indignation as if it were a shield to protect her from her own vulnerability.

"Stop dawdling, Elspeth. I've never known a woman who took so long to undress."

"Afraid you're losing your touch, Captain?"

"What I'm losing is my patience," he snapped.

With a sigh of resignation, Elspeth stuck her hand into

her waistband to untie the padded sash. The silk cushion, weighted with barleycorns, hit the floor with a faint thud.

"Was it a boy or a girl?" Niall asked wryly, still staring straight ahead.

Tears of frustration sprang to Elspeth's eyes. Obviously Fate had decided she needed an extra measure of misery. It wasn't enough to have a deceptive father and a homicidal, unfaithful fiancé. It wasn't enough that she'd been cursed with a face and temperament more suited to a Viking warship than a Victorian drawing room. No, Fate had decided her life deserved a little more bedevilment in the unlikely form of Niall Glenlyon. He was like a shadow you couldn't shake, the dominant figure in a recurring dream.

"Are you all right, Elspeth?" he asked softly.

She rubbed her eyes with the back of her wrist. "I'm the very picture of contentment, Glenlyon," she said in a dry voice. "I can't imagine why you'd think otherwise."

Clenching her teeth, she knelt to unlatch the battered old trunk which held her own clothes. The pleasant aroma of dried moss and heather wafted upward as she raised the lid. Now that she'd had a moment to recover from the shock of seeing Glenlyon and feeling sorry for herself, she was beginning to recover her wits. Ali Baba couldn't have developed shin problems. Why, she'd fed him his red bran mash and walked him herself less than three hours ago. He'd been as sound and spirited as the first day she had fallen passionately in love with him in the duke's stables.

And Samson would never suffer a stranger to spirit her away. Why in the world had she allowed Glenlyon to intimidate her? The gypsies were probably only placating him until the Council of Elders decided how best to send him packing.

Her confidence began to return, imbuing her with a warm glow of security. She counted on her friends' loyalty toward her, their sense of fairness, their instincts of survival and love of freedom to protect her.

Unfortunately, what she hadn't counted on was the tribe's reluctance to become embroiled in a non-gypsy dispute with possible legal ramifications, the inherent Romany belief that a daughter owed even a dishonest father unquestioning obedience. She certainly hadn't counted on the gypsies' immediate feeling of fraternity with the legendary hunter who'd mysteriously appeared on the moor with his dark-skinned mentor who instinctively appreciated their ways.

Like the gypsies, Niall Glenlyon had suffered years of persecution and had been forced to survive on his wits. Like these children of the darkness, he viewed life with a certain cynical humor. Like the gypsies, Niall Glenlyon claimed no land as his home and yet enjoyed a mystical kinship with the earth and all its wild creatures.

As it turned out, the gypsies were only too relieved to entrust Elspeth to his care.

Nineteen

Elspeth listened in shock while Delilah shamefacedly broke the bad news to her in Ali Baba's van early the following morning: The Council of Elders had held a midnight meeting and voted unanimously to send Elspeth away. Traitors. Hypocrites. Shallow-minded, mean-hearted, double-dealing dimwits.

"De elders don't despise you or nothing, Elspeth, but that man has put a big hobbiken on them." Delilah shoved her spectacles back onto the bridge of her nose, her shoulders slumped in dejection. "We got trouble with de law enough."

Elspeth's chest ached with the effort it took not to break down and cry from sheer desperation. She sat up from her bed of fresh straw, her joints stiff, her eyelids burning from fatigue. She and Samson had spent half the night poulticing the young horse in the hope he had nothing worse than an inflammation that would subside. But her bad luck had held true.

Just an hour ago, Samson's cousin Gethel had admitted he'd ridden Ali Baba down a narrow cobblestone street yesterday to impress a haughty shopgirl. As a result, the horse would never run in the Ayr or Derby next year, or the St. Leger. The duke would never trust her judgment again. Her friends at Mrs. Grimble's house would lose all their investments, money needed to save them from lives of prostitution.

Delilah hunkered down beside her. "Who can tell, eh? In two, three months, de damn horse could be stronger than ever. I seen Samson bring back worse."

"He's going to auction Ali Baba off," Elspeth whispered. Guilt compounded her despair as the horse nickered and nuzzled her ear. "We can't afford to keep him."

"There's other horses, Elspeth. Yer got to look at it with a philosophical attitude like Samson do."

"Samson, the exalted philosopher," Elspeth murmured, biting her knuckle to stifle a humorless laugh while tears welled in her eyes. "Oh, damn. You aren't really going to make me leave, Delilah?"

Delilah stared down at the floor in defeat. "I done my best. When did anyone ever listen to me?"

"You're going to let a stranger take me away when I've loved you like a sister?" Elspeth's voice was rising in a very real panic, but she wasn't above a little emotional manipulation to save herself from being handed over to Glenlyon's guardianship. "After I rode out in the freezing rain and spent my savings to drag a doctor across the moor to save your mother? Your poor dying mother."

"It was only indigestion, Elspeth."

Elspeth pulled herself to her feet, her face pale and frightened. Somehow she hadn't really believed her friends would betray her. She'd depended, naively perhaps, on the fierce degree of loyalty she would have shown in their place.

"Please, Elspeth," Delilah said, her gaze remorseful. "Maybe it's all meant to be. When I looked into my crystal, I saw you and yer captain together as clear as I'm looking at yer now."

"For heaven's sake, he's not my captain," Elspeth cried, clenching her fists in frustration. "He's my—he's my curse."

"Sometimes a woman needs a man to watch out for her proper."

"Well, he's the wrong man." Elspeth's eyes flashed with resentment. "He doesn't want to protect me at all, or he wouldn't be forcing me to go back home."

"You take a big chance, a woman traveling dese lonely moors with winter on its way," Delilah muttered direly, shaking her head. "I saw bad things for yer in that crystal. Fire, water, and an evil man."

Evil. The face of Francis Barron crept into Elspeth's mind, temporarily crowding out her immediate worries and raising rows of gooseflesh on her forearms. It wasn't exactly reassuring to think of meeting him alone on the moors.

"Save the prophetic warnings for a paying customer, Delilah. I've never believed in that nonsense." Her voice cracked with emotional strain as she bent to snatch her belongings from the floor before Ali Baba could work his velvety muzzle into her bag. "I know it isn't your fault, Delilah. I know your father didn't want me traveling with you in the first place, but I-I don't have anyone else to turn to."

Delilah put her hand on Elspeth's forearm. "If de posh-rat lays a finger on you once, Samson and me will take care of him good."

Elspeth smiled wanly. The thought of the hapless couple harming a man like Glenlyon seemed almost comical.

"Hey, don't you worry," Delilah continued. "I already made a wax doll in his image and got my kids poking pins into his private areas every hour." She lowered her voice. "I hid a packet of sleeping herbs in the bottom of yer bag if he gets perverse again. Dere's some of my special pies for yer too, but don't take the powder by mistake."

A bubble of helpless laughter caught in Elspeth's throat even as the tears she was fighting back began to well in her eyes. "I *am* in trouble if your magic is the only thing I can depend on to save me."

Suddenly the thunderous vibration of a fist pounding against the side of the wooden van shocked them into silence. "Magic or not, I'd like to get you on that coach this morning, Miss Kildrummond," Niall said loudly.

Cold rage filled Elspeth as she struggled on with her cloak. "Tell Samson he shouldn't sell Ali Baba until he talks to the duke first." Her voice shook. "Not that any nodcock is going to buy him in his condition."

Delilah nodded glumly, her eyes widening in alarm as Niall banged on the van again. "Elspeth, I swear," she whispered. "I'll spit in a cock's mouth at midnight in all de graveyards we pass, and call up every dead spirit in Scotland to bedevil that man."

"Don't worry about me." Elspeth looked at her friend with a courageous resolve she prayed fervently wouldn't desert her when she came face to face with Niall again. "There's no person on earth who can make me turn back until I've learned for myself what cost Tormod his life, and that includes the famous Captain Glenlyon."

Twenty

Elspeth scrutinized Niall in dispassionate silence for several moments before approaching the strawberry mare Samson had obtained for her from a farmer outside Tarland. After the humiliation Glenlyon had subjected her to in the brothel, and the undeniable sensuality that had smoldered between them, she had hoped to heaven she would never spend another minute in his company. And now she was practically his captive.

The image of their interlocked figures reflected in the brothel mirror burned in the back of her mind. It undermined her efforts to walk past him as if he didn't exist. But no matter how she tried, she couldn't make herself forget the warm confusion of being crushed against his chest, the sensual play of his strong fingers on her shoulders, the tender seduction of the kiss he'd stolen in the summerhouse. The remembered sensations rippled over her skin like a summer breeze.

Flustered, annoyed with herself for following the pointless train of thought, she almost lost her footing as she hoisted herself into the saddle. Glenlyon didn't smile or say a word or offer to help her. In fact, she suspected he didn't even notice her. He appeared to stare past her to the moor. His shoulders were stretched in an unyielding line that reminded her of the suppressed strength he could summon at will.

But Niall noticed her, all right. He noticed her with

every rampant nerve ending that had remained in a perpetual state of arousal since their clash in Mrs. Grimble's "Finishing School." In fact, he ached with noticing her.

His impassive face masked the tumult of his private thoughts. He only pretended to ignore her struggle to secure her traveling bag and battered violin case on the saddle. He wasn't about to touch her again. Not on his life. The enticing memory of his mock seduction in the brothel had mocked him ever since, and he found his mouth suddenly dry with a desire that could never be quenched. An absurd, dangerous desire to tumble her to the mossy ground and finish the foreplay he'd started that morning.

Her cold fury challenged all the male impulses a man of his age was supposed to have mastered. She heightened his awareness of all his inadequacies and unexpressed needs to a painful degree. She made him feel so angry— and alive. Ah, yes, that was it. Far more potent than sexual attraction. She made him feel alive again.

Elspeth wound the reins around her fingers until her knuckles whitened. Her voice dripped icy scorn. "Well, are you going to snap a collar round my throat and lead me away?"

"A tempting thought. Is it necessary?"

She sniffed, deliberately not looking into his amused face. Obviously she had underestimated both his determination and greed for the money her father had offered for her return. Well, he wasn't the only one who could play dirty in this game.

She spurred her horse away from the encampment, a smile tightening her lips.

Niall wheeled the stallion around to follow her. "I don't trust that smile, Miss Kildrummond."

Elspeth didn't respond as she nudged her horse into an easy canter toward the open moor. Delilah and her children had gathered around the campfire to watch her leave, but the other gypsies, aside from a few apologetic glances,

refused to acknowledge her. Elspeth's confidence in her
ability to handle whatever lay ahead took a dizzying
plunge as she noticed Delilah's hand lift to the silver crucifix at her throat. Things had to look very bad for her
if her friend had to resort to not only magic but religion.

"Dammit," she heard Niall mutter as she cantered past
the last of the Romany *vardos.* "Don't ride so far ahead
of me."

She spurred the horse forward, faster, toward the beck-
oning freedom of the moors. Heavy autumn mist brushed
her burning face and enshrouded the fallen boulders that
flanked the path. Niall's angry voice was absorbed into
the void she left behind.

To her delight the sturdy young mare rose to the challenge.

"Yes," she whispered, leaning low with her hair stream-
ing loose. "Let's take him on a wild, wild, ride."

Her heartbeat accelerated as if in rhythm with the
horse's hooves. The possibility of escape tantalized her,
made her reckless. Why not? Why not? She glanced over
her shoulder. Exhilaration sang through her veins.

Glenlyon had fallen behind, the mist enveloping his
dark figure in a cloak of invisibility. He might be a world-
famous hunter, but he was no horseman. In fact, she was
tempted to believe she could outride him, outhide him.

The craggy hills ahead promised shelter. The waves of
pearlescent mist offered protection. It didn't matter that
there was only the faintest hope she'd get away; she would
thoroughly enjoy making him earn her father's money.

After twenty minutes of riding hard, she slowed the
mare and listened to the silence. A family of crows cawed
from a distant hilltop cross, noting her approach. Her erratic breathing eased as she studied her options for escape.
To ride along the open ridge would be inviting attention.
Her best chance was to skirt the moor and find a burn
to follow, hoping the boggy soil would absorb her tracks.

Even if she didn't lose Glenlyon for long, she could conceivably make them miss the coach.

She slid to her feet, easing the reins over the mare's neck to lead her. She decided to head for the purple-brown rise of hills to the west. For another ten minutes she believed herself safe, and she started to envision how she would spend the night, hidden in some dry cave with her cloak wrapped around her while she devoured the tasty potato-onion pies Delilah had packed in her bag.

She had almost reached the stone cross on the hill, where the crows were observing her with their unblinking black eyes. She felt her mouth begin to water, anticipating the taste of those pies. It wasn't even an hour since she'd abandoned Glenlyon, but with a sense of disquietude as she began to climb higher ground, she realized the mist was thinning out. With a pair of field glasses, he could pick her out like a cat on a rooftop.

The crows watched her in silence. The mare trod with painstaking slowness between tussocks of fading gold broom and loose stones, hooves sucking into the spongy peat. The stillness wore on her nerves, that and the growing sensation of being observed.

She tilted her head back to stare at the crows. She imagined she saw a shadow fall below the Pictish cross. But the birds hadn't moved, coal-black eyes glinting with what she sensed to be some evil secret. Nasty things—carrion-eaters. She fought a sudden impulse to wheel the horse around.

Stupid. Fear, senseless fear. There was nothing to be afraid of on these moors. Not the weather, not the wild creatures. She coaxed the horse higher, refusing to indulge the niggling resistance of intuition that rose against her intellect.

And then she saw him.

She saw the thin plume of smoke curling upward from the cigar he had just lit while lounging back against the cross with his long legs outstretched. Perched on this desolate hilltop in all his dark beauty, he reminded her of a fallen archangel surveying the world with self-indulgent disdain.

"Well?" He smiled coldly, staring down at her with heavy-lidded eyes. He flicked the burning cigar back over his shoulder with his thumbnail, leaning forward as if to spring at her. "I've been waiting such a devilishly long time for you to get here, *chérie.*"

Delayed panic made her reckless. She knew it was too late, but she forced the horse around anyway, urging the frightened animal back down the hill as the crows burst into flight above the cross. She heard the heavy flapping of wings, their mocking caws, and the devil's own laughter drawing closer. And closer until its echoes shivered down her spine.

He caught her at the foot of the hill. His gray eyes promising punishment, he grabbed her by the wrist and wrenched her sideways off the horse onto his shoulders. Outraged, she dug the ball of her foot into the stirrup, but he only pulled her the harder. The force twisted the saddle to dangle beneath the mare's heaving belly.

"What are you doing?" she cried as he hoisted her higher and bore her back up toward the cross. He didn't answer. He curled his left arm around her neck like the iron collar she'd dared him to use earlier. With his right arm he held the calves of her legs imprisoned, his elbow thrust into her bottom.

She felt like a sacrificial calf being borne to a pagan altar.

"Mephistopheles!" she shouted with deafening fury into his ear.

He hesitated for a moment before continuing up the hill. She wriggled to break his hold. She struck at his face, his head, his throat, gratified when she finally clipped him in the jaw, and his mouth tightened. A steady hiss of pain escaped his gritted teeth.

"You've pushed me too far," he said with a quiet intensity that temporarily stilled her. "If we miss that coach and I arrive too late to meet my uncle, well, let's just say I wouldn't want to be in your place."

She was so humiliated, so angry, she would have killed him if she'd had a weapon. He was her father, he was George and Robert Campbell, and Francis Barron and Samson—all the men who had lied and tried to thwart and mold her with their arrogant male assumptions about how a woman should behave. All the men who had destroyed her confidence and fledgling attempts at independence.

But he was bolder than all those men combined.

Bolder, wilder, darker. She had known him a shorter time than the others, but in that brief interval, there had been moments, flashes of awful realization when she sensed they shared an inescapable bond, that something stronger than the force of their two personalities was drawing them together. He was the most infuriating, and fascinating, man she had ever met.

At the hilltop, he tumbled her down onto the plaid he'd laid out earlier. She sprang back onto her feet before he could finish removing his coat. Her eyes were dark with fear. He swore at her in French. She swore right back at him in the Gaelic learned in her grandfather's house.

He shoved her back down. Grasping handfuls of his shirt, she forced him to fall full-tilt on top of her. A little surprised at her strength, he used the weight of his body to hold her immobile before she could roll them down the hillside in an angry, adult parody of Jack and Jill.

And even in the midst of tussling with her, of having her pound her fists on his head, of pressing her flush to the plaid to subdue her, arms and legs flailing like the spokes of a wheel, Niall was acutely aware of how absurd they must look.

But he was out of control. His emotions had erupted like a fireworks display when she had run off on that mare into the mist. His anger was a clean, pure thing he understood. He only wished he knew why he was wasting his time trying to teach her the lessons she should have been taught at her father's knee a good decade ago.

Rachel. He told himself he was taking temporary responsibility for this handful of trouble as a sort of unspoken bargain with God that somewhere another stranger might intervene to save his sister from her own stubborn will, or God forbid, from a man like Francis Barron.

But Rachel and Francis Barron had nothing to do with the protective anger this woman made him feel, with the sexual dominance she made him ache to wield.

He reared back onto his knees, staring down into her white enraged face. "Get up," he said grimly.

"Go to Hades, you stupid dog!"

He pulled off his coat and flung it into the air. Elspeth's eyes widened. A vein began pulsing purple-blue in the pale hollow of her throat. "What . . . what are you going to do?"

He gripped her by the wrists and lifted her toward him, then swung her face-down over his outstretched knees before she could shake out of her shock to stop him.

"I'm going to do what your papa should have done years ago when he caught you smoking his pipe in the barn."

The calm determination in his voice made her shiver. Her papa, the barn. She had barely registered the distant memory than she felt Glenlyon thrust her skirts up over her head, and she realized he intended to spank her like a bairn. She wriggled around and shot to her feet, backing up against the cross.

"Don't you dare touch me again, you miserable per-

We've got your authors!

KENSINGTON CHOICE is the only club where you can find authors like Janelle Taylor, Shannon Drake, Rosanne Bittner, Penelope Neri and Phoebe Conn all in one place...

...and the only service that will deliver their romances direct to your home as soon as they are published—even before they reach the bookstores.

KENSINGTON CHOICE is also the only service that will give you a substantial guaranteed discount off the publisher's prices on every one of those romances.

That's right: Every month, the Editors at Zebra and Pinnacle select four of the newest novels by our bestselling authors and rush them straight to you, usually *before they reach the bookstores.* The publisher's prices for these romances range from $4.99 to $5.99—but they are always yours for the guaranteed low price of just $4.20, up to 30% off the publisher's price!

All books are sent on a 10-day free examination basis, and there is no minimum number of books to buy. (A postage and handling charge of $1.50 is added to each shipment.)

As your introduction to the convenience and value of KENSINGTON CHOICE, we invite you to accept

4 BOOKS FREE

The 4 books, worth up to $23.96, are our welcoming gift. You pay only $1 to help cover postage and handling.

Plus as a regular subscriber....you'll receive our free monthly newsletter, Zebra/Pinnacle Romance News which features author interviews, contests, and more!

To start your subscription to KENSINGTON CHOICE and receive your introductory package of 4 FREE romances, detach and mail the card at right *today.*

We have 4 FREE BOOKS for you
as your introduction to
KENSINGTON CHOICE
To get your FREE BOOKS, worth
up to $23.96, mail the card below.

FREE BOOK CERTIFICATE

As my introduction to your new KENSINGTON CHOICE reader's service, please send me 4 FREE historical romances (worth up to $23.96), billing me just $1 to help cover postage and handling. As a KENSINGTON CHOICE subscriber, I will then receive 4 brand-new romances to preview each month for 10 days FREE. I can return any books I decide not to keep and owe nothing. The publisher's prices for the KENSINGTON CHOICE romances range from $4.99 to $5.99, but as a subscriber I will be entitled to get them for just $4.20 per book or $16.80 for all four titles. There is no minimum number of books to buy, and I can cancel my subscription at any time. A $1.50 postage and handling charge is added to each shipment.

Name _____

Address _____ Apt._____

City _____ State_____ Zip_____

Telephone (____) _____

Signature_____

(If under 18, parent or guardian must sign)

Subscription subject to acceptance. Terms and prices subject to change.

KP1095

We have
4
FREE
Historical
Romances
for you!

(worth up
to $23.96!)

Details inside!

son." Her voice increased in volume. "You secondhand-shop swine. You—you effing bawdyhouse pimp."

He blinked, lowering his head. He hadn't made a dent in her red-hot temper, but she had done terrifying things to his. He took a deep breath and stood to tower over her, horrified at how close he had come to emotional anarchy. He was amazed to discover there was that much passion left inside him. This woman had managed to penetrate every defense he'd spent years struggling to erect.

"Don't run away from me again," he warned her.

"You b—"

He silenced her with a look, then pushed around her to snatch his coat from atop the cross where it had landed. *Dieu,* this was exactly the stuff that had sent Archie Harper's gossip-hungry readers to the newsstands in droves. He could see the headline now: FRENCH SOLDIER OF FORTUNE SPANKS SCOTTISH HEIRESS BENEATH SACRED CROSS!

"—billiard-table fornicator!" she concluded at the top of her very forceful lungs, trembling from shoulder to toe while tears of anger etched tracks down her face.

"And don't swear at me either," he added with an infuriating smirk, turning away from her.

A stone hit him on the ear, followed by the colorful invective: "Filthy piss-pot son of a French whore!"

He pivoted slowly, his face darkening, but the incredible woman held her ground, tempting him to toss her over his lap to finish what he had started.

"Some people have to learn their lessons the hard way, Elspeth. Apparently you're one of them." He gripped his coat to his chest before he could destroy the effect of what he'd almost done by brushing the hair from her tear-stained face. "I'm sorry I lost my temper." He softened his tone. "Would you like to wash your face in the burn down there in the moor? We've missed the damn coach anyway."

"Would I like to wash my face in the burn, he asks?

Would I like to *wash* my face in the burn? No, Glenlyon, I'd like to drown you in it. I'd like to put my foot down on your dark head and hold it under the water until your eyes pop out like marbles, until your tongue lolls out of your mouth, until—"

"That will be all, Elspeth." He started backing down the hill to his horse, waiting behind a massive fall of rocks. "Your papa didn't pay me enough to swallow your insults."

She rushed after him, her face burning with indignation as she scrambled down the stony incline. "My papa didn't pay you to abuse me either!"

He fingered the scratches on his neck, his ringing ear. "It's a matter of contention which one of us has suffered the most abuse."

"I'm going to tell my papa what you almost did to me."

He slid sideways to the foot of the hill on the insoles of his boots, whistling softly for his horse, pretending not to care that Elspeth looked as if she could thrust a dagger through his heart. He didn't know what to do now. He didn't even know what he had hoped to gain by threatening to spank her. He didn't know anything except that he had lost control, it was all her fault, and suddenly, instead of making things better, he'd made them worse.

And they'd missed the last coach for a week. Now he was either stuck with dragging the impossible woman along with him, or losing what would probably be his only chance to meet his uncle.

She strode up before him and punched him on the chest. His face like granite, he caught her fist in his hand as she reached to strike him again.

"Good," he said. "Tell your papa what I did. Tell Archie Harper too while you're at it. You can even send my mother a letter describing my misdeeds, and I guarantee she'll be horrified, but it might take years to reach her in the jungle."

"I'll tell the police you abducted me, Glenlyon. Let go of my hand."

"I'll tell the police about the body if you do," he said before he could stop himself, and at the stricken look that crossed her face, he wished he could retract the hollow threat.

Au diable—the devil—he thought in alarm as he recalled the image of her standing before him in the hall in her bloodstained nightdress, there *had* been a body. Damn if the unguarded guilt on her face didn't finally confirm it.

He raised her hand to his mouth, and grazed her knuckles with a kiss, confused by the concern he felt. "Forgive me if I frightened you," he said, more uncertain now than ever what he should do. Despite everything, he felt compelled to help her.

Her voice shook with hurt and humiliation. "You did, and I'm not ever, ever going to forgive you."

"Then that is your choice," he said gravely, "but if you run away from me again, so help me God, Elspeth, it will be worse next time."

She wrenched her hand from his. "How could it possibly be any worse?" she whispered. And yet she had a rough idea, alone with this unscrupulous man on the moors, in his power, so to speak. Yes, Archie Harper would appreciate the scandalous aspects of her dilemma. HEADSTRONG SCOTTISH HEIRESS ABDUCTED BY DISHONORED JUNGLE SOLDIER AND RAVISHED UNDER ANCIENT CROSS!

She made an unconscious sound of distress in her throat, stumbling back a step. "You'll be sorry you did this, Glenlyon."

He shoved his arms into his coat, his face harsh with honest disagreement. "I'm sorry about a lot of things in my life, Elspeth. One more won't make much difference at this point."

Twenty-one

"I am hating this place that called Scotlands," Hasim announced to Elspeth by way of initiating a friendly conversation as they rode abreast on the moorland ridge behind Niall. "Very nice peoples, but very bad weather."

Elspeth stared grimly ahead. She didn't want to like Glenlyon's valet, she really didn't, but he'd ignored all her attempts at overt hostility; he didn't understand, or pretended not to understand her naked insults. In fact, he seemed determined to win her confidence, and she was damned if he hadn't succeeded. Besides, it wasn't in her nature to hold her tongue for long.

"I'll tell you what I hate, Hasim. I hate that big coldhearted snake riding right ahead of us. I hate him more than I hate midges and cold lumpy porridge."

Hasim gaped at her in genuine astonishment. "You hates Tuan Captain?" He shook his head as if he could not believe such an emotional aberration. "All ladies, babies, and animals loves Tuan. It embarrassing how much the ladies loves him."

"I'm quite sure," Elspeth said crisply, then fell silent as the object of universal appeal himself wheeled around to wait for them.

"Interesting conversation?" Niall asked, glancing at Elspeth and then Hasim.

"We talking about bad weather," Hasim replied, in a high, unconvincing voice.

Elspeth didn't even bother to acknowledge him. She kept gazing far ahead to the dark thicket of trees in the distance. So far they'd avoided the main road, and Niall had yet to tell her their destination. The ridge track they were following had begun to dip into a deeply wooded ravine where traces of late morning mist drifted from a swift-flowing river. The dank aroma of humus rose into the cool air to blend pleasantly with the perfume of pine.

They'd passed only one other person in hours, an elderly shepherd coming down from the hills. Elspeth had been strongly tempted to throw herself at the man's mercy and explain how she was being abducted by a madman, but Glenlyon had given her such an intimidating look that she had lost her nerve.

I'll tell the police about the body if you do.

He didn't know anything about that night. How could he? It was just an empty threat to hang over her head. Still, she wouldn't put it past him to turn his hunting talents on finding out the truth just to satisfy his curiosity. Sooner or later someone would discover what had happened.

Her gaze lit suddenly on a small tangle of twigs to the left of the track. The patteran of passing gypsies? Yes, yes, it was. Her heart beating hard, she eased off the mare and pretended to walk ahead to stretch her legs, all the while studying the track for the secret Romany messages left by traveling bands to help other fellow gypsies.

SMALL FARMHOUSE TWO MILES AHEAD
HIDDEN IN HILLS
WOMAN IS A WIDOW—FRIENDLY TO GYPSIES

"Looking for something, Miss Kildrummond?" Niall asked, dismounting to peer over her shoulder.

Elspeth whirled around, feeling hemmed in by the two horses and the latent power of Glenlyon's large body. "I was making sure I didn't walk into a—a bog."

"A bog? Really?"

"Yes, really. The ground is getting damper by the inch, Glenlyon. An idiot couldn't miss it, let alone a man who's built his reputation on studying such things."

"Would you like to show me exactly how a native daughter goes about deducing the safety of the ground? I'm humble when it comes to learning something new."

"No, I wouldn't," she replied evenly, swinging beneath her horse's neck to remount. "But I would like something to eat and possibly a chance to wash behind that waterfall."

"Still a bit upset with me, *chérie?*" he asked softly.

When she refused to answer, he glanced down at the falls, where white frothy water was splashing against a basin of smooth gray boulders. He frowned.

"It looks damn cold for a wash if you ask me."

"Some of us are rather particular about our cleanliness, Captain."

He grinned, eyeing her muddied dress, her multicolored hair. "It's a very well-kept secret."

He hesitated and then walked to the edge of the track, his feet a centimeter from the configuration of twigs and feathers and dried heather the gypsies had left. Elspeth held her breath.

"I'll just climb out to those rocks and rinse my hair in the falls. As you said yourself, Delilah did a hideous job of dyeing it."

"I don't know," he said slowly. "Your papa might not like it if his little princess comes home with a bad case of the sniffles."

"He'd die of shame if I walked into his house looking like this."

Niall looked down unexpectedly at the ground.

"I don't know," he repeated. "You have a mane of hair like Rapunzel. It could take all day to dry."

She was already dashing past him and clambering down

the ravine, skirts, cloak, petticoats swept up in her arms. Niall glanced back at Hasim before hurrying after her.

"This wouldn't be another ploy to escape me, would it?" he shouted over the sound of the cascading waters.

"Captain Glenlyon," she shouted back, "as far as I can tell, we're at least fifteen miles from the nearest village. I'd have to be entirely stupid to think I could outrun you on open moorland, now wouldn't I?"

Niall braced his feet against a clump of bracken and slid down toward her. She was standing amidst a tangle of reeds, struggling to remove her cloak. Her face was flushed with impatience; he could make out the shape of her body, its tantalizing contours, through the damp blue silk of the traveling gown she wore. His throat tightened with involuntary longing as he remembered the luscious fullness of her breasts, the honey and cream smoothness of her skin that morning in the brothel.

"Do you want something, Glenlyon?"

Only you, he thought, but he didn't say a word; he just swallowed and felt heat pool in his groin as she stretched her arms over her head to toss her cloak at him.

"This had better not be a trick," he warned her as he crushed the blue-violet wool to his chest.

She spun around, her skirts snagging on the reeds to reveal a bare muscular leg to his scrutiny. She had obviously removed her stockings after he had tossed her over his knee; he'd thought at the time how torn and dirty they'd looked, but now he could only stare, astonished that the sight of this frustrating woman's naked ankle was arousing him.

"Stop looking at my feet!" she yelled. "Go away."

"No."

She ducked into the reeds, her face flaming at his long unwavering stare. "You ought to be ashamed of yourself, Glenlyon."

"If I had a shilling for every time I've heard that."

"Turn your head."

He crouched down, chin resting on his fist, and continued to study her with unabashed enjoyment. Suddenly he wanted to know all of her womanly secrets, to learn the private scent of her flesh, the texture of her skin. He wanted to bite her neck, her bottom, and to smother her rude mouth in kisses when she climaxed beneath him. He wanted to seduce her in a hundred ways, to work whatever magic he could conjure to make her his. He would use every sexual and emotional technique he had learned from his courtesan friends and past lovers to bend her to his will. And then he would pleasure her beyond her wildest imaginings.

"Are you going to sit there all day staring at me like a half-wit, Glenlyon?"

He gave her a lazy smile. "Perhaps."

All his life he had searched for a woman exactly like her, but it wasn't until this shocking instant, as he looked down into her sweet wrathful face, that he realized it. When was the last time a lover had touched his heart, or made him laugh? *Bonté divine,* when had he ever gotten hard listening to a woman insult him?

He sighed, letting the spell of dangerous temptation dissipate. Elspeth's cool resignation to returning home was too uncharacteristic to trust. Of course she would try to run away again. He adored her animal cunning, but he'd be glad enough when they parted company.

"I'm going to be watching you through that waterfall," he told her sternly, then, "No, don't move, *no,* get away from that yellow grass—"

She took a few inadvertent steps back only to shriek in alarm as she began sinking into the shallow bogmire concealed beneath the tussocks. Cold muck sucked at her bare ankles and gushed into the folds of her skirts. She grasped a handful of reeds, but they slipped through her fingers. Within seconds she was immersed up to her knees.

Then Niall was standing on the solid ground before her. His lips twitched into a wicked grin. "There's a saying in the Orient—'From the dark mud the beautiful lotus blossoms.' "

"Well, we're not in the Orient, you pea-brain, we're in Scotland, and while you're standing there grinning yourself silly, I'm sinking up to my arse in freezing muck."

He clucked his tongue. "Your language is foul even by my standards, *chère.*"

"Oh? You mean my arse is good enough for you to wallop, but not for me to discuss?"

He leaned across his knee, his eyes dancing. "I thought you knew how to detect a bog."

"And I would have noticed it too, if you hadn't made me so nervous with that horrid leer. No. Never mind. Don't bother helping me out. I suspect I'm better off sinking."

He had hopped down toward her, feet planted on a tangle of roots, and grasped her under the armpits to pluck her out of the mud. Her heart was beating in triple time. She heard him grunt with exaggerated effort as he hefted her higher and shook her free like a rag doll.

"What a mess," he said quietly.

She couldn't deny it. Mud was sliding down her petticoats and plopping onto his boots, adhering his buckskin trousers to her skirts. She shivered and deflected her gaze. She couldn't believe the strange sensations that assailed her, the burning heat where her breasts pressed into his coat, the icy slime caking on her legs, the current of something dangerous and delicious that passed between the pair of them.

She inhaled slowly. "Put me down."

"Back into the bog?"

"Yes. Put me back into the bog. Hang me on a tree. Just leave me alone, Glenlyon."

He pulled her closer, backing up clumsily until he walked them into a boulder and sat down with her still entrapped in his arms. A shiver of pleasure darted through him at the pressure of her soft breasts against his forearm. She twisted around. He grunted and gripped her harder, cupping her buttocks through her skirts to hold her still.

"Do you think you could trust me, Elspeth?"

"Trust . . . *you?* That's a laugh, isn't it, you trying to blister and then fondle my bum while asking me to trust you?"

He grinned. He was moving his large hands up and down her back, learning the enticing shape of her through her skirts with a bold familiarity that rendered her speechless. But what was even worse, she *liked* the false security of being protected, comforted, cradled against his big warm body.

"You have incredible gall, Glenlyon, asking me to trust you."

He had an incredible erection, too, and he was afraid to move another inch before his rampant impulses got the better of him. He shifted her onto his other knee.

"I don't think I've ever had a woman who was such a mess, or who had such an impertinent tongue."

"You're not 'having' one now, at least not if I'm given any say in the matter."

His unabashed gaze drifted down her throat, over her breasts, the tantalizing arch of her lower body where her bottom pressed into his lap. "You're going to run away from me again, aren't you?" he asked, sounding resigned to it.

She swallowed and fell still, aware of a trail of invisible fire smoldering beneath the surface of her skin where his gaze had touched her. "Of course I am, Glenlyon."

He sighed quietly at her too-disarming frankness. "Tell

me what really happened that night when I met you in the hallway."

"I—I'm getting a terrible cramp in my legs from lying across—"

"Tell me." His grip on her tightened. "Why was there blood on your gown? Was it your own, *ma chère?* Tell me what was so important it sent you running out into the rainstorm with a knife."

"I bought it from the gypsies."

"Tell me," he demanded, wondering why it even mattered to him as much as it did, how she could lie one second and break his heart with her honesty another.

She moistened her lips, closed her eyes as the graphic memory of Tormod's death destroyed the unwelcome sense of intimacy building between them. "But I told you before, Glenlyon, there was a stable door banging in the wind."

"And I didn't believe it then, either." He gave her a scathing look, then thrust her back unsteadily on her feet. "You have five minutes to wash yourself."

"Ten." She swept up her muddied skirts with a flourish, her heart hammering at how foolishly tempted she'd been to tell him the truth for one reckless moment. "And don't watch me through your field glasses either," she added impertinently.

Twenty-two

Twenty minutes passed, and Niall knew she was gone. Lying flat on his back with his hands folded under his head, he stared up at the spiked fingers of the pine branches overhead. He figured he'd give her a good hour of hiking across the moor, just to wear her out, before he started after her. He grinned at the thought of another clash.

Niall needed that hour too. He needed to empty his mind, regain control of his body, the erotic urges engendered by the memory of her standing naked behind the falls. He wanted to make love to her, yes, but he felt a compulsion equally as strong to help her, to understand her. He wanted to protect her from whatever painful secret she was trying to hide. He ached to earn her trust and couldn't say why. He wasn't prone to kindly impulses.

"It has to be because she reminds me of Rachel," he said aloud.

"Yes," Hasim agreed complacently, engrossed in peeling back the skin of a toadstool he'd picked.

Niall frowned and sat up, brushing pine needles off his back. "She doesn't trust me."

"I not blames her, Tuan. You very mean sometimes. Your heart is like volcano lava that was once full of fires of life and now is stone."

Snorting, Niall fed a twig into the small fire they had

built. "You know, Hasim, you could at least pretend to show me a modicum of respect."

"Respect? Huh. How I respect you, Tuan, when you not even married mans?"

Niall settled back down on his plaid and pulled Elspeth's battered tapestry bag into his lap. "Look, she forgot her bag and violin case. Now what do you suppose the well-heeled runaway deems important enough to cart around?"

"I not know, Tuan. Remembering her room, I afraid to look."

Niall grimaced as he emptied the bag's contents onto the plaid. A hoof pick and a silver-chased hairbrush, a rose-scented soapball studded with lint, several lumps of rancid scone, a racing schedule, five shriveled apples, then—

"Mon Dieu," he breathed softly, running his fingers over the jewel-gripped hilt of the dirk that fell out of its worn leather scabbard. "What a beauty this is. I never really got a close look at it that night."

Hasim hunkered down beside him, his eyes aglow with appreciation. "It very old weapon. Very powerfuls. But it is *hantu,* Tuan, haunted."

"Haunted or not, it must be precious to her," Niall said reflectively. "In fact, I don't believe she'd have deliberately left it behind."

"What you mean, Tuan?"

Niall rose slowly to his feet. A worried frown furrowed his brow as he scanned the shadowed stalker's path that wound through the trees. "Ride ahead to the woods and see if she's hiding there," he instructed Hasim quietly. "I'm going back down to the water. Damn if I wasn't so convinced she'd run away that I never considered someone else might have happened to find her."

* * *

Her wickedness must be stopped.

Francis Barron is rumored to have drowned his own betrothed . . . drowned his own betrothed . . . drowned . . .

They say he doesna have the desires of a normal man.

The remembered voices rang like discordant bells in Niall's brain, mingled chillingly in his blood. As he careened down the rocky embankment, he pictured Elspeth bound and gagged, snagged between the submerged rocks. He pictured Barron's bony hands closing around her throat. He imagined finding her body floating under the falls, and his heart hammered wildly against his ribs. He should never have left her unguarded for even a second. He swore in self-contempt.

He kicked off his boots and sent them flying into the reeds. He had almost unbuttoned his trousers when he spotted her. Wrenching a comb through her horrible tangle of hair with one hand, grasping fistfuls of reeds with the other, she was pulling herself by fits up the embankment several yards to his right. An indescribable emotion twisted his heart.

She glanced up, frowning at the sight of him. His lungs felt as if they'd collapsed with relief, expelling a breath that took the last of his energy from him. "What the hell have you been doing?" he demanded. "I said five minutes."

"Have you ever tried getting dressed with nothing but a screen of reeds for modesty?" she asked. "No, of course not. You probably pranced about in the altogether like Pan in your jungle swamps and enjoyed it."

In spite of the fact that only moments ago he was wild with worry over her disappearance, Niall couldn't resist a nasty smile at the sight of her puffed silk muslin petticoats floating downriver behind her. "Missing something, *chère?*"

She jerked her head around, panic widening her eyes.

"Mother of God, I stretched them out to dry on a boulder!
Well, don't just stand there grinning, Glenlyon. Do something. Rescue is supposed to be your line of work, isn't
it?"

"Not underwear." He climbed down toward her, grasping her forearm to guide her up over the rocks. "Rescuing
reckless women who lose their drawers is another matter."

She snorted at that and allowed him to help her, her
face turning purple when she realized what he was holding in his other hand. "What the blazes were you doing
in my bag, Glenlyon? Lord, you have to be the nosiest
man I've ever met!"

He released her and danced back up the embankment,
chuckling as she chased him through the thin stand of
trees where his small fire still smoldered. Damn him, Elspeth thought. The warmth of the alluring fire and the
fact that she'd forgotten the dirk, had prevented her from
making good on her impulsive plan to escape.

He twisted onto his elbow in a half-reclining sprawl on
the plaid, taking a bite out of one of her apples before
she descended on him. Damp hair showering him with
chilly beads of water, she swooped down to reassemble
her belongings in the bag.

"I hope you haven't eaten all the pies, Glenlyon!"

"Pies?" He sat up abruptly, staring at her bag with renewed interest. "You have pies in there too?"

She ignored him and tugged his hairbrush out from under his hip. His senses exploded at her nearness, her skin
and hair smelled so fresh and clean, he had to close his
eyes to subdue a violent longing to pull her down beside
him.

Falling back onto his elbow, he allowed himself the
safer indulgence of watching a string of water droplets
trickle down her throat into the cleft of her breasts where
the bodice of her blue silk gown had been carelessly left
undone. He swallowed the bite of apple, not tasting its

sourness. He was afraid to move a muscle, not trusting himself, aware he was only a heartbeat from making a few of his dark fantasies about her a reality.

"You're staring at me again," she said with an admonishing sigh. "Didn't anyone ever teach you any manners?"

"My mother would be deeply offended if she heard that."

"Then I suppose it's a good thing the poor woman is so far away and saved the embarrassment of witnessing what you've become."

"Hasim is far away too," he said quietly. "I sent him off to the main road in search of you, and now we're all alone."

"Alone?" she said, her fingers stilling at her laces.

He eased up higher onto his elbow, his deep voice frank with desire. "Yes, alone. Shall we call a truce, do you think?"

She dragged in a breath, feeling the sexual energy he exuded reach out and wrap her in invisible coils that seemed to lure her toward him. A smile touched his lips, as if he were privy to her thoughts, his effect on her. Slowly he let his eyes travel over her, not bothering to suppress the seductive heat simmering in their depths. Elspeth pressed her hand even closer to her speeding heart.

"Well?" he prompted with a sleepy grin. "Shall we call a truce or not?"

She had no idea what he was talking about. All she knew was that suddenly the bones in her body seemed to liquefy. Her breasts strained against her damp clothes with a sense of unaccustomed heaviness. The muscles in her belly contracted with a quivering warmth she would have liked to label anger, but what she secretly feared was the stirring of a wicked excitement. Heaven help her. He was melting her with his eyes.

"I-I would have shared the apples with you if you'd asked," she murmured in a nervous attempt to break the mood. "If you're really hungry, I suppose I could give you one of the pies Delilah made for you—" She slanted him a curious glance. "You haven't felt any queer sensations since we left the encampment, by the way? No little twinges in certain parts of your body?"

A deep chuckle rumbled in his chest. "Do you really want to know about the sensations I'm experiencing in certain parts of my body?"

"Only if they're fatal," she said drolly.

He leaned into her. Unnerved by the devilish glitter in his eye, by the sultry flush of warmth through her own body, she inched back to the edge of the plaid.

But the damage had already been done to Niall's nervous system. He tossed the apple core over his shoulder and clasped her by the wrists, slowly drawing her between his long buckskin-clad legs.

"What if your friend's magic backfires?" he asked wickedly, his hands encircling her waist. "What if she only succeeds in strengthening my 'certain parts'? You'd be in trouble then, eh, *chère?*"

Warm eddies of forbidden excitement swept over her. "I think I'm in enough trouble as it is," she said, swallowing dryly.

"I want you," he said without the slightest hint of humor in his voice.

She shook her head in mute denial, her heart lodging like a stone in her throat, but when he withdrew his hands from her waist and lowered her to the plaid, she didn't protest. She tensed her shoulders and tried to breathe over the wild palpitations of her pulse, taking in the exhilarating scent of his skin, musk and smoke and the fresh tang of the pine needles he had slept on. When he kissed her, pinning her down beneath him with a soft groan of anticipation, she felt a flash of panic, but it dissolved, washed into the waves of erotic abandonment that immersed her.

She lifted her hands to his neck and closed her eyes,

drugged insensible with desire as his tongue flicked against hers and penetrated deeply into her mouth. Moisture seeped from the aching place between her thighs, shaming her. She made a half-hearted effort to rise, but her trembling muscles disobeyed the fading objections of her mind. The hot rush of blood through her body ruthlessly obliterated what remained of her resistance.

And then it didn't matter. Then he was pressing his lower body to hers, rubbing his hard shaft against the apex of her thighs. An answering heat flared in the pit of her belly. She moaned against his mouth. She dropped her hands to her sides, shivering at the raw assault of sexual awareness he was so easily awakening inside her.

"Glenlyon."

He was lost. He was wild at the feel of her soft yielding body under his, her sweet plump breasts, the warm hollow of her thighs that welcomed his rhythmic thrusting. He plunged his hands into the sensual tumble of her hair, his fingers massaging the taut muscles of her scalp. She gasped at the pleasure. Her breath quickened. *Dieu,* she excited him.

"How sweet you are," he murmured, trailing a strand of burning kisses down her delicate jaw to her throat. "Let me look at your breasts."

Her eyes flew open. "For God's sake, Glenlyon," she said, struggling up onto her elbow. "What a thing to ask. What if Hasim comes back to see us groping at each other like a pair of peasants?"

"He's at least a mile away by now. A pair of peasants, indeed. Here, put my coat over you if it makes you feel better."

"No—take that ugly old thing off me. It probably has bugs if it came from a loanshop."

He looked insulted. "Only the evening coat was borrowed. For your engagement party, I might add."

"My engagement party," she murmured sadly, falling back against the plaid.

"Well, don't let's reminisce about it now." His voice held a note of selfish urgency, and he kissed her hard on the mouth, as if by not mentioning George's name, she wouldn't remember that formally she belonged to another man. "Concentrate on us."

"Us?" she whispered, searching his face.

"Yes." He stared down at her. "On you and me. We've had a special bond from the beginning, *non?*"

His heart hammering, he worked loose the silk bindings of her gown and buried his face in the bounty of her breasts, rubbing his cheek against her silky pink nipple. A moan of ragged longing broke in his throat. He'd planned only to play with her, tease her, kiss her, but suddenly he couldn't control the elemental urges pounding through his blood, the fierce need to make her his before reality could intervene. The balance of power had shifted. He was under her enchantment.

"God help me," he said tightly, raising his gaze in a desperate plea to hers. She looked too luscious lying beneath him. Her eyes were dark with desire, her breasts lushly heavy with arousal. Longing pierced his heart. With his weight braced on his wrists, he flicked his tongue to first one pouty nipple and then another, drawing the engorged peak between his teeth, lust flooding his loins at the breathless little gasps of arousal that escaped her.

She gripped a fistful of his shirt. "That's enough, Glenlyon," she whispered.

He shook his head, looking tortured, intent, hell-bent on conquest. "I need to feel your flesh against me," he said without apology. "Put my coat over your shoulders, Elspeth. You're shaking, and your hair is still wet."

She was shaking, but less from cold than from the aching sweetness swirling through her and the shocking urges that inundated her senses. Even when she felt the intimate brush of his strong brown hand against her bare ankle, his long fingers sliding up her calf to the moist delta between her legs, she didn't utter a word to discourage him.

Oh, no. She just melted. She held her breath. She waited.

Every nerve ending in her traitorous body tingled in unashamed suspense, caught in the spell of his seduction. Every muscle contracted in expectation as he parted the slit of her drawers and eased his forefinger into the slick warmth of her sensitive passage.

He withdrew his finger, then sank it back between the plush folds of dewy flesh. She lunged upward, her body pulsing with the powerful sensations his skilled probing elicited.

"Glenlyon," she whispered, and this time the name was spoken more as an urgent appeal than a refusal.

He dropped onto his side, resting his face on her inner thigh. Elspeth sank back onto the plaid with a soft moan of mortification as she realized he was studying her exposed woman's flesh with dark fascination.

"Niall," she whispered uncertainly.

"You're beautiful, Elspeth. Every inch of you is beautiful."

He drove his finger deeper, relentless in his quest to strip her of all her inhibitions. He rubbed his thumb against the hooded nub hidden below her fleece of curls, savoring the helpless shiver of surrender she gave.

"This is what you've needed all along, isn't it?" he asked, his voice a murmur of sensual enjoyment. *"Mon Dieu,* how soft and wet you are in there."

She arched into his hand, eyes wide with a need he was all too tempted to fulfill. That sweet bewitchment had grown stronger, rendering her incapable of all but the involuntary tremors shuddering upward from where he teased her.

"This should be me inside you," he said hoarsely, raising up again to kiss her on the mouth while he continued to coax her toward that tantalizing edge. "Open your legs even wider, Elspeth. Soak my fingers with your sweetness."

She sobbed into his mouth as the first wild pulsations of pleasure rippled through her. Burying her face in his shoulder, she felt his free hand cup her bottom as she rocked against his hand. Then he was kissing her neck, her hair, her breasts again. They were laughing, and she sighed in selfish contentment when he tucked his coat around her, then reached behind him for her traveling bag to pillow her head.

"I can't believe we went that far," she whispered, her eyes lowered in demure amusement.

He smiled morosely. "I can't believe we didn't go farther."

"I should have stopped you sooner."

He squinted up into the treetops. "All I can say is that it's a damn good thing this didn't happen in that brothel."

She sent him a mischievous grin. "I shouldn't think a man of your talents would let a minor inconvenience such as the lack of a bed deter you."

"Normally it wouldn't."

She sighed. "I know I shouldn't say this, Glenlyon. God knows you don't need any encouragement, but it was quite, well, it was quite wonderful."

He swallowed a groan, her careless admission arousing his desire for her all over again. "No, you shouldn't have said it," he admonished her sternly, "but thank you anyway."

"I find it difficult to detest you now, Glenlyon."

"Thank heavens."

"I never really did, you know."

He lowered his gaze. Studying her impish face, its glow of satisfaction fading into a becoming flush, he picked up a pine needle and tickled her on the nose. His heart had filled with a strange heaviness that had nothing to do with physical need. "Truce?" he asked softly.

"Hmmm. Perhaps."

"How about sealing it with one of those pies you're hoarding in your bag?"

She nodded slowly and reached up behind her for the bag, the movement casually languid, bringing her body up against his. For a dangerous moment, Niall thought he was going to lose the battle for self-possession, after all. His craving for sexual completion twisted like a knife in his gut, a physical ache intensified by her wanton dishevelment, the musky perfume of her that clung to his skin, her unguarded softness. She was audacious and adorable.

She brushed his inner thigh with her elbow as she leaned across his lap to pass him the bag. He sucked in a sharp breath and swore. Flustered, Elspeth snatched her hand away; the contents of the bag tumbled out onto the plaid: apples, the pies wrapped in brown paper, the jeweled dirk, slipping from its frayed scabbard to fall on the dark wool.

She sat up slowly, her gaze transfixed on the dirk. *Remember.* She closed her fingers around the grip, unaware of her appealing half-nakedness as Glenlyon's coat slipped off her shoulders. Unaware of the concern replacing the desire in his eyes. Unaware that the horror in her mind was etched starkly on her face.

She looked up after several moments, but Niall knew she didn't see him. No, her focus had turned inward to that place he couldn't reach.

"Elspeth." His voice had become urgent. He seized hold of her shoulders to shake her out of her trance.

There it was again in her eyes. That repressed horror, that secret she wouldn't share with him. He could help if she'd let him, but she wouldn't. Dammit.

"Elspeth," he said again, gripping her harder because

he could feel her fear even more keenly than he had that night. He could feel her fear because they had just shared something wonderful and exciting, and even though the sight of that dirk had spoiled the passionate spontaneity of the moment, even though he was so stiff with wanting her his trousers felt like a tent, he knew that the beautiful wildness between them had passed.

She released the dirk and pushed his arms away. "You have to let me go, Glenlyon."

And he knew she wasn't talking about this moment. No, she expected him to let her ride away again on her dangerous quest, with Francis Barron at her heels like a bloodhound, and the musk of her arousal so fresh on his skin he felt lightheaded with lust.

"No. No. I'm not letting you go. Don't even ask me. My uncle is waiting for me on his deathbed—*Dieu,* I'll probably arrive too late for his damned funeral. You're mad. If I don't make you go home, you'll end up getting hurt, and I don't need that on my conscience."

She tossed her head. *"Your* conscience. Your obligations. Well, has it ever occurred to you I have my own responsibilities to fulfill?"

He lifted the dirk and held it between them, his voice hard. "And those responsibilities have something to do with this?"

"Please," she said in a dry whisper.

"I'm confused, Elspeth," he continued harshly. "Perhaps if you'd been honest with me from the start, I might be a little more sympathetic."

Her voice shook with emotion. "It belonged to my grandfather."

"I heard a pistol fired that night, didn't I?"

She stared at him in anguished silence.

"Someone was killed that night, and you know who, don't you, Elspeth?"

She clasped her hands in her lap to control their trembling.

Frustrated by her refusal to trust him, Niall tossed down the dirk and caught her wrists. "If you did kill someone, then I'll wager you had a damn good reason, and I understand why you're trying to run away. I know what it's like to be accused with no chance of self-defense."

Elspeth stared up into his dark compelling face. A humorless smile started slowly forming on her lips as she realized what he was leading to. Dear God above, did he really suspect she was an escaped murderess? Had the deluded man been worrying that she'd slip the dirk into his ribs the whole time he was seducing her, dangerous female felon that she was? It had to have put a perverse edge on his pleasure.

"Can I truly trust you, Glenlyon?"

"On my soul, Elspeth. I swear it."

She leaned forward, suppressing the pang of guilt that his earnest face evoked. "All right then." She drew a deep breath. "I'll tell you everything—yes, you guessed the truth. I did murder someone. I—oh, God, it's so bad, Glenlyon. I'm so ashamed to admit it. I lost complete control of my faculties."

Niall swallowed and squeezed her hand, straining to hear her low penitent voice over the soft roaring of the waterfall and the sick fear throbbing in his temples. "It's all right," he said, hoping it was. "Believe me. I've probably heard much, much worse, and I'll help you, but you have to tell me everything first. Tell me who."

She gave a soft despairing sob that sounded almost like a giggle. *La pauvre petite,* he thought in alarm. Just discussing this makes the poor little thing half-hysterical.

"Who, Elspeth?" he urged.

"I—I shot . . . the gardener."

Niall blinked. "The *gardener?*"

"In . . . the summerhouse." She dropped her gaze, sud-

denly afraid that even though he deserved such an outlandish lie, he wouldn't appreciate the humor in it. "I-I
can't say any more."

"The man attacked you?" he asked quietly, his hold on
her hands so tight, her fingers lost their feeling.

"No-o-o. Not exactly. He—he attacked the ivy vines
that grow under my bedroom window as I was climbing
down in the dark."

"Your gardener works at midnight?" he inquired dryly.

"Well, he'd been put off schedule by the party, and he'd
had to help string up all the lanterns." She peeped up at
him through her lowered eyelashes, suddenly realizing by
his skeptical frown that she was rapidly losing his sympathy. "I almost broke my neck, Glenlyon. I'd warned him
time and time again not to clip my vines, and when I
caught him out in the summerhouse a little later—I, well,
I lost control of my senses."

"What did you do with the body?" he said in a clipped
voice.

Elspeth slowly summoned the nerve to look him directly
in the eye, ashamed of herself but unable to keep the lie
from growing. She cleared her throat.

"Samson and I dumped it in the river."

"Then you're a very dangerous woman, aren't you?" he
asked softly.

She began to squirm under the pressure of his dark
stare. "I prefer to think of myself as desperate, Glenlyon."

"And you're an imaginative if terrible liar." Giving her
a droll smile that acknowledged his temporary defeat, he
released her hands and glanced distractedly toward the
road. "You ought to consider writing some of Archie Harper's lurid stories for a living."

"But it's the truth—"

"Save your energy, sweetheart," he said quietly. "In
fact, instead of entertaining me with more of your ama-

teurish theatrics, I suggest you cover your enticing little body. Hasim is coming."

"You believed me for a moment, Glenlyon." Elspeth chuckled wickedly, working at the laces of her gown. "At least have the grace to admit it."

He flushed. "Laugh all you like, but I *am* going to find out the truth, one way or another. And Elspeth—" He grasped her hands again and drew her to her knees. Her face looked rebellious and afraid. "—if you ever give me another chance like the one I just let slip through my fingers, I'm going to make love to you until you're too exhausted to even consider lying to me again or leading me on another chase."

She couldn't resist a grin. "What if it turns out I am a murderess after all?"

He released her without warning as Hasim strode into the clearing, his brown face creased into lines of concern.

"Troubles, Tuan. Three men coming."

Niall took Elspeth by the elbow and dragged her to her feet, wondering if a more perplexing or desirable woman existed on the face of the earth. "There's no need to panic," he said. "Unless we're on private property, we haven't broken any laws." He glanced meaningfully at Elspeth, who with her head downbent pushed around him to collect her things. "At least I don't think we have."

Hasim frowned, following Niall down to the river's edge where the three horses had wandered. "It man from joy house who frighten ladies, Tuan."

"Joy house?" Niall repeated, puzzled. "What are you talking about?"

"He's referring to Coffin Face at Mrs. Grimble's," Elspeth explained as she came up behind them, her eyes dark with anxiety.

Hasim nodded in agreement. "He with other man who look like polices."

"I'll bet he's brought the sheriff with him," Elspeth said

worriedly. "Dammit, Glenlyon, he's going to make me go back to George. He'd never have found me if you hadn't interfered and dragged me away from the gypsies."

Niall swung around, his voice low. "He hasn't found you yet. Hell. Wade back out under the falls and wait for me. Leave your things with Hasim."

She bit her lip, backing away. "He'll see the extra horse—"

"We'll take care of it. Go!"

As she hurried off, he returned to the plaid and stared down at the dirk. He knelt and slipped it into one of his saddlebags. He didn't know its significance, but clearly it meant something to Elspeth.

Twenty-three

Niall watched her from the corner of his eye as he led the horses back up the embankment. Whatever crime she may or may not have committed, her fear of Francis Barron was genuine enough, and it aroused every protective instinct he possessed.

He entrusted the animals to Hasim's care and proceeded to remove all traces of Elspeth from the campsite. His face darkened as he found one of the stockings that she had half-stuffed into her violin case. *Bon Dieu,* he was lucky the careless female hadn't left him holding her drawers.

He glanced back at the waterfall, frowning as he reassured himself that she wasn't visible behind the white cascades that frothed like lace around the borders at its base. His nerves were on edge with the possibility that Barron would find her.

Yet a few minutes later, as Francis and two other men cantered into the clearing, Niall managed to appear the picture of indolent unconcern, munching the last of Elspeth's savory pies while Hasim curried the horses with unhurried deliberation.

The three Scotsmen slowed their horses to climb the embankment. One of the men, boyishly handsome and broad-shouldered, scanned the riverbank with an intensity that set off warning signals in Niall's head.

"Elspeth?" the man called in a soft brogue, sliding off

his horse. "It's Robert, my love. Robert Campbell. Do ye remember me?"

My love? The pie congealed into a sour knot of surprising jealousy in the pit of Niall's stomach. He stared with renewed suspicion at the handsome young Robert, restraining himself from giving the man an unfriendly shove into the river.

Francis dismounted. His sallow face was smug as he strode directly to where Niall lay sprawled out on the plaid. "Where is she, Captain Glenlyon?"

Niall stretched his arms over his head and yawned. "I wish I knew. There's another thousand pounds for me riding on that answer."

A muscle ticked in Francis's elongated jaw. "Ye're in possession of three horses, ye insolent blackguard. Are ye ignorant of the fact that abducting a woman is a crime in a civilized country? If ye are, allow my friend the sheriff over there to enlighten ye."

Niall lumbered to his feet, feigning an air of utter ignorance while his muscles tightened in instinctive dislike of the good-looking sheriff who was examining the reeds that fringed the shore.

"On my island, Mr. Barron," Niall murmured, "a man who abducts an unwilling woman can have his genitals cut off and sewn to his mouth."

Francis recoiled, staring at Niall in disgust. The heavyset older constable, still astride his horse, winced and folded his hands across his lap at the graphic description.

Niall allowed himself a smile. "As you can imagine, very few men on Kali Simpang mistreat their women, the occasional human sacrifice the unpleasant exception. However, we're improving in that area." As he reached down for his coat, his heart stopped at the few blond strands of Elspeth's hair that glistened against the dark wool. Straightening, he forced himself to stare Francis in the eye. "I found her horse several miles outside Balmuir. A few people recalled seeing her in the area. She can't have gotten far on foot."

"The gypsies lied when they told me they hadna seen her either." Francis glanced unexpectedly toward the river, his voice brittle. "How do I know she hasna cast Eve's spell of enchantment over ye too, Captain?"

The young sheriff with the massive shoulders had just motioned for the constable to join him at the river's edge. Niall schooled his features into a mask of impassivity to conceal his rising fear.

The two men had spotted something; Niall could only hope to God it wasn't Elspeth. Whatever it was, even Francis seemed suddenly fascinated by the swirling rush of water over the rocks.

Niall took a reflexive step forward, clenching his hands at his sides as if to restrain himself. The look on Barron's face suddenly had him worried.

Or was Barron remembering his own lost love, the girl he had allegedly drowned? Niall covertly stuck his left hand into his pocket to stuff down the stocking hidden there. All he needed to completely ruin his life was to be caught in possession of a missing woman's underthings.

He came up behind Francis. "Women are such treacherous creatures, aren't they, Francis?" he asked quietly.

To his surprise Francis nodded; his gaze was still riveted to the water. "Aye, Captain," he murmured. "There's no surer path to a man's destruction unless—"

Francis stopped, a low whistle of satisfaction escaping him as the constable clambered up the embankment, waving Elspeth's sodden petticoats above his head like a banner. The sight stopped Niall's heart cold.

Resisting the urge to call out a warning to Elspeth not to move, he looked back over his shoulder for an instant. Hasim stared past him, unseen in the shadowy pine grove by the others where he waited with his kris drawn in anticipation of a fight. Presumably he had hidden Elspeth's belongings high in the treetops.

But her *petticoats*.

Niall cursed his own stupidity for the oversight. What had been so amusing less than an hour ago would probably get him hanged. What a fitting end to a life of undeserved infamy.

Francis turned; triumph glowed in his deep-set amber eyes. "Well, Captain. What do ye have to say for yerself now?"

Niall lifted his head, annoyed at the absurd evolution of events, alarmed at the self-righteous determination on the sheriff's face as he took it upon himself to examine Elspeth's dripping petticoats.

My love, he'd called her, Robert Campbell, pretty-boy bastard.

"I have nothing to say for myself," he snapped. "Why don't you search the river for whoever the petticoats belonged to? They certainly aren't mine."

Campbell strode up the slope and stopped in front of Niall, flinging the petticoats down between them like a gauntlet. A wave of cold wind ruffled the trees overhead. Niall forced himself to remain calm, aware Hasim was waiting for a sign.

"I knew the reckless girl would come to a bad end," Francis murmured.

Campbell gestured to the heavy-set constable. "Search the bastard."

A few seconds later Campbell rushed him like a bull, and Niall readied his body for a fight when a movement behind the waterfall distracted him. Elspeth, peering out like a frightened kelpie at the strange mortals fighting on shore.

Stay hidden, you little fool. Stay hidden.

The moment of inattention cost him. Robert Campbell and Francis wrestled him to the ground, and the constable pounced on his chest like a pudgy gargoyle. Hasim, while looking concerned, had not lifted a finger to help or emerged from his hiding place because Niall hadn't instructed him to do so.

Gloating, Campbell dangled the torn stocking before Niall's face. "Ye dirty scum. Explain to the magistrate how this happened to be hidden in yer pocket."

The night threatened to last forever. Niall sat for countless mind-numbing hours in the dim draughty parlor of an old magistrate obsessed with deer-hunting while his own attention wandered to the chill wind that blasted down from the mountains and rimed the casement windows with frost.

Of course Niall hadn't actually been suspected of abducting that improvident young woman, and even the savage Highlanders understood habeas corpus, and possession of someone's underwear did not a murder make.

Of course Captain Glenlyon was free to go. Why, the elderly justice had himself followed Niall's exploits in the papers, and wouldn't it be grand sport to shoot grouse together some time before the weather worsened?

Besides, what point was there in the captain languishing in prison while waiting for the circuit court to hear his case when the missing woman would no doubt turn up in the interim?

What point was there, indeed? Niall wondered. They wouldn't need to hang him. He'd be talked to death by dawn.

Still, he managed to nod at appropriate intervals and exclaim in polite rapture over His Honour's collections of European butterflies. He drummed his fingers. He hoarded a plateful of barley bannocks in his pockets and prayed to a God he suspected was laughing into His beard that Hasim and Elspeth had managed to find warm shelter from the cold, and that Robert "My Love" Campbell hadn't taken it on himself to return to the river to search for other clues.

Two hours later, when he finally managed to gain his freedom from His Honour's century-old house, he found the cocksure young sheriff waiting for him out in the small detached stable. There was no sign of Francis Barron.

Niall tensed as he walked slowly toward his horse, throwing off the tiredness that had crept over him in the magistrate's parlor. "What a shame you've been waiting around to see me hanged, Sheriff. I'm free to go."

Campbell pushed away from the stall door. Elspeth's stocking was wound around his wrist. "Ellie Kildrummond," he mused quietly, a reminiscent smile on his face. "So the wee temptress is still raising hell."

Niall stopped several feet from the stall, his eyes narrowing. "I was under the impression you thought I'd murdered her."

"Och, no. She never much liked to wear fancy female things like stockings and petticoats in the first place. I only brought ye here to placate that Bible-breathin' Barron."

Niall's bland expression gave no warning of the dangerous turn his thoughts had taken. "Then you did know her?"

"Know her? Aye, I 'knew' her. I took her maidenhead on a bed of straw after her mother died. Sympathy, ye ken. Is there a woman who can resist it? Christ, she had the sweetest body this side of heaven, and a sharp tongue too, ye mind. But I'd have left my wife fer her had Mary's father-in-law not sat on the Privy Council and held the key to my future."

"This charming romance took place some time ago, I assume?" Niall asked in a tone that might have put a more intelligent man on guard.

"Oh, aye. Years. I heard a rumor once at a fair that I'd

got a bairn on her, but obviously 'twasna true." Campbell's smile turned sly. "I'd not mind meeting Ellie again under similar circumstances. I think of that afternoon often, Captain, when I'm lyin' in bed wi' my wife. I can still smell the wild roses that grew outside that barn door, and the scent of fresh straw—well, between you and me that alone is enough to make my cock hard—"

Campbell never saw the fist that slammed into his relaxed abdomen, then up into his face like a cudgel.

He never had time to defend himself before the dark foreigner propelled him backward into the stall door and sent him sprawling into the bed of manure-littered straw around the white stallion's hooves.

The big horse agilely sidestepped the fallen man with a whicker of annoyance.

Niall shook out his bruised hand and stared down at Campbell's unmoving figure, afraid of the force of his anger, that he might have just given that old magistrate good cause to have him incarcerated for murder.

Then finally Campbell stirred, blood trickling down his nose as he struggled to raise his head.

"Remember the smell of horse shit the next time you're lying in bed with your unfortunate wife," Niall said succinctly, stepping over Campbell's legs to reach the stallion. "And remember this too, you pathetic little prick: A man takes care of the woman he makes his own, and any children that might come of their mating. A man doesn't use a woman as a receptacle."

His breathing harsh, he bridled and saddled the stallion, then led the animal from the stall and out into the frosty night, listening with ambivalent relief to Campbell's grunts of pain as he tried to rouse himself.

And then there was only the deep silence of the night, punctuated by the uncontrollable pounding of his own heart. How many other dark secrets did Elspeth Kildrummond harbor? he wondered as he mounted his horse and studied the long stretch of moonlit road.

Would he indeed be incited to commit murder before his association with her was done? He supposed it was a moot point. Right or wrong, he was committed to helping her. Regret it or not, he had decided he wanted her for himself and nothing would stand in his way.

Twenty-four

Elspeth was gone when he reached the clearing. This time it wasn't a reasonable deduction, or even a fear. Niall knew in his heart as he rode his horse up the wooded ridge to the river that he would not find her there. The little brat had abandoned him without a blasted by-your-leave.

"Where did she go?" he demanded of the silent figure wrapped from head to foot in a fur cape before the fire.

His face grave, Hasim gestured to the configuration of feathers, twigs, and stones he had reassembled on the ground. "I studies secret symbols, Tuan, I think she hidings in a house on hill. Which house, which hills, I not know."

Niall pulled out the food he'd filched from the magistrate's table and dropped it into Hasim's lap. Call it pride. Call it sheer stupidity. But he had yet to touch a penny of the money her father had given him, not even to buy them food. "I thought she would have waited for me. Damn her," he growled. "I thought I'd finally convinced her to trust me."

"Why should she trusts you, Tuan?" Hasim's softly chiding voice cut into the bitter cold of the night. "Why should wounded tigress trust hunter who chases her for his own gain?"

* * *

For four hours she had wandered lost on horseback in her soggy clothes through the dark unfamiliar hills. By midnight she was convinced she had misread the gypsies' patteran and would never find the home of the lonely widow who had befriended them. She was probably riding in circles.

She almost wished for that scapegrace Glenlyon's company, aye, even hoping he'd appear on the desolate hillside track. But, och, where was her dignity then? Had the bastard not tried to spank her like a misbehaved bairn that very morning? Did he not deserve to sit for a spell in a dank Scottish gaol? Wasn't it better to wander alone than to submit to his dominant presence?

She rubbed her gloved hand across the tip of her frozen nose. Sad gray eyes, self-deprecating smile. His face danced through her weary mind. In fact, she'd just been on the verge of showing herself to Coffin Face, of sacrificing all her own interests to rescue Niall when she had spotted Robert Campbell on the embankment with her petticoats. Recognizing that lying cad had brought back all the shame and bewilderment of her seventeenth summer. She hadn't been able to move, not to save Glenlyon, not even to save herself. She had stood shivering behind the waterfall, sneaking out only after Hasim had gone to the main road to watch for his master.

And what had she learned from her past mistakes? Where was the self-control and emotional stability the intervening years should have added to her character?

She'd learned nothing, to judge by her disgraceful display of abandon on Glenlyon's plaid. She blushed hotly at the memory of it, a memory of sinful pleasure and aching need, and laughter, of a mysterious man who was both ruthless and gentle, a man who had created a horrible conflict in her heart.

Nothing she did seemed to unsettle him. He handled

whatever she threw at him with that unholy sense of humor and aplomb.

She shouldn't feel the tiniest bit guilty he'd been arrested on her account. Hadn't he dragged her off across the moor against her will? Hadn't he intended to send her back home for the reward her father offered? She sighed deeply, her breath fogging the frosty air.

She shouldn't feel anything but relief. She shouldn't be missing him so much that she searched for his tall figure behind every shadow she met. She ought to concentrate instead on finding a warm haven for her and the horse. She ought to banish Glenlyon from her thoughts for good.

She stared down into the corrie of the hill, at the abandoned bothy built into the snug little hollow. Well, it wasn't home but it would have to do. Ignoring a prickle of foreboding, she eased her horse down the brae. The frozen bracken that crunched under the mare's hooves warned her that the first winter frost had set in. The race was on in earnest to reach the glen.

But her buoyant confidence in her ability to make the journey alone had begun to deflate. It was one thing to travel with your family in a crowded coach on a chilly night, the heat of packed bodies serving as insulation and a charcoal brazier burning at your feet, singing loudly as you barreled down a mountain pass. . . .

It was another thing to ride these desolate hills alone on a bone-chilling November night. Her nerves were definitely on edge.

The moon had disappeared behind a bank of clouds, throwing the corrie into inky blackness. She dismounted beside the burn that gurgled down the hill. Before she had turned from her horse, she noticed a peat cart and a pair of harnessed ponies behind the bothy.

Her first impulse was to remount and flee.

And then she noticed the plaid folded over the back of

the cart—Glenlyon's notorious plaid. Unwilling warmth surged through her.

She swallowed a relieved laugh and impatiently pulled her horse across the shallow burn. Why had she been so worried about Niall? She should have known the rogue would wangle his own release, and acquire a cart and ponies into the bargain. Of course he could take care of himself.

"Glenlyon?" she called in a tentative voice. "Hasim? Good Lord, is all this mystery necessary? I realize you're probably a wee bit annoyed about being arrested on my account, but—"

"—but what is another man's downfall to be added to the list of men ye have led astray?"

The morose voice had barely made a dent in Elspeth's awareness than Francis Barron emerged from behind a stack of winter peat. Flexing a coil of rope in his thin white hands, he frowned down into her shocked face.

"You," she said, whipping around to run back up the brae.

He clamped his hands down on her shoulders. She stiffened, then swung around to hit him. Her fists only grazed his jacket. Before she could utter a cry or curse, he clapped his calloused palm over her mouth and worked the rope around her waist.

"Yes, it's me, Coffin Face." He sounded breathless from struggling to subdue her. "Dinna bother screaming, Elspeth. There's no one for miles to hear ye. We're quite alone, the two of us."

Niall didn't doubt for a second that Francis Barron had abducted Elspeth. The indisputable signs of a struggle had only been a few hours old when he'd finally tracked her to the bothy. Sifting on his hands and knees through the humus, decaying willow leaves and damp red dirt, he'd found her violin case—and the mate to the discarded stocking that had gotten him into so much trouble. Cold panic had paralyzed his ability to think as he grasped it. It was too personal, too private a possession, and the implications that ran through his mind had him staggering to his feet in helpless fury.

It had taken all his self-control and Hasim's calming influence to subdue that panic, to rely on his skill and experience to follow Barron's washed-out cart tracks, riding through rain and mist on unfamiliar roads with the witch doctor lagging behind.

The sight of them must have startled the placid Highlanders through whose peaceful hamlets they flew—a black-caped stranger with a killing fury in his eyes and a native in a ruby-studded turban, stopping only to water and rest their overexerted horses, to ask if anyone had seen a fair-haired woman matching Elspeth's description and the man who accompanied her.

But Niall had managed to find the odd pair in just under twenty-four hours. Striding through the crowded public room of the popular wayside inn to where he'd traced them, he wondered for not the first time why Barron had made no effort to hide his abduction. Unless the man had blackmailed Elspeth into compliance with information about that mysterious night. Or had she arbitrarily changed her mind and decided to return home with George's cousin of her own free will?

The latter possibility infuriated Niall, indulging in these ridiculous Highland heroics, delaying his own plans and talking his way out of a nasty prison sentence for a woman who'd abandoned him with the same casual disregard as she would yesterday's newspaper.

He stared wildly around the smoky room. The Highlanders stared back in open curiosity, some muttering "Sassenach" in knowing tones as if that explained his apparent agitation. Before he could ask the harried innkeeper about Elspeth, a disturbingly familiar voice called to him from a corner table to his left.

"Cor blimey, Captain, don't tell me you dunno where she is either?"

Niall whirled in disbelief and stared down into Archie Harper's earnestly disconcerted face. Catherine Kildrummond, snuggled in a red fox-trimmed cloak, sat beside him, her mouth taut with anxiety.

"We hoped you'd saved her, Captain," she said in a voice so edged with disappointment that Niall realized she actually believed all the romantic fiction she'd read about him.

He approached the table slowly, his face white with the shocked realization that Archie Harper and Elspeth's sister were the man and woman he'd been following with such flamboyant arrogance. Self-disgust welled inside him, accompanied by a panic spawned by the fact that he had no idea where Elspeth actually was, that while he was chasing the two well-meaning twits seated below him, Francis Barron could have taken Elspeth anywhere.

"The gypsies told us you had taken her, Captain," Catherine said in a broken voice. "I had planned to stay here while Mr. Harper kindly offered to travel ahead in the hope he would catch up with you and Elspeth. Auntie Flora has retired to a bed upstairs, unable to endure all the excitement."

Niall lowered himself into the chair Archie pulled out for him, his mind still reeling from the blow. Hell, he must be getting old; he'd lost touch with his instincts. Incredibly, he had lost her tracks. He felt useless, seething with fear and frustration. He needed to hit someone, break a chair or two. Restless energy surged through him like a tidal wave.

"I'm wasting time even talking to you," he said tersely. "Unless there's some information you can give me on where Barron would have hidden Elspeth."

"Francis has her then," Catherine said in a choked whisper. "Oh, no."

Archie patted her consolingly on the elbow, his round face devoid of its usual urbane amusement. "In view of all the distressing evidence that 'as recently come to light, Captain, I'd say we put aside our differences and combine our talents to find 'er."

"What recent evidence?" Niall asked in a tight voice.

Archie tugged a red silk handkerchief from his vest pocket to pass to Catherine. "The corpse that disappeared the night of the engagement party."

With a distracted nod of thanks, Niall took the mug of untouched tea that Catherine pushed toward him. "The night of the party—Oh, come on, Harper, you tried this bluff before."

Archie frowned. "I'm afraid it ain't a bluff," he said softly.

"There *was* a body?"

"Yes."

"Then we're talking about murder."

Something about the way Harper evaded his gaze made Niall suspect the man knew more than he was willing to tell. "Murder?" Harper mumbled. "It could 'ave been an accident, Captain. Who's to say?"

"A body. Sweet Christ." Niall slumped back tiredly in his chair, rubbing his eyes as if to erase the picture of Elspeth's face the night she had stood before him in that blood-stained nightdress.

If she hadn't killed someone, she knew damn well who had.

And no wonder her papa had been so against involving the local authorities. No wonder political-minded Sir George had scurried off to England where no shadow of a murder scandal could taint his career. But even so, Niall found it difficult to believe Elspeth capable of murdering anyone without extreme provocation.

And now Francis Barron had her, possibly intending to silence her before she could incriminate . . . Niall's mind slammed against another frustrating wall. Incriminate *whom* for murdering *whom?*

"Just whose body was it anyway?" he demanded, fatigue, hunger, and anxiety conspiring to diminish not just his mental capacities but his patience as well.

"Lower your voice, Captain," Catherine murmured, giving her nose a dainty little blow.

Niall scowled and leaned forward. "This had better not be another one of your literary exaggerations, Harper."

"It isn't." Catherine's eyes welled with a fresh flood of tears. "An unidentified man's body was found near the docks the same morning I left Falhaven. The p-poor person had been shot in the chest, and . . ." She shook her head, unable to continue.

Harper took over the explanation. "A woman's shawl was wound around the man's mortal injury, Captain. A pretty Paisley thing from London, it's been said."

Niall looked steadily at Catherine. "It belonged to Elspeth?" he asked in a low voice.

She gazed down at the table, allowing Harper to answer for her again. "All either of us are willing to say at this point is that Elspeth Kildrummond's life may be in jeopardy unless we find 'er right soon, Captain."

"Oh, Elspeth," Catherine whispered, squeezing her eyes shut. "God help you."

Twenty-five

"God help me, Elspeth Kildrummond," Francis Barron said to himself, though not without a certain wry amusement as he walked through the lonely graveyard toward the woman cursing him to the heavens from his cart. "Ye are a trial to yer Maker, as well as to those who care for ye."

She strained wildly against the rope tied around her waist. "Stay away from me, you crazy bastard! I'm warning you, Francis."

She fell silent, her empty threat hanging in the quiet of early evening. Waves of pain rolled over her, radiating from her swollen kneecap into her thigh. At the bothy she had tried to disable Francis with a sharp kick to the groin only to twist her leg and stumble over her own damned stupid violin case. Putting any weight on that leg caused her so much agony, she doubted she could run far even if she did manage to untruss herself from his cart.

But if she could reach her bag and then her mare, hitched between the two little ponies. . . .

Francis closed his bony hand over her wrist. "Raise yer skirts, woman."

She shook her head, mute with horror at the unexpected request. She had run out of bravado. Her nerves were strained to snapping with waiting for him to commit one of the sexual atrocities he was capable of. For two whole days she had dreaded this moment, too terrified to even sleep but in snatches for fear he'd decide to strangle her and leave her lying on the desolate deer trail he was following to avoid detection.

He motioned impatiently to the skirts, and Elspeth broke into an icy sweat at the sight of the length of bandage and small tin he was brandishing in his other hand. "Will ye raise yer skirts for me or no? I havena got all day. Stubborn, sinful creature."

She kicked his hand, swallowing a cry of pain at the wrenching ache the movement caused in her knee. His long face red with anger, Francis stared down at the bandage that had landed in the dirt. "I was going to put horse liniment on yer knee and wrap it for the night. But perhaps the pain will serve as a reminder of the price one pays for wantonness and false pride."

She glared at him, breathing so hard her chest hurt. "You're the one who ought to pay for his sins."

"Aye." He nodded wearily as he straightened, retrieving the bandage from the dirt. Then, without warning, he worked the rope loose from around her waist and jerked his head toward the small fire he'd kindled on the outskirts of an abandoned abbey.

"We'll bide here the night."

"In a graveyard?" Elspeth whispered, buckling at the knee as she jumped to the ground and blood rushed back into her legs.

"I'll not be seen wi' ye in public," he muttered before he strode back to his fire.

Elspeth reached back into the cart for her bag. Clutching it to her chest, she hobbled around him to the opposite side of the fire. He had bound his hand in the bandage to take his tea water off the boil, careful bugger that he was. As she watched him, measuring out precise spoonfuls of tea, unwrapping a package of scones, she realized for the first time that the lonely boy she remembered from the past had grown into a lonely man, and she remembered suddenly how he had never had a friend to play with until George arrived from London.

In fact, George was still his only friend in the world.

"Sit down, woman, if ye want yer supper. I'll no wait on ye like a servant."

She complied reluctantly, stretching out her sore leg with a grimace of pain. "Where are you taking me?"

"The Lord has yet to guide me on how to handle ye."

She snorted and took the tin cup of tea he handed her. "You're not going to get away with this, Francis."

"Get away wi' what, Elspeth Kildrummond?" he said, indignant. "I've not harmed a hair on ye stubborn head, have I?"

She banged her cup down on the ground. "You've dragged me around in your cart like a prize porker on its way to a harvest fair! You've spied on me, stolen my freedom."

" 'Tis a woman's husband who decides how much freedom she should be allowed. I've only saved ye from yerself as George would have done in my place."

"George isn't my husband," she retorted. "Not now, or probably ever. Not after what he did to Tormod Mac-Queen."

She was a little surprised when Francis didn't leap to George's defense, glancing down into the fire with a shadow of what looked like guilt crossing his face.

"Finish yer tea," he mumbled, rising to his knees. "I've bread and cheese in the cart."

He froze, halfway to his feet, at the expression of tense expectancy on Elspeth's face, her gaze riveted to irregular rows of gravestones and stone crosses that rose on the darkened slope of the abbey behind them.

"What is it?" he asked quietly, narrowing his eyes.

She slipped her left hand into her bag, waving the other toward the slope while she started to shout, "Over here, help me! He's holding me prisoner!"

Throwing her a disgusted look, Francis straightened fully and broke into a run toward the cemetery, snatching his cudgel from the cart on his way to investigate whatever it was she had seen.

Which, in reality, was nothing; she had needed a distraction to withdraw the packet of sedative herbs Delilah had given her to use as a last resort on Glenlyon.

Scarcely daring to breathe, she watched Francis skulk about the gravestones for another minute. Then, her hands shaking, she leaned around the fire to dump the powdered herbs into his pot of tea, singeing the hem of her cloak in the process. Belladonna, henbane, blue vervain. She hoped to hell Delilah hadn't accidentally given her a pack of the aphrodisiac herbs that sold so well at the fairs.

When Francis strode back to the fire, glancing down at her in suspicion, she'd just settled back in her spot and was staring innocently into the flames.

"Ye're seeing things," he said tersely. "And what if there had been someone there, I ask ye? Who in his right mind would want to help a woman like you?"

She blinked and looked away as he reached for the teapot. "What the blazes is that supposed to mean?"

He refilled his cup from the steaming teapot. "Ye've been a destructive influence on all the men whose misfortune it has been to love ye. First, there was George, and then that sheriff's officer ye tempted into adultery. Oh, aye, dinna look so startled. I knew ye'd seduced Robert, that yer lust of each other had taken root only to perish in yer womb."

Shaking his head, he reached around the flames with the teapot to fill the cup she was gripping in her hands. "I hoped George would forget ye when he went to sea, but he didna, no, he was convinced ye were his talisman. And now that rogue soldier ye've taken up with."

"Rogue soldier that I've taken up with? Are you referring to Glenlyon?"

"Aye." Francis frowned. "The pair of ye are the perfect match. If it weren't for breaking George's heart, I'd have said let the soldier have the joy of ye."

He took a loud nervous sip of tea, clearly having worked himself into a state over the evil she'd unleashed on the world. His mind was twisting facts to suit his own warped views. And, true, he hadn't hurt her, at least not yet, but she had suffered unspeakable emotional indignities being carted about as his captive, listening to hour upon hour of his insults and boring Biblical sermons.

But to match her up with Niall Glenlyon, the most imperfect mate she could imagine. Mercenary. Crude. Irreverent. Honest, yes, she had to grant the devil his due. He was the most honest man she'd ever met.

In fact, she'd give anything to be looking across the fire at his honestly beautiful face instead of at this pious madman's.

"What if Glenlyon decides to come after us?" she asked.

"I dinna think the man will want to tangle wi' the authorities again on yer account." He grimaced. "Fah. The tea's gone bitter in the pot."

"What do you expect from burn water that flows through a cemetery?" she said before she could stop herself. "The bodies buried on the hill have probably seeped into the soil." She looked down at her cup, her heart lodging in her throat. Lord help her, that she should bring up the subject of dead bodies to Francis Barron. That she should put any more lurid ideas in the lunatic's head.

To cover the heavy silence that followed, she put down her tea and made a show of rummaging through her bag, withdrawing the lone bruised crab apple Niall hadn't managed to find.

She felt a surprising pang of bittersweetness at the memory of their last afternoon together, the silliness, the sexual intimacy they had shared. She should be blaming him for her troubles, not wishing him here.

He had bedeviled her life from the start. Brought her bad luck. But he was the only man she had ever met who was strong enough to stand up to her without batting an eye at her outlandish behavior because his own was worse.

She held out the apple to Francis. "Take it."

He swallowed his first cautious sip of tea, accepting the apple with a look of surprise. "Thank ye," he said, then hesitated. "Yer generosity has always been one of the few traits in yer character I canna fault. 'Twas once said Ronald Kildrummond never let a stranger go by his house hungry. He was kind to me, yer granddad was. I was with him a lot at the end, ye ken."

Elspeth blinked in astonishment. "You were with my grandfather when he died?"

"Aye." Francis lowered his troubled gaze. "Me and puir dead Tormod."

Elspeth glanced away as he took another sip of tea, grimaced again, then seemed to relax. She didn't know what to make of what he'd just told her; it played hell with the evil image of him that she had held for so long in her mind.

"I wanted to be yer friend once a long time ago," he said softly. "Aye, well. I suppose yer hatred of me stems from the time I was forced to put down yer horse when it was hurt and ye were away."

She blinked, wondering what in God's name Delilah had mixed in that packet to have loosened the man's tongue so.

"You didn't have to burn the poor beast, did you?" she asked, shuddering at the memory. "I'd have buried him myself, on my special place on the moor."

"Elspeth," he said, sighing deeply, "did no one ever tell ye that a wildcat had attacked it after it had fallen from a ledge into the ravine? The poor creature was mutilated beyond recognition."

She stared down into the fire, frowning in confusion. Rarely did a wildcat attack except when its prey was old, or in weakened condition, but Francis's voice did ring with a disturbing sincerity. Still, she wasn't about to take the word of a murderer over her own common sense.

"Aye, no," Francis said, his voice faintly slurred from the tea's soporific effect. He bit into the apple and chewed it slowly, his large teeth crunching the bruised flesh and spurting juice onto his hand. "The crofters would have wanted to protect ye. In those days ye were their cherished princess and could do no wrong."

In those days? The rueful tone, his usage of past tense, tolled an alarm bell in Elspeth's brain, but she was too absorbed in willing him to finish the tea to analyze it.

Soon, soon, *soon.*

Even if she had been mistaken about her horse, she knew the prostitutes of Falhaven dreaded his visits. She knew he'd murdered his sweetheart and was probably intending to do the same to her. She knew he had abducted her and brought him to this lonely abbey ruins . . .

She glanced uneasily at the gravestones protruding on the hill. Was this where he had buried Isobel, where he would bury her? An abandoned cemetery. What better place to commit a murder and not be caught?

"I canna decide . . ." His voice trailed off. "I canna decide what to do wi' ye."

She exhaled slowly, gripping the cup. "Let me go, Francis."

"To Glen Fyne? Now that would be a sin, lass."

"What do you mean?"

He shook his head, sweat gathering around his hairline. "God has instructed me to protect ye . . . from yerself and the others."

"The others?"

Her nerves were tingling, the suspense of waiting for the tea to take effect was almost more than she could bear, and yet she couldn't move, sensing he was on the verge of revealing the answer to all the mystery surrounding Tormod's death.

"What others, Francis?" she asked quietly.

Without warning he tossed the remainder of his apple into the fire and stared across the dying flames at her with accusing horror in his eyes. The tin cup fell from his other hand, and she shrank back, gazing up into his face as he lurched to his feet and staggered toward her.

"Eve—the apple . . . ye've poisoned me," he said in disbelief.

She struggled to rise, to run toward the cart. Francis grabbed the tail of her cloak. Jerking it free, she heard him fall behind her. She heard him cry out to her in the dark as she worked frantically to unhitch her mare, but her mind was too focused on escape to make sense of his hoarse warning.

"Ye thought I meant to harm ye. Foolish woman. Ye're running . . . running toward yer own death."

Twenty-six

It took Niall another three days to find her. Although rain and strong southeast winds had obliterated most of her tracks, he sensed by the haphazard trail he pieced together that she was desperate, determined to reach her childhood home.

He also had the word of Francis Barron that Elspeth was headed for grave danger. The two men had met again by accident on the old cattle drover's road around Loch Abermaddy. More than that Barron refused to explain. His face haggard, he claimed only that the "wee witch" had tried to poison him. He said surely he had misinterpreted God's guidance and that he was done helping such a wicked creature. He said that she would understand everything when she reached the glen.

And Niall knew then he had to intensify his efforts to find her, glad he had forced Hasim to remain behind at the inn with Catherine and Archie Harper. The weather had worsened. Autumn was deepening into early winter, and he remembered Duncan Kildrummond's warning about the savage blizzards that could come shrieking down from the Cairngorms. Even Elspeth's bravado couldn't compete with the elements. He ached to protect her.

She had veered off the well-traveled remains of the military road. The terrain had grown wilder, more desolate and beautiful if possible. As far as Niall could tell, Elspeth was following a rain-swollen river which twisted through a pine forest and tumbled down the distant mountains over a barrier of low wooded hills that broke into moorland.

At night he camped in those hills and watched formations of wild geese flying across the shifting clouds. He tried to picture Elspeth, where she would take shelter, how she would survive. He listened to the wind stirring the tall conifers, and he was afraid for her; she was desperate, and he remembered the wounded tigress he had tracked into her hilly lair years ago. The man-eater, the murderess. The celebrated hunt that had been told and retold, embellished and exaggerated until it had evolved into a minor legend. It had made him a hero, and no one had ever known that he had captured the tigress and taken her to an unpopulated island in the archipelago because he'd been unable to destroy such rare beauty. He had nursed her back to health and released her to her fate.

He could not sleep.

He studied this land that had sired his ancestors and felt an unexpected kinship, a curiosity about their long-ago dreams. He thought of his uncle, dying without ever knowing Niall had traveled across the world to meet him. He thought of Rachel, his little sister, her fate unknown. He thought of his brothers, Alex and Dallas, and he hoped that the reckless fools had not gotten themselves killed, and if they had, pray God that Niall would not have to be the one to break the news to their mother.

But mostly he thought of her, of Elspeth, and of how she had brought him back to life with her irrepressible passion for living, and of how he wanted to help her even if it turned out she had done something wrong, at least according to the law. He wouldn't rest until he saw that winsome light in her eyes again.

Because he knew that even though he might never understand what had motivated her actions, there had to be a cause, and because she had made him laugh and believe in his own inner strength again.

Because she had made him care.

He spotted her horse sheltering from the wind in a circle of standing stones on a secluded moor that spread like a fading carpet over a succession of hills. For a moment he thought he'd made a mistake, that the gloaming shadows and his own desperation had deceived him, that the dispirited-looking mare grazing amidst the frost-shriveled ferns could not belong to Elspeth.

As much as she loved horses, it seemed unlikely she'd have abandoned the animal of her own free will.

And then he glanced up, distracted by the raucous croaking of a pair of carrion crows above the stones. The scent of death hung in the air. His heart in his throat, he urged the stallion up the rocky escarpment.

Halfway to the stones, he vaulted off his horse and ran the remaining distance. His black greatcoat flapped in the wind. Fear contorted his features; he imagined his appearance would strike terror into the hearts of the three raggedly dressed Highlanders he descended upon. Squatted over a flat-surfaced boulder, they were intent on some grim task when he surprised them.

The gaunt faces of a white-haired man, a much younger woman, and two adolescent boys gaped at him as if he were the devil himself. He stared down and saw the glint of an old knife in the woman's hand. Elspeth's dirk, and there was fresh blood dripping from the blade.

He felt so physically ill at the sight that it took him several seconds before he realized that the object stretched out for slaughter on the boulder was only a red pheasant grouse.

"Where did you get the dirk?" His voice sounded hoarse; the blood roaring in his head made him feel as if he were falling down a hole. "And the horse? I warn you, I'll make you regret it if you lie."

The woman, her stringy hair stirring in the breeze, drew her threadbare shawl around her. "We've done no wrong." Her face was fearful but belligerent. "We found the horse wanderin' aboot by itself. The dirk were here on the ground."

"They belonged—belong—to someone I know."

The young mother stared up at him in defiant silence.

"Didn't it occur to you that the knife and horse belonged to someone?" he demanded, his fear and frustration overwhelming even a semblance of self-control.

One of the woman's sons sniggered, eyeing Niall with contempt. "What's lost by one is found by another."

He drew a deep burning breath. "Didn't it occur to you that the horse's rider may have been thrown and was lying hurt somewhere, unable to get help?"

"My lads looked," the woman said with an unconvincing shrug. " 'Tweren't no one to be helped." She wiped her runny nose on her shoulder. "Besides, what woman in her right mind'd be crossing the moor in this weather?"

She went back to the chore of cleaning the bird, hunger evidently a stronger motivation than whatever threat this dark stranger represented. Niall studied her for a moment, suspicion and worry crushing any empathy he might have felt for their impoverishment.

"I don't believe I mentioned I was looking for a woman," he said quietly, his gaze burning into her.

" 'Tis a woman's mount that," she retorted with only a slight trembling of her mouth to betray her as she slit the grouse's breastbone.

Wishing for the rifle he'd left on the white stallion, Niall walked past her to examine the pathetic array of possessions scattered around the stones—a charred stool, a broken clairschach, some cooking utensils, but nothing else that belonged to Elspeth.

Yet he wasn't reassured.

"Where do you come from anyway?" he asked the woman over his shoulder, whistling to Elspeth's horse as he foraged in his pocket for that last apple of hers he'd stolen.

And kept for some ridiculously sentimental reason to remind him of their sweet romp on his plaid.

The woman's hair swung forward to obscure the expression on her face as she wiped her bloodied hands on a rag. "Glen Fyne," she said with a sneer. "Why do ye care?"

Niall whirled around, Elspeth's mare devouring the apple in the palm of his hand. "Glen Fyne? That's Elspeth's home—the woman I'm looking for. Perhaps you know her. Perhaps you were friends. Elspeth Kildrummond—"

He broke off at the savage hatred that twisted the woman's face. "Och, aye. I know the little traitor, called her friend once, my husband did." She sniffed, tossing her head. "So it's her that's maybe lyin' dead wi' the black crows plucking out her eyes. Weel, may she rot in hell wi' the devil her da, I say."

"Duncan Kildrummond?" Niall asked, struggling to make sense of her emotional diatribe.

She licked a bubble of spittle from her lips. "May the entire lot of them perish in hell fer what they did to us!"

Niall took an involuntary step backward, fighting the impulse to turn away from the raw pain in her eyes. "What happened to you at Glen Fyne?" he asked intently.

"Do ye want to know?" Her voice rising into an inhuman screech, she leaped up and scrambled over a pile of rubble to get to him. "Are ye another one of those newspaper men from London, eager to hear the details of how my family was destroyed?"

"No." He shook his head, told himself he was dealing

with a madwoman and that he'd find Elspeth faster by
himself.

He turned away. She clawed at his arm, holding him
back with an alarmingly strong grip. "Ronald Kildrummond swore his granddaughter would take care of us.
Fools we were to believe him while Ellie dallied wi' that
fat Sassenach fop who was scarit of his own shadow."

"George, you mean," he said, breaking free. "Sir
George Westcott?"

She made a sound of contempt and flung the bloodied
dirk at him; it landed between the forelegs of Elspeth's
horse. Panicking, the animal whipped around and knocked
Niall aside. Before he could stop it, the horse had broken
away from its long tether of bramble twine.

"Dinna let the horse go," the woman cried to her sons.
"We'll feast on it tonight while the crows are stripping
the flesh from its mistress's body!"

The horse had descended the crag and was tearing
across the moor as if chased by the hounds of hell. Niall
watched it for only a fraction of a second before realizing
it could lead him to Elspeth. He swooped down to retrieve
the dirk and barreled past the woman.

"They burnt us out of our homes like wasps!" she said,
falling to her knees. "They made me lose my bairn."

Niall jumped onto his horse, ducking the mouthful of
curses and spittle she hurled at him. Her elderly father
and sons were collecting stones to throw. He didn't doubt
he'd be a dead man by now if they owned a gun.

He pressed his heels to his mount's sides as a stone
grazed his ear. The stallion, though not in peak condition
itself, lunged down the escarpment and cantered for its
life. Niall gave it its head and rode hard until almost a
mile later, it overtook the mare on the moor. He grasped
the dangling reins and slowed both horses to a walk, staring in every direction for a trace of Elspeth. Despair rose
up like a wall to block his intuition.

Nothing.

Even the wind had died to a whisper. He rode slowly with a sinking sense of defeat and the lingering horror of that family amidst the stones.

The strawberry mare seemed only weary and confused, too listless to lead him anywhere. Soon it would be dark. Unless he found Elspeth's trail, he would lose another night to this godforsaken moor.

The hunter followed the wounded tigress high into the hills, his heart heavy with the prospect of what he had to do. The native porters had abandoned him long ago. Stalking the twilight shadows of montane forest, Niall Glenlyon was a man haunted by his own failures, in competition with his own reputation.

Elspeth snorted and hurled the popular magazine toward the mouth of the high hillside cave that concealed her. A second later, she regretted the impulsive act. The paper would have been better fuel than the dried ferns she'd tried to build into a fire since realizing she was sharing the cave with a small inhospitable wildcat.

A wildcat. She thought moodily of Glenlyon, imagining him stalking that tigress in those jungle hills. She imagined his long lean body, bronze muscled chest glistening, a knife strapped to his waist. She wondered if he'd given up on her by now. If he was cursing her name from the bowels of a prison cell. No. Not Glenlyon. Nothing could hold his restless spirit for too long.

The wildcat released a low warning snarl and shuffled on the ledge above her, sending a spray of dust and stones down onto Elspeth's head.

"I'll bet I'm hungrier than you," she muttered, taking a fortifying swig from the bottle of whisky she'd stolen from Francis's cart, along with the short-barreled gun she held in her hands. "I'll bet—"

Her voice faded on an involuntary groan of pain and bone-deep exhaustion. Curling her fingers tightly around the gun, she leaned back against her bag and closed her eyes. She hated guns. They were undignified weapons in her opinion, and their power frightened her. Still, if that pious bastard Barron came after her again, she was prepared to sacrifice her personal beliefs . . . and blast him to kingdom come.

Twenty-seven

Mist shimmered against the crevices of the bare crag. Niall glanced up from the magazine that had landed in a clump of withered crowberry at his feet and assessed the daunting climb to the black orifice where Elspeth had taken refuge. At least he hoped to hell he'd find her hidden up there.

Twenty minutes later he had scaled the crag and entered the cave, swallowing hard at the absolute stillness that engulfed him. "Elspeth?" he called quietly.

He ducked under the overhanging ledge and crawled over a pile of stones and dried ferns. He smelled smoke and the scent of a wildcat in the air and felt his chest tighten with apprehension.

Don't let me be too late.

A faint click from the shadows of the wall stopped him cold.

Releasing his breath, he stared down at the gun barrel leveled at his groin.

"Glenlyon . . . you d-damned nitwit. I could have . . . shot off your cue stick." She struggled to roll up from the wall, the gun wobbling dangerously between her upraised knees. "I should warn you I'm a wee b-bitty drunk, Glenlyon. In fact, I'm not even sure I've got this damn thing loaded properly."

He glanced up at the shifting movement on the ledge.

"Give it to me just in case, Elspeth," he instructed her in a calm undertone.

She grunted and handed him the weapon, her mouth tightening into a seamless line of pain. "There's a wildcat hiding up on that ledge," she whispered, allowing herself to relax for the first time in days. "I-I don't think she's in a mood for company."

"Those snarls don't strike me as very sociable either."

He hunkered down beside her, holding back the barrage of emotions that he'd believed himself incapable of feeling. Relief, profound relief that he'd found her (and hadn't lost his tracking skill). Desire tempered with an aching tenderness that savaged his self-control. Affection for this troublesome woman that went beyond words.

But his lean face revealed none of his thoughts. Silent, he pocketed the gun and passed his hands over her body for obvious signs of injury. Only when he reached the tattered piece of fabric she'd inexpertly wound around her swollen knee did he allow his concern to show in his eyes.

She winced at the probing pressure of his fingertips, then tried to cover her discomfort with a weak smile. "Trying to take advantage of an invalid?"

"Naturally."

"I—" She released her breath as he withdrew his hand. "I knew you'd find me."

He studied her face, resisting the urge to wipe away the dirty tracks of the tears that had dried on her cheeks. "I never dreamed you had that much faith in me," he said wryly.

"Let's just say I had faith in your determination to collect my father's money."

He laughed reluctantly and slid his hands under her rump to hoist her into his arms. She didn't even stiffen, just sighed and snuggled against his chest like a kitten that had been rescued from a tree.

"Where are you taking me, Glenlyon?" she asked contentedly.

"I passed another cave on the moor. It was a hell of a lot cleaner and more accessible than this." He sniffed, his nostrils flaring in distaste. "Is that whisky on your breath?"

"Um-hmm. I stole it from Francis along with the gun. He only used it for medicinal purposes. Dreadful waste of fine liquor in my opinion."

He grunted, hefting her derrière up higher with his knee. "No wonder you're so damned congenial."

"I'm heavy, aren't I?" she whispered, her voice muffled by his coat.

"I've hauled lumber barges that were lighter," he admitted with a smile that belied the sudden terror that had seized him.

Cannibals. Enemy soldiers. Border wars. Crocodiles and jungle cats. Not all of those past dangers combined, in fact and fiction, had prepared him for the traitorous softening of his own heart. The small fingers curled around his neck, and the defenseless body snuggled into him were the most potent weapons he had ever encountered in his life. The battle had been lost from the beginning. The hunter had been brought to his knees by his quarry.

Elspeth peered through the curtain of bracken Niall had laced to make a windscreen across the cave's entrance as a barrier to the raw wind that swept across the moor. "My horse looks like hell, Glenlyon," she exclaimed. "What did you do to her?"

He frowned and continued feeding twigs into the fire, refusing to tell her that in another few hours her mare could well have been someone's dinner. She wasn't recovered enough from her ordeal with Barron to assimilate another horror. Besides, he was enjoying the primitive in-

timacy of sharing a cave with her too much to spoil it
with tales of reality.

"We'll bring them both in after we eat," he reassured
her.

"You have food?" she asked eagerly.

"Just some old cheese and stale bannocks."

Elspeth made a face and hobbled back to the fire.
"What are you brewing in that pot? It smells rather like
boiled socks."

"It's my island-grown coffee," he said with a wry
chuckle. "Would you like a cup? I'd give you mine but
it's laced with quinine."

"Quinine?"

He glanced up at her from beneath his heavy black
brows, his heart quickening at her nearness. "I'm prone
to malarial fever." He pointed to the small green bottle
propped between his saddlebags. "Hasim and I have to
take the quinine as a preventative."

"Oh," she murmured, sitting awkwardly, trying not to
stare at his beautiful face in the firelight. "Couldn't you
have bagged a pheasant, or a blue hare to roast, you being
such a big-game hunter, I mean? I spotted some deer a
day or so ago."

"Foraging for food. The does looked pregnant." He
passed her a tin of steaming black coffee. "Careful, it's
hot. And as to hunting, well, you were more than enough
to keep me occupied. I have to give you credit for getting
this far."

She sniffed at the cup with a suspicious frown. "I was
so hungry this morning, I almost broke my leg snaring a
rabbit, but I didn't have the heart to kill it when I finally
caught the poor little thing. My grandfather would be disgusted with me."

"Aren't you going to taste the coffee?"

"Why? Is it poisoned? I-I drugged Francis, you know."
She lowered her voice, her eyes dark with guilt. "Glen-

lyon, I keep telling myself he deserved it, but I'm afraid, well, I think I might even have killed him."

"Along with the gardener?" He hid a smile at the faint blush that rose to her face. "You didn't. I saw Francis on my way here. I saw your sister a few days before, too."

"My sister?" she repeated, incredulous. "My little sister followed me from Falhaven all by herself? That's impossible, Glenlyon. Cat couldn't find her way to the privy without an atlas."

"Well, as it turns out, she did have some help. She's brought Archie Harper and Aunt Flora along for the journey."

"Good heavens. Good God."

"Yes, I was a little shocked to see them myself. With any luck, however, Hasim will make sure they don't venture any farther."

She almost dropped her cup. "You left your headhunter guarding my sister?"

"Actually, he was casting deer bones to read your aunt's horoscope the last time I saw him." He pushed one of his saddlebags around the fire. "Find something in there for us to eat. And I think it's very sweet that your sister came after you. At least she cared enough to bother."

She glanced up slowly, dragging his bag onto her lap. "Meaning George and my father don't care?"

Chère, those are your words, not mine."

He stared down into the fire, pretending not to notice when she pulled his plaid from the bag. It was a flagrant reminder of how close they'd come to making love that afternoon, of how badly he'd wanted her, even after his miserable night with the magistrate. The mere sight of that plaid possessed the power to make him shake, bringing back the memory of soft melting kisses, and creamy white flesh, of intense emotion and aching desire.

He wanted her more now. And he didn't care what anyone said. She hadn't murdered anyone. Hell, she couldn't even bring herself to kill a rabbit.

"I know what you're thinking," she said quietly.

He jerked his head up. "You do?"

"You're thinking about that afternoon at the waterfall when we . . . when you and I almost . . ."

Her voice trailed off. Niall exhaled and stared up at the ceiling of the cave, intent on subduing the spasm of sexual impulse that twisted in his belly. He might have made it through the night if she hadn't mentioned that afternoon aloud, but now that she had, he couldn't force it out of his mind.

Suddenly he was obsessed with touching her again, pressing her flesh to his, taking her right here on this dirt floor with the wind rushing around the cave and no one for miles to disturb them. He could almost smell the musk of their lovemaking. He gritted his teeth until his jaw ached.

"It was a mistake, Glenlyon," she said, gripping the plaid. "You have to stop thinking about it. It isn't normal."

"I wasn't thinking about it at all," he snapped. "I was thinking I needed a cigar, but since I only have one left, I'm going to save it to smoke in peace." He stabbed at the fire with a stick. "That afternoon was the farthest thing from my mind. In fact, I'd completely forgotten it until you brought it up just now."

Elspeth set down the plaid and bag, bending forward to massage her knee. "Well, you were looking at me like that again, and I assumed—"

He threw the stick into the fire. His eyes reflected the searing heat of the flames. "I was looking at you in what way? *Dieu*, it's that imagination of yours at work again. I wasn't looking at you at all."

The fire in his eyes flustered her. Biting back the impulse to argue, she distracted herself by hiking up her skirts to examine her knee. She had to admit it felt better since he'd poulticed and bandaged it less than an hour ago. Despite his pretense of harsh detachment, he had the gentlest touch she had ever known.

He frowned. "Is something wrong with the bandage?"

"No. It doesn't hurt half as much as before."

"I'd better look at it again."

"Oh, good heavens, no."

But she fell silent as he stood and crossed the short distance between them, crouching at her side to probe his index finger under the wrapping.

"I don't see anything wrong with it," he muttered, his brow furrowed.

"I never said there was, Glenlyon."

He looked up appraisingly into her face. Elspeth was conscious of the fire's smoky warmth, of a pleasurable tension radiating up her thigh from his hand as it tightened around her knee.

Releasing her breath, she said, "I suppose you learned your medical skills in the army."

"Some." His voice was as thick as hers was thin-pitched with nervousness. "My grandfather was a physician."

Her heart missing a beat, she let her hand slide boldly down her side to cover his. "I think I read that somewhere. It must have been in one of Archie Harper's articles."

Niall gave her a chastising smile, turning his palm up to intertwine their fingers. "And I thought you were above reading such rubbish," he said softly, amused, aroused by her minor act of aggression.

"To be perfectly honest, I am," she said earnestly. "But I brought along a few of Cat's magazines because I was curious about you." She shuddered a little, closed her eyes in sublime relaxation as he began to trace his initials with his thumb over her wrist.

"Curiosity killed the cat," he murmured. *"Ciel,* what I could do if I had half the power attributed to me."

Her eyes gleamed in the fire glow. "What would you do if you really knew magic?" she whispered. "I don't believe in it myself, but how would you use your power?"

He glanced down at their interlocked hands, loosened his grip to run his long elegant fingers up and down her forearm. As he smiled, the creases on either side of his sensual mouth deepened with what Elspeth imagined was some secret knowledge of sexuality. Suspense gathered in the smoky silence. Her eyelids grew heavy. His playful touch made her quiver, made her feel faint, made her ache.

"I don't need to put a spell on you, do I, Elspeth?" he asked softly. "All I'd have to do is keep touching you like this and you'd melt like hot wax in my hands."

"The hell I would, you conceited numskull," she said, her eyes flying open. "I'm just too lazy and tired to pull my hand away."

"All that passion—" He shook his head. His low voice was mocking, seductive. "—all that passion hidden behind your shield of bravado just begging for the right man to set it free."

She swallowed, the smile that touched her lips acerbic. "Was that what you did in that brothel of yours, Glenlyon? Helped women 'free' their passions?"

She was enjoying the moment too much to notice the brief silence that fell, the glimmer of remembered pain in his eyes. She had no idea that her carelessly spoken words had broken his heart.

"Drink your coffee before it gets cold, Elspeth," he said in a subdued voice. "It will make the food more palatable. And thank you, *chérie,"* he added with a cynical smile, lifting his hand from her arm.

A tiny sigh escaped her at the loss of pleasurable contact. "Thank me for what?"

"For reminding me what I was, what I am. You see, there are times when I'm with you and I forget that ugly life I've led. I look at you, and it almost doesn't seem possible that once I lived only to rummage in a rubbish heap with pariah dogs for my next meal."

Tears of self-reproach stung her eyes. He always put up such a cynical front himself that it had never occurred to her until this moment that he was deeply ashamed of his past. "Niall, I'm so sorry."

"—it doesn't seem possible that I dragged opium-crazed customers off young girls who'd been sold into prostitution by their parents."

"Please," she whispered, tormented by the images he had painted of his past. "I never think before I speak."

"It doesn't matter."

"Yes, it does." She shifted upward to grab his arm, ignoring the shaft of pain that shot through her knee. "Just a few minutes ago, when I accused you of looking at me and having lustful thoughts about that afternoon—"

"Par Dieu, sweetheart, don't start that again."

"It was because I've been thinking about it, Glenlyon, wishing it would happen again." She wiped impatiently at the tears trickling down her face. "Damnation, I don't know why I'm crying. I don't even know what I'm saying to you, or why I care so much when it's obvious you don't give a groat about me."

He hadn't moved, hadn't said a word, but then suddenly his face darkened; he caught her hand and was reeling her into his lap, his eyes glittering with unmistakable intent. Elspeth gave a shaky laugh of relief through her tears and hugged his shoulders, arching her neck when his arms tightened around her and he buried his face in the silken tangle of her hair.

"You think I don't care?" he whispered harshly.

"I-I don't know what to think."

"I'll be damned if you don't make me feel as eager

and as awkward as an altar boy with his first woman," he said with a catch in his voice. "Tell me again how you wished it would happen again."

She wiggled into a more comfortable position across his lap, leaning her head back to gaze up into his face. "Are you going to seduce me, Glenlyon?"

"In a cave? You must think I'm an animal. How do you unbutton this dress, hmmm?"

Elspeth rubbed her cheek against his shoulder, the strong musk of his skin, the acrid tang of smoke, seducing her senses. One by one he plucked loose the buttons at her back, artful little pops against her vertebrae. A wave of cool night air caressed her bare flesh, followed by the proprietary warmth of his palm.

"That's much better, isn't it?" he whispered.

She blushed. She shivered. She closed her eyes only to open them as a twig on the fire exploded into a burst of sparks. He leaned back and molded her body to his, giving a low excited groan as he untied her chemise and eased it up over her arms. She fell limp against him. The hard ridge of his sex pushed into her buttocks through her drawers.

"It still isn't too late," he said quietly. "I'll take you home to Papa and Georgie in the morning, and no one will be the wiser."

She didn't answer. She could barely tip her head back and stare up into his unsmiling face, mesmerized by the raw need it reflected.

"Didn't you hear me?" he said roughly. With his face deliberately cold, intending to frighten her, he shoved his hand under her skirts and forced his fingers into the damp crevice of her drawers. "I want this," he said, clenching his jaw. "I want you here, on the ground, just like the animal you accused me of being."

"Glenlyon—"

"I want to teach that impertinent mouth of yours to do

things you've never even heard of," he went on in a dangerously soft voice, "I want you the way the hill warriors used to take the whores I was paid to protect."

Elspeth flinched at his deliberate crudeness even as an arrow of heat shot through her at his touch and splintered inside her belly. Dangerous. Mercenary. Womanizer. But perhaps she was just as bad, a creature of passions that ran too deep, too wild to control. Perhaps she was simply too dispirited and confused to care anymore. Or perhaps, her heart countered in a hopeful whisper, perhaps she had found the love she had secretly ached for all her life.

"I think I'm delirious, Glenlyon," she said in a husky whisper. "I'm beginning to imagine myself in love with you. Feel my head."

"In love . . . with me?"

He laughed in unrestrained delight and lowered his mouth to hers. His kiss was infinitely tender, chasing away every last vestige of her resistance. Moments later, she couldn't have explained how, she was lying beneath him on that plaid again, her gown bunched up to her hips, and his graceful body draped over hers as if she had been made for the sole purpose of giving and receiving pleasure.

"Glenlyon." She moaned his name, in surrender, in regret, in pure female desire. She wet her lips and shivered as he ground his lower body to hers, staring down at her face.

"I'm delirious, too," he whispered. "You've been a fire in my blood since that night we met. *Chère,* your fate was sealed the moment you let me kiss you."

He bracketed his jaw with his left hand; he teased the moist outline of her lips with his tongue while he worked his other hand between her legs. She whimpered, unable to restrain herself from moving against his fingers. Her hot response was all the encouragement he needed to penetrate her damp passage, to play with the little nub of exquisitely sensitive nerve endings he had found.

"Trust me?" he asked her quietly, his eyes closed briefly in fierce enjoyment, the scent and softness of her overwhelming his senses.

"That's the trouble," she murmured. "I've trusted too many people."

"The wrong people."

"What are you saying?" she whispered, hardly daring to hope.

"Dieu, je ne sais— All I know is I need you to trust me. I need this."

"Yes," she whispered shakily.

He swallowed as he felt her stroking his neck with her fingertips, a tenderness he hadn't experienced for too many years in her touch. "I know something else," he said, his voice almost inaudible. "I can't let you go again."

The intensity of his face made her catch her breath. Her one sexual experience with Robert had been clumsy, painful, humiliating; he had shattered her with his betrayal. She wasn't sure if her heart had mended enough to withstand whatever the future held with this enigmatic man.

"It's too late to change your mind," he said, reading the indecision in her eyes. "I'm sorry—no, I'm not. You should never have let me touch you if you weren't sure."

"But I wanted you to," she whispered. She ran her hands down his broad muscular back. "I want . . . to feel you inside me."

Primitive desire ignited in the unfathomable depths of his eyes. He kissed her again, and Elspeth felt a frisson of fear-edged anticipation ripple over her, aware that this time he wasn't playing, that his hands were shaking as he untied her skirts, shoving the wool and her thin drawers down her legs.

He deepened his kiss, not breaking away until blackness swam in her head, until she'd forgotten where they were, until she waited beneath him with her heart and body laid bare, her languid acquiescence inviting him to assuage the aching need he had awakened.

He muttered something in French. He swore as he reared back to pull off his coat and knocked over her cup of untasted coffee with his foot. Elspeth swallowed a nervous laugh, but she couldn't look away, not even when he began to undress, sending his shirt, his trousers, his boots flying across the cave.

No, she couldn't look away; she stared with unabashed curiosity at his body in the fire shadows. Naked, he was even more beautiful than she could believe, his long muscular torso deeply tanned almost down to the thick penis that jutted from the black pelt between his legs.

She rose up on one elbow. "Merciful heavens, Glenlyon—you're brown right down to your bum! Don't tell me you swim nude on your island in broad daylight?"

"Why not?" Grinning, he positioned himself between her thighs, his powerful biceps straining with the weight of balancing his body above hers. "Would you like to make love on my private beach with the waves washing against us? Or do you prefer in a volcanic pool by moonlight?"

"Only if the water is very warm," she whispered mischievously.

He lowered his head. She gasped, arching involuntarily at the intimate shock of his mouth blazing a trail down her throat, her collarbone, her shoulder. He showed her no mercy, nipping her flesh like a wolf cub, kissing the swollen aureoles of her breasts until she was writhing to evade or encourage him, she could no longer tell.

Glenlyon. Oh, yes. There was magic in the name.

And Elspeth needed him, too, not only to satisfy the physical yearning he had aroused in her, but to anchor herself against the turbulence of the past fortnight. In a world that had suddenly tilted on its axis, Niall had proven to be the only person she could rely on. Without pretension or false promises, he had caught her every time she had stumbled.

He had stolen her heart like a thief in the night.

"No, Niall." She gave a soft moan, moved her hands restlessly down the muscled plane of his back. "How did I let this happen?"

"It's all right, Elspeth," he soothed her.

"It isn't all right unless you promise me you won't break my heart."

"Promise you won't break mine," he whispered back. "Promise me you won't go back to George no matter what."

"I'm through with George," she said vehemently, but there was enough doubt in Niall's mind to make him narrow his eyes, to make him wild at the thought of another man possessing her after he had staked his claim.

"What can we promise each other beyond the night, *mon coeur?* Do you want marriage? All right, I'll marry you."

"Dammit, don't make a joke of this."

"A joke?" He caught her face in his big hands. His voice, a virtual growl in the silence, terrified her even as it sent a thrill of primitive satisfaction coursing down her spine. "I'm not the type to plant a babe in your belly and abandon you. I keep what's mine, do you understand?"

"What I understand is that passion makes people stupid, Glenlyon. It breaks hearts and ruins lives."

"I know about Robert Campbell," he said, his hands tightening around her face before she could pull away. And the shame and sadness in her eyes filled him with bitter regret that he hadn't left the callous bastard with more than a broken nose.

"Goddamn you, Glenlyon," she whispered in a voice that shook with shocked humiliation. "How could you know?"

"Never mind now. All you should care about is that somehow in this insane world, you and I have found each other, and if I take you tonight, there'll be no turning back for either of us."

She pressed her face into his palm. "Then take me, Glenlyon," she whispered passionately. "I don't intend to turn back anyway."

The warmth of the fire washed over them, wrapped their straining bodies in gilded shadows. The wind, promising winter, howled across the Highland moor. Lost in each other, they did not notice.

He drove into her body. He thrust, his shoulder muscles straining. He clenched his jaw and released a purring groan of animal pleasure into the silence. She was tight, so sweet, her flesh plush with arousal, slick and sheathing him, and he gripped her hips in his hands and penetrated deeper. He filled her until his possession of her body was complete, until he knew he could hold back no longer.

Yes, she belonged to him now, and he reveled in his domination. She was responding to his every stroke as he intended she should.

She was his.

She couldn't speak; soft animal sounds broke in the back of her throat. She couldn't even be sure if her heart was still beating, gripped by a shock of wonderful anticipation. The power of his rhythmic thrusting drove her into the rough folds of the plaid; it sparked a sweet friction in her body that had to be eased or she would die. Sensation and emotion overlapped, ignited into white-hot wavelets that weakened, warmed her, swept her in a relentless rush toward a faraway shore.

"Chère," he said, his breathing ragged. "I can't get enough of you . . . can't get deep enough inside."

Overcome with her own restless compulsion, she raked her hands down to the hard contours of his hips. She lifted her legs to lock together as he rode her. His gaze unfocused, he gripped her buttocks in his hands and jerked her against him with such force that she stopped breathing, impaled to the hilt.

"Mine," he whispered, his face contorted in the firelight with fierce male triumph.

The tension that had gripped her nerves and muscles suddenly uncoiled to electrify her with a thousand pinpoints of pleasure that darted through her veins. Her senses shattered like fine crystal. She sobbed his name. She fisted her hands, and quivered. Watching her face with erotic intensity, Niall threw back his head and surrendered his own control. His body was shaking with the primal force of his orgasm and unleashed emotions. His hold on her was almost bruising in its possessiveness when he finally lowered himself onto his side to drag her against him.

"And now it is too late," he said with heartfelt satisfaction.

She shivered, her voice a dry whisper. "Yes."

He wrapped his big arms around her shoulders, absorbing the convulsive shivers that shook her from the force of her emotions. Elspeth heard her heart beating like a wild bird against his damp chest. With a secret smile of wonder, she realized she could detect the racing counter-rhythm of his. She had shaken him, too.

"Glenlyon," she murmured, "you damned rogue."

She closed her eyes, touched her tongue to his shoulder to taste the salty musk of his skin. In a distant corner of her mind, she registered the uneasy nickering of the horses outside, the thudding of loose stones down the hill. Then there was quiet.

She didn't move. Contentment was blanketing her capacity to worry. And even before she could rouse herself to demand he at least cover their naked bodies with the plaid, he had rolled away from her and leaped to his feet, utterly naked, his rifle in his hand. Bewildered, she barely had time to blink at him before he grabbed his coat and rushed toward the covered entrance of the cave.

He returned several minutes later with their horses, looking highly annoyed as he led both animals past the fire to the back of the cave. Elspeth didn't know what to make of him, parading around in the freezing wind with his caped coat barely reaching the line of his bare knees. The man was untamed to the marrow.

"I thought I heard something," he said curtly, in such a tone of voice she decided that the less said about his bizarre appearance, the better. "It must have been the horses—at least they'd broken their tethers, but don't ask me how."

"What else could it have been, Niall?" She pulled the plaid tighter around her shoulders, covertly admiring his lean brown buttocks as he bent to rummage in his bags. "We're miles away from the main road, at night in a cave."

He was quiet for a moment. "There are other people on the moor besides us, Elspeth."

"I imagine that there are, Niall, but as long as Francis hasn't followed us, I can't see any reason to worry."

He frowned, obviously not agreeing, and went about the business of feeding and brushing down the horses for the night. Elspeth listened to the wind and tried inexpertly to rebuild the fire. It wasn't all that late, really, it just seemed so because of the shorter days and the piercing cold that Niall had let into the cave when he'd pulled aside the windscreen.

But when she thought about what they had done only a half hour ago, she didn't feel at all cold, just a little bruised and deliriously happy and terrified. Niall seemed so preoccupied that she wondered if he was going to pretend nothing had happened between them. Her heart sank at the prospect of their intimacy not surviving past the sexual act.

She reached into her bag for her stolen bottle of whiskey, hiding it in the plaid as Niall unexpectedly strode back to the fire to hover over her like a thundercloud.

He folded his arms across his chest and frowned. "Are you ready to go home now?" he asked, his voice rasping.

She looked up at him, past his long bare legs, to his face. "I'm not going home, Glenlyon," she sputtered, hurt and indignant. "I can't believe you'd even ask me that after we—well, after I've come this far."

He was silent.

Her face defiant, she pulled the bottle out of her bag and uncorked it. "Are you ready to give up on me?" she challenged as she took a swig that half choked her as it trickled down her throat.

"No."

His expression unreadable, he crouched down beside her and sorted through their clothes, separating his shirt and trousers from her rumpled gown. Elspeth's mouth went dry as their hands touched, as he looked up briefly into her face.

"Get dressed," he said. "It's cold in here."

"I don't want to go back, Glenlyon." She gripped her bottle with fingers that had suddenly gone numb with fear. "You can't make me. Just because we—you don't have the right to stop me."

He gave her a silencing look, his face grim.

Smoke wafted between them from the balls of bracken fern she'd heaped on the fire. Fanning the choking air from his face, Niall dressed, then settled down to watch her with brooding absorption as she pulled off the plaid to do the same.

Firelight gleamed in the alluring hollows of her body; the wisps of smoke that screened her made her seem like some elusive nymph, a teasing creature of his deepest fantasies who might disappear if he reached out to claim her with his grasping mortal hands.

But he had claimed her. He drew a deep breath into his belly as if to bank the flames of desire that stirred at the memory of their mating. Her nakedness, her nearness enticed him. He forgot what they'd been discussing, fascinated by the plump fullness of her breasts, her hips, the golden triangle of hair between her thighs. He ached to bury himself in her softness all over again, to taste her secret nectar. He tried to look away but couldn't. He balled his hands into fists to stifle his longing to touch her. Once hadn't been enough—it had only broken the first barrier between them. It had made him face the dark well of his feelings.

He was so afraid of what he felt for her, the physical obsession only the surface of a deeper, more dangerous involvement. He didn't want it to end here.

She pulled her gown over her head, wriggled into her skirts with an unintentional sensuality that wrought an audible groan from Niall. "I'm not going back to George or my father, and you're not giving up on me," she said as if to challenge him. "Where does that leave us, Glenlyon?"

He smiled darkly, considering his answer as he retrieved his dented coffeepot from its bed of heated stones. "Where does it leave us, *chère?*" he asked with a slow elegant shrug. "About five days or so from Glen Fyne if the weather doesn't worsen."

They warmed some of Niall's barley bannocks over the fire and ate them with chunks of white cheese while the wind blasted across the moor and banged against the breaker Niall had constructed. Elspeth ignored his disapproving looks and sipped the potent liquor in her flask. The raw Highland whisky warmed her insides, but had scant effect on her churning emotions.

No, she hadn't learned a thing from her experience with Robert Campbell. She was as enslaved to her baser nature as when she'd believed the empty promises of a married man. But this time it was far, far worse.

Glenlyon hadn't told her he loved her, or that she meant anything more to him than one of the many other women he had undoubtedly known in his notorious life. No, she hadn't learned a blessed thing about love and passion.

Her heart skipped a beat as he threw his saddlebags against her legs, then stretched out himself beside her. "I don't intend to haul a drunken woman across the Highlands."

She turned her head to stare down at him, her voice lifting in excitement. "You're really going to come with me?"

"If you tell me the truth. The real reason you ran away."

Panic closed her throat. "I can't, Niall. I just can't."

"Then I'm taking you home." He gazed morosely into the fire. "You know damn well you can't make it all the way to Glen Fyne without my help."

She leaned her chin against her updrawn knees, her eyes reflecting the glow of the fire and the fear she had lived with since Tormod's death.

And then in a soft halting voice she told Niall everything, not looking at him once but feeling as if a stone had been rolled off her chest from the release of tension. He didn't interrupt her. She was afraid to even look at his face for fear of the horror it might reflect.

"It—it was murder," she finished, feeling emotionally drained as the damning words were spoken. "George is a good enough marksman that it couldn't have been an accident."

"And yet George claims he was only protecting you." There was more than a trace of doubt in his voice, but he wanted to be fair. "What will you do if when you reach Glen Fyne, you find out he was telling the truth all along?"

Elspeth lifted her face from her knees. "What do you mean?"

"Will you forgive George, forget your past misadventures, and live the life you and he had planned? After all, a gentleman can hardly be faulted for defending his fiancée. Tormod might indeed have been mad. George, although I admit it stretches the imagination, might turn out to be a hero."

She blinked in confusion. "How can I marry George after he and Susan . . . after you and I just. . . ."

He sat up to refill their coffee mugs, his voice rich with irony. "I'll never tell any of your secrets if that's what you're worried about. As for Susan—" He gave a Gallic shrug. "—a man is allowed to take a mistress in George's position, *n'est-ce pas?* It's acceptable, even encouraged in European society, isn't it?"

Elspeth made a face, refusing the mug he held out, and raised the flask to her mouth. "I didn't expect you to understand," she muttered.

"Ah, so despite everything, you still believe in love, is that it?"

"Don't you?" she challenged, feeling a wave of intense dizziness weave through her head as the whisky worked its magic.

Biting off a curse, he pried the half-empty flask from her hand and pulled her against his side. "You should have told me the truth that very night instead of running away. You'd have spared us both a load of grief."

"I didn't trust you then." She gave a desolate sigh,

dropping her head against his shoulder. "I'm not even convinced I should trust you now."

"Because my clothes are five years out of fashion, and I wasted part of my youth in a whorehouse waiting for my sister?"

She tilted her head back and stared up into his shadowed face. "Poor Glenlyon," she whispered. "Listen to me going on, and you have your own woes, don't you? Well, I'll tell you this, and I mean it. I hope with my whole heart that your sister comes home one day soon, and that your sad, scattered family is reunited, and—"

"Shut up, Elspeth," he said, shaking his head in gentle reproof. "Nobody in my sad, scattered family has a home to come back to anymore. Besides, that whisky has gone right to your head, and you're starting to sound like a rambling drunkard."

She closed her eyes, sighing again. "I'm afraid you're right, Glenlyon, about the whisky going to my—"

He caught her chin in his big hand and interrupted her with a long penetrating kiss. When he finally released her, Elspeth snuggled into his arms with a drowsy smile of satisfaction.

"Get some rest while you can," he said, stroking her hair. "We're leaving in only a few hours, and we'll be riding hard if we're to beat the first blizzard to Glen Fyne."

"I can't believe you're coming with me," she said softly.

"I can't either."

But he knew as he laid her down beneath him on his bedroll that he couldn't let her go on alone. And he refused to return her to her father and George, uncertain of either man's motives as far as her welfare was concerned.

"Glen Fyne," she said sleepily. "We'll find the answer there, Niall."

"Yes." He nodded absently and glanced around the cave. He wasn't sure they would find any answers at all,

but he was afraid there would be danger. Even if Francis
Barron had not predicted it, Niall could sense it, heard it
whispering in the wind. Less than an hour later, he wished
fervently he had listened to the intuitive warning.

Twenty-eight

Smoke!

The acrid scent stung the back of Niall's throat and invaded his confused dream by insidious degrees.

He disentangled himself from Elspeth's arms and sat up stiffly, wasting precious moments peering into the low-burning fire to seek the source of the smoke. The contained flames glowed back benignly at him from the circle of stones he'd carefully assembled. For all his experience in the wilds, he wouldn't have been surprised to discover he had burned his boots in his insatiable passion for Elspeth during the night.

From the back of the cave the horses nickered and stamped restlessly, dark shifting shapes against the tendrils of gray-brown smoke that drifted across the cave from the windscreen he'd woven.

Smoke—

"Sacrebleu!" He lurched to his feet, jerking the plaid out from beneath Elspeth with enough force to send her rolling away from his feet like a sow bug.

"Wake up! Elspeth, wake up! *Jesu,* cover your mouth and nose with this. No—crawl on your belly. Don't try to stand up yet. Elspeth, stay on the ground!"

She stared up at him, disoriented, and automatically caught the piece of clothing he had doused in cold coffee and thrown down at her; it was her own chemise. She had been in such a deep, exhausted sleep when he'd started shouting that even now she wondered if everything happening around her didn't belong to the tail-end of a vividly frightening dream.

Bitter smoke filled her nostrils with every breath she drew. The horses turned circles in bewilderment, forcing her toward the circle of glowing stones. The repeated thudding of metal against a dull object echoed through the cave. It was a scene straight out of hell.

She glanced up in astonishment to see Niall hacking like a wildman at the smoldering windscreen with his knife, a native parang. The curved steel blade flashed quicksilver in the dark. Chips of burning cinders flew across the cave like a trail of tiny shooting comets. She couldn't understand why he was having so much trouble breaking through to the outside of the cave, why she could not see through to the moor.

She rose to her knees, then froze in horror, realizing that the untucked tail of his shirt had caught fire. Flames raced up his arm, singeing the ends of his longish black hair, which swung to and fro with the frenzied rhythm of his movements.

The odor of scorched linen and hair combined with the intense smoke to choke her. Pressing the chemise to her face, she ignored Niall's warning cry and leaped up, grabbing the plaid to smother the flames on his shirt.

A blessed wave of bracing fresh air washed over her. He had managed to break several openings in the tightly woven screen. Her eyes wide with shock, she stared past him and saw that the mouth of the cave had been obstructed by an enormous wall of loosely piled stones. Swearing, he savagely kicked a hole in the wall. The rocks collapsed around him in a slow groaning cascade.

Her face grew waxen as Elspeth moved beside him to stare outside. "It wasn't an accident," she whispered, shuddering with the gruesome realization.

"Not a chance in hell."

Kneeling, he found and raised his water flask to empty it over his face and sweating throat. His breathing uneven, he staggered to his feet and flicked a few smoking plugs of wood from the screen. Wisps of smoke rose from the dirt as he viciously stamped them out.

"Bog-fir torches," he said slowly, rubbing his burnt sleeve across his eyes. "Someone stuck enough of them in the windscreen to start a bonfire and then sealed us inside the cave like a burning tomb."

Elspeth shook her head in instinctive denial, searching her mind for another explanation to counteract the grim horror of what he had just said: Someone had gone to incredible lengths to burn them to death while they slept.

She swallowed over the tightness in her throat. Tears from the smoke and shock were irritating her eyes. "Who? *Why?*"

He frowned down into her face, his hair disheveled and sprinkled with ash. "None of my friends, *doucette,*" he said tiredly. "Nor my enemies, either, I'm sure."

"Francis Barron," she whispered. She threw the plaid down angrily on the pile of charred rocks that might have proven to be their gravestones. "What a fitting way for a woman he believed was a witch to die."

Niall shoved his hand through his hair, a cold glimmer of logic piercing his own rage. It was true that Barron had seemed furious enough at Elspeth to murder her. But the man had also looked unwell, and unless he possessed hidden talents for tracking and inhuman regenerative powers, he couldn't possibly have walled them in the cave. And call it a sixth sense, but Niall was beginning to suspect Barron did not have a violent bone in his body, no matter what had been said about him.

The disturbing memory of the homeless family he had encountered earlier on the moor broke through the exhaustion blanketing his mind. *They burned us out of our homes like wasps.* Now, there was a reason for revenge.

"Perhaps I was wrong." Elspeth stared at him with an innocent hope that wrenched his heart. "Perhaps I'll find out George and my father aren't guilty of anything worse than protecting me after all. Perhaps they were trying to save me from the truth."

He blinked and brushed a particle of ash from his eyelashes, hating the selfishness in himself that hoped George would not emerge from this mystery as a hero. "Well, who knows?" he said, in a voice raspy from heat and smoke and fatigue. "I suppose they deserve the benefit of the doubt."

She swallowed hard. "I'm so afraid they don't," she whispered.

He saw her lower lip tremble with the strain that had begun to undermine her courage. "I think we might be safer traveling in the dark," he said slowly. "It's almost dawn, and I'll feel better once I get us back onto the hidden strath road."

"Glenlyon." She exhaled quietly and turned her pale face toward the moor. "I don't want you to come with me, after all. Go back to your uncle and have the happy reunion you deserve. And don't forget to insist my father pay you in full. You've earned that money. I appreciate what you've tried to do for me, but I think I have to face whatever lies ahead by myself. Thank you."

She picked up her cloak and climbed over the collapsed barricade of rocks to the moor, her face averted. Niall threw down his flask and knife, shaking with hurt disbelief and anger. Throwing his coat over his shoulders, he jumped over the rubble to block her escape before she could reach the moor.

"Excuse me," he said in a voice of menacing restraint. "I believe you and I became more to each other last night than passing acquaintances. Am I imagining things?"

He had backed her up to the fallen rocks outside the cave, causing her to stumble, to brace herself against the

barren face of the hill that had sheltered them. Hurt fury
rolled off him in waves that battered her own numb misery.

"Damn you, Glenlyon," she said between her teeth as
a single defiant tear rolled down her face. "You don't
have to k-keep pretending."

"Pretending what?" he demanded impatiently.

"Th-that you care about me. You don't have to pretend
that last night meant anything more than a mistake made
by two lonely people."

Anger flared in the depths of his eyes; for a moment
she was truly afraid of him. "Are you telling me that you
were only pretending to love me last night?" he asked her.

She quailed at the deadly calm of his voice, at the naked
vulnerability he had unwittingly revealed. "I knew what I
was doing," she whispered miserably, lifting her chin.

He nodded, a muscle ticking in his jaw. "Yes, and so
did I, and it wasn't a mistake. I wanted you, I took you,
and now you belong to me." He drew a long searing
breath into his lungs, staring up at the sky before he returned his gaze to hers. He was insane at the thought of
losing her. "If I say we are going back to my island, we
will go. And that's the end of it."

"No, it isn't," she said with a quiet dignity that might
have made him laugh at any other time. "This is Scotland,
Glenlyon. We're not savages. I have a responsibility to the
people at Glen Fyne."

He smiled coldly and braced his hands against the hill
to flank her small shoulders, imprisoning her between his
arms. "You have a responsibility to me now. That comes
first, last, forever."

"No." Her heart began to pound against her breastbone.
She didn't doubt for an instant that he meant every word
he said, but so did she. It was a clash of intractable wills.
"I'm going to the glen."

He stared down at her, studying the enchanting face

that had haunted him from the moment he'd first met her. Yes, he could bend her to his will with physical force, or even emotional manipulation for that matter. He knew the right words to say to melt a woman's resolve, even this woman. He could seduce her within seconds; he had spent half the night learning the keys to awakening not just her body but her mind.

The silence lengthened. Elspeth gazed up into his face, his eyes shadowed with emotions too dark for her to fathom. Then just when she thought he would let her go, he took her face in his hands, rammed his body flush to hers with such force that she gasped, and kissed her. Shaking, she pushed at his shoulders, but he didn't budge.

It was a punishing kiss, bittersweet and urgent, a gesture of domination and heart-rending appeal, and she was shocked to find herself responding with a hunger as primal as his. She wrapped her arms around his waist and closed her eyes. She kissed him back until neither of them could breathe. Her spine ached from the crushing pressure of his weight. A dry sob broke in her throat.

She was shaking violently when he released her to sag back into the rough crevice of the hill. The sky had lightened to a watery violet-gold, but the wind still blew with a chilling intensity that cut to her bones the instant Niall drew back from her.

"Come away with me, *chérie*."

"Glenlyon," she said in soft despair.

He studied her intently, his face drawn into stark lines that might have meant regret or realization, perhaps both. She thought he looked more than wild, his black hair stirring on his powerful shoulders, his cheekbones smeared with ash. The emotions that he exuded were so elemental she could feel them tearing through all her upbringing, her defenses. She could feel herself abandoning everything she believed in, to belong to him. Just like that. He held complete power over her foolish heart in his hands.

"Get out of my life, Niall Glenlyon," she whispered in anguish. "You like being alone, isn't that what Archie Harper wrote about you? You hate parties, you hate people. You need solitude in order to survive."

"I need you," he said quietly.

"Do you?" she asked, her voice breaking. "For how long?"

He saw through her apparent rebuff. He saw through the fear of loving and of being loved, the fear of rejection and betrayal. He felt her pain, and his sense of empathy only made it worse, made him want her more. He felt these things because he had suffered them himself and let them scar his heart.

"I am not Robert Campbell," he said slowly. "I'm not George or any other man who ever hurt you."

"Then who are you?" She tilted her face up to his, felt her heart tighten with anxiety as she threw out a challenge he did not expect. "What do you believe in, Glenlyon? What do you stand for?"

He shook his head. He searched his soul and was stricken by his inability to form an answer. All his life he had run away. From the horror of his father being tortured to death when he had been too terrified to intervene. He had run from the seminary where he'd passed two abysmal months flirting with the priesthood.

He had spent years of his life finding lost people when in truth he had been running from himself; and when his days as a tracker had ended, he had hidden away on his island, giving the local Resident and Rajah strict instructions that his privacy must be protected.

And it had taken this woman with the heart of a tigress to show him how empty he'd become, that his withdrawal from the world had come with a price too high to pay— the slow death of his soul.

"Who am I, *chérie?*" he asked softly. "I'm a fool, that's

who I am." Then, shaking his head again, he whirled from the sight of her heartbroken face and strode past the cave.

He walked into the wind, fighting against its brutal force, its turbulence reflecting his own bewildered thoughts. He and Elspeth could not have been more unlike. Life was so easy for someone like her, who saw everything in terms of black and white, who fought tooth and nail for what she believed in.

Of course, at least she believed in something, whether based on reality or romantic illusion, he didn't know. But it was more than he could say for himself. Unfortunately, she also had it in her stubborn head to save the world.

Well, it was a hopeless cause. Niall had figured that out by the time he turned fifteen. There was too much evil for one person to battle, and before long the world would squelch all her admirable spirit. Ultimately, in his opinion, a person faced only two rational options: You either became part of the insanity, or you withdrew from it and lived in peaceful, if lonely, isolation.

"Glenlyon!"

He heard her calling him and quickened his pace, no logical destination in sight. He was running again, but it would seem there was no safe haven from the fervent desires of his heart.

He wondered for a moment if he had it all wrong. Perhaps she didn't really need him at all. Perhaps there were guardian angels who watched over those intrepid souls like Elspeth Kildrummond, the self-appointed champions of humanity. Perhaps no matter what danger she got herself into, and with her headstrong nature, danger was assured, there would be some invisible power waiting to pluck her up, brush her off, and set her charging back into the me-lee. She would fight the good fight to the end.

But *he* needed her. He needed her faith, her courage,

her incorruptible enthusiasm for life. It would destroy what faint spark of hope that kept his wounded soul alive to lose her. Perhaps in the world's eyes he had nothing to offer a woman of ideals, but he would protect her, cherish her with his whole being, make her life the endless adventure her vibrant spirit deserved. How could he let her go? No, he wouldn't. No one, nothing, would take her away from him.

Nothing except her obsession with a murdered old man and the remote Highland glen that she called her heart's home.

Elspeth stared after his receding figure, panic and hope clutching her heart. She'd told him to go, but she hadn't meant it. She had denied her own feelings, how much she needed him, how deeply she loved the rogue.

She loved him. Heaven help her, it had happened despite all her efforts to resist it. And he felt something for her too, which only complicated the outcome because neither of them could be counted on to behave in any reasonable manner whatsoever. What better example than their wild mating the night before?

She ran out across the moor after him. High winds tore at her hair, and she imagined she must look like Medusa. Niall had already climbed the hill and was striding along the exposed ridge to God only knew where, his black caped coat billowing out behind him. They were starting to act like a pair of players in one of Shakespeare's comedies.

"Glenlyon!"

He was either too far away to hear, or he had given up on her. She hitched up her skirts and clambered up the hill, gasping in anger, at the raw assault of cold.

She thought he was half mad, abandoning her, the horses. She stumbled onto the ridge, ran, and caught a handful of his coat, jerking the frogged fastening to the side of his neck.

He spun around, staring down at this wild creature clinging to him as a falcon would at a fox.

"Dieu," he muttered, reaching into his coat pocket for a cigar before he remembered he had only one left, in the cave, and how would he smoke it anyway in this wretched Scottish wind? *"Sacré nom d'un chien!"*

"If you're going to swear at me, Glenlyon," she said breathlessly, her throat aching, "you could at least have the courtesy to do so in English."

He glared down his nose at her. He was furious at her idealism, keenly jealous of her ties to the past and to a heritage that did not deserve her fierce loyalties. He craved every last ounce of her passionate attachments for himself.

He'd meant it when he had told her he would take her back to his island. His motives were primarily selfish, of course; he wanted her without any competition whatsoever. But it was also the only way he foresaw protecting her. True, he might have phrased his proposal a trifle more poetically, waited until he was not so desperate to pump into her sweet little body that he would have said anything to please her. But her answer today had been blunt enough.

She preferred her lofty battle of ideals in lieu of a life with him. He could not bear it.

He gripped her wrist, furious at the thought of losing her, and hauled her to her feet. "Let go of my coat. It's the only decent piece of clothing this worthless pimp owns."

"I was afraid you were leaving me," she said in a hoarse whisper.

He pulled her toward him, his heart beating fiercely as she laid her head against his chest. He could feel his anger draining away, replaced by a tenderness, a poignant stab of despair that was a far more dangerous emotion.

"Elspeth," he whispered. "Do you know something? I'm well and truly lost for the first time in my life."

"Lost?" she said, catching her breath at the hope slowly sparking in her heart.

"Yes, ironic, isn't it?" he said with a smile of resignation.

She exhaled slowly and stared into his sad gray eyes, shaken by the naked emotions he had allowed to surface. "Are you going to run away from me, too?" she asked softly, aware he had fought some kind of battle within himself, and not knowing where she stood.

"Will you come with me?"

"Yes." She felt his fingers grasp hers. "You know I will. You . . . you've won."

The coils of tenderness tightened around his heart, and he flinched at the painful rebirth of feelings so long repressed. Relinquishing her hand, he gestured toward the pine-bristled hills that rose like footsteps into the dawn horizon. "There's a track through those hills that leads away from the loch road and cuts into your beloved glen."

A gust of wind raced across the ridge, buffeting their bodies, and then there was stillness.

"I know the bloody way to the glen," she said, swallowing tightly at the sacrifice she had made. "What difference does it make anyway?"

He smiled again, the cynical glint back in his eye. "You're not afraid of Francis Barron, of people who try to roast you alive during the night?"

"I'm more afraid of what you make me feel," she said solemnly.

He laughed softly at that, and lifted his face into the morning light. "And I'm terrified, *ma chère,* but the alternative, to feel nothing, is much, much, worse. Come on. We're wasting time. Take me to this place you love so well."

Twenty-nine

Niall had once led his regiment into a war-ravaged Burmese village. Now, as he rode slowly toward Elspeth's glen, he felt that same sense of desolation forewarn him.

It was the haunting despair of a ghost village, the aftermath of human tragedy and abandonment. It was the sad echoing of a way of life forever gone.

He saw it in the absence of hoofprints and cart tracks on the old drover's road they followed. He felt it as they crested the last foothill and stared through the autumnal haze that blanketed the glen. No curling wisps of smoke in the distance from home fires to season the air and welcome the weary traveler. He felt sick inside for Elspeth and wished fervently to have been proven wrong. The idyllic little glen she loved no longer existed.

"Elspeth," he said in concern as she rode past him, her eyes glazed, refusing to read the clues that were so obvious. "The horses need rest and food. We need food and shelter for the night."

"Soon," she murmured, shortening the reins. "We'll be home soon, Glenlyon."

As they descended into a dark stretch of fir thicket, he studied the ground. He spotted several deer beds among the low-growing junipers. A hind darted out from behind a tree and disappeared.

He wanted suddenly to turn around, to protect Elspeth from whatever grim discovery awaited them in the glen, which held so many fond memories for her. But unlike him, she would refuse to run away.

"Is it as you remember it?" he asked quietly.

She hesitated; her face was flushed pink from the cold air that swept down from the Cairngorms. She was disappointed, yes, that she hadn't met an old friend or two in the hills, but then there was a sharp bite of snow in the air, it was late afternoon, and the shortness of daylight demanded chores be done before dark.

She drew a deep calming breath, refusing to give in to the anxiety that had crept over her happy anticipation. "I wish you could see it in summer, Glenlyon. Masses and masses of white briar roses smother the stone hedges for almost three miles."

"It sounds delightful," he said in a subdued tone. "I'm sorry to have missed it."

"Perhaps we won't miss it, after all," she said, excitement returning to her voice at the idea. "We could stay here all winter. We'll hibernate at Liath House, and when summer comes—"

"We'll make passionate love on a bed of rose petals?" he suggested, leaning forward on the pommel of his saddle with a lazy smile. "Why wait that long, *doucette?*"

"Good Lord, Niall, not this close to home."

He caught her by the waist and lifted her across his horse, his strong thighs gripping her when she would have wriggled away. He did feel like taking her right where they sat, easing his hands under her skirts as he kissed the back of her neck, but it was too damned cold for such love play, as tempted as he was by the idea.

"Are you still sore, *chérie?*" he whispered, giving her bottom a possessive pat before he set her back on her own horse. "I loved you hard last night in that shepherd's hut, I know, but I couldn't help myself."

"You've loved me hard every night since we left the cave," she said wryly.

"And who was chasing whom in that barn the other morning, hmmm?"

She blushed, the place between her legs still burning where his leather-gloved hand had briefly caressed her. Yes, she was sore, not just from making love, but from riding for days on end and exercising muscles she'd forgotten even existed. But it would be all right once they reached Liath House. She would take a lovely tub and make Niall rub her aching back.

"It's getting dark," he said, a frown darkening his face. "You'd better start leading the way."

She slid to the ground; fallen fir needles rustled under her feet. "There's nothing to worry about now. I can find my way home blindfolded from here. Even if we don't make it to Liath House tonight, there are plenty of crofts along the way where we'll be welcome."

He said nothing and slowly scanned the long shadows of the woods. The fine hairs on the nape of his neck had begun to prickle. He was positive they had not been followed and just as certain that all of a sudden they were being watched.

"We're not alone," he warned her in an undertone.

"Of course we're not," Elspeth said blithely as she began leading her mare through the maze of firs. "All the woods of Glen Fyne are haunted, and the bogles always come out at gloaming. Perhaps they're welcoming me back. Oh, look, Niall, you can see the old kirk through the trees. I was christened there, you know."

"Really?" he said, reaching covertly into his waistband for his gun.

"Yes. I wonder if the old reverend will invite us into the manse for tea and scones. I'm famished, and don't you dare make any comments about how we've been spending our nights if he does."

He followed her on his horse, ignoring her cheerful

chatter until they broke out of the woods and his feeling of unease faded.

"Oh," he heard Elspeth murmur in disappointment. "What a wretched mess the place has become, and to think of Mama and my grandfather resting beneath all that muck."

He dismounted in silence and placed his hand on her shoulder, gazing down the incline into the desolate little cemetery of the village kirkyard. The autumn rains had formed furrows between the weathered gravestones. Quite a few recent gravestones, he thought, tightening his grip on Elspeth. She had to notice the aura of sad abandon here.

A thin wind fluttered across the treetops and set clanging several of the peculiar rusty cages that sat pierced on stakes at the far end of the graveyard.

Elspeth turned toward Niall, her eyes mischievous. "Those cages are ancient, built in the days when people believed you could hold a dead man's spirit captive. I used to make George sneak down here with me late at night so he'd lose his fear of ghosts."

"And did he?"

"Och, no. Tormod dressed up one Samhain Eve in a white sheet complete with ball and chains, and jumped out at us from one of the cages. George never recovered."

Niall forced a smile. "George is liable to end up with a cage of his very own if I ever see the little swine again. Tell me, have there always been so many gravestones here?"

Elspeth hesitated, the nostalgic glint fading from her eyes. "No. Well, no. There haven't, but I suppose a few deaths are inevitable among the old crofters."

"Time passes," he murmured. "People die. Things change."

"Well, Glen Fyne never changes. That's its charm— Oh, don't look so bloody skeptical. It's my own private heaven, Niall, and all its people my personal army of angels."

Thirty

The reverend was not home at the manse when they arrived.

Ignoring Elspeth's loud objections, Niall forced a window open and unceremoniously hoisted her rump first over the sill before climbing in himself. While she landed in a disgruntled heap on the floor, he proceeded to step over her and explore the house. He whistled a Christmas carol through his teeth to counteract the oppressive silence that greeted him.

The place stank of cats, neglect, peat smoke and mildew. Numerous pails and barrels cluttered the hall to catch the leaks crisscrossing the ceiling beneath the heather thatch. The parlor was a comfortable clutter of legal treatises, books, and unwashed whisky glasses.

Elspeth frowned in disapproval from the parlor doorway as Niall poked around. "The reverend is obviously getting on in years," she murmured uneasily. "His housekeeper must have married and moved away."

Niall didn't reply, staring down at a book on the sofa entitled *The Legal Process of Eviction*. "Where's the kitchen?" he asked as he noticed her melting back into the darkness of the hall.

"In the back, but we just can't help—"

"—God helps those who help themselves," he said with mock piety as he caught up with her and grabbed her hand, guiding her around the pails of stagnant rainwater.

"I'm sure the reverend would agree. All I've had to eat today is a bowl of sour juniper berries. We're not leaving this house without a decent meal."

"Can't you at least wait until we reach the crofts and we're invited to supper?" she asked in chagrin.

"No, Elspeth. I can't."

She rushed after him as he strode with unswerving determination into the kitchen, examining the contents of a tin on the table, sampling the cold porridge on the hearth.

She tapped her foot on the flagstone floor. "You're behaving like a barbarian, Niall."

"Do you want some?" he inquired amicably, dipping a long wooden spoon into the pot of lumpy porridge.

"Certainly not!"

He stole a look at her face. There weren't going to be any crofts or cries of homecoming or invitations to share a meal by the fire. No fond reminiscing either.

But he couldn't bring himself to tell her. God forgive him, he didn't have the guts for it. She was going to find out everything George and her father had done anyway. Knowing Elspeth, she'd insist on seeing the damage for herself. He could only be there to hold her when her heart broke.

He ransacked the oak pantry and found a well-preserved shank of ham, a wheel of crumbly yellow cheese, plus a few fat onions that had sprouted trailing roots. Elspeth watched, wide-eyed, as he stuffed the food into his pockets and up his sleeves like a magician performing before the queen. Then he calmly tucked a canister of tea under his coat. Clearly he had done this sort of thing before.

"You're stealing, Niall, and from a man of the kirk to boot! You can't just break into a person's home and pilfer his cupboards like a—a wolf."

Grinning, he extracted a coin from his boot and tossed it onto the table. "For that price, I think he ought to include the crock of marmalade too, don't you?"

Throwing up her hands in disgust, she spun on her heel and marched out of the kitchen. Three mewing kittens materialized from the shadows to escort her. His grin fading, Niall patted the various bulges of hidden food under his clothing and hurried after her. He had a very unpleasant premonition they were going to need every bite he had filched. He'd been forced to forego his principles and spend half her father's money on lodgings and food to get this far. But all the money in the world did no good without shops to spend it.

In the concealing darkness of the hallway, he tore off a piece of ham and popped it into his mouth, savoring the salty flavor before disentangling his ankles from another pair of kittens. He thought he must have lost half a stone this past fortnight, what with chasing after and then ravishing Elspeth halfway across Scotland.

"Couldn't you have restrained yourself until we were back in the woods?" she whispered disparagingly from the front door.

"No." He straightened, squaring his shoulders in self-defense. "A man needs to eat well to keep up with a woman like you."

They shivered as they reemerged into the brisk afternoon air. Elspeth went striding ahead while Niall hesitated at the door to rearrange his onions. Elspeth slowed, then broke into a run as she caught sight of the horses finishing off a bag of oats that had been propped inside the reverend's pony byre.

"Dear God! Moldy oats, no doubt, and now I'll be walking home with two colicky horses and a man who has a stolen ham in his trews!"

Frowning, Niall squatted beside her and helped her scoop the scattered oats back into the sack. Wind whipped through the forlorn garden, over piles of dead broom and a pathetic patch of turnips, chaffing their bare hands and faces. Elspeth's small shoulders drooped in dejection.

"This is the lowest point in my life," she muttered.

He looked into her face. "And because of you it's my highest," he said in a hoarse voice, putting his hand over hers. She swallowed tightly, squeezing his fingers in gratitude.

"We might want to stay here the night in case it snows," he suggested, lowering his gaze. "In the morning I'll ride ahead to make sure everything is all right."

"There's nothing wrong, Glenlyon. Stop talking that way. Francis mentioned months ago that the crops had failed again and that a few families had chosen to move to the Lowlands to make a decent living. But it's going to be all right, you'll see."

She stood, her eyes bright with emotion, and backed away from him. Then almost at the same instant, they noticed a gray-haired man in tweed watching them with a ferocious scowl from the end of the irregular stone pathway to the manse. Leaning heavily on his gnarled walking stick, a creel of peats on his back, he started at a limping stride toward them.

Niall sprang to his feet and attempted to plant himself in front of Elspeth, the ham protruding from his pocket. The man obviously didn't believe in the ancient custom of Highland hospitality.

"Reverend MacCuag," she said in a rush of embarrassed relief, pushing Niall into the background. "Please don't be afraid. I was so hoping to find you home—it's me, Elspeth Kildrummond," she added in confusion as he strode past her without a word, hostility emanating from his face. "It . . . it's me."

"Aye, I ken. I watched ye break into my house and help yerself to what little I have."

"Elspeth," Niall said gently, gripping her elbow. "Let's go."

She shook herself loose. "It's me," she said again in a soft hurt voice. "I've come all the way from Falhaven."

The elderly minister hesitated on the steps, staring back at her with such a look of loathing that she subsided into silence. Niall's head began to pound, with hunger, anxiety, and the intolerable realization that he could protect her from physical harm but not from this. She had given her heart to this place.

"Och, aye," MacCuag said with a snarl. "I remember ye, the wee Kildrummond whore."

The color drained from Elspeth's face. Niall reached for her arm again, but she shrugged away. The pain in her eyes was more than he could tolerate.

In fact, he wouldn't tolerate it.

He began moving toward the steps, not having the faintest notion what he was going to do, but he heard Elspeth telling him to stop, to keep his temper, and he ignored her. The crock of marmalade slipped out of his sleeve and shattered in a sticky puddle at his feet. He ignored that too. A blood-red haze dominated his brain, demanding a primitive response.

The old reverend glanced up from the broken crockery to the dark man approaching the steps. "A whore and a thief," he said with contempt. "Charming, charming. Are ye here to gloat over the spoils of yer destruction?"

Elspeth ran up alongside Niall, trying to intercept him. "Don't antagonize him, Niall. He's old. He doesn't know what he's saying."

"Don't I?" MacCuag raised his twisted juniper cane at them as if he were warding off a curse. "Like buzzards come to feast on the flesh of the dead, ye are. Well, there's a half-dozen buried in the graveyard because of yer family's greed. Puir old Maggie MacQueen, her pregnant daughter and two-year-old grandson."

"No," she whispered dryly, shaking her head in denial.

"Aye, burned out of their homes to make room for a load

of stinking sheep. Seven dead in all, killed by Kildrummond avarice."

His eyes shining with tears of bitterness, he hurled his cane at Elspeth. It missed her by a foot, but it was close enough to snap the frayed threads of Niall's self-restraint. He jumped over the cane, over the willow creel the man had dropped on the path. Anger pulsed through his veins.

"Don't do anything stupid, Niall!" Elspeth cried. "Please—"

She was plucking at his coattails, yanking him back, horrified by the violence in his eyes. The ham popped out of his pocket. The onions he'd stuffed up his sleeve rolled out next. Her looked preposterous, like a walking grocer's cart, and he looked killing mad.

MacCuag must have thought so too. His eyes round with fear, he scurried inside his house and slammed the door just as Niall reached the sunken front steps with a roar of outrage like a wounded beast.

He banged his fist on the door in frustration. Elspeth snagged his wrist on the upswing and pulled him back down the steps, shaken less by MacCuag's naked hatred of her than by Niall's reaction to it.

"Let's leave here, Niall," she begged.

"Like hell—I want my guinea back."

"Niall, we *have* to leave."

He turned reluctantly and glanced down at her, his heart constricting at the bruised disbelief in her eyes. He drew a deep breath into his lungs. He could have strangled that old bastard for upsetting her. He'd swallowed too many years of similar abuse and taunting rejection to stand by and allow someone he loved—

Someone he loved.

The thought met far less resistance now than it had the first time, and he was amazed at how easily, at how eagerly, he had come to accept it. With love followed the possibility of loss and all the complications of involvement he had protected himself against.

Yet suddenly his own pain seemed to take second place. Elspeth mattered more. He loved her more fiercely than he had ever loved anyone or anything in his life. The scope of emotion she aroused in him almost brought him to his knees.

He touched her cold pale cheek in a tentative caress of concern and wonder. For the moment, she belonged to him. He would fight till his last breath to keep her. But if her father and George got hold of her, he was very much afraid the fragile intimacy between them would dissipate like a dream.

"Let's not stay where we're not wanted," he said gruffly, reminding himself that the worst still lay ahead. "I want you to ride in front of me, and don't stop for anything."

She frowned, glancing back at the manse as he grasped her hand and propelled her toward the two horses. "What are you going to do?"

He boosted her onto the mare. "Take my gun. *Take it.* No, sweetheart, don't point it at your feet. Just hold it against the pommel the way you were holding Barron's pistol in the cave. Meet me in the woods."

"But I—" She jerked her head up as the dormer window of the manse scraped open. MacCuag glowered down at them with an ancient fowling musket piece positioned on his shoulder.

"Be gone from the kirk's property, Elspeth Kildrummond! This is nae yer land to destroy. Be gone before I mete out the same mercy yer family showed those who trusted ye!"

She gave a quiet sob and averted her face, but not before her eyes met Niall's and he saw the horrified realization in them. She finally knew now. Perhaps she had suspected all along, and she hadn't been able to face the truth.

His face grim, he swatted her horse on the rump and watched with relief as Elspeth wheeled the mare around and cantered for the woods. He heard MacCuag squeeze the trigger above him, but he refused to move until Elspeth vanished into the dark stand of firs. Then, with an audacity that only the memory of gut-gnawing hunger can engender, he calmly picked up the ham and onions he had dropped before he vaulted onto his own horse to follow her.

Thirty-one

A drizzling mist that promised rain muted the traces of destruction. Piles of charred rubble stood where there had once been tidy rows of crofts. Dying bracken choked the barren oat fields; family plots lay buried between hillocks of mud where now only thistle grew. Everything of beauty cleared away, people, homes, herbage.

Sheep bleated at their solemn passing, wandering haphazardly in front of the horses until Niall cursed and dismounted to chase them away.

"Na Caoraich Mhor—the Great Sheep," he heard Elspeth murmur in contempt, the only words she had uttered in an hour. Then, "George and my father destroyed the glen to fill it with fields of filthy worthless sheep. Damn them. *Damn* them."

Not exactly worthless, Niall observed in cynical silence, remembering the article on the subject of the Highland Clearances that Archie Harper had written with a surprising amount of compassion for the displaced crofters. The renting of the glen to the men who owned those sheep must yield an easy profit. Certainly more than the Kildrummonds had ever made from the impoverished tenants who'd been lucky to eke any living at all from this land.

And those profits would soon belong to Sir George Westcott, as Elspeth's fiancé, the promise of marriage between them legally entitling him to all her worldly goods even before their vows had been exchanged. In a cold monetary sense, George had made a shrewd business decision with his betrothed's dowry, but the price had been untold human suffering.

The families that Elspeth had counted as her dearest friends had been forced from their homes with only the belongings they could carry on their backs so that hundreds of sheep could breed. And prosper the landlord.

He was hesitant to break the silence that had fallen again. He trailed Elspeth on foot into a winding lane that had once bustled with little shops. The wooden shutter of an apothecary's creaked forlornly in the breeze. He would have praised her composure, but he feared it concealed a heartbreak beyond words. The evidence of mass eviction, a way of life erased perhaps forever, depressed even Niall, who had no emotional investment in the glen. He could imagine the blow it had dealt her.

"Where are we going, Elspeth?" he asked, unwilling for night to find them wandering without shelter in a fierce storm.

"Into the heart of hell."

"I'm sorry, Elspeth. I really am."

She sighed deeply, pushing her wind-tangled hair from her face. "And I'm sorry I dragged you along to witness my family's shame, Glenlyon. You ought to go to your uncle before it's too late."

He reached up for her hand, but she threw him a look that was half despair, half defiance. Her back stiff, she spurred her mare toward a solitary black hut that sat amid a grove of skeletal birch trees.

"The witch's hut," she said when he finally reached her, her face so pale and bereft of its lovely spirit it hurt to look at her. "Old Una Innes."

He thought he heard a movement within the hut, but it might have been the wind. The mist was giving way to a trickle of rain. "Are you going to go inside?" he asked Elspeth quietly.

It seemed forever before she answered, but when at last she said, "No," he was relieved, casting an uneasy glance around the strange patterned plots of herbs planted around the hut. A sense of dormant power lay over the place, neither good nor evil.

"Why was her hut not burned like the others?" he wondered aloud.

Elspeth stared dully at the shriveled rowan cross nailed to the door. "Perhaps her magic protected her. More likely, though, the vicious bastards left her alone out of superstitious fear for their own lives."

Niall walked slowly toward the hut and felt a smattering of cold raindrops hit his forehead. "Would she put us up for the night?" he asked as he reached the broken garden gate.

Elspeth didn't respond. When Niall looked around to repeat the question, he saw that she had gone, riding hard for the little forest that fringed Loch Fyne.

"Elspeth!" he shouted in frustration, in panic. "What the hell are you doing?"

Thunder rumbled across the sky before he reached his own horse, and he knew that she couldn't hear him, that she probably wouldn't have stopped anyway. He also knew she had ridden in the opposite direction of the hillside track to Liath House, headed for where he couldn't imagine. Surely not for the loch—not in this weather.

"Ye'll have to go after her," a frail voice advised from behind him. " 'Tisna safe for her to be ridin' out in the open anymore."

He whirled in surprise, staring through the veil of steadily falling rain. A diminutive old woman with compassionate blue eyes and curly silver hair stood in the black hut's doorway. Clad in a soft-gray woolen gown, she looked more like a fairy godmother than a witch.

"The others might hurt her," she said in concern.

Niall was mesmerized by the gentle humanity of her face and reminded of Hasim. "What others?"

"Not all of the crofters left. They were some who waited for vengeance."

He backed away, his blood running cold. "And you?"

"I waited for Elspeth to return to make everything right."

He didn't have the time to decide whether the old witch could be believed or not. The panic that had seized him was as primal as the storm breaking. Wounded and confused, Elspeth was capable of any rash action, vulnerable in the extreme, and fear gripped his heart as he remounted his horse to find her.

Mortally wounded, the tigress lured him high into the wooded hills where she had been born. In the words of the Far Eastern mystics, hunter and hunted had become one. The chase had evolved into a compassionate obsession. The shikari knew that if his quarry wandered back down into the village, the people would savagely kill her in retaliation for the deaths they believed she had caused.

Twenty minutes later, he broke out of the little forest and emerged onto a rocky knoll. The sun had completely disappeared behind a bank of black-violet clouds. The rain was deafening. His heart stopped when he saw her cantering in a reckless fury down the precipice of a deep ravine; she had apparently forgotten he even existed, hell-bent on her wild descent.

He couldn't see through the driving downpour of rain to decide where she was going, if she even had a rational destination in sight. Surely she wasn't riding for the loch below. Its black waters had been lashed to the boiling point by the wind and were breaking violently on shore.

If there were any refugee crofters hiding out in the glen, she was a damned vulnerable target.

He galloped across the knoll and down into the ravine, losing sight of Elspeth again somewhere in the quavering shadows of the naked larches that bordered the loch. His horse slid to a halt, hooves splashing in the mud. Vaulting to the ground, he ran against invisible waves of cold wet wind until he caught up with her on the little stone pier that protruded into the loch.

He wrenched her against him, the wind whipping her skirts around their legs. "In God's name, Elspeth, where do you think you're going?"

She shivered convulsively, trying to pull away. "Niall, please, please. I have to be by myself."

"Fine, Elspeth, I understand. I realize you're upset, you're hurt and you need to think this awful shock through. But we're standing on a pier in the middle of a rainstorm that's about to rage into a gale. I'm soaked to the teeth, and so are you."

"I love you," she said, tears thickening her voice. "I didn't want to, but I do, and I-I want to be alone."

"If you love me, then let me take care of you," Niall said softly, pretending that what she had just told him made perfect sense. "Let me take you back to Liath House. I'll build a fire, make something to eat, leave you alone for as long as you like. But not here."

"Liath House?" She twisted out of his arms, her anguish more than even his loving concern or logic could pierce. "I can't go back to Liath House until I've decided what to do, Niall. I don't deserve to set even one foot in that house. I've broken my word."

He took a deep breath, wishing they could have this conversation anywhere but on an exposed pier in a storm. He was concerned for her and deeply worried they would end up spending a bitter night outside.

"Elspeth, I understand."

"Of course you don't," she said with so much vehemence that he couldn't help but feel insulted. "You couldn't possibly understand any of this. All my life I was brought up to believe I would be responsible for Glen Fyne, that the responsibility was a sacred trust handed down from generation to generation. Every death, every broken home is on my hands. You—" She stumbled back from him, staring out at the agitated water. "How could you understand when you've never stayed anywhere long enough to form attachments?"

He saw her eyeing the small rowboat that the waves were banging against the pier, but he couldn't believe she'd even consider taking it out in this weather.

"You think I'm incapable of abiding loyalty or love, is that it, Elspeth?"

She threw him a cursory glance. "I never said anything of the sort, but all right, how *could* you understand what it feels like to fail the people who trusted you to take care of them?"

"I understand far more than you realize," he said flatly.

She turned away, and he doubted that she'd even heard him, lifting her rain-swollen skirts to run to the end of the pier. He followed her like a shadow, remembered pain and shame still alive in his heart after all these years. Yes, he knew what it felt like to hurt the people you love. He had failed to save his father's life, and Lamont Glenlyon had died in agony while Niall listened in secret horror, not knowing whether he should risk trying to save him or whether he should remain guarding his mother and siblings. There had been no easy choice.

He had even failed to fulfill his father's last wish before Lamont was captured and taken into the enemy compound: to protect the Glenlyon family.

For a moment the memory of he and his father's last meeting was so vivid Niall could feel the sweltering humidity of the underground tiger pit where Lamont had hidden his family while enemy soldiers swarmed above. He could feel the needles of sharpened bamboo piercing his side. He could hear his mother's whispered prayers to her saints, and his father's low strong voice.

Alex may be older, Niall, but you're the responsible one, the one I'm entrusting with this grave duty. You're the one I choose to take care of the family should I not return.

But Niall hadn't protected his family. He had panicked and led them on a hellish journey through the jungle. He had lost Rachel. He'd watched Alex and Dallas waste irredeemable years of their lives. He had seen grief break his mother's spirit. And he had led his regiment of raw young recruits into a bloody ambush which only he and a Welsh soldier had survived.

Cold rain pelted his face. The memories receded, leaving only the lingering traces of fear, of loss, and shame aching in his heart.

But he wasn't inclined to explain any of this to Elspeth now. Not with the wind blasting across the loch, rattling the bare branches of the trees behind him. Not when it was left to him to protect her.

He set his jaw and scooped her up into his arms, setting off at a determined run up the pier toward the woods. The rain was pouring down his neck in rivulets before he reached the shore, and Elspeth was bouncing against his chest, not fighting him but not exactly helping anything either.

He was starving. He kept thinking about his ham and onions, and his head ached. In fact, he thought he was going to faint when he finally deposited her at the edge of the little forest with its black shadows and wet flailing limbs, the sort of secret woods in a fairy-tale world where bad children might get lost.

He leaned back against a trunk to catch his breath while Elspeth paced around him, oblivious to the wretched weather.

"Catherine told me once that some Highland families

were forced to emigrate to New Zealand, Niall. New Zealand. Dear God. How will they survive in a land like that when most of them could barely raise a crop of potatoes in the glen?"

"People manage, Elspeth," he murmured wearily. "People find strength to survive when there's no other choice. I ate snakes and smoked opium to ease my own hunger pangs when—"

"I won't be satisfied until I find them all," she said, circling him again. "Francis had to have known. God in heaven, I'll *never* forgive George and my father for this. I'll bring everyone back to the glen if I have to go to New Zealand myself."

"New Zealand?" he said bleakly, his hopes for a peaceful future fading before his eyes.

"They can't all have gone, Niall, can they?"

"No," he said dryly, "there was the friendly gang on the moor who tried to torch us."

"Oh, God, Glenlyon, what am I going to do?"

"You're going to get back on your horse, Elspeth, or I'm throwing you over mine."

Hasim would have said that Niall's threat must have been an irresistible challenge to the gods because scarcely had he spoken than from the corner of his eye he saw a limb crack and crash to the ground behind the two horses who had taken shelter in the underbrush. Terrified, the animals bolted in opposite directions.

"Oh, no." He pushed away from the tree, panic and self-disgust breaking through his physical fatigue. "Oh, hell—there go the horses and my saddlebags!"

Elspeth looked up without great concern, too dispirited to bother helping him chase after the horses. He rushed past her, stopped cold, and looked back in warning.

"Wait," he said. "Don't be stupid. Wait for me."

* * *

Actually, he was amazed that she did wait. He was amazed and relieved when almost a half hour later, he returned and found her standing in the very same spot, staring desolately through the trees across the loch. She spun around when she heard him and flung herself into his arms, making him not care that they'd lost the damn horses and would have to sleep in the woods all night like the bad children in a story.

She loved him. She needed him. They would be together no matter how bad they were, how badly life had treated them.

Elspeth burrowed against him in shamefaced gratitude, astonished that he'd returned to her when she had been ranting like a madwoman and she couldn't have blamed him for running off.

"I thought you might not come back," she whispered brokenly, feeling the beat of his heart against her face. Strong. Vital. Pulsing with power and a love that was palpable.

"And where would I go without you?" he demanded, swallowing hard as he gripped her.

"When the storm is over, take me away, Glenlyon. Take me to your island with you. I've lost everything anyway."

"Yes." He frowned, stroking her damp, tangled hair, knowing she didn't mean a word she said. "But we have to find somewhere to stay tonight—a shepherd's hut, a bothy."

"My grandfather's shooting lodge is in those woods above the loch. It's where I wanted to go, to be alone. It's the most private place in the world."

He held her away from him. "Above the—*Corbleu,* you don't mean on the other side of the loch?"

"With both of us rowing, we'll reach the shore in no time, Niall."

"If we make it. Look at that water."

"It's the loveliest lodge," she said with a beguiling

smile. "Look, there it is—hidden behind that hill in a little pine grove."

He glanced up the crag that towered ominously over the black turbulent waters of the loch. "That isn't a hill, Elspeth, it's a mountain, and at the moment, I sincerely doubt I have the strength for another invigorating hike."

She slipped her warm hands under his coat, inside his shirt to his chest, not above a little artful seduction of her own. "It's probably too secluded anyway," she whispered. "We'd be bored stupid, lying about under Grandda's plaids in front of a huge fire with nothing to do. We'd wear on each other's nerves."

Niall frowned. The muscles of his belly began contracting as she ran her fingers down his rib cage to the verge of his waistband. "And if a band of hostile Highlanders are lying in wait to crack our heads with one of Grandda's claymores?" he asked hoarsely.

"The lodge is said to be haunted by my grandmother's ghost, a rumor I suspect my grandfather instigated to protect his peace and keep everyone away. Yes, it's a safe place. It's a secluded place. That's why I wanted to go there alone."

The wind raged across the loch, tearing through the treetops and dislodging icy droplets from the shivering limbs. Niall grasped Elspeth's hands, filling them with his stolen ham, the onions, the cheese. "Guard these with your life," he said gravely.

She didn't move for a moment, clutching his foodstuffs as he strode past her through the trees to the shoreline. And while she watched him on the pier, struggling against the wind and rough waves to unlash the bobbing rowboat to secure her bag and violin case, it seemed he belonged to the glen as much as she did.

She darted down the pier with his pilfered booty jiggling in her skirts. She could hear his rich deep laughter resonating in the air like a god who knew he could conquer the elements. He raised his dark head for a moment and waved at her. Lightning flashed across the loch, illuminating his face into a sculpture of pagan beauty.

She slowed at the end of the pier to study him. The love she felt was overwhelming, frightening because she knew it would last all her life, would grow even stronger. She was not a woman of halfway measures. She swallowed dryly as she reached his side.

He gripped her around the waist as she reached him and lowered her into the rowboat. The onions, cheese, and ham thudded off the thwarts, at their feet.

"You've made me insane," he said cheerfully, and with the rain washing down on them, he settled her into the bow before he dipped the oars into the choppy waters.

"You're a Scotsman at heart, Glenlyon," she called across the boat, shoving her hair from her face. "It's that French blood that's gotten you into so much trouble."

He gave her an ironic smile. "As I said before, I'm a damn fool. I can't blame my heritage for that."

She huddled into her soggy cloak while he propelled the rowboat into the loch's dark heart. "I'm sorry," she cried, aching with guilt at how hard he had to work to compete against the undercurrent, at the strain on his face as the bow lifted like a cork and lurched into a violent trough. "I never meant to involve you in my woes."

"I'll find a way for you to repay me," he shouted back, and the smile he sent her was blatantly sexual, warm and encouraging. "We'll start tonight in this secluded lodge of yours under Grandda's plaids in front of a huge fire."

"All right," she whispered.

And they both smiled, staring into each other's eyes, neither of them noticing the figures who had come to stand at the edge of the forest, their eyes burning with suspicion and contempt, the weapons they held gleaming in the shadows of the rain.

Thirty-two

George took a deep drink of his whisky and stared with open contempt at the crowd of Highland couples singing a ribald ballad around the stinking peat fire of the taproom. Why would anyone *choose* to live in these freezing wilds? Why would any gently bred woman scorn the cultural stimulation of London for these socially inept savages? Why did his own betrothed prefer these hulking oafs to his own circle of high-born friends?

But Elspeth didn't have a gently bred bone in her body. That ignorant old goat of her grandfather had seen to that, making her believe she was a man's equal, that she possessed rights and responsibilities. In fact, the entire Kildrummond clan seemed to be united in an ugly conspiracy to ruin George's life.

He had been forced to cancel his politically crucial hunting party, only two days out of Falhaven before the papers erupted into gleeful reports claiming that the Scottish heiress fiancée of Parliamentary contender Sir George Westcott had gone missing, and that a man's body had been found near the company warehouse draped in an English-made shawl.

Duncan had presumably been questioned by the police; George might have been next if he hadn't come chasing after Elspeth to insure she said nothing to incriminate him in a murder he'd never intended to commit. To complicate the situation, an unnamed servant in the Kildrummond household had reported to the press that Elspeth had run off on a romantic adventure with that dishonored soldier of fortune.

The whole bloody mess had played hell with George's political support—Lord Howard had already withdrawn his backing. It was only a matter of time before the dead man was identified as Tormod MacQueen, and God only knew what lurid associations would be drawn from there.

He tightened his grip on the whisky glass. "I should have known she'd be attracted to a low sort like Glenlyon. What a shame I hadn't shot him too while I was in the mood."

Francis, seated across the table, looked shocked at the remark. "And hasn't there been enough of that? Ye talk as if murderin' a man were as commonplace as steppin' on a snail. We'd not be in this coil if ye'd found another way to handle that wretched old man instead of killing him."

"Lower your voice, dammit," George hissed, his gaze darting around them. "I hardly need to be reminded of the price I'm paying for that night. But you, Francis, well, you're in no position to talk, are you?"

Francis slumped forward, pain darkening his face. "How can ye even say that to me, Georgie? Ye know Isobel ran off to spare her family the shame of an illegitimate child. Ye know I offered to go through wi' our wedding, but if she couldna wed the bairn's true father, she wanted no one. She ran off, George, because he broke her heart. I didna lay a hand on her, and well ye know it."

"Do I?" George curled his upper lip in derision, his own mood too black to believe the best of anyone. In Francis's case, however, he did believe the bloody fool. No, Francis hadn't pushed his faithless village slut off the bridge; he didn't have the guts for it. He didn't even have the nerve to admit what had really happened between him and Isobel because he was afraid the truth would upset her aging parents.

He stared at Francis in cruel amusement. Who else but the zealous idiot would pay for an hour of a prostitute's time only to tie her to the bed to lecture the poor creature on the wages of sin? There wasn't a whore in the entire northeast of Scotland who hadn't heard of Francis. Every mercenary madam dreaded the pious Highlander's visits, fearing he'd convert her girls back into God-fearing behavior.

He laid his hand on Francis's arm in a comforting gesture. "Come now, Francis. Who else can we trust but each other?"

Francis stared down at the table in misery. "What of Elspeth then? The crofters who stayed behind are liable to stone her to death if they see her in the glen. They barely tolerated the sight of me."

"Perhaps her pagan soldier will protect her," George said bitterly.

"And if she turns ye in for the murder of Tormod MacQueen?"

George didn't answer, swallowing convulsively. His love for Elspeth had always been more a compulsion than a choice, more an irrational dependence on her that had developed during childhood than an association of mutual caring. Elspeth had been his champion, and now she had betrayed him. It wasn't the first time either.

Obviously she neither understood nor appreciated a man of his emotional complexity and capabilities. She scorned the most basic concept that it was a woman's duty to obey a man, to support him no matter her own personal desires or beliefs. He was disgusted by her reckless conduct, her selfish obsession with a plot of land that barely supported its ignorant peasantry. She owed *him* her loyalty, not the people who were the cruel phantoms of his boyhood, who had laughed at his fears, his weaknesses.

"I'll nae be a party to another act of violence," Francis said quietly.

George held Francis's arm immobile before he could pull it away. "But you will stand by me, Francis? You will tell the police that it was Niall Glenlyon who shot the old man?"

"Dear God," Francis whispered. "The turn of yer mind, the twists of it, frighten me, George."

"Listen to me, Francis, and listen well, for we're both in this together. I did not shoot the man. You did not drive his corpse down the street and dump it at the docks."

"I didna know what else to do! I swear that I was being followed. Oh, God help me, George, the evil in yer heart is more than I can bear."

"But it's the evil in the world I mean to eradicate, Francis—the poverty that drives men and women to drunkenness and prostitution, the low morals that threaten the very fabric of society."

Francis shook his head like a confused child.

"Satan has unleashed so much sin upon the earth," George continued softly. "He is so subtle, so clever. I'll wager his voice is whispering in your mind this very moment that you shouldn't trust me, that you should turn me in."

Francis drew a sharp breath. "Aye, 'tis so, 'tis so."

"Sometimes the devil must be overcome with force, as repugnant as a decent man finds the idea. Your faithless Isobel and my wicked Elspeth. Mad Tormod MacQueen who flaunted the laws of the land. Did they not all lead us down the paths of our own destruction?"

Francis swallowed a sob.

George squeezed Francis's arm, his voice trembling with emotion. "The Lord has spoken to me, Francis, and told me I must carry out His will. Who are we to question His methods?"

Thirty-three

The northerly gale swept down from the mountains all that night. Sleet lashed the stone and mortar hunting lodge. In fact, before they had even secured the boat on shore and struggled up the craggy slope, hail was breaking against their backs. Niall caught only a blurred impression of Ronald Kildrummond's hidden sanctuary before he carried Elspeth, violin case, bag, and stolen food, over the threshold. His own saddlebags had vanished with the horses. All he had were the clothes on his back, his parang, pistol, and field glasses.

The lodge was sturdy. Secluded. Built deep within a coniferous woodland against a backdrop of snow-laced mountains. Below it the loch gleamed darkly through a circle of naked larches. Niall decided he would have liked Elspeth's grandfather. The man had understood the value of solitude.

He dropped Elspeth to her feet inside the door, suppressing a groan of relief. He glanced up appraisingly from the large stone fireplace to the hand-hewn blackened rafters. "It isn't your grandmama's ghost that keeps them away, Elspeth, it's the row across the loch and Herculean climb."

She was already returning from the storeroom, stacking an armload of dusty logs in the fireplace. "Ronald Kildrummond wasn't much for shooting." Her voice echoed in the cavernous gloom. "But he did like to be by himself."

She stifled a startled cry as she felt Niall's hands close around her backside, caress her for a moment, then lift her out of the way. Within minutes he had coaxed a beautiful fire from the logs and was shedding his clothes in the circle of spreading warmth.

Elspeth glanced up at the ceiling. "Grandmother, if you're watching, you'll have to excuse this man his appalling lack of modesty. He was raised in the jungle."

Niall chuckled, continuing to undress in casual unconcern until he stood completely nude before her. Elspeth stared blindly into the fire, pretending not to notice him, which of course proved impossible. His perfection was too compelling, too evocative of the nights they had shared, the forbidden delight he had taught her. She could have gazed at him for hours.

"Get out of those wet clothes, *chère*," he urged her, giving her shoulders a light squeeze. "Since you're going to need all your strength over the next few days, I wouldn't want you to take a nasty chill."

"I won't ask you what I need to keep my strength up for, Glenlyon."

A slow grin spread across his face. "It does seem a redundant question."

"Doesn't it though?"

He gave a low devilish laugh and brought his hands to her throat to unfasten her sodden cloak. Firelight glinted off his sharply defined features, his brown muscular chest and belly. With his long hair slicked back over his scalp, his faint beard, and unadorned masculinity, he resembled to every raw inch the dangerous character Archie Harper had painted him to be. He was also the most immodest person she'd ever met.

He let her cloak slide off her shoulders. "Relax, Elspeth," he said as he brought his hands down her back to the hooks of her gown. "We were strangers to each other that first night in the cave. We're so much closer now, *non?*"

Desire tingled through her veins like a warm rich wine. She swallowed dryly and took an awkward step back, disengaging his hands only to discover he'd already unhooked her gown.

"You're soaked to the skin," he said reproachfully. "Let me undress you. We'll warm each other up before we eat."

The heat of his large body, his seductive voice, overwhelmed her dwindling resistance. "For pity's sake, Glenlyon, is that all you can think about—sexual gratification and your stomach?"

"A good part of the time, yes." With a flick of his wrist, her gown dropped to her waist. "Is there a bed?" he murmured, bending his head to nuzzle her neck.

"Yes, but . . ." She took another step back and bumped into the oaken settle. Her gown sank to the floor, entangling her feet. As Niall started to laugh at her efforts to extricate herself, she snatched an old musty plaid from the settle and threw it at him.

"Ah, another plaid—you know what that means, Elspeth." Grinning with unabashed enjoyment, he wrapped it around his naked shoulders and began to advance on her. "About that bed?" he demanded, grasping her by the wrist and forcing her back against him.

The pleasant shock of physical contact with his naked warmth stole her breath. Her pale body shone like a pearl against his deeply bronzed skin. The well-defined planes of his torso were cast into relief by the firelight. She could only laugh at his single-minded determination even as she felt the familiar ache of wanting him unfurl deep inside her. "Not in my grandfather's bed, Niall. It wouldn't be proper."

"You mean I rowed all the way across that blasted loch—I had hailstones hitting me on the head as big as

oulders—to have to sleep on a stone floor out of respect
or your late grandfather?"

"We can sleep in his bed, Niall," she said primly. "It's
ust that I'd feel, well, odd, I'd feel very uncomfortable
loing certain other things."

He shrugged. "All right," he said slowly. "According to
he press, I'm supposed to be a resourceful man."

"You're a wicked man," she said.

"Wicked, and resourceful."

And before she realized what he meant, he was sinking
lown onto the hard wooden settle, clasping her across his
ap to pull her drawers down to her ankles, with the plaid
lraped over their bodies. She caught her breath and sat
ip, swinging her feet to the floor. Without the least hesi-
ation, he jerked her right back between his thighs so that
ler legs were straddling him, and the thick knob of his
)enis was pressing into her womanhood. He cupped the
indersides of her breasts, lowering his face to kiss the
ipe flesh that filled his hands.

"Ride me," he said roughly.

Her breathing quickened. It would have been pretense to
efuse him. Still, she was amazed at her quick response,
ler willingness to please him, the wild passion he could
summon from her with a word, a casual touch. She should
lave felt ashamed for what they were about to do in her
grandfather's lodge, but she didn't. Somehow she sensed
that Ronald Kildrummond would approve of this man who
lefied the world to follow his own personal code of ethics.

She arched her neck as he started to sink inside her,
then slowly impaled her on his rigid sex. He brought his
mouth back to hers to smother her startled cry with a
deep, hungry kiss. She lunged upward as he filled her,
gripping her hips, pumping into her.

"Je t'aime, mon coeur sauvage," he whispered, his
voice ragged. "My wild heart, I'm so in love with you."

He was staring down at her with a dark possessive pas-

sion, watching every nuance of expression on her face
whispering to her in French, words that were tender an
rough, words that she did not understand but her bod
did, answering his demands with an urgency of her own
There was sweet desperation in their mating tonight, a
unconscious reaffirmation of their love, of life itself.

"Yes," he whispered, coaxing her, his face contorte
with a pleasure that hovered on pain, his desire for he
so fierce nothing could have stopped him. He was so har
so excited, he was afraid he would hurt her and did no
know how long he could last.

Still, he waited, his powerful body trembling with in
credible restraint. He waited until she was mindless wit
her own wanting. She pleaded softly and rocked her hip
up against him. She twined her fingers in his long we
hair, flexing her inner muscles to grip him tighter. An
he waited as a pressure like molten lava built in his loin
He held back until the first quivers of release ripple
through her slender frame.

Only then did he squeeze his eyes shut, gripping he
soft white buttocks, and drive to the tip of her womb. H
heart thundered with emotion and the satisfaction of sav
age need. Shuddering, his body drained, he drew the plai
around her shoulders and took her face in his hands.

"Elspeth, look at me."

She did, tears filling her eyes.

He frowned and caressed her face, his calloused finge
following the contours of her cheekbones. "I won't le
you be sad, at least not for the little time I have you t
myself," he said quietly. "I've been so jealous, *chère*,
all the others who laid claim to your heart."

"Who broke it, you mean."

He shifted her onto his other side, his circulation im
peded by the weight of her utterly relaxed body. "B
you'd never have to see any of them again if you can
away with me."

"The glen," she murmured sleepily, burrowing into the heat of his warm glistening chest. "All those poor people, Niall. I can think of nothing else."

He sighed and eased onto his feet, hefting her over his shoulders and letting intuition guide him to a surprisingly clean bedroom. Possibly Francis Barron had come here from time to time to escape his troubles. It couldn't have been easy overseeing the glen while helpless families were burned from their homes. Little wonder the crofters despised the Kildrummonds, not realizing how innocent Elspeth was of George and Duncan's selfish machinations.

He lowered her gently onto the old boxwood bed and covered her with the plaid. The scent of faded heather sprigs rose from the mattress as she stirred.

"My violin," she murmured. "Och, you left it by the door, out in all that sleet."

"Don't worry," he said, smiling faintly. "I'll rescue it."

Shivering, he headed back for the blazing fire he had built and his stiffly drying clothes. He saw little point in planning for the distant future when there were more imminent matters of survival to contend with.

The rowboat had washed out into the middle of the loch, and Niall had no intention of ploughing back out into the frigid water to retrieve it. As he turned in disgust from the wave-battered shore, he noticed a blur of movement across the loch within the woods. He looked up slowly, wondering with a mixture of unease and irritation what had happened to their horses.

His entire body went rigid when he realized what he was watching—ragged figures flitting through the trees with wavering bog-fir torches, and in the blackest shadows, the glint of a shovel hitting the hard earth in a repeated mechanical motion. Surely it was the wind, the waves of the loch rushing shoreward, and not a woman's keening wail he could hear.

Were those the vengeful crofters the witch had warned him about?

He straightened and backed away from the shoreline, grateful for the stretch of loch that isolated the lodge from the glen. He didn't know what those figures were doing in the woods, but the eerie tableau shadowed his thoughts as he hurried back up the hill.

Yet it wasn't until much later, when he was safely back at the lodge and half-asleep beside Elspeth that it occurred to him what he had witnessed, why it had disturbed him so. He sat up, staring at the door, apprehension stabbing at his awareness.

A grave being dug in the dead of night.

But for whom? For someone who had just died . . . or for someone who was about to be killed?

Thirty-four

Four days passed. Snow swirled down from the northern peaks, lacing the hills in pristine whiteness. Remembering the old witch's warning, the wisdom in her eyes, Niall grew as restless as a caged lion in the lodge. Every hour found him staring out the window at the loch with a brooding absorption that began to wear on Elspeth's nerves.

And he was worse at night—he'd rigged up the most ridiculous contraption she had ever seen at their bedchamber door—a design using rope, fishing poles, and leather buckets weighted with stones from the loch, all of which were presumably intended to bash any would-be intruders on the head when the door was opened.

"I'm truly concerned about you, Glenlyon," she confided in him one evening as they lay huddled together in bed under a hillock of old hunting plaids. He'd hidden Francis's old gun beneath the pillow, and one of Ronald Kildrummond's ancient crossbows was positioned across his knees. A Lochaber axe lay at the foot of the bed. "We're both liable to end up with a mortal injury if one of us rolls the wrong way during the night."

He compressed his lips, leaning back to accommodate her as she snuggled under his armpit and buried her freezing feet between his ankles. "Elspeth, call me a killjoy, but I tend to feel a little nervous knowing someone wanted to make a human inferno out of us not that long ago."

"That was on the moor, and miles and miles away. For all we know, it could have been Francis."

It hadn't been, but Niall felt it futile to argue. "Listen to me, Elspeth. They were a displaced family, they were angry and wild, and they knew your name."

"Who spoke my name first, Niall? Was it you or them?"

He scowled. "It was me, but I don't see what difference—"

"Then how do you know that if you hadn't said to them, 'Do you know Mary Ross?' they'd not have spat and cursed and behaved in exactly the same abominable way?"

"They had your dirk and horse."

"They *found* my dirk and horse."

"I know, Elspeth. I just know."

"This is my home, Niall. My land."

He grunted. "Home or not, I don't want you walking about the woods without me anymore. And don't go out after dark at all."

She stared up at his chiseled profile in sympathetic vexation, wondering what dangers he had faced in his life to have torn down all his trust. "I'll tell you what we should worry about—we should worry about running out of food. Your awful ham broth didn't go very far."

"Well, there's always venison and onion. Or grouse and onion. Or, God forbid—"

"Mutton and onion," Elspeth said dryly. "Yes, the thought crossed my mind too, but all the bloody sheep are in the glen, aren't they?"

In reality, they had already begun to ration their meager food supplies. Niall had almost killed himself catching two trout in the chilly depths of the loch, and Elspeth managed to produce a daily breakfast of watery porridge from the oats that Francis had presumably left in the storeroom for his infrequent visits to the lodge.

"We won't be here much longer anyway," Niall thought aloud.

"No," Elspeth murmured, worrying him with the lack of conviction in her voice.

The loch could not be crossed until the boat was repaired. The mountain pass in the back woods behind them was too slick with ice to even consider traveling on, and besides, it only led toward the snow-blasted domes of the Cairngorms.

He flipped onto his side, working his hand under her grandfather's old nightshirt. "You don't feel undernourished to me," he remarked with a rude grin. "You aren't eating for two, by any chance?"

She stared up into his face. "With my luck and your animal tendencies, Glenlyon, I probably am."

His grin faded into an expression of pleased contemplation. "I like the idea very, very much."

Elspeth liked it too; it buoyed her broken spirit with a fragile hope and happiness she was afraid to admit aloud. "I don't feel any different from last month," was all she could manage to say. Because, for all their intimacy, she couldn't bring herself to confess to him one of her most powerful fears, a fear entangled with shame and one of a woman's deepest yearnings—a fear that the miscarriage she'd suffered in the witch's hut might have left her unable to carry another child.

"Five children would be nice," he said softly, his tapered fingertips tracing over the curve of her belly. She forced a smile, remembering their heated discussion at her father's dinner table the first night they'd met. So, that much of Archie Harper's fiction had been true at least. Niall did want a large family to populate his jungle domain.

"Did you really come to Scotland seeking a bride, Glenlyon?" she asked, wondering how much else she'd read about him was true.

Wrapping her in his arms, he looked down at her sweetly expectant face. "I came seeking you, *ma tigresse*. Would you mind spending the rest of your life living under a volcano?"

"I don't know." She lowered her eyes to hide their teasing light. "You have the most horrible reputation. Someone once told me that no woman in her right mind would want to marry you."

"Queen Hippolyta of the Amazons," he mocked gently, nudging her knees apart and maneuvering himself between her legs, his organ as heavy as a club. "Did she have many children? Did she even like men?"

"I believe she made slaves of them."

He rubbed against her. "Well, you've certainly enslaved me."

"Good God, Glenlyon, you're insatiable."

"Only with you."

"And I'm supposed to believe that?"

"Don't judge me by how George treated you, *chérie*," he said, giving her shoulder a light punishing love bite.

"George." She sighed and pushed his head off her shoulder, the name spoiling the moment. "He's going to lose his election, you know."

"Do you care?" he asked sharply, his expression resentful.

She gazed up at the ancient targe mounted on the wall, her grandfather's small shield draped in tartan. "I knew he was selfish and carried away with his ambition. I knew he wasn't as attached to Glen Fyne as I am, but I never thought he was capable of such cruelty and deceit."

"You thought he loved you," he said with a frown.

"Yes." She brought her troubled gaze back to his. "Yes," she repeated softly.

A raw pain ripped through him at the traces of bewilderment that lingered in her voice. For all she might hate George now, she had shared an emotional history with the little bastard, the closeness of childhood, the first stirrings of adolescent love with all its attendant sweetness and confusion. She and George had probably taken such attachments for granted, but they seemed to Niall all the more threatening because he could only imagine them. There had been no poignant courtships in his brutal youth. He had been plunged from a boy's innocence into a remorseless adult reality overnight.

"Did you sleep with him?" he asked bluntly, his hand tightening where it rested on her hip.

"Would it matter to a man who worked in a brothel?" she asked coolly.

"I don't know." Her answer displeased him for reasons too complex, too deeply ingrained in cultural standards, to bring to light. "Would it matter to you?"

"I didn't. He wanted to often enough—"

His bitter laughter silenced her. "I can imagine."

"You're jealous," she said softly.

"I'm going to carve his heart out with Tormod's knife."

"That's a wretched thought, and very barbaric."

"I'm a wretched person—and a barbarian into the bargain. I believe you've mentioned that more than once."

"Niall?"

"What?" His face was angry, closed.

She ran her finger up his arm. "George is a shadow."

" 'George is a shadow.' That's lovely, *chérie,* more touching than I can tell you. But what does that make me?"

She hid a smile. "You, Glenlyon, are the sun . . . in all its fierce glory. You are the center of my universe."

He closed his eyes, his brow furrowed in an effort not to show her how deeply her words had penetrated into his heart, how badly he had needed to hear them.

"I think I might have wanted to marry George because he seemed safe," she continued softly. "I believed that because I could control my feelings for him, he couldn't hurt me."

"Sometimes what appears safe is the most dangerous illusion of all."

"And what appears dangerous?" she whispered.

He opened his eyes, his gaze warm and adoring, easing that unspoken fear. "I won't leave you."

And if I can't give you children? If the urge to run again overwhelms you? If my father is brought before a court of law, implicated in Tormod's death, and I must stay here to help his defense?

But the questions drifted unanswered in her mind, disappeared into nothingness as Niall drew her closer to him and she fell asleep in his arms. For the moment she was content to trust in their simple intimacy. She was so content that she even managed to ignore the arsenal on their bed, the wariness that returned to his eyes as he turned his gaze in his nightly ritual of watchfulness at the door.

Are you going to run away from me too?
Run away . . .
Run . . .

Niall awoke with a violent start, the words a counterpoint to the pulsing of blood in his temples. He stared around the darkened bedchamber, wincing at the thin shafts of light piercing the partially shuttered windows. The lodge. Why had he expected to find himself at the edge of a steamy jungle swamp?

Slowly he released his pent-up breath as he realized it was his own internal anxiety and not a past or present threat that had broken his sleep. His heartbeat slowed into a dull tatoo.

Elspeth stirred beside him. Warm body, full breasts, and silky white skin, she curled into his back, and he felt the irrational panic dissipate.

"Mmm," she said, "what is it?"

"It isn't snowing." He turned to take her into his arms, his voice husky. "In fact, the sun is even shining, and I can't see a cloud in the sky."

They stared at each other in bittersweet silence. They'd both known that reality would intrude sooner or later, but it shook them nonetheless. Time had hung suspended during their sweet interlude in the lodge.

She sat up awkwardly, and Niall sighed as he felt himself growing hard again. The sight of her graceful back, her long muscular limbs thrown across the bed was all it took to excite him. He lifted his hand to touch her, then let it drop, aware of a tightening behind his eyes.

"You look a bit queer, Niall."

"My head hurts." He frowned and unconsciously put his hand to his eyes.

"No wonder then, the way you carry on all the time. You've probably shaken something loose."

He caught her by the elbow and dragged her down between his legs to kiss her. His hands curved around her rump. She landed back between his legs with a soft laugh. The feeble sunlight fell across them like an intruder, a reminder of the world they'd have to reenter. Her laughter faded on a soft groan of despair.

"Oh, Niall," she whispered, gripping his arm.

Resentment consumed him. His eyes dark with reluctance, he released her and managed a smile. "Make us breakfast, *ma belle.* We've work to do down at the loch on the rowboat. With a bit of luck we'll find those damned horses before dark."

Elspeth's face clouded over. "Och, you just reminded me—I had the most horrid dream last night that they were being eaten."

He got up from the bed and shivered, waiting a moment for the buzzing in his ears to subside. Straightening, he caught himself a split-second before he walked into the low pine wood chest on which Elspeth had untidily piled their clothes. A shadowed memory flitted like a warning flag across his mind. He had felt like this before. Something wasn't right.

He turned slowly. He looked at the primitive alarm device he had rigged to the door. Those figures he had seen in the woods, the gravediggers, could only have been the wind lashing the trees into weird shapes. He'd watched every night since through his field glasses and had never seen another trace of human activity. He shivered again.

"Unless it was our horses," he muttered, glancing at the window. "A bridle could glint like a shovel, I suppose."

Elspeth frowned, wriggling up against the pillows. "You haven't been eating any of those mushrooms we found growing in the storeroom, by any chance?"

"Don't be impertinent, *chère*," he said cheerfully, pulling his shirt over his broad shoulders. He grinned. "As perverse as it may sound, I find your rudeness is starting to excite me."

"Good Lord," she grumbled, pretending to hide under the plaid. "Everything excites you, Glenlyon."

The boat had been damaged beyond repair, the hull smashed up against the razor-sharp rocks submerged in the roots of the reeds that grew along the frozen edges of the loch. Niall could barely salvage on oar from the wreckage.

"We're stuck here all winter," Elspeth announced, striving to sound dejected when deep inside she wanted to shout for joy. "Damn. Talk about terrible luck."

Smiling wryly, Niall unwrapped her grandfather's battle axe from its sheepskin casing and stood, thin patches of snow crunching like sugar under his feet. "I'll have to make a raft."

"A raft?" She gazed out across the cold gray water of

the loch, burying her hands under her cloak. "And what if it sinks and we fall in? No, thank you very much."

He sighed and cast an appraising look at the pines that sprouted from the snow-swathed ridge above the lodge. "Hell. There's some work ahead."

"Well," Elspeth said, attempting to appear concerned, "I suppose I'll have to walk up to the burn and see if I can find any more of those godawful water grasses for the broth. They're nourishing if somewhat disgusting. It sounds as if we're going to be here for weeks."

He straightened before she could turn away. "Never mind the godawful water grasses. I need you to collect as many birch twigs for twine as you can."

"Bog-fir roots serve the same purpose," she said reluctantly. "I could cut some for you from the ravine."

"Fine," he said. "But mind the ice. Your boots are in shocking shape."

"Yes, Mother."

"And don't go any farther than I can hear you scream."

" 'Hear me scream'? What should I be screaming about, pray tell?"

He ran his gloved fingers through his hair, grinning crookedly. "I don't know. Witches who live in black huts. Villagers who eat horses. That sort of thing."

She drew her hand out of her cloak and touched his face, frowning at the flushed color highlighting his strong cheekbones. "You don't look well," she said softly, "and for the second time today, you're making absolutely no bloody sense. Are you all right?"

"Yes," he said impatiently, turning back toward the lodge while Elspeth stood watching him with a stirring of uneasiness, her hand falling to her side.

Her concern mounted throughout the day as Niall hurried to finish the birch-branch raft before the winter light faded. She brought him hot tea and broth while he worked, but his strange spells of silence, the oblique look on his face as he studied the loch, heightened her intuitive worry until she could no longer ignore it.

"I'm going with you across the loch to find the horses." She crawled over the pointed rocks that separated them and faced him with her arms folded across her chest as if she expected a fight.

"Yes," he said, his eyes glassy. "You and me."

Her heart gave a little lurch of alarm. Biting her lip, she rose unsteadily and began to back away. "I'll fetch our things from the lodge. Why don't you sit and finish that mug of tea while you're waiting?"

She hadn't taken three more steps before she heard him muttering under his breath.

"I can't believe how hot it is out in the snow."

Startled by the senseless remark, she stopped in her tracks and swung around just in time to see Niall stagger up onto one knee and then fall face-down in a dead faint into an inhospitable bed of frozen bracken.

Malarial fever.

God help them both.

Sickness had always secretly terrified Elspeth; her mind recoiled from the memory of how swiftly her mother had died from the complications of a simple cold.

The precarious path carved into the crag seemed a thousand feet high. The ice-rimmed whortleberry that rose from its rocky borders snagged her cloak and nearly sent her careening back down into the stalwart pines below. Her grandfather had designed the approach to keep the outside world at bay.

She half-dragged, half-carried Niall, breathing through gritted teeth, her knees and spine aching from the strain. It seemed to take forever. The sky had already darkened to a sullen wine-gray with the remaining daylight thinning to needle-points of silver behind the mountains.

At last they reached the lodge. Breathless, Elspeth buckled against the iron-hinged door and let Niall collapse where they stood. He opened his eyes and stared up intently into her face, but she felt a cold shaft of fearful certainty that he didn't even recognize her.

She dropped down beside him, her voice urgent as she fought back a helpless despair. "Tell me where your medicine is. How much am I supposed to give you? Answer me, Niall. Where is your bottle of medicine?"

He caught her hands in a bruising grip and frowned in concentration, shuddering so violently she felt it through her own body. "It's with the horses across the loch. But you can't find it now. There . . . there are too many snakes on the other side."

She refused to give him up to the darkness; she refused to give way to the fear that whispered her sweetest dreams would die stillborn in this room. The children they had hoped for. A future of laughter and fulfillment, the weaving together of their broken lives to form a seamless tapestry of love. She had lost too much already.

As if it were a pagan sacrifice to a capricious deity, she threw her violin, case and all, onto the bonfire in the hearth, perspiration trickling down the cleft of her breasts. Although she'd stripped down to her chemise and drawers, the bedchamber was as stifling as a bakehouse. But even then, with every sheet and blanket in the lodge heaped over him, Niall continued to shake and thrash his arms, to moan incoherently.

Repeatedly she had sponged down his face and throat with melted snow, but the last time she had tried, he'd hit her so hard in the shoulder that she could barely lift that arm, the muscles deeply bruised by his delirious strength.

In desperation she had torn apart the cupboards of the storeroom for a medicinal cordial, but all she'd manage to unearth was an old jar of dried rosemary, and she couldn't remember if the herb helped fevers or fertility. With nothing to lose, she brewed some tea, sweetened with sugar, and added the aromatic gray-green leaves.

She forced three spoonfuls into his mouth before he shoved the cup to the floor and sat bolt upright beneath his covers, knocking her clear down to the foot of the bed.

"Shave my head," he said tersely, his face fierce in the firelight.

Tears of fear and frustration pooled in her eyes. She didn't know how to help him. Her inexpert nursing might prove more harmful than good, and she could only blame herself that he'd fallen sick in the first place. If she hadn't run off in a frenzy that afternoon on the loch, he probably wouldn't have weakened his system; for certain his medicine would not have been lost when the horses ran off.

"Elspeth," he said with a sudden urgent calm that was more ominous than his earlier spell of violence, "you have to shave my head. The fever is burning into my brain."

She slid to her feet, staggering back in weary confusion as he collapsed back down onto the bed. She knew so little about healing; she couldn't even be sure he was lucid enough to believe, or whether he was ranting from delirium. But somewhere in her distant memory of growing up in the glen, it did seem that Una had once shaved a young boy's head to bring down his body temperature when he lay deathly ill with scarlet fever.

"Do it now," he said, closing his eyes. *"Now."*

By the time she'd managed to hunt down a rusty pair of scissors (there was no razor), Niall was lying in alert silence, watching her every move through narrowed, bloodshot eyes. But the moment she brought the scissors to his head, he panicked. He went insane, an animal sound of distress breaking in his throat as he gripped the bed-clothes.

"Bastards . . . frigging little bastards are hiding in the mission chapel . . . It's *Christmas*. My men wanted to . . . worship."

"It's all right, Niall," Elspeth whispered, clasping his hand. "I won't do it now. Let me put this honey poultice on your head instead."

Horror contorted his face. He grasped her forearm. *"Non, je vous prie . . . n'employez pas . . .* not honey."

"Honey? The honey will hurt you?" Elspeth asked, searching his terrified eyes to understand.

"General Chin . . . ambush in the chapel. Warn them . . . Thomas, Smitty. I—I'll kill him . . . bare hands . . . kill."

"It's Elspeth," she said urgently, wrapping her arms around his shaking shoulders. "Elspeth." But he wasn't coherent. He didn't see her at all. He was confronting the ghost of the Burmese general who had slaughtered his regiment on Christmas morning in a jungle mission church.

A succession of shudders racked his frame. His gaze was black, focused inwardly on the shadows of his past. "B-buried us up to our necks in the jungle. Covered our heads with h-honey so the . . . white a-ants and giant wasps . . . eat us alive. *Mon Dieu,* they made me watch . . ." He threw his hands up over his eyes. ". . . spared me so I could watch."

She drew back, tears spilling down her face. He was so hot, his skin burning through the bedclothes, that her mind began to spiral in panic. "Oh, Niall," she whispered, gently pulling his hands from his face. "It's all right now."

"Goddamnit, don't you understand anything? *Shave my head.*"

He frowned, staring at her in fierce concentration as she lifted the pair of scissors to his neck and started to cut his hair. Her hands shook. Tears blurred her vision. Then suddenly he caught her wrist and thrust his entire weight upward, burying her beneath his body and the woolen blankets. The blades of the scissors pricked her throat, drawing several droplets of blood. She felt him shaking, staring down at her, struggling to understand.

"They're all dead," he whispered hoarsely. "Only Thomas and me . . . left."

"Niall," she whispered, in pity and in fear that he would not recognize her until it was too late for either of them. "P-please don't hurt me."

His eyes went blank, then filled with tortured remorse. "Elspeth," he said, rearing back with a dry sob catching in his throat. *"Dieu,* what have I done?"

"Nothing." She swallowed dryly, took a searing breath of relief. "Nothing. I'm all right."

He groaned and sank back onto the bed, his fingers still curled around the pair of scissors until Elspeth gently wrested them from his grasp. His gaze clung to her face. "Don't . . . don't let me die, *chère."*

"Tell me what do, Glenlyon," she pleaded softly. "Help me, please."

He closed his eyes, drew a shallow rattling breath, then fell utterly still.

And for one unspeakable moment, her own heart stopped beating with the fear she had lost him. She touched his neck, searched frantically for the faint throb of a pulsebeat.

He was sleeping. His breathing was so shallow she could barely detect it. She kissed his cheek, the black stubble of his beard abrading her own flushed skin. There was only one hope left to her. She had to take the risk.

Niall heard the door open and close, felt the stillness fall over the lodge as she left. It was dark outside, too late for her to be collecting elding for the fire. A sense of unease throbbed inside him until it grew too powerful to ignore.

"Elspeth?" he called in a raspy whisper, forcing himself to awaken fully from the feverish fog that shrouded his brain. Then, rolling onto his side, the blankets clutched to his chest, he fought a wave of intense dizziness to bring his feet to the floor.

"Elspeth!" he bellowed, shaking with the energy he exerted to call her.

Panic gripped him, underlaid with his own humiliating sense of helplessness and an almost infantile anger that she'd abandoned him.

But where would she go?

Not through the dangerous mountain pass in the middle of the night. Not to the burn because they had buckets of water to spare in the storeroom.

The raft. Sweet Jesu.

Praying he was wrong, he snatched his battered field glasses from the nightstand and wove across the rough stone floor to the window. His head pounded with sharp hammers of excruciating pain behind his eyes. His leg muscles felt like tree sap, liquefying under his weight.

He raised the field glasses and leaned his hip against the rough-hewn windowsill. The onslaught of frosty air from outside brought gooseflesh to his overheated skin. For a minute he couldn't locate her in the darkness of the craggy slope, and he felt weak with relief that he'd been wrong; she was probably rummaging around in that unlit storeroom looking for another remedy to cure him. Perhaps she was even—

God help her.

He gripped the field glasses, groaning softly. She had already poled herself halfway across the loch, flailing inexpertly, propelled more no doubt by sheer nerve than physical strength or skill. The moon, rising above the ragged horizon of pines, shone down on her wild mane of hair. A pair of pipistrelle bats flew out of the treetops and circled over her.

She looked so small, defenseless, alone.

She looked like a single candle flame challenging a world of darkness.

He shuddered, sagging against the sill. The throbbing in his head intensified until he could no longer focus on her receding figure. Then just before he dropped the field glasses, he spotted a flicker of light in the woods on the opposite shore.

Someone was waiting for her on the other side.

Gravediggers, witches, ghosts. Blood rushed up into his head to compete with the dark figures that danced through his imagination. He glanced around wildly for his clothes. He took a step toward the chest and stumbled over the blankets he had wrapped around his waist. He fell. The coldness of the stone floor caressed his burning cheek as consciousness receded.

Someone was waiting for her on the other side.

A tear trickled down onto his temple. He sobbed dryly. Just as it had happened when he'd watched his father die, just as when he had lost Rachel, when his regiment had been slaughtered, Niall could only watch, helpless to intervene.

Thirty-five

George extinguished the tin lantern he had lit to dispel the shadows pressing in around him. He wouldn't be afraid now, not with Elspeth finally pulling the raft onto the banks of the loch. Yes, he was outraged at what she had done, but he could breathe more easily now, reassured he didn't have to endure the dark silence of the forest alone for much longer.

Francis, the bloody fool, had abandoned him at the crossroads two villages ago, swearing the glen was haunted by the ghosts of the seven crofters who had died defending their homes from the eviction orders George had put into motion. They had argued and George had been forced to ride into the glen himself—at night.

And George had been terrified of the dark since he was five years old, when his father had locked him into the family crypt overnight with his elderly aunt's coffin—a day after the old woman's funeral—to toughen the boy's oversensitive character. The smell of decaying flesh seemed to fill the darkness around him even now, and he darted out of his hiding place with a clawing sense of panic.

"Elspeth?"

He stepped out in front of her. He was shocked and fascinated at her appearance, her hair as snarled as that of a Samhain witch and framing her white tense face. She looked older, more worldly. She looked more sexual and

more mature than he remembered her, and the raw pain
in her eyes, followed by the flash of hostile recognition
when she noticed him, made him flinch.

She swept up her waterlogged skirts and strode toward
him. "Get out of my way, George Westcott, you dirty little
bastard. No—wait." She inclined her chin at his horse.
"Take me to Una's hut, then ride straight to fetch a doctor.
Pay him whatever it takes to get him here tonight. Move
your goddamned feet, George. Move or I'll murder you
with my bare hands."

He stared at her, at the torn, stained gown she was
wearing under a man's gaping black greatcoat. For days
he'd allowed himself to hope she would forgive him for
what he had done to the glen, that she'd come to see the
future from his perspective. And perhaps he might have
had a chance to win her back, despite everything, if it
hadn't been for Niall Glenlyon.

"You are ill, Elspeth?" he asked guardedly.

She brushed past him to his horse. "If anything happens
to Niall, I'll make you suffer, George."

The unexpected emotion in her voice broke through his
entrancement. "Niall?" His face hardening, he strode
alongside her and the horse. "Niall, is it, you whore? So
the sordid little scandal with Robert Campbell didn't teach
you a lesson, after all."

She raised her head, a spark of shock briefly obscuring
the dark worry in her eyes. "Francis told you. I should
have guessed."

"No, I told him," he said bitterly. "I came home from
port to surprise you that summer I went away, to spend
a stolen day with my beloved before we set sail, but I
was the one who had the surprise."

"I—"

"You little slut," he said softly, "swiving a sheriff's substitute in a barn."

She gazed into his face, realizing the handsome mask

hid more twisted secrets than she could ever fathom, or forgive. "I'm past explaining my behavior to you," she said quietly. "Are you going to help me save Niall's life or not?"

He made a sound of contempt, reaching inside his coat for what she assumed was his pistol. Even then she refused to let him intimidate her.

"You accepted my proposal of marriage, Elspeth," he said with a look of self-righteous scorn. "I offered you my name when any other man in my position would have cut you out of his life."

She listened to him with a weary detachment, the cruel words beyond damaging her self-esteem. Deep inside she had always suspected he harbored such feelings. Why had she ever believed she could turn his selfish arrogance into caring?

"Did you hear me, Elspeth?" He forced her back against the horse, his voice shaking, his fury rising at her lack of response. "No other decent man would have you. You aren't pretty or rich enough to overlook your lack of breeding."

The loch glinted coldly through the trees. Elspeth fought back a growing panic at how alone she was, how much Niall needed her to help him.

She took a breath. "The only *decent* man I know is dependent on me to fetch him help. I'm not afraid of you. No, I'm not. I'm taking your horse—"

He pulled out his pistol, not pointing it at her, but laying it against the horse's neck with his arm uplifted like a barricade to prevent Elspeth's escape. Her face dark with contempt, she merely edged around him and hoisted herself awkwardly into the saddle with her skirts rucked up to her knees.

"Will you shoot me then, George?" she asked, grasping the reins.

"You know I could never hurt you."

"But you have," she whispered. "More than anyone I've ever known."

His mouth trembled. "I will shoot the bloody horse if I have to, if you leave me."

"Please," she said, her control breaking, this dark little drama more than she could endure. "Please let me go. If you can't bring yourself to help me, at least let me go."

He grabbed a handful of her skirts, his face tormented. "Did you ever care for me as much as you do for that man?"

"How can you even ask me that?" she cried. "Did I not defend you when we were children? Even after you murdered Tormod, I wanted to prove to myself you had good cause." Her voice broke. "You were my first love."

"But you don't love me now, do you?" He dug his fingers through her skirts as he searched her face for the answer he would never find. *"Do you?"*

"You destroyed our love with your deceit, your greed."

He looked wild. "You mean the bloody glen? I saved this wretched mass of cold gray stones and barren fields, you sentimental little fool. For the first time in decades, it's actually turned a profit."

"You never even consulted me, George. Oh, goddamn you—get out of the way."

She drew back on the reins and kicked his hand away, thinking of Niall, the time wasted.

"I did what was within my legal rights as your future husband." He jumped in front of the horse, his eyes flashing with desperation as he tried to wrestle the reins from her hands. "I killed a man to protect you."

"You killed him to protect yourself!"

"Don't you dare leave me here, Elspeth. I—I saw a freshly dug grave just a few feet from here, and the marker b-bore my name."

"The ghosts of the glen will find you, George," she taunted, refusing to yield to the pity he aroused in her even now. "All the spirits of the crofters who perished in fire when the constable torched their huts. I'll wager it was them who dug that grave."

He shook his head, swallowing in fright. "I had no control over how the eviction notices were executed."

She pried his hands from the reins. The gun hit against her wrist when he groped at her skirts, but she was too skilled a rider to be unseated. She urged the frightened animal to backstep, then wheel onto the overgrown bridle path.

From the edge of her eye she saw him raise the pistol to her back, his face grimly determined, but she didn't slow pace, pressing in her heels and letting memory guide her back toward the glen. Tears slid down her cheeks, stinging in the cold, tears of fear for Niall, for herself; tears for the friends lost and promises broken, even for George whose past was inescapably interwoven with hers.

And when she guided the horse across the small frozen burn into the white mist that swathed the glen, she heard him shouting, "I'll ruin your father, Elspeth!"

But she didn't stop.

"Elspeth, for the love of God, I can't live without you." He gave an anguished cry, and she closed her eyes. "Elspeth, I am *nothing* without you."

The gunshot exploded into the night. She flinched, remembering all the times when they were young that he had threatened to kill himself, all the times she had intervened.

But she didn't stop.

As she cantered down the steep brae into the ruins of the glen, a stray sheep darted into a corrie at her violent appearance. The gunshot echoed in her mind even as she thundered over the bridge that led to the solitary black hut where old Una lived, her one desperate hope to help Niall.

She dismounted, running, to let herself into the hut. Icy darkness enveloped her.

The woman was gone, the hut deserted.

She gazed around her in panic, at the unlit hearth, the scant belongings stripped from the crude wall shelves. In a frenzy she wrenched open the doors to the tall single cupboard to hunt for some of the woman's healing herbs.

Nothing.

Nothing.

I am nothing without you, Elspeth.

Remember.

Don't let me die, chère . . .

She ran out into the desolate winter garden, around frost-coated beds whose plants held the secret to life or death. Drained of hope, bereft of human assistance, she lifted her face to the sky.

"Help me, God," she whispered. "Show me what to do."

The silence of the night engulfed her, mocked her simple faith that she had only to make a request from the depths of her heart and it would be answered. How naive.

When would she ever learn to stop believing? How much evidence of life's ugliness did it take to break her childish spirit?

She walked slowly across the frozen earth and buried her face between the horse's hot lathered neck and mane. She had to decide between riding into the nearest village herself to fetch a doctor, or returning to the lodge to stay with Niall. Either way, she couldn't waste time crying to the moon.

Raising her head, despair an aching knot in her throat, she reminded herself she had to think of the horse's welfare if it was to carry her back and forth through the night. She exhaled quietly and turned in grim resolve.

A weird shadow fell across her path, distorted by the moonlight. Choking back an instinctive cry, she stared at the strange apparition that came striding toward her. With its painted features and body draped from shoulder to ankle in a cloak of striped fur, it was neither animal nor human . . . like nothing she had ever seen before—

Until it grinned and announced, "It damn freezing colds in this place you loves."

She pressed her hand to her heart, relief sweeping over her in waves. "How—oh, God, Hasim, how did you find me?"

Hasim pointed back with a long curled fingernail to the tall gaunt man standing at the end of the bridge. Her mare and Niall's stallion moved behind him by the burn.

"My good friends bring me here," Hasim explained as if it were the most natural thing in the world. "Find horses that belong to you and Tuan."

My good friends. Francis Barron. And at that moment Elspeth could only stare up again at the sky, unable to speak for the mysterious wonder and grateful humility that filled her.

Francis approached her, his face weary, his voice hopeful. "You are all right, Elspeth Kildrummond?"

"I'm fine," she whispered, her voice, her control cracking. "But Niall needs help—he needs Hasim at the lodge."

Francis nodded solemnly. "Aye, so we have both misjudged each other when judgment is reserved for Him alone. Is it too late for us, do ye think? Can we make our peace on this pagan ground?"

Thirty-six

They would still attract gawking stares as they traveled northeast through the Highlands to the gentler Grampian hills; the dark Captain Glenlyon and his intended bride, the witch doctor who ambled after them, wrapped in so many plaids and furs all you could see of him was tea-brown eyes narrowed in mystical contemplation.

They rode out of the glen on a misty January morning. Elspeth was subdued as she stared for perhaps the last time at the land she loved. Niall, however, could not escape this ghostly village a minute too soon. Or, more precisely, he couldn't carry Elspeth away fast enough to please his jealous heart. He was seriously considering taking her back to the island by force. Hell, if he was going to be accused of abducting her, he might as well commit the crime.

He would not breathe freely until they left this place far, far behind, even though their storm-isolated days at the lodge, his slow recovery, had been uneventful with no interference from George, who had apparently disappeared without a trace. The fact should have relieved Niall. Instead, it worried him deeply.

And Hasim, Niall noted uneasily, had been on edge himself all morning, lapsing into impenetrable silences and then running off alone every few minutes to blow his conch shell in supplication to the mist-loving Scottish gods.

The arched stone bridge that led from the glen to the open moors loomed into view. Niall's heart began to pound with anticipation. Or was it anxiety? He reminded himself that he still was not completely recovered from the fever. A film of cold sweat had broken out between his shoulder blades. His skin began to crawl with warning sensation beneath his heavy clothes.

"Hurry up," he said. "Hurry."

He glanced around with a scowl at Elspeth and Hasim, still several yards behind the bridge. His emotions overcame his usual calm, fear and love clashing into a sense of urgency too strong to ignore.

"Come on, dammit. Pick up your heels, Hasim. Elspeth, beloved, stop bloody crying. We have a long way to go."

The burn that ran sluggishly in icy channels beneath the bridge sounded too loud. The air wafting across the moorland carried an eerie sharpness.

He noticed the Highlanders as he swung back around in the saddle. He spotted the first of the shadowed figures materializing to block the road, and he cursed himself for once again ignoring his inner guidance.

A tiny band of the glen's former crofters emerged one by one from beneath the ramparts of the bridge, those too old or too stubborn to be dislodged by any unjust Sassenach law. Niall counted thirteen of them. Although he knew their surprise appearance portended trouble, he had no inkling of how far-reaching it would be.

Elspeth and Hasim rode up beside him, utterly silent. He didn't spare them a glance, inching his hand inside his coat for his gun, returned to him by Francis Barron along with one of his missing saddlebags. As far as he could tell, the Highlanders carried no weapons, but their worn plaids and ragged homespun skirts could easily conceal stones and rusty dirks, perhaps a musket or ancestral claymore or two.

These were the ghosts of the glen, whom George had

feared, and apparently with good cause. Had they gotten to the Englishman after all and taken their revenge before he could escape the woods that night he confronted Elspeth?

Niall could only hope so.

His face deliberately neutral, he glanced from the corner of his eye at Hasim. To his amazement, the little idiot was nodding and smiling at the hostile crowd as if he were a foreign dignitary being honored by a public farewell party.

A worn-faced woman disengaged herself from the silent group of Highlanders and walked across the bridge toward Elspeth. Niall sat up straighter, thinking how closely the woman resembled the destitute young mother he had met weeks ago on the moor. Alarmed at the memory of that woman's violent behavior, he reacted instinctively and forced his horse in front of Elspeth.

"It's all right, Niall," she said in an undertone.

"The hell it is."

But as usual she did what she wanted, dismounting to face the woman who stood waiting in wary silence.

"Sorcha Davidson," she said with a smiling calmness that Niall could only admire, despite his intense concern for her safety. *Bon Dieu,* how would he and Hasim handle an entire mob of Scotsmen gone wild if violence erupted?

He risked a closer look at the unmoving cluster of men, women, and children obstructing the bridge. Malnutrition, fear, and hopelessness as well as exposure to the elements had etched indelible lines in their faces. He felt genuine pity for their plight, empathy for the unfairness dealt them. Even so, he couldn't forget that such desperation could lead to outbursts of irrational violence.

"Elspeth Kildrummond," the woman named Sorcha said, her face so gaunt with lingering grief that Niall was astonished when he realized that she was actually close to Elspeth's own age.

"It's been a long time, Sorcha," Elspeth said.

Sorcha's mouth curved into a cynical smile. "Hasn't it just? Years in fact since we stood on this same spot and ye promised ye'd be back in the summer before the white briars bloomed again."

"Oh, Sorcha."

"There are no more roses."

"I had nothing to do with this," Elspeth said fiercely, fighting for control, her gaze lifting to the other Highlanders assembled behind Sorcha. "Where is the rest of your family?"

"My da, my sister, and her children are as good as can be expected for havin' lived these past months on the moor. Her husband killed a man over a cow, ye ken, and no one's heard of him since."

"Someone tried to kill me on the moor," Elspeth said slowly.

"None of us." Sorcha's chin trembled.

"Where is your husband then?"

"New Zealand, hoping to make a home before he sends for us. He's a proud man, Hugh is, ye'll remember. He wouldna be pleased to know I'd disobeyed him to stay in the glen, forced to live on what your sheep have left of the land."

"I had nothing to do with this," Elspeth repeated, her eyes blazing.

Sorcha lowered her voice. "Did ye not even try to stop them?"

"My God, Sorcha, do you think I'd have sat idly by sipping tea while you were burned out of your homes? I had no idea what George was doing."

One of the older men on the bridge raised his voice. "Where is Tormod MacQueen? 'Tis no secret he escaped the asylum."

Niall sensed Elspeth's indecision, her anguish, and before he could warn her not to admit the truth, she had already begun to speak.

"He was shot." The words quavered in the sudden quiet. "He died in my arms, and I'm here because of him."

"Who shot him?" someone shouted.

Elspeth lifted her chin. She looked so brave and vulnerable, defending herself against a crime she hadn't committed, or understood, that Niall's heart pounded as if it would burst with the pressure of pride and fear it contained.

And when she said softly, "George shot him," and a buzz of anger broke out around them, he jumped off his horse and forced himself in front of her. He didn't care if she resented his interference. She was his now, she didn't belong to these people, and he couldn't pretend to control his emotions for another minute longer.

"Hasim," he said quietly, never taking his eyes off the band of Highlanders below the bridge, confident that his friend was already reaching for the fighting kris he wore under his cloak. Not that the pair of them, a shivering little shaman and a man still weakened from malarial fever, would last long if this mob decided to launch an attack.

"It's time for us to go now, Elspeth," he said with as much self-control as he could manage.

"They wouldn't hurt me, Niall. I know them."

"Open your eyes, *chère,*" he said harshly. "The fairy tale is over and it didn't have a pretty ending. Your prince turned out to be a monster, and he even managed to escape his punishment. There is no poetic justice."

She shook her head in denial, that irrepressible light, undimmed by disillusionment, back in her eyes. "Poor Glenlyon," she said in a gentle voice. "Don't you understand yet?"

"I'm only trying to protect you," he said angrily, aching to shake her out of her stubborn faith. "You make me hate myself for forcing you to confront the truth."

"Where is old Tormod buried, lass?" a woman cried. "Where has the puir murdered soul been laid to rest?"

Elspeth shook her head, too unsettled by the question herself to conceal her own sense of guilt. "I wish I knew."

A shocked silence fell, then, "Ye said he died in yer arms—"

"He sent me here to help you on his last dying breath," she answered slowly. "Please . . . I'll seek legal counsel to find out how we can regain control of the glen. I still don't know the extent of my father's involvement."

Her voice trailed off. She had exhausted her own defense, and unlike Niall she was too damned honorable to lie to save her neck. His hand closed around the gun under his coat. The muscles of his neck ached with the tension of waiting.

She trusted in the truth. He knew better.

There was an angry jostling, a restless surge of energy from the end of the bridge. A young boy tossed a handful of stones in the air. Niall thought he heard the phrase, "Someone hold her hostage," or God knew, it could have even been, "Someone hold my sausage," but the effect on his tinder-dry nerves was the same, triggering an automatic response.

People started to shove, surging toward them, and he stationed himself in front of Elspeth, shoving back the swell of bodies. He saw the prongs of a pitchfork stabbing air. He drew out his gun, and waved it in a vague menacing gesture over his head. His heart was racing at the horrified gasps around him, Elspeth's the loudest.

Then all at once an elderly woman pressed to the fore, the same magnificent silver-haired beldame he had met outside the hut. The gentle reproof in her faded blue eyes mocked his violent reaction.

"Let them pass," she instructed the crowd of Highlanders, her quiet voice carrying a power that calmed the restless energy in the air.

"But Una—"

She raised her hand impatiently. "Do ye want peace or revenge? If it's peace ye want, then let them pass."

The crowd drew apart, faces averted in shame, suspicious glances giving way to hopeful resignation as Niall took advantage of the moment to heave Elspeth back onto her mount.

She and Sorcha were staring at each other, tears of regret and forgiveness in their eyes.

Hasim glanced down from his horse at the old wise woman and gave a slow nod of acknowledgment of her power. She returned the compliment with a gracious nod of her own, then raised her gaze to Niall.

" 'Tis time to let go too, laddie," she said with a little sympathetic smile before she turned away, melting back into the subdued mob.

He swallowed hard. He felt suddenly like crying and didn't know why. Hell, he didn't know what she was talking about, unless it was the gun he was still clutching in his hand.

Let go.

Of who . . . of what?

He jammed the gun back into his waistband and remounted his horse, so flustered he was halfway across the bridge before he realized Elspeth hadn't followed. Swiveling around in the saddle, he watched her lean down to clasp Sorcha's hand in farewell.

"I'll be back," he heard Elspeth say.

Sorcha was crying, shaking her head. "Ye may have more of a fight on yer hands than ye realize."

"I'll do everything I can," Elspeth promised with a sincerity that Niall didn't doubt for a second. "And I will be back."

The Highlanders drew apart to allow the three riders across the bridge. If Niall had been in a more forgiving mood, if he hadn't been so numb from what he had just heard Elspeth promise, he might have realized that she'd had no choice.

He might have seen the hope and mutual respect, the bond built between the laird's beloved granddaughter and the people who looked to her as their last link to the only way of life they understood.

But his mind refused to follow any logical course. In fact, a single dark thought dominated it, again and again: He had lost her. She had only been on loan to him, like the evening coat from the pawnbroker's which he had leased (and neglected to return).

And just as he had left a bag of smuggled Siamese rubies in the pawnshop for that damned coat, so had Elspeth taken his heart as collateral.

She was staying here. There would be no bride for him to take home to his island, no spirited children to learn the magical secrets of the jungle. There would be no wild-haired Scottish wife to make love with in the warm monsoon winds.

"What is it, Niall?" Elspeth said, her voice breaking into his self-pitying reverie as she rode up beside him.

He slowed his mount, his face unfathomable. They had reached the moor and the freedom he had hoped it would lead to, which now only seemed to represent a future of familiar loneliness. Stealing her from George had been child's play. Taking her away from the land and people she loved would be tantamount to sacrilege; visions of wrathful angels rose in his mind at the very prospect. Heaven certainly wouldn't be on *his* side in such a holy war.

"What is it, Niall?" she asked again.

"You're not a coat," he said curtly, spurring his horse past hers.

"Not a coat?" She shared a worried look with Hasim, mouthing, "Could it be the fever again?"

"It is not the fever," Niall bit out before Hasim could even open his mouth to venture an opinion.

He didn't bother to explain his dark feelings for the remainder of the ride. What would have been the point? She was too self-absorbed in playing Joan of Arc to her crofters to consider what she'd done to his heart. She took him for granted.

The glen. The damned glen. It owned her, not the other way around. And for the first time, he felt a reluctant glimmer of understanding about why George had conspired to get rid of the place.

[faint text from facing/previous page bleeding through, partially legible]

Thirty-seven

Elspeth opened her eyes, then yawned in self-indulgent satisfaction as Niall lowered her onto the bed. After five harrowing days on horseback through the Grampian passes in sleet and melting snow, she had fallen sound asleep over a plate of chops and buttered tatties in the inn's dining room downstairs. The past few weeks had taken a toll on her healthy constitution; she didn't seem to have her usual Viking stamina. Her appetite, however, was as robust as ever.

"What did you do with my lovely supper?" she murmured, snuggling under the goose-down comforter he tucked around her.

"Hasim took the potatoes to offer to his gods," he said wryly. "I'm having the chops sent up with a tureen of soup and some hot tea." He tossed his saddlebags into the corner. "If you're awake, I think it's time we had a serious talk."

She blinked, following his restless movements around the room until he returned to her side. "I don't know if I like the sound of that."

He sat down on the edge of the bed, studying her with such a penetrating stare that she began to fidget under the comforter. And to realize that something must be wrong.

"What is it?" Instantly awake, she imagined the worst. His fever had returned, and he was going to die. Or, he'd had news during supper that his uncle was already dead.

"What happened, Niall? Don't keep it from me. I'm not the trembling virgin type."

He smiled faintly, studying her concerned face, feature by feature, the dark dramatic eyebrows, the sweet red mouth, the strong chin. "When are your courses due, Elspeth?"

"My courses?" She pushed up onto her elbow, her expression blank.

"I'm not entirely ignorant of such things, *chérie*. I've seen the signs."

"The—oh, you mean the horse races. Honestly, Niall, I would have told you if I'd won. And I only took five bob out of your purse to bet when we stopped for supper at the last coaching inn. Well, there might have been one or two other times before that."

"What?" he said quietly. "Are you trying to tell me you've been gambling with *my* money behind my back?"

She moistened her lips nervously, sleepy and confused. "Isn't that what you were talking about?"

He closed his eyes as if to compose himself. "I'm not talking about horses' courses. Your *courses*. Monthly things. Red poppies as they say in France." His own face was turning a similar shade. "For heaven's sake, must I be more explicit? Eve's curse, Elspeth."

"Eve who?" she whispered, staring at him in bewilderment. Then, understanding struck and she released her breath in a rush, sinking back onto the bed, every particle of her being alert to the possibility of this intriguing complication.

"Those courses," she said softly. "My goodness."

"Yes," he murmured in amusement, turning back to the window, but there was a dark gleam of satisfaction in his eyes that gave her a hint of how he felt about a potential pregnancy.

"I'm two weeks overdue. How stupid. How incredibly

stupid. I kept thinking my appetite had increased because of the cold."

"You've been feeling unwell every morning for a week," he pointed out.

"Yes, and I've been drinking that nasty-tasting coffee you and Hasim prepared." She chewed the corner of her lip. "Pregnant. Well, I'm in shock, Niall."

" 'Shock' has unpleasant overtones," he said quickly. Their eyes met, emotion rising like smoke between them in the silence. "Do you want this child, *chère?*"

"Of course I do," she said, indignant he could even suggest otherwise.

He took her hands, covering them with his own. "Then why do you look so terrified?"

"Because I am terrified, Glenlyon. I can't believe how I feel. A few moments ago this child did not exist to me and now, well, now there is nothing more important."

"That is nature," he said with a nod of approval, rubbing his thumb across her whitened knuckles, clutched into knots of tension. "The tigress's most powerful instinct is to protect her offspring."

She gazed down at their hands, interlocked in a taut uncomfortable tangle. "I don't know much about wild animals, or tigresses, or whatever particular metaphysical meaning they might have in your life—"

"Metaphorical," he said, trying not to smile. "That's what you wanted to say."

"Yes, well, I haven't lived the life you've led, Glenlyon," she said irritably. "I haven't picked up your vocabulary." She released a deep breath. "Do *you* want this child?"

Sadness tinged his smile. "I'm afraid I want this child so badly, I may have to fight you for it."

She looked up slowly, into his face, and felt an indefinable fear grip her heart. Not once since they'd left Glen Fyne had he mentioned marriage, or whisking her off to his island plantation. The playful warmth, the intimacy they had enjoyed at the lodge had, in fact, dwindled away like the aftermath of a heavenly dream.

His obligation to her father had ended. Their misadventure, a mere chapter in the amorous life of the infamous Captain Glenlyon had come—to what? A close? A pregnant pause? Somewhere along the way, while he was stealing her heart, she had forgotten that when a man felt lust it did not necessarily equal love. Men sired children. Men left those children behind like so many sad wee wildflowers and went on to sow riper fields. But Niall was an unpredictable element. She frowned at him.

"What do you intend to do, Glenlyon, spirit my baby away like a bad fairy the moment it's born?"

"Our baby. And yes, I'll do whatever is necessary to take the child home where it belongs, if it has to come to that."

"Charming. And where does that leave its mother?"

He narrowed his eyes. "Did I or did I not hear you promise you'd return to the glen and restore as many crofts as you could?"

"Of course you did." She sniffed at his lack of understanding. "What else was I supposed to do? My grandfather left the responsibility of it to me."

He felt like shaking her. "For five days, Elspeth, I have been convincing myself you made that promise under duress and had no intention of keeping it."

"That's wretched, Niall. To even think that of me. I keep my promises. Dear God."

"And we promised the future to each other in the lodge, or did I imagine that in my fever?"

"You said something to the effect that you wanted to swim naked with me in a volcanic pool, Niall. You mentioned marriage only when the urge to rut came on you. I could hardly interpret that as a lifelong commitment."

"The commitment was understood," he said in astonishment. "I want you and my baby to go back to the island with me. It's that simple."

"Couldn't we decide all this next year?" she asked in a small hopeful voice.

He gave her a reproachful look. "The coffee plantation is in its fledgling stages, and I've been chasing around Scotland a good month longer than I ever meant to. There are people dependent on me for work, too, Elspeth. Families who live on a bowl of rice a day. I've promised them permanent employment. You understand my position."

"But I promised them I'd come back," she whispered miserably.

"Hell," he said, feeling guilty for her predicament and wronged by it at the same time. "Am I selfish because I want my children to grow up in a land where they can be the lords of their own lives?"

"You want your children to run away from the world just as you've done all your life," she retorted before she could stop herself.

He recoiled; the barb had sank deeper than she had ever intended. "Well, that's frank enough, isn't it?" he asked softly. "And even though I admire frankness as a rule, I find it hard to keep hearing the woman I love calling me a coward."

"That isn't what I meant at all!"

"Hell, it doesn't matter."

"Yes, it does."

"No." He shook his head self-righteously, glad to see he'd made her feel guilty, too. "It's the child that matters. Not the glen. Not George. Not my pathetic coffee plantation, which of course I'll need to make a success of to support our growing family. No, Elspeth. None of it matters."

"Except the child."

He frowned. "Yes. I thought I said that."

"You really want to return to your own world, don't

you?" she asked, suddenly feeling immeasurably selfish as she studied his face.

He hesitated; it was a struggle to explain what he had only now begun to realize himself. "Sometimes I think that part of me is still an angry and frightened young boy wandering in those jungles. Searching."

"For your sister Rachel?"

"Partly. And for my soul." He stared across the room, looking as sad as the first night they had met. "I'll never forgive myself for not finding her. *Dieu,* I know all this must sound stupid, sentimental."

"It doesn't, Niall."

He lowered his gaze to stare down at her, at the outline of her full white breasts against her gown, the golden tumult of her hair gleaming in the candlelight. He thought of how her body would expand to accommodate his child, how the stunning mess of his life had somehow managed to evolve into such a miracle, and he was humbled, delighted, afraid to trust this unexpected state of grace.

"I think we'll have to return to those jungles and find that lost boy, Glenlyon," she said gently. "I can't bear the thought of him wandering there all alone."

"Ah, but he isn't a very attractive character, *chère.* He's tall and thin and frightened of his own shadow, pretending to be so mean and brave because he doesn't want anyone to know what he really is."

Her tigress eyes shone with tears. "But he grew into such an attractive man."

"Did he?" he asked, swallowing tightly.

"The rogue stole my heart."

"Well, you see, he isn't actually all that nice then, is he? Stealing things like hearts and second-hand coats."

"He was kind to an old vagrant who broke into my father's house when any other man would have been indignant. And he's led such an interesting life."

"How much do you love me?" he asked quietly.

"More than I should, I'm sure."

"Enough to sell your soul for my sake, to follow me to the ends of the earth?"

"Good heavens," she whispered.

"I need your love," he said, closing his eyes. "I need your loyalty."

"You are a lost cause, Captain Glenlyon."

"Of all your causes, *chérie*," he said hoarsely, "there is little doubt that I am the most lost."

She slipped her arms around his shoulders and ran her fingertips down the ridge of his spine, feeling his muscles flex with involuntary pleasure. "I'll never reform you, will I?" she whispered.

"I think . . ." He drew a breath. "I think you already have."

"I'd sell my soul for your sake," she echoed softly, pulling him down against her. "I'd follow you to the ends of the earth, or to an active volcano if that would make you happier."

He laughed reluctantly and pressed her down into the pillows, his large body moving over her with masculine grace and mastery. "Let's hope it never comes to that," he whispered. "But if it does, I'm going to hold you to your promise."

He studied Elspeth in the predawn stillness. Tousled yellow hair, purple circles under her eyes, her hand resting on her cheek, she lay sweetly plundered and curled up in a ball, dead to the world under the comforter. With her wild golden mane of hair in disarray, she looked like a dandelion lying in a field after a windstorm.

Just the sight of her, vulnerable and warmly inviting, carrying his baby, made him feel as if an arrow had pierced the last wall of self-isolation around his heart.

Bull's-eye.

A sudden stirring of anxiety chased away the afterglow of sexual satisfaction he should have savored. He wouldn't know a moment's peace until they were on his island where they could create their own memories and pretend the past never existed.

He began to pack their few belongings, having checked last night that the coach for the Grampians would leave in less than two hours; he'd feel better not having her continue on horseback. The predawn quiet reinforced his irrational feeling of urgency, the need to put as much distance between them and Glen Fyne as possible.

He shuddered to think what the papers would make of this, abducting an heiress, a pregnancy, and subsequent elopement. Hell, it just occurred to him that escaping Scotland before Tormod MacQueen's murder trial came due was reason enough to rush. Niall didn't fancy being anyone's scapegoat.

And he was going to be a father. Incredible. He rubbed his thumb across the large ruby of his ring for luck, unable to hold back a smile.

He dressed. He stacked peats in the fire so Elspeth would not wake up to a cold room. Then, humming softly, he left and started down the stairs to order breakfast and arrange their passage.

His anxiety receded as he observed the inn coming to life, pots banging, doors opening, pumps creaking, customers hurrying on their way. The thought crossed his mind that this was how *other* people lived, and for an absurd instant he was profoundly content that he was so close to achieving that state of anonymous normalcy that everyone else took for granted.

He was suddenly like the self-important men he passed on the stairs, ordering breakfast, respectable. He worried about the future of his children, about the weather, about getting a good seat on the coach for Elspeth. He had a reason for being. The mundane had become elevated to the sublime.

When he returned to the room, the cause of his uplifted mood was sitting at the very edge of the bed, totally ignoring the tray beside her on which sat two bowls of porridge with cream, two pots of tea, and a plate of buttered toast.

He walked up beside her and tapped her on the head with his gloves. "I paid an outrageous price for that meal you're letting go cold and—"

His heart took a sick plunge in his chest; his mind went wild with possibilities. Her posture was too stiff, her averted face hinted at something too painful to consider. "What is it?"

"I'm sure it's nothing," she said with utter misery in her voice.

He knelt before her, gazing up into her distressed face. *"Jesu,"* he whispered, bringing his big hand to her cheek. "Tell me what's wrong so I can make it better."

"It's just a little cramping . . . a little blood."

His chest constricted with fear, and anger—at himself, the more fool he for believing his luck had changed; at life, for threatening such precious innocence.

"No," he said. "No." Somehow he managed to keep his voice steady. He refused to show her how frightened he was, or how he would blame himself because he had made love to her all night if she miscarried the child.

"I knew it, Niall. God is going to punish me again."

"No." He straightened, realizing how closely her fears reflected his, how unfair, how ridiculous to worship such a vengeful deity. "No. God is not like that, *doucette*. And this is our child, strong, resilient, and stubborn, just as we are."

She forced a brave smile at that. "Have faith for us, Glenlyon." Her voice fell an octave. The despair on her face shook him to the core. "They say that you know magic."

He backed toward the door. "I'll find Hasim."

"You're going to ask a witch doctor to save our child?" she whispered, her eyes widening.

"I've seen him do it before—save unborn children, that is."

"A midwife might be a wee bit more appropriate, do you not think?"

She was a little calmer now, more like her old self, and Niall took reassurance from that. "I'll bring in Hasim, a doctor, the village midwife—whoever will help you, Elspeth. Now get back into bed and eat your porridge like a good girl."

She bit her lip and picked up her spoon. "Use whatever magic you know, Glenlyon," she pleaded softly.

"Don't worry," he promised her from the door. "I'll move heaven and earth if that's what I have to do."

Thirty-eight

Niall sent Elspeth an apologetic smile from the bottom of the bed where he stood guarding her from the battle raging in the room. He refused to leave a single stone unturned where his child's life was concerned. Accordingly, he'd summoned not only Hasim to look at Elspeth, but also the village midwife, a traveling dentist, and the local doctor. He was beginning to wonder if he'd overreacted.

The traveling dentist had examined Elspeth's teeth and offered to extract her molars and bleed her. Niall, who still bore leech scars from his jungle days, had sent the man and his instruments of torture packing. The doctor had still not arrived.

But in the meanwhile, for almost an hour now, Niall and Elspeth had waited in apprehensive suspense for the conclusion of the fierce if friendly debate building between Hasim and the ruddy-cheeked midwife Mrs. Gordon.

Niall expelled a long sigh. For his own part he had spent considerable time alone in the local kirk in heartfelt prayer. He hadn't even known what denomination it was, certainly not Roman Catholic, memories of its ritualistic solemnity returning to his awareness in a rush of surprisingly poignant images. Papa snoring during Mass, Maman pretending not to notice, he and Dallas playing finger puppets with Rachel, Alex slipping a frog down her back.

Ah, yes. Rachel. That was the last time Niall had formally prayed, down on his knees, trousers threadbare, in a Jesuit mission on the Burmese border. He had prayed earnestly then, unselfishly, for his sister, but nothing had come of it.

Lord, I believe. Help though mine unbelief. Don't let Elspeth lose this baby. I want it too much. Don't let anything hurt her.

"Niall." She nudged his hand.

He blinked. His attention returned to the room. An agreement apparently had been reached between midwife and witch doctor.

The woman, twice Hasim's height and breadth, had recognized the similarities between the heathen beliefs of his culture and those in these remote Scottish Highlands. After a cursory examination of the patient, including a few critical frowns directed at Niall, she claimed that an evil fairy was trying to expel the child from Elspeth's womb to take possession herself.

Niall's eyebrows lifted at the bizarre diagnosis. "An evil fairy? Hasim, do you concur?"

Hasim nodded solemnly. "It is so, Tuan, I very afraids to say. A *leyak,* yes."

"An evil fairy," Niall muttered and, at a loss, yanked out his broken pocket watch to wonder when the doctor would arrive. "Assuming there exist such things as evil fairies, how the blazes would one have entered Elspeth's body?"

Mrs. Gordon glanced up at him grimly from the hearth. "Has the patient recently spent time in a graveyard?"

Niall swallowed a curse, his patience eroded. "Of course she hasn't spent time in a graveyard. What a stupid question."

"Yes, I have," Elspeth said in a meek voice. "I spent an evening with Francis in the abbey kirkyard, and you and I rode through the graves right after you tried to ravish me on your horse, Niall. Don't you remember?"

"Dear, dear," the midwife said, giving Niall another look.

He frowned at Elspeth. "I think we'd better wait for the doctor, after all. How do you feel?"

"Fine, actually." She smiled sheepishly. "I'm rather hungry."

Mrs. Gordon moved to one side of the bed, Hasim to the other; between them they effectively bumped Niall into the background.

"Here," he said in alarm, catching sight of Elspeth's pale startled face in the center, "what do you think you're doing?"

The midwife began fanning Elspeth's cheeks with the pages of a well-worn Bible. "For a start, sir, we'll give her a guid dose of raspberry-leaf tea wi' goats' milk and honey of roses."

"That sounds harmless enough, I suppose," Niall said reluctantly.

"She's to sleep wi' a nail under the mattress."

"A nail?"

"She not to eats any yams, turtle, or dragon lizards, Tuan."

Elspeth giggled unwillingly. "That shouldn't be a problem."

"She's to name the child right after its birth, sir," the midwife added.

"Small frogs fine to eat, Tuan."

Mrs. Gordon removed a bundle of herbs from her basket. "I must insist that all the doors of the inn be unlocked, sir."

"You're joking."

Hasim glanced up. "All bottles must be uncorked also, Tuan."

"The doors," Niall said. "The bottles."

"Immediately, sir," urged Mrs. Gordon.

He nodded, wondering as he left the room how he

would force the innkeeper to comply with such outlandish requests. But these were the Highlands, superstition was rife, and comply the poor fellow would because Niall would stop at nothing to save the child that neither he nor Elspeth could see or touch, but who represented the essence of their love. Their future.

Elspeth had fallen asleep again; the midwife had packed up her kettle and herbs, and Hasim had gallantly offered to walk her home, explaining on the way how he had once exorcised an evil genie from the subterranean vaults of a sultan's palace.

Sitting in the hushed candlelit room, Niall examined Hasim's strange arrangement of volcanic stones on the hearth and felt a return of his earlier tension, but it was so overlaid with relief, he could easily ignore it.

Elspeth showed every sign of completing a healthy pregnancy. All the powers of heaven and earth had combined to answer his prayer. He was deeply grateful. And emotionally drained.

He had just pulled off his boots and socks when a cautious knock sounded at the door. Frowning at the disturbance, he walked barefooted past the bed to open the door a quarter-inch. Elspeth needed rest more than anything now.

"What is it?"

The innkeeper blinked. His heavily bearded face was apprehensive. "May we lock the doors and cork up the bottles now, Captain?"

Niall swallowed a smile, remembering the veiled threats he had made in the taproom not that long ago. "Yes," he said, "and thank you."

He started to close the door only to hesitate at the nervous glance the innkeeper cast back into the hall. "I did pay you for your trouble, didn't I?"

"Aye, sir. But, uh, ye're wanted in the courtyard."

"I'm what?" Niall frowned in annoyance. "Who wants me?"

"I couldna say, sir," the man replied, hurrying back toward the stairs in his hobnailed brogues.

Hell, Niall thought as he returned to the stool to retrieve his boots and socks. It was probably only the doctor, no doubt expecting a fee for his call despite the fact his services were thankfully no longer needed. Well, it wouldn't hurt to have the man take a look at her, even though she would complain when they disturbed her, the spotting had stopped, and she had been pinching their dwindling cash reserves to bet on horses all over the Highlands.

Carrying his boots and socks, he crept past the bed. As he closed the door quietly behind him, he did not hear her call out his name, her voice low with uncharacteristic fear.

Elspeth had drifted back into the throes of an uneasy dream and then came awake with a startled cry. Her heart began racing as she gazed up at the two cloaked men who flanked the bed. They had once been poignantly familiar to her. She had loved and trusted them with all her stubborn heart, but now the mere sight of them filled it with only sadness and trepidation. George and her father had become her enemies.

She struggled to sit up, feeling vulnerable as they flanked the bed, exchanging shocked glances at her appearance. Well, let them look! She pushed off the comforter, glad she still wore Hasim's tiger claw talisman around her throat, that the soles of her feet were still painted with red Malayan clay, and that the room still reeked of the herbs Mrs. Gordon had burned in the fireplace.

"Dear Jesus." Duncan Kildrummond shook his head in

disbelief. "What has that bastard done to you, my reckless daughter?"

George glanced down at the clothing on the floor. Glen-lyon's shoddy black coat was spread like a protective shadow over the costly cloak George had bought for her in Edinburgh. "I told you, Duncan," he said with malicious satisfaction. "I didn't exaggerate, did I?"

A flush of anger flooded Elspeth's face. The damned hypocrites! "Aye, I'm ruined, Papa," she said, her voice stiff with the strain of keeping her self-possession. "Despoiled, defiled, seduced, ravished, and—"

"That's enough," Duncan said, the veins in his temple pulsing.

"—and pregnant with a pagan coffee-planter's bastard," she concluded.

"What?" Duncan said. *"What?"*

She shrank back against the headboard, her righteous anger wilting at the shock on her father's face.

"No." George shook his head, his skin like chalk. "No."

"Yes," she whispered.

George stared at her, then walked in a speechless daze to the window, shaken enough by her revelation that he had to lean the heels of his hands against the sill before he could draw a normal breath.

Duncan began to pace around the bed. "Well, you've really done it now, lass. I don't know how we can help you out of this one."

"I don't want to be helped," she said quietly. "I've never been happier in my life."

"She'll have to go to the Continent," George murmured, recovering his composure. "Susan could travel with her. I have a friend who owes me a favor."

"Goddamnit." Duncan kicked Niall's coat against the hearth. "If that press reporter gets wind of this—Catherine and Aunt Flora are *not* to be told."

"We'll go straight to Devon." George frowned. "She'll need new clothes, of course."

"But you've done so much for me already," Elspeth said, her voice deep with sarcasm. "Plundering my inheritance behind my back, sleeping with Susan, destroying the lives of the people we'd agreed to protect."

"Susan?" Duncan came to a stop a foot from the bed, his mouth curling in disgust. "You committed adultery with my niece on top of everything else?"

George met his gaze without blinking. "Catherine made the whole thing up out of her fertile imagination just as she labeled my poor cousin Francis a murderer."

Elspeth looked over at him in cold anger, witnessing firsthand how easily, how well he could dissemble to suit his purpose. To think of all the years he had used her sympathy, her dumb loyalty, as a weapon against her.

She rose abruptly from the bed, wondering where Niall had gone, when he would return. "George and Susan's dallying with each other doesn't matter, but the glen does. You've ruined it, Papa. You've broken hearts and homes."

Duncan shook his head sadly. "I never knew the details, lass. I was ignorant of how the whole sorrowful affair was handled."

"You knew enough." Her eyes blazed at him with hurt accusation. "You could have told me."

George plucked her worn dress from the chair where Niall had draped it. "Put this on," he said in distaste. "You're barely decent."

"It was a business decision, Elspeth," her father went on, deliberately ignoring George. "At the time I believed it was for your own good."

"For my own good, Papa! Really. Oh, just leave me alone—both of you. Get out of here and save Niall the trouble of throwing you out when he comes back."

George thrust the dress at her. The vicious glint in his eyes turned her blood cold. "I wouldn't count on your 'captain' coming back for quite some time. He's been arrested, you see."

"For abducting me?" Elspeth snorted and ducked behind the dressing screen to remove her loosened nightdress. "Oh, stuff it, George. Trying to have Niall arrested for abducting me didn't work before, and it won't work now."

He hesitated a heartbeat. "Except that this time he's been arrested for the murder of Tormod MacQueen."

Elspeth stepped out from behind the screen, her initial reaction of indignant contempt fading at the look on his face. "No." She swallowed, the sour taste of fear filling her mouth. "No one would ever believe that. He'd never even heard of Tormod before the night of the party. What possible motive could you have invented for him, George?"

He waited, clearly savoring the fear she could not manage to hide. She felt her chest tighten as the silence lengthened, as her father sank down into a chair and stared morosely at the floor.

"Papa," she whispered, her heart pounding at the suspense. "Tell me you're not going to let this happen."

Duncan slowly raised his head. "Tormod's death need never have happened if you'd stayed in your room that night. Unfortunately your rash behavior has set into motion a chain of events that force us into an unpalatable position."

"You'd let an innocent man be convicted of a crime he didn't commit?" she said in shock.

George readjusted his neckcloth. "He doesn't have much choice, darling."

"No one will believe you," she said, her voice hard. "No one will believe Niall shot a man he'd never met without reason."

"It was robbery, Elspeth." George leaned back against the windowsill, crossing his ankles. "Everyone knows Glenlyon is a low sort who'd do anything for cash—including seducing silly young runaways. The sad but sordid truth is that he robbed Tormod of the priceless antique dirk the poor old fellow had carried all the way down from the Highlands to give to you and me as a wedding gift. Dear God, Glenlyon couldn't even afford a decent evening jacket. Of course he'd steal a costly treasure."

Elspeth fought against her mounting panic to keep her head. "But I have the dirk, you swine." Throwing George a killing look, she reached down under the bed for her bag. "It's somewhere in here, I know it."

"No, it isn't," George said softly. "I found it in Glenlyon's saddlebag in that haunted little forest of yours that night you and I had such an enlightening chat. Naturally, I turned it over to the authorities. Evidence, you know."

She straightened, her voice shaking with fury. "You can't keep distorting the truth and get away with it, George."

He smiled coldly. "If it's the truth you want, Elspeth, then ask your papa about the changes in MacAllister's will, or about that last fire at the warehouse."

She glanced down unwillingly at her father.

"No one has ever been hurt because of me, I swear it," Duncan said with fervent conviction. "The glen was bleeding me dry. We were in danger of losing everything, including your precious land, and I—I never dreamed it would turn into such a tragedy."

"Why did you not let me know?" she whispered, still wanting to trust him, unable to relinquish that last hope that he loved her, that he was the honorable man she had grown up to adore.

"George thought it best." He shook his head. "I thought he was securing the future of my grandchildren. It all made sense on paper."

She grasped the back of the chair that stood between her and George. "If I weren't pregnant, George," she said softly, "I might try—"

He uncrossed his ankles, pretending to look surprised. "But darling, there are ways to end an unwanted pregnancy—there are old women who take care of such nuisances, but then you already knew that, didn't you?"

It was the cruelest taunt imaginable to make, especially in front of her father, who until now had known nothing about her ill-fated association with Robert. And even though she realized that her unintentional betrayal had hurt George, her well of pity for him had run dry.

Duncan slowly rose, staring at her for an explanation. "What is he saying, Elspeth?"

"Thank you, George," she said tersely.

"Oh, didn't you know about your daughter and big, brawny Robbie Campbell?" George's voice struck the superficial chords of a man discussing nothing more important than the weather. "Everyone else did. Everyone else knew how she'd spread her legs for him in your barn while you were bawling like a baby over your wife's grave."

Elspeth snatched her cloak off the chair, too upset to meet her father's bewildered gaze. All the years of trying to hide what had happened from Papa, praying he would not hear the rumors. All of the unspeakable shame, and now it was out in the open. Now he could justify his neglect, his lack of faith in her. Now he could twist the impulsive mistake of a bereaved young girl into a plausible rationale for handing George control of her inheritance.

Duncan reached for her arm in concern. "Are you all right, Elspeth?"

She lifted her eyes uncertainly to his. "I'm fine, but, oh, Papa . . . how did we ever come to this?"

"Is it true—are you pregnant, lass?" he asked under his breath.

She nodded numbly, brushing past his outstretched arm. She could see one of Niall's socks folded into her cloak, and she might have smiled at the thought of him hauled off to gaol, one sock missing, if the situation hadn't been so frightening.

"I'm going to the authorities, Papa." She clutched the sock to her chest. "I'm going to tell them the truth."

George shoved the chair across the room. "Goddamnit, stop her this time, Duncan. Stop her, I tell you."

Duncan turned slowly, his face sad but resolute.

"No," he said, shaking his head. "Let her do what she will. It's over, George."

She ran outside past the stables to avoid the rush of evening arrivals to the inn, realizing as she reached the drinking trough that she had no money, no idea of where or how to find Niall. She didn't even know whether he'd been taken to a proper gaol or to a lonely farmhouse that served as the local lock-up. She didn't even have her own shoes on. Her bare toes contracted as she slowly walked across the cold shining cobbles.

She began to pace in circles around the courtyard, her face dark with frustration. She supposed she would have to wait until Hasim returned from his walk and could help her.

Her cloak slid to the dirty cobbles. She shivered and felt the loss, but made no move to pick it up, still holding the sock. She didn't believe for a minute that Niall would be brought to trial for a murder he hadn't committed. There was still a stubborn uncorrupted streak in her character that clung to the inevitable triumph of truth and justice.

Quite frankly, what she feared most was that after Niall got free, he would flee to his island haven without her, so disgusted by the trouble she'd caused him that he wanted only to forget her. She wouldn't let him, of course. She would follow him and bedevil his life again until he married him. Then she'd make him bring her back to Scotland, which in her opinion was the only proper place in the world to bring up a child.

The approaching clatter of wheels and hoofbeats coming toward the inn interrupted her tangle of thoughts. Alarmed, she watched a small coach appear out of the mist and barrel into the courtyard with such blatant disregard for whatever stood in the way that she ducked instinctively behind the horse trough to protect herself.

The coach ran over her cloak.

Indignant, she darted out to shout at the driver. But he didn't so much as glance at her as he slowed his heaving horses and remained on the box while his two male passengers alit from the coach.

"Glenlyon?" she whispered in disbelief.

She ventured closer to the taller of the two men who had stooped out of view to wrest her cloak from beneath the coach wheel.

"Mon Dieu, Elspeth." He swung around, his lean face admonishing. "I can't believe how careless you are! I'm not gone even two hours and here I find you running after a coach like some romantic heroine in a novel. Your cloak is ruined, but you'll have to wear it anyway because all our money is almost gone. If you can't think of your own welfare, think of the little one's."

She swallowed tightly, holding back laughter and tears of relief as he draped the cloak around her shoulders. Despite his perplexed tone of voice, she felt his hands tremble slightly where he touched her, and only when she turned back toward him did she notice the dark shadows of a bruise that covered his left cheek.

"Why are you even down here?" he asked, anxiety deepening his voice. "Is everything all right with the baby?"

She nodded and studied his discolored cheek, biting her lip in sympathy. "You look like—" She sniffed the front of his coat, pulling her head away in distaste. "My God, what is that atrocious odor?"

"You might smell too, Elspeth, if you'd been beaten, manacled, and held for an hour in a turnip cellar by Robert Campbell and his two oafish constables."

"Oh, Niall."

"The beating wasn't the worst part either. The worst part was imagining that George had spirited you away to some lonely moor and that you'd——" He gripped her around the waist, his voice uneven. "Well, and here I find you out in the January cold, waving my sock and shouting at strange coachmen."

"You look like hell, Glenlyon," she whispered.

He smiled, wincing slightly at the reflexive tightening of his facial muscles. "You should see the other fellow, *mon coeur*," he said darkly. "Poor Robert Campbell won't be quite the ladies' man from now on, I'll warrant."

"Not his nose again, Niall."

"No." His eyes glinted at the satisfying memory. "It was one of his front teeth. Now why aren't you resting in bed and breathing in all those stinking herbs that are supposed to be so good for my baby?"

"Niall——"

"And where is Hasim? *Sacrebleu,* I despair of ever having an obedient wife or valet."

"George and my father are upstairs in our room," she said quietly.

He withdrew his hands from her waist, murmuring, "Are they indeed?" He stared at her for a moment, the warmth in his eyes becoming a winter chill. "Get into the coach. If I'm not back down in five minutes, the driver will take you to my uncle's house. And don't come back for me."

She pulled on his arm. His face emanated a dangerous energy that frightened her. "We'll go there together, Niall."

"I'll help you into the coach." He shook off her hand, looking wild and angry and dissolute. "Now."

"Where did you get hold of a coach anyway?" she

asked in alarm, her imagination running wild. "Please God, don't tell me you stole it."

"Once again your faith in me is astonishing—as out of character as it may seem, I didn't steal anything." He glanced back wryly at the man who had remained beside the coach. "Someone offered evidence on my behalf, and Campbell was forced to release me. I even got your damn dirk back."

"Evidence?" she said in confusion.

"Somebody else witnessed what happened in the summerhouse that night, Elspeth."

Stunned, she stared past him, remembering the unidentified passenger who had accompanied him. Several moments passed before she recognized the short man standing by the coach. "Archie Harper? That awful press reporter got you free?"

That awful press reporter, his stout figure clad in an ermine-lined cloak, strode toward her with an ingratiating grin. "We journalists are not entirely without a little influence, my dear. Or moral conscience."

Elspeth found herself grinning back at him in grudging admiration. "I don't know how you managed to do it, Mr. Harper, but—I don't suppose you could use your influence to persuade Niall that he can't kill George?"

Archie's grin vanished into a look of alarm. "Oh, no. We can't 'ave that kind of conduct, Capt'n. It would make an 'orrible end to your story." He looked up into Niall's tense face. "Go on then. Take a stroll in the night air to cool that temper. I'll manage things from 'ere on. I'll take care of Sir George once and for all."

They stood at the edge of the roadway and stared out at the distant hills, letting the tension of the past hours dissolve. Duncan watched them from the shadows of the inn for several minutes before he dared to intrude on their intimacy. Even from where he stood, he could sense the loving tenderness between them, and he thought achingly of his own Helen, who no doubt was relieved that Elspeth's future had been decided. He could only hope that Helen would understand and forgive *him* for closing off his heart after she'd died.

Had their troublesome daughter found the affection, the attention that Duncan had neglected to give her? God knew he'd never have chosen this Glenlyon, this comeouter, with his reputation, as a husband for her. But then look at George. Appealing on the outside, rotten to the core.

He cleared his throat, slowly walking forward. "When do you intend to marry her, Glenlyon?"

Elspeth pulled away from the peaceful Scottish landscape to face her father. "When do you intend to atone for the wrongs you've committed, Papa?"

He sighed. Aye, he'd lost her forever, her precious trust. "As soon as I'm able, lass."

"But you'll pay back all the money that you took by fraudulent means, won't you, Papa?"

He glanced up, wondering if it was his imagination or if that was a glint of enjoyment he'd seen in Glenlyon's eye. He hoped so. The man would need an endless reserve of humor to keep life with his hellion wife in perspective.

"You'll help restore the glen and find the scattered families, Papa?"

Duncan snorted, unable to spoil her happiness by explaining that all the money in the world would never restore Glen Fyne to the idyllic life she remembered. Or was *he* wrong, too old to share her courageous vision?

"I asked you when you were going to take her off my hands, Captain," he said sternly.

"Well, we have a slight problem, sir," Niall replied. "You see, Elspeth will never make a well-behaved wife until her mind is at rest on this issue of the glen. And unless you promise to help her, all my efforts to get her out of Scotland will be useless."

"You're taking her away then?" Duncan asked over the lump that had risen in his throat. "Away to your island?"

"Yes." Niall smiled. "The sooner, the better."

"Well, this sounds a wee bit like what is known in the Gaelic as *mail-dubh*," Duncan said, scowling. "That's blackmail, Glenlyon."

"It does sound like it, doesn't it, sir?"

Duncan swallowed and glanced back down at his eldest daughter, love and regret deepening his voice. "Aye, well, I've been considering retiring and settling down in the glen myself. That is, if you'll let me. The land is yours, after all."

"George might challenge that in court, Papa."

"I have a feeling George will have his hands full challenging other matters." He sighed heavily. "I've not been the best of fathers, have I, little girl?"

She gave him a level look. "No, Papa, but then I've been more than a minor disgrace and worry to you all these years."

He held out his arms and she went to him, feeling him grip her hard as if he were the child seeking comfort from a parent. "It's all right, Papa," she whispered.

"I've not slept one restful night since Tormod died," he said in an anxious voice. "You should never have been there, child. If George had missed—"

"But it's all right now, Papa. We'll do what Tormod wanted, and that would please him. Just promise me his remains will rest in a place of honor beneath the highest cairn on the moor."

"Aye." He drew back, covering his emotional display with a gruff laugh. "But look at you, lass. What would poor Tormod and your granddad think, you standing here barefoot and pregnant by that big foreign fellow?"

"It's not entirely a hopeless cause. After all, he is half Scottish, Papa."

"Aye, that's the half that accepted my offer of money to chase after you." He pretended to glare at Niall. "I hope you intend to take better care of her than this, Captain."

"I'm dying for the chance." Niall couldn't suppress a devilish laugh. "In fact, with your permission, sir—" And before Elspeth could escape him, he caught her around the waist and hefted her over his shoulder, swinging her around to face her father.

"He's a brute, Papa! A perfect barbarian!"

"With all due respect, Duncan," Niall said, "I think it's time for me to start living up to my name. Oh, by the way, if my uncle is well enough for it, we'll be getting married at his home in Glasmagh. A small wedding sometime before the end of the month, I expect."

"All the blood is rushing to my head, Papa! Make the bully put me down."

Niall fell back a step, pretending to gasp as he hoisted Elspeth to his other side. "I think your daughter has given me a hernia, sir."

Duncan smiled reluctantly. "It's a good thing you're a strong man."

"Sir?"

"She'll run you ragged, Glenlyon. You'll be crying on my shoulder in another month."

"Blame it on those damned Vikings," Elspeth said gleefully, gazing upside down at her father through the crook in Niall's arm.

And Niall grinned his most roguish grin, shifting his weight until he had her draped over his shoulders like a hunter carrying away his captured quarry. "We'll see about that, sir, but I may surprise you. They say I have a way with wild creatures."

* * *

Archie Harper smiled to himself at the heartening sight of Glenlyon striding past the waiting coach with his future bride slung over his shoulders. Turning away from the window, Archie picked up his pen and diary journal. His readers, bless their little purse strings, dearly loved a happy ending.

Blowing out a sigh, he glanced beneath his brows at the man sitting on the opposite side of the coach with his well-manicured fingers covering his face. Sir George Westcott, deeply immersed in his own defeat and, one would hope, the first stirrings of a healing shame. The poor bastard thought his political life was over.

But Archie had other ideas.

Although Sir George didn't know it yet, he *was* going to win that election—on the platform of legal protection for the evicted crofters all across the Highlands. Yes, indeed, George would rise to political prominence as the British champion for Scottish social reform. It was either that or spend a hell of a long time in gaol.

"Gallows fiction," Archie said aloud with a wistful shake of his head. "Mental opiates for the masses. It breaks me 'eart, Sir George, to 'ear the cruel things the critics say about my writing. I pour my bleedin' guts into my work, I do."

George lowered his hand, his face bleak. "I tell you, at that moment when I pulled the trigger I truly believed that old man was going to kill either her or me for what had happened in the glen."

Archie stared down at his journal.

"Dear God," George groaned softly. "I can't believe she actually fell in love with that . . . that soldier."

Archie nodded absently and continued to scribble notes. The smile came creeping back across his face. He'd love to print an article on the tumultuous events of these past few weeks: a murder, an abducted heiress, a corrupt political aspirant brought to his knees.

But now wasn't the time. No, he'd hoard the exciting details, embellished a little for dramatic effect, of course, to one day write a brilliant novel. For now a juicy article would have to do.

Well, Dear Readers, it must be true what they say about the mysterious Scottish mist breeding romantical fancies. For that fascinating rogue, subject of so many scintillating serial novels, has at last found a bride to carry back to his heathen hideaway.

Thirty-nine

February had arrived well before they reached the river valley in the Grampian foothills where Oliver Glenlyon lived. Snow had thawed in patches, revealing layers of soggy sphagnum moss. Burns overflowed with melted water to roar down gullies into misty lochans. As the coach labored down a wooded brae, icicles cracked off bare branches and hit the roof like tinkling shards of crystal.

Oliver Glenlyon, retired solicitor, made his home in a grand Georgian manor house of soft apricot stone that was sheltered from the mountain winds by a stand of silver firs. Staring at the half-hidden estate, Niall wondered if he and his uncle might share a passion for privacy. He hoped he had arrived in time to at least meet the man.

"We're here, Elspeth."

She gave an enormous yawn and opened her eyes, leaning around Niall to stare out the window. "Good Lord, look at the size of that house, Glenlyon. Your uncle must be filthy rich—ooh, do you think he's leaving you his estate as an inheritance?"

"I sincerely hope not."

"Dear heaven, do those beautiful fields behind the house belong to him too?"

"And they call me a mercenary," he said wryly. He stretched forward to help her out, giving Hasim on the opposite seat a friendly nudge in the arm. "What would

I do with a house in the Highlands anyway? I have enough trouble trying to manage a coffee plantation."

She slid down into his arms, and he held her close, nuzzling her neck in full view of the tiny group of people who had crowded out on the entrance steps to meet them.

"Glenlyon, put me down. Everyone is watching."

"Not until you promise you won't persuade my uncle to leave us his land so he can move your displaced Highlanders here and start a potato farm."

"The thought never entered my mind."

"You're such a liar, *chérie*."

"They're staring at us, Niall, wondering what that foreigner is doing to such a sweet Scottish lassie in their driveway."

He let her fall down the length of him, drawing a breath as her full breasts brushed his chest. "I know what I wish we were doing."

"Well, you're going to have to wait another week."

"Yes, but there are other—" He plunked her down onto her feet, falling silent as he stared past her. At his expression of amazement, Elspeth glanced around in curiosity to see a tall, distinguished-looking man with silver hair disengage himself from the others on the entrance steps to approach them. Her heart gave a painful lurch. The man's elegant grace of movement, despite his age, his chiseled features, were so reminiscent of Niall that she felt as if she were witnessing a vision of Niall in the decades to come.

Damn if Glenlyon wasn't destined to retain that roguish attraction well into his seventies.

"Assuming that this is your uncle, Niall," she said in an undertone, "he doesn't exactly look as if he's at death's door, does he?"

"There goes your hope for another inheritance," he teased her. "But you're right. He looks fit enough to outlive us both."

Up close, as Oliver slowed to circle Niall, the resemblance between the two of them struck Elspeth even harder: the same gray eyes, smoldering with arrogance and irony; strong unapologetic features that might have made the sum total of the face cruel but for the humor around the mouth.

"You took your time, Niall." Oliver's voice crackled with a vitality that belied not only his age but the likelihood of his imminent demise.

Niall looked flustered. "Well, I— This is Elspeth Kildrummond, Uncle Oliver. You are Uncle Oliver, aren't you?"

"Not if you've gotten yourself into serious trouble, I'm not. Pleased to make your acquaintance, Miss Kildrummond."

Elspeth felt compelled to intervene on Niall's behalf. "Niall's delay in getting here was all my fault," she explained politely. "I ran away, and he came chasing after me all the way into the Highlands."

"What did the rogue do to make you run away from him?" Oliver demanded, scowling at Niall from beneath his lowered eyebrows.

"Actually, I was running away from my home in Falhaven, but I thought a man who was my enemy was following me, so I took refuge in the brothel until your nephew came storming into my room—"

"A brothel?" Oliver repeated in shock, taking a step back from Niall. "Do you mean to say I've been defending you to all my friends when those filthy scandal sheets were really recording the truth? Good gracious."

"To be perfectly fair to Niall," Elspeth tried to explain, "I have to admit that this was my brothel, not the one where he worked in Mandalay."

Oliver glanced rapidly from her to Niall. "Are you telling me, young woman, that you and my nephew struck

up your romantic association while the pair of you were
employed in a—a School of Venus?"

"No," Niall said in annoyance. "She wasn't 'employed'
at the time, and neither was I for that matter." He paused,
putting his hand on Elspeth's shoulder instead of across
her mouth as he was strongly tempted. "Sir, I don't mean
to be rude, but I've come a great distance to see you, and
under considerable duress."

"Duress?" Oliver huffed. "I can well imagine from the
sound of what you two have been up to."

"Actually, I was under the impression that you were,
well . . . you know."

"No, to be honest, Niall, I don't."

"I thought you were dying, sir."

"Dying? Whatever gave you that idea?"

"You did, sir," Niall retorted. "You wrote that I was to
come to you immediately on a matter of grave importance."

"Which you of course interpreted to mean I had one
foot in the grave."

"See for yourself. Here's the very letter," Niall said, his
face perplexed as he reached into his vest pocket to produce a crumpled piece of paper.

" 'Two bob on Arthur's Angel in the second. The
miller's wife likes his legs,' " Oliver read slowly, shaking
his head. "I never wrote this nonsense, Niall. Why, I don't
even know what it means. And all these scribbled numbers
don't make a bit of sense to me."

"It's mine," Elspeth admitted in a low embarrassed
voice. "My racing sheet, which Niall rudely took it upon
himself to confiscate. I think he's forgotten I burned your
letter in the lodge along with my violin after we sailed
across the loch in the storm."

Oliver stared at them in silence.

"Elspeth insisted on rowing to her grandfather's lodge,

the boat was smashed, and then I took a bout of fever," Niall said with an impatient sigh.

Oliver blinked. "I see," he said slowly, which he obviously didn't.

"We thought we might like to be married on your estate, Uncle Oliver," Niall added, lowering his voice.

"Before or after my funeral?"

Niall cast a hopeful look at the house. "Look, you do remember inviting me here, Uncle Oliver, don't you?"

"There is nothing wrong with my memory, Niall, nor with my health." Oliver looked at Elspeth with amused sympathy and offered her his arm. "Come along to the house, my dear, and let me reassure myself my nephew has not mistreated—"

He took a step, then froze in his tracks, gaping at the sight of Hasim grinning from the coach window, the ruby in his turban glittering in the winter gloom. "My word," Oliver whispered. "We don't see many of his kind in the Highlands, do we, Miss Kildrummond?"

She accepted his arm with a smile. "That's Niall's valet."

"Indeed?"

"He's a witch doctor, too."

"A witch . . . Ah, yes, of course. What else?" Oliver glanced down at her, his eyes warm and speculative. "I realize Niall is an attractive man. He's led quite the life, as they say, but have you read the stories published about him?"

"Shocking, aren't they?"

"And you still want to marry him?"

She looked straight ahead. "I'm going to have his child."

Oliver glanced back dryly at Niall. "I can't say that comes as any great surprise."

Niall cleared his throat as he fell into step behind them.

"Is it too much to ask why you summoned me here in such urgency?"

"In due time, Niall." Oliver maneuvered Elspeth around the coach, smiling in satisfaction. "All in due time."

Forty

Oliver added a liberal measure of whisky to Niall's tea, passing it over the tea table with a distracted frown. "Well," he was telling Elspeth, "it never hurts to find out where one stands with the courts, my dear. I can recommend excellent counsel in Aberdeen."

"Aberdeen?" Niall slumped back, scowling, in his chair. "We won't be in Scotland long enough to bother with legal counsel."

Elspeth scooted her own chair closer to Oliver. "I'm hoping George will relinquish all claims to the glen once a certain press reporter gets through with him."

She smiled ruefully over her teacup at the thought of Archie, how she had misjudged him. She'd misjudged Francis, too, but at least she could atone for that mistake by inviting him to stay on as factor at Liath House. That was where the strange man was happiest, living alone and reading his Bible, removed from all worldly temptations.

And on the subject of worldly temptations . . .

She swallowed a scalding mouthful of tea at the shapely auburn-haired maidservant who had just burst into the room brandishing a silver coffeepot. Hovering over Niall's chair, she looked like a vixen about to pounce on her next meal.

"I've read all about yer exploits, Captain, if it isn't out of place to say so!" she gushed. "How brave ye must be. What a thrilling life ye've led."

Elspeth noted that while Niall colored and fidgeted in his chair, he didn't bother to deny his bravery, his "thrilling" life. He just sat there with a stupid grin spreading across his face, allowing the gushing twit to top off his whisky-laced tea with coffee.

"Care for some milk, Captain Niall?"

"Uh, no."

"Some lovely brown sugar?" the young maid persisted.

"No. No thanks."

"A bit of heather honey, Captain Niall?"

He glanced sheepishly at Elspeth. "Definitely *no* honey, thank you."

Oliver pursed his lips. "You may leave the room now, girl."

"Oh, do ye not want some scones, Captain Niall? Such a bold adventurer must have a hearty appetite."

Niall shrank down in his chair. "I'll ring if I do."

The girl slipped out of the room, giving Elspeth an unexpected conspiratorial wink over her shoulder. Elspeth blinked in confusion, feeling suddenly very pregnant and possessive. Only when Niall took a taste of his tainted tea and nearly choked did she see the humor in the situation.

"Too bitter for your palate, *Captain Niall?*"

Oliver chuckled softly, settling back in his chair. "You realize, Elspeth," he said, resuming their earlier conversation, "that if this former fiancé of yours had elected to sell your property, legally he would have been within his rights? This would not be considered larceny since he could not steal from himself."

Elspeth lowered her cup. "Hell's bells."

"Furthermore," Oliver said soberly, "if *you* had attempted to dispose of your property without your fiancé's consent, the transaction could be considered legal fraud on your part."

Elspeth swore. "Did you hear that, Niall?"

"Yes, I heard it," he replied, irritation sharp in his

voice. "It's all I've been hearing for the past hour, George and Glen Fyne this, George and Glen Fyne that. Elspeth, I realize you're a woman obsessed and I knew that when I fell in love with you. But you, Uncle Oliver, well, don't tell me you summoned me all this way to have a cozy chat over tea?"

"No," Oliver said slowly. "I didn't."

Never one for subterfuge or social niceties to begin with, Niall had reached his boiling point. "Uncle Oliver," he said, throwing back the curtains to gesture outside, "that serving girl is actually waving to me—she's motioning me to go outside even as we speak. Just who the blazes does she think she is?"

Oliver glanced past Niall to the window with a rueful smile. "Go into the garden and find out for yourself, lad. Elspeth and I will bide here by the fire and discuss the finer points of the law."

Niall spotted Hasim as he strode past the outbuildings. The witch doctor was holding court by the brewery door, impressing the cook and her scullions with his ability to stand on his head. Polite applause followed the feat as Hasim started unfolding his supple frame into a series of hand springs.

Their gazes met, and a strange prickle of premonition rippled over his skin as he saw the tears well in Hasim's dark kindly eyes.

"This Scotland, Tuan," he said softly, "it very magic place where dreams of the heart come true."

"Mon Dieu," Niall breathed, turning back toward the garden in shock. "It was her, wasn't it? It was her all along."

He couldn't believe he hadn't recognized her. He couldn't believe she was hiding out in the garden some- where, playing games as they had as children in the jun-

gle. It was twilight, that mysterious interlude in the day
which the Scots called gloaming and which was known
in the Far East as the hour of the tigress.

He could sense her presence, girlish mischief and secrets, and he wondered how he had ever missed the emotional anticipation that vibrated all around him, how he
had failed to see through his sister's silly charade.

"I know you're out here, Rachel."

He took a deep breath. Sensing her sneaking up behind
him, he stood perfectly still with his gaze lifted to the
hills that rose like a ladder to heaven.

"Ooh, fancy my guid fortune in findin' ye all alone,
Captain Niall! Ye'll be ready fer those scones now, and
I've another nice pot of coffee on the hob to wash 'em
down with—"

He pivoted, his bronzed face so forbidding in its ironic
contemplation that she jumped back with an involuntary
squeak of alarm.

"You always had the wickedest temper, Niall," she said
quietly. "You always could frighten me with a look."

He stared and stared. His throat closed around the
words that formed but would not come. His heart began
to pound so hard that he brought his hand to his chest.

"Oh, no, Niall," she cried in distress, and rushed toward
him. "Don't you dare die on me just when I've finally
found you! Maman's own heart almost gave out from the
shock when she recognized me."

He shook his head, struggling to speak as he felt her
gripping his wrist. Her hands were strong. Her accent held
a trace of Parisian French and an intriguing Far Eastern
flavor he hadn't the wits to place. And he was going to
faint, like a girl, at her feet.

"Rachel," he said at last, clasping her hands in his and

studying her face in the fading daylight. "Rachel, here in Scotland, rude and all grown-up. Here in Scotland."

He caught her up in his arms. She giggled in delight, letting him spin her around and around until he stumbled back against a low stone bench.

"Rachel." He stared at her in wonder, a striking young woman with blue-gray eyes and sun-kissed skin, strong cheekbones; she had Glenlyon arrogance stamped in every feature of her face.

"They tell me you're the veriest rogue," she whispered with tears thickening her voice. "Maman said you have been such a naughty boy."

He grinned. "Not me, Rachel."

"Don't think I haven't read the papers, you scoundrel."

His amusement faded. This was too wonderful, too painful, too sudden, and so many questions clamored for answers, he didn't know where to begin.

"Where have you been? Not in Scotland all this time. No, it isn't possible. Don't tell me you 'lost' your memory either. *Jesu,* Rachel, do you have any idea how many years we spent trying to trace you?"

She bit her lip. "Don't start me crying, Niall. I'll never stop. Yes, Maman told me all the sacrifices made on my behalf." She paused, disengaging her hands from his. "I've been living for the past year as a postulant nun in a Siamese jungle convent."

"A nun?" he shouted in disbelief, eliciting a startled giggle from her at his reaction. "Tell me it isn't true. No, Rachel, really."

"Of course it isn't true." Her voice became somber. "But I needed that year of peace and purity, to recover, to readjust before I entered the civilized world."

Peace and purity—to recover from what? He tried not to let his imagination torture him.

Rachel looked away. The sadness in her eyes hinted at soul-deep wounds which he instantly wished to heal. "But what did you need to recover from, *ma petite?* Why didn't you try to find us? For pity's sake, where have you been?"

She didn't look at him; he suspected that she was ashamed, or fighting to control her emotions. "I didn't know until this past year that any of you were still alive, Niall. I'd been told by my captors that my entire family had been slaughtered in the war."

He drew a breath, picturing a nine-year-old girl lost in the jungle, believing everyone she loved had been killed.

"I suppose I was in shock when I was taken," she continued. "After a few years of that life, I barely remembered my real name."

She glanced up, her face almost defiant, and he realized in astonishment that she wore a long curved knife strapped around her waist beneath the borrowed apron she hadn't bothered to remove.

"Your *captors,* Rachel?"

"I was sold into a tribe of hill bandits by a renegade British soldier. Slavery, as you know, is still common in that part of the world."

A British soldier. Siamese hill bandits. His little sister. He refused to think of what she had survived. *"Bon Dieu,"* he said, too upset to pretend he wasn't shocked. "Now I am going to have a heart attack."

"There's more," she said softly.

"You don't have to tell me. Not yet."

"I married the leader of the tribe, Niall. I became the queen of the hill bandits, if you will."

Niall pulled her down beside him onto the bench because this was news he really could not take standing up. "Where is your husband now, Rachel?"

"He isn't my husband anymore. I divorced him before I entered the convent."

"He was cruel to you?" he asked, his mouth tightening

at the thought, his anger at what she had undergone need
ing an object for him to attack.

"No, actually, he wasn't. Not to me. For the most par
I was pampered like a princess. But he was rather nasty
to other people, and his men were positively barbaric. Tc
his enemies he was brutal beyond belief."

Niall studied her profile, realizing in amazement tha
she had actually loved this man. And look at her now, sc
cool, so composed, so lovely and broken, his little Rachel
Queen of the Hill Bandits. What a story she could peddle
to Archie Harper, he realized, more than a little disgustec
with himself at the thought.

"Rachel," he said after a deep silence, "I'm grateful
that you're home. Nothing else really matters."

She gave him a thoughtful smile. "Is this Scotland you
home then?"

"No. Well, no."

"I don't have a home either," she said wistfully.

"Yes, you do. I'll take care of you."

"And bring me out next season as a debutante?" She
laughed as she asked, "Oh, Niall. Can you imagine? Whc
do you suppose would have the courage to ask me tc
dance?"

"A hundred men."

"What respectable man would be seen in public with
me?"

"No one has to know," he said guardedly.

"But I know, and I can't change what I've become. I'n
half heathen, half Catholic, in my heart as well as in my
behavior. I am half French and half Scottish. I woulc
rather sleep outside in this garden tonight than in a bed
As far as sexual matters are concerned, I've been in
structed to please a man in nearly every manner imagin
able."

"Rachel, stop it."

"I embarrass *you,* Niall?" she asked in surprise.

"No," he said quietly. "It's just that some things are better forgotten."

She touched his arm, and the old mischief returned to her face. "But you look happy, Niall. Was that lovely young woman in the parlor your wife?"

"Not yet." He grinned with irrepressible pleasure at the thought of Elspeth, their baby on its way. "Almost. Why, you'll be here for the wedding—you'll be a bridesmaid, Rachel. It's a grand start to your social training, although God knows that Elspeth and I aren't exactly models of acceptable behavior ourselves."

She gazed up fondly at his handsome face. "So the stories about you were at least partly true. You have found a bride. I'm dying to meet the woman who's tamed my wild big brother."

She rose, her smile so impish he couldn't believe the life she'd led. But then, look at him, settling down with a wife and family.

"Perhaps your meeting Elspeth is a mistake," he teased her. "You'll be comparing lethal weapons before the night is out, and—is it really necessary to carry a knife around in Uncle Oliver's garden?"

A shadow crossed her face, and he wished he had not mentioned the subject, not with the joy of their reunion still breaking over him like sunrise.

"No, Niall, it probably isn't necessary, but I made an enemy or two in those lawless hills. Self-protection is second nature to me, I suppose."

Forty-one

Niall walked stealthily across the room to the pier glass where Elspeth stood, too deep in a self-critical analysis of her appearance to acknowledge him. He could have reassured her she looked wonderful, but that Valkyrie scowl of hers stopped the impulse.

She'd just emerged from Oliver's ancient copper bathtub; the seductive fragrance of roses and jasmine (a gift from Rachel) hung in the steam. She was holding one of his sister's sarongs to her nude body, studying the effect of the diaphanous ivory silk with displeasure.

"You've got it upside down," he whispered in her ear.

She glanced at his grinning satyr's face in the mirror. "I know that, Glenlyon, but either way I model the damn thing, it still looks like an undergarment."

"Well, take it off then."

"No. I won't."

She snapped the sarong around the other way, but he was faster, catching the loose folds around her waist to tug her into his arms.

She stumbled toward him, warning, "You'll be in deep trouble if you tear this. Rachel thinks I should wear it for the ceremony on Monday, but, honestly, I won't be able to repeat my vows for shivering."

"Wear Hasim's sun-bear cloak over it," he advised her, using the sarong to walk her back toward the bed.

"Do women really dress like this on your island?" she

said a split-second before she fell against him, the bed-board broke, crashing to the floor, and the chambermaid, just bringing up fresh towels for the captain's bath, banged on the door in alarm.

"Ye didna slip on that bare floor and do yerself an injury, miss?"

Elspeth grunted, giving Niall an elbow in the ribs to stop his laughter. "I'm fine, thank you. My boots fell off the—the bed. Please leave the captain's towels by the door."

And when the woman's footsteps had faded down the hall, Elspeth leaned over the edge of the four-poster to examine the splintered bedboard. "Oh, look at this."

He studied the long curve of her back, the heart-shaped rise of her bare white bottom. "Yes, it's a lovely sight."

"You've broken the bed with your horseplay, Glenlyon. How embarrassing."

He ran his hand from the swell of her right calf to her hipbone. "And us not even wed yet. Do you know your legs are more muscular than some of the young recruits I had in my regiment?"

She rolled onto her side with a wicked smile. "I never knew you liked to look at other men's legs. Fancy that."

He smiled reluctantly. "I dressed enough wounds to have made the observation."

"You're sitting on my sarong, Niall."

He raised his leg, allowing her to pull the flimsy garment free before he twisted around to entrap her in his arms. "Actually, some of the women on the island wear nothing across their breasts at all."

Elspeth stared at him. "Heaven knows I'm liberal-minded enough, Niall, but that must be horribly uncomfortable when one goes riding."

"No one on the island 'goes riding'—well, at least not for pleasure. I own only one horse myself."

She sat up slowly, appalled at this revelation. "No

horses, Niall. No pleasure riding. How does one get about?"

"Usually in carts pulled by water buffaloes. Those are bullocks," he added at her blank expression.

"Bullocks? Isn't that rather primitive? I don't suppose there's any horse racing either?"

He stretched out flat on his back, pretending to be absorbed in unbuttoning his shirt. "Well, I seem to recall the natives racing lizards. Life there is a wee bit different from what you know."

"A wee bit," she moaned, hiding her face in her hands.

"Ma chère," he said in concern, sitting up to stare at her. "Don't tell me you're having second thoughts?"

"Of course I am," she whispered. "I do love you, Niall, but all of a sudden I'm pregnant and getting married in a silk handkerchief and going to live in a place where people race *lizards* for fun."

She dissolved into tearful giggles, and Niall forced himself to laugh along with her, hoping humor would counteract the dark fear of losing her. It didn't. "You're going to leave me standing at the altar, aren't you, Elspeth?"

"No, I wouldn't dare. Not with Rachel there wearing that weapon."

"Reassure me."

She smiled into his eyes. "The ends of the earth, remember?"

"Yes, I remember. It's your memory that worries me."

He twisted unexpectedly and forced her down beneath him. His large body was burrowing her into the featherbed. "You'd better put some clothes on before we continue this conversation, Elspeth. I'm stiff as a pikestaff looking at you and—" He raised his head, his gaze moving to the window. "Do you hear music?"

"Not yet, Niall. It usually takes a little more than this."

He frowned and allowed her to wriggle out from under him, giving her bottom a regretful pinch. His eyes were smoky with raw sensuality as he watched her struggle into her lawn nightdress. Sighing in resignation, he threw his legs over the bed and walked purposefully to the window.

Elspeth sank back against the bed and studied him, her heart quickening with the same dangerous fascination she might feel if a beautiful but unpredictable wild animal had wandered into her room.

His muslin shirt hung open to the waist, revealing a glimpse of his powerful build, the sun-burnished melding of muscle and sinew that formed his chest. The late evening shadows accentuated the dark elegance of his features, heightened the aura of suppressed power around him.

Her husband. It was overwhelming, intoxicating, to imagine what the future would hold with such a man. He had experienced so much darkness in his life that she knew it would always form at least part of his character.

"Elspeth." He motioned her over to the window. "Look at this. Rachel is walking out there alone again. There's something sad about her, don't you think?"

She left the bed to stand beside him, suppressing a shiver of longing as he drew her into his arms. The warmth of his bare brown chest, the protective shelter he offered more than compensated for whatever she would sacrifice to live with him; without him, there would be no life.

"Perhaps she's pining for her barbarian," she murmured. "Perhaps it hurt more than she'll admit to leave him."

"That makes no sense to me at all," Niall said solemnly. "If you love someone, you stay with that person, *non?*"

"He was a brute, Niall."

"He was her husband, though, and she claims he never lifted a hand to her in violence."

"But—"

"—but nothing," he cut in, staring down at her with such an unforgiving expression that she felt herself flinch.

"If he'd loved her, he wouldn't have let her go either. And if—"

He pulled away from her so abruptly that she found herself leaning into midair and staring in annoyance at his back as he wrenched open the window to stare outside, his eyes going wide with surprise.

"Bon Dieu!" he exclaimed.

"What is it now, Niall?" she said peevishly. "Isn't Rachel sobbing loud enough to suit you?"

He swung around, looking like a madman, and nearly knocked her over in his haste to fetch his field glasses from his saddlebag on the chair. Speechless, she watched him stride back to the window, swearing a blue Gallic streak while the oddly familiar rattle of wagon wheels over the hill grew in volume.

"I don't believe it," he muttered, fishing in his bag for a cigar. "This is the end. It must be true what they say about me. I'm cursed."

He was raving like a lunatic, and she pulled him by the hand, afraid he'd taken another feverish delirium. But the insanity appeared to have spread through the house. Servants were pouring out of the outbuildings onto the moonlit grounds, their excited chatter competing with the gay Moorish strains of a fiddle.

She even felt it herself, infected by this enthusiasm of an unknown origin. In fact, everyone else in the house appeared to have already gathered outside as if a falling star had landed in the driveway.

There was a childlike sense of magic in the air.

Squeezing around Niall, she stared outside. Without the field glasses she could only make out a train of shadowy blurs crawling down the hillside toward the house. But it was a familiar enough sight that the fine hairs on her forearms began to tingle with anticipation.

She laughed. She leaned out into the cold February

night, scooping up the heavy folds of her white nightdress to wave like a flag.

"It's them—it's my gypsies!" she said happily. "Just in time for the wedding."

Niall stared down at her in affectionate exasperation, the field glasses dangling around his bare chest. "It's going to be a fight for you until the very end, isn't it, Elspeth?"

Forty-two

The gypsies clamored for the bride and groom to observe a traditional Romany ceremony, jumping the broomstick and smashing an article of crockery afterward, the idea behind the ritual that for every piece that shattered, the newlyweds would enjoy a year of wedded bliss.

Elspeth loved the idea, and so did Rachel, the pair of pagans. But Niall put his foot down. After all, he'd been raised a Roman Catholic, not that religious custom had ever mattered overmuch to him until this eventful morning. But he was entering this new phase of his life with a solemn sense of responsibility. And he did feel as if he'd already compromised himself to begin with by marrying his pregnant bride in a Scottish Presbyterian kirk.

That is, if they ever made it to the little strathside church.

The wedding party had just piled into Oliver's ancient coach—Niall, Elspeth, Oliver, Hasim, Delilah, and Rachel—when Duncan Kildrummond, his daughter Catherine, Auntie Flora, and Archie Harper arrived. Niall stared in amazement as their huge rented coach, festooned with swags of blue silk ribbons and rosettes, came rattling up the drive.

"Did you think I'd miss the opportunity to give my daughter away?" Duncan shouted jovially from the window as his driver pulled alongside the other vehicle.

Catherine squeezed her head out beside her father's to

exclaim, "Ooh, it's all too romantic, isn't it, Captain Glenlyon?"

Niall could only pretend to agree, allowing Elspeth, Delilah, and Rachel to crawl over him to transfer to the other
coach. And just as he dared to draw a breath, Archie Harper jumped into the vacant space beside him and Hasim.
The three of them couldn't move a muscle, squashed together on the lopsided cushions with tufts of horsehair
sticking into their behinds.

"Nice hat, Mr. Harper," Samson, Horse Trainer, Knife
Thrower, and Curer of Warts, said from the adjacent seat
as he squeezed down beside Uncle Oliver. He looked his
dapper best in a brown frockcoat with a scarf cravat and
tweed trousers.

"Thank you, Mr. Petulengro," Archie replied. "You cut
an 'andsome figger yourself, sir."

Niall lifted his brow. "You two know each other?"

"Indeed, we do, Captain," Archie said stoutly. "I wrote
quite a few articles on Mr. Petulengro 'ere in our salad
days. Gypsies, you know—violins and fortunetelling. My
female readers are mad for 'em. Speaking of which,
Capt'n, whatever 'appened to that beautiful violin what
belonged to your lovely bride?"

"It was . . . sacrificed, sent up in smoke, you might
say."

"Ah, well. All in the name of love, eh?"

Samson whistled through the gap in his teeth. "You
couldna bought yourself some new boots, Captain, some
new clothes and plenty more with de money from selling
that violin. Now you and Elspeth won't get rich until our
horse runs next year."

"Horse?" Niall didn't like the sound of that at all.
"You're not talking about Elspeth's lame horse, Ali Baba,
I hope?"

"Hey, that horse—lame last week, perfect today, Captain. Yer witch doctor, he gave me some potion that

worked the trick. I tell yer, in another year, with me training him good, that animal is gonna be a champion just."

The matrimonial coach circled the drive and rumbled off toward the kirk, followed by a cartload of colorfully dressed gypsies and Oliver's small domestic staff. Elspeth gave Niall a wicked grin from her window as her coach shot past his.

"We won't be here in another year," Niall said, leaning forward with a frown to watch her.

Archie rapped his knuckles across the top of his hat, his voice museful. "Well, who knows, Captain? As they say, 'The final page ain't been written yet' . . . now 'as it?"

The young minister had thinning red hair and a nervous tic in his left cheek. Not that Niall couldn't sympathize with the man. You had to feel sorry for the fellow as he cast a bewildered look over what Niall suspected was the strangest wedding party ever assembled in the humble kirk.

Oliver's servants mingled with the band of gypsies who lounged in the doorway to serve as witnesses. Samson sprawled across an entire pew by himself, humming and cracking his hairy knuckles. Delilah was on her hands and knees, searching for one of the marbles her children had shot down the aisle before someone slipped on it. Archie Harper was sketching the scene with rapt interest. Aunt Flora dozed.

Hasim stood, the best man, dabbing at his eyes with the lace hanky Catherine handed him. Duncan waited in anxious silence to give away the bride. And Rachel was motioning furtively to Delilah that the marble had rolled into the nave toward the minister.

Heaven help me, Niall thought. I'm not marrying a

woman. I'm marrying an institution of eccentrics, and my side of the family is just as bad.

Elspeth caught his eye, her expression mirroring his own amused disbelief and love. "I have a present for you, darling," she said in a low sweet voice that filled his mind with delicious anticipation of the days to come. "Take it," she urged.

He blinked in surprise and stared down at the jewel-hilted dirk she held toward him. "It's beautiful, Elspeth, I'm honored. I know it has great meaning to you, but what exactly am I supposed to do with it?"

"It's a dirk, Niall."

"I can see that, Elspeth, but I'm not going to have to perform a ceremonial dance at a crossroads around it, am I?"

"A dance?" she said, as if he were a simpleton. "You wear it in your right sock, Niall."

The young minister cleared his throat. "Is something wrong?"

"No," they said in unison, sharing a private smile.

Everything was right, for the first time in Niall's life— the strange warm-hearted people who surrounded him, the heavy knife, fraught with meaning and memories, that he struggled to slip inside his sock, the woman who giggled softly as she watched him stab himself in the calf, passion and love and the promise of forever in her eyes.

He wanted to weep and laugh and whisk her away to his private corner of the world before . . .

No sooner had the minister spoken the opening words of the traditional ceremony than thunder boomed outside like musket fire, rattling the kirk's ancient rafters, and rain poured down against the triple lancet windows in a deafening roar. Shadowy dampness permeated the church.

Niall smiled reluctantly. "I knew it. This family circus was too great a temptation for heaven to ignore."

The wedding guests stirred before falling silent in a

spell of superstitious unease. Delilah straightened, her face a mask of melodramatic enjoyment as she curled her fingers into the horned sign to warn off evil. Then Elspeth dared to giggle, the dour minister deigned to snuffle, and Rachel best summed up the consensus of opinion with a philosophical shrug.

"They say that a tempestuous marriage is the most enduring. Judging from what I know of my brother and his bride, I can only predict a lifetime of sunshine interspersed with a fair share of storms."

Forty-three

For the fourth time that afternoon, Niall Glenlyon, reluctant Laird of Glen Fyne, had sneaked away from the confusion of his household to read a magazine in the library. Never mind that the news it contained was almost a month old. By the time he found an uninterrupted moment, it would probably be Christmas. People occupied every nook and cranny of the house.

Architects were tramping about waving costly plans under his nose for refurbishing the creaky old manor; workmen hammered slates onto the roof, and repaired pumps. There were gypsies in the garden. Gypsies exercising racehorses in fallow fields. Tenants putting up snug stone crofts and inviting him down every five minutes to mark off their generous allotments of land.

He thought with a transient pang of longing of his island home where Rachel would soon reside and take up the task of growing coffee. He missed Hasim, who had accompanied her, and hoped his shaman mentor would soon convince his own family to make the sea voyage back to Scotland. Still, Niall was glad he'd made a last-minute decision to stay.

There was a knock at the door. Before he could look

up, Elspeth strode in, oblivious to a husband's need f[
privacy.

"Look what's just come, Niall."

"Not more bills?"

"Yes, and it looks like we've got a wedding present
She hugged a long battered box in her arms. "I wond[
if it's another christening gown for the baby from Georg[
He's trying so hard to prove he's changed."

Niall scowled and drew a cigar from the rosewood b[
on his desk. Although he bitterly disagreed, Elspeth b[
lieved that Tormod would prefer that George devote h[
life to the crofters' cause rather than to face imprisonme[
for murder. "He has a damn long road to travel."

"Dear me, the present isn't from George at all." A smi[
brightened her face as she began to tug at the knotte[
twine. "How sweet. It's from the girls at Mrs. Grimble[
bawdy house. Oh, by the way, we've been invited to
ceilidh in the glen tonight to celebrate the birth of So[
cha's son."

Niall looked up, halting his hunt for a match under a[
the unpaid bills on the desk. "The present is fro[
where?"

"The finishing school." She swept around the desk [
pluck the cigar from his hand as if it were a dead mous[
"You don't have time to read magazines and smoke th[
smelly thing, Niall. You have to start getting dressed f[
the party."

"Elspeth, I will no doubt dedicate the rest of my day[
to being a doting father and loving husband. I may eve[
take up growing potatoes and shearing sheep in the gle[
but I will never, *never,* agree to attend or even host a[
other party."

"Shall we finish discussing this upstairs, Niall, so th[
servants working in the hall aren't forced to overhear wh[
could well turn into a very ugly family dispute?"

She sauntered around the desk with that bewitchin[

smile which usually brought him buckets of trouble. Digging into her package, she littered his carpet, his sanctuary, with crumpled brown paper and bits of twine.

As he examined the mess made by his wife, resisting the impulse to tidy up after her, he realized there were some things in life, some people you could never change, some people who didn't need changing because they were good enough already, precious despite or even because of their flaws.

She was as resilient as Scottish heather, she was as determined and bold-hearted as her Viking ancestors, but a man had to draw the line somewhere.

"I am reading this magazine, Elspeth." And shooting her a defiant look, he returned to his chair and began flipping through his copy of *Le Bon Temps* in search of that certain article.

"Hasim said you were to pamper me, Niall."

"Would you like me to catch you some small frogs for supper?" he inquired without looking up.

"Rachel said you should humor me."

He propped his feet upon the desk, pointedly ignoring both her and the old sheepdog who had jumped up uninvited into his lap.

"I'm going upstairs now, Niall, to dress for our party." She began to back away from him, sniffing in disapproval. "If the girls sent us chocolates, I'm not giving you a single one."

"Close the door behind you," he murmured.

She slammed it. The dog sighed, resting its head on Niall's sternum. A rare silence fell over the room.

Ah, yes. Niall scratched Clootie's ears, frowning in absorption. Here it was . . . the final installment in the series of *"The Thrilling Misadventures of Captain Glenlyon,"* sandwiched between an advert for Peach's Pearl Dentrifice and a titillating little piece entitled *"Illicit Goings-Inside the Cathedral!"*

The subhead read: *"The Fruit Never Falls Far from the Tree!"*

> *Captain Niall Glenlyon, late of Burma and the British Protectorate of Kali Simpang, has not only taken a Scottish wife, but has also decided to make his home in the secluded Highland hamlet of Glen Fyne. And so our story ends.*
>
> *Swapping a billiard table for a bridal bed, his military rifle for a farmer's yoke, our erstwhile misadventurer will soon be settling down to an exemplary life as Laird of the Manor. Who'd have ever thought our rogue hunter would be off chasing sheep instead of man-eating tigers?*

Niall laughed appreciatively and swung his legs down from the desk, gently setting the dog on the floor. How Harper had possessed the precognition, or brazen audacity to print such a headline two weeks before Niall had decided himself to stay in Scotland, he couldn't guess.

But this was one tidbit of gossip he wouldn't try to deny, or hide from his wife.

"Elspeth!" He stood and strode from the room, ran up the massive oak staircase and down the portrait-lined hallway to their bedroom. "Elspeth, you just have to read this."

She turned slowly from the dressing-room mirror, shaking loose her chignon so her hair tumbled down her shoulders in a dramatic cascade. "It wasn't chocolates," she said with a naughty smile. "But it was something Mrs Grimble's girls thought we should share."

He closed the door and leaned back against it, his heart hammering as he stared at his young wife, at the seductress she had become. His eyes darkened in appreciation. For his life he could not remember why he had come rushing into their room. But there was no doubt he was going to stay.

The dog whined and scratched from outside in the hall. There were workmen arguing above them on the roof. A slate tile flew past the long casement window, down into the garden, and hit Samson on the head. The subsequent Romany swearing from the rhododendrons turned the air blue.

Niall didn't notice.

Elspeth was too nervous to care.

"Well?" She moistened her lips with the tip of her tongue. "Do you like it?"

Coherent speech eluded him. He could feel his body temperature rising. Black silk stockings, black satin pumps, see-through frilly white apron over a black lace corset with a whalebone gusset that cinched in her waist and thrust her breasts up into two tempting handfuls of creamy flesh.

"Mon Dieu." He shook his head, trying to breathe, and pushed away from the door. "Your body is unbelievable. That costume does incredible things to the imagination."

She lowered her eyelashes demurely. "I'm supposed to be a French maid."

Niall circled his wife, his fascinated gaze traveling up the length of her black-stockinged calves, past lacy garters to her heart-shaped derrière, displayed to prurient advantage in the risqué costume.

"I daresay you won't get much housekeeping done in that thing, *chère*." His face harsh with desire, he caught hold of her apron strings and drew her toward him. The magazine protruded, forgotten, from his pocket. "Not as long as I'm master of the house."

"Niall, I could barely get the damned corset on over my stomach."

"Then take the damned corset off. In fact, I'll even help you, shall I?" he murmured solicitously, turning her around by the apron strings as they reached the bed, working his hands under the frilly bib to the row of hooks and eyelets.

"You are going to come to the party with me tonight, aren't you?" she whispered.

"A little of the old *mail-dubh,* eh, Elspeth?"

She glanced across the room, catching her breath at their reflection in the mirror. "I knew I'd come to a decadent end, Glenlyon."

"Your decline was my salvation," he said, his hands tightening around her waist.

Their eyes met in the mirror.

"I do love you," she said softly.

"Mrs. Glenlyon, my very life depends on it."

He released her to unbutton his black waistcoat and white muslin shirt, pulling the magazine from his trousers pocket and tossing it to the floor where it landed, page open, to the final installment of his life.

He and his wife would have a good laugh over it later . . . after the party, after she performed her "domestic duties" as his maid. And much, much later, he might even take it upon himself to drop Archie Harper a line, pointing out the one part of his story that he'd gotten wrong.

Marrying Elspeth Kildrummond wasn't the end of Captain Glenlyon's misadventures at all.

It was the sweet beginning.

Dear Reader,

Some books come straight from the heart. The characters seem to take on a life of their own as soon as they hit the first page, and all the writer can do is follow them wherever they decide to go.

In the case of Niall and Elspeth, it was an exhilarating roller-coaster of a ride. From the moment this spirited pair of misfits met, I was off and running to keep up with them. Of course a man as provocative and unpredictable as Niall Glenlyon needed a strong-willed woman to match wits with him. Elspeth gave him a run for his money, and more.

I hope that reading Niall and Elspeth's story brought you a few hours of enjoyment. As always, *your* letters delight me. If you'd like to drop me a line, my address is:

Jillian Hunter
P. O. Box 3074
Long Beach, CA 90803

Wishing you love and laughter,

Jillian Hunter

If you liked this book, be sure to look for the November releases in the *Denise Little Presents* line:

Something Wild by Anna Eberhardt   (0192-5, $4.99)

Chloe Pembrook has her whole life under control—and that's exactly how she likes it. She's a lifestyle expert—a sort of Miss Manners meets Martha Stewart. It's her job to be a control freak. Ashley Clayton Ellsworth III has always had a fondness for chaos—and a real talent for causing it. Naturally, these two people are destined for each other. From the moment they meet, sparks (and bullets) fly. Soon Chloe and Ace are involved in a high-speed, high-stakes chase from Chicago to the Hamptons, and nothing will ever be the same—especially their hearts!

The Bargain by Francis Ray   (0174-7, $4.99)

Heiress Alexandria Carstairs is a woman with a problem. Well-bred young women in 1859 have to marry, and she has no intention of ever signing away her freedom to a man! Thorne Blakemore, the Fifth Earl of Grayson, has no intention of marrying either, but could use a convenient fiancée. Between the two of them, they find a solution. A short engagement, a little dalliance, then freedom. Their only problem—they forgot to include love in the equation! It's a merry romp through the best of England, in *The Bargain!*

$\mathcal{R}$OMANCE YOU'LL ALWAYS REMEMBER...

$\mathcal{A}$ NAME YOU'LL NEVER FORGET!

Receive
$2 REBATE
With the purchase of any two
$\mathcal{D}$ENISE $\mathcal{L}$ITTLE $\mathcal{P}$RESENTS
Romances

To receive your rebate, enclose:
+ Original cash register receipts with book prices circled
+ This certificate with information printed
+ ISBN numbers filled in from book covers

Mail to: DLP Rebate, P.O. Box 1092
            Grand Rapids, MN 55745-1092

Name_____

Address_____

City_____ State_____ Zip_____

Telephone number (   )_____ (OPTIONAL)

COMPLETE ISBN NUMBERS:

0-7860-_____ 0-7860-_____

This certificate must accompany your request. No duplicates accepted. Void where prohibited, taxed or restricted. Offer available to U.S. & Canadian residents only. Allow 6 weeks for mailing of your refund payable in U.S. funds.

OFFER EXPIRES 5/30/96

**If you liked this book, be sure to look for others
in the *Denise Little Presents* line:**